It's Reigning in London

J.P. Robideaux

A Rick Blaine Novel

It's Reigning in London

Book and cover design by Kevin Breen
Cover image derived from Adobe Stock photos

ISBN: 979-8-218-31457-6
Cataloging-in-Publication Data is available upon request

Manufactured in the United States of America

Published by Deep Breath
The author may be contacted at johnprobideaux@gmail.com

Dedication

For my wife, Lorrie, who inspires me.

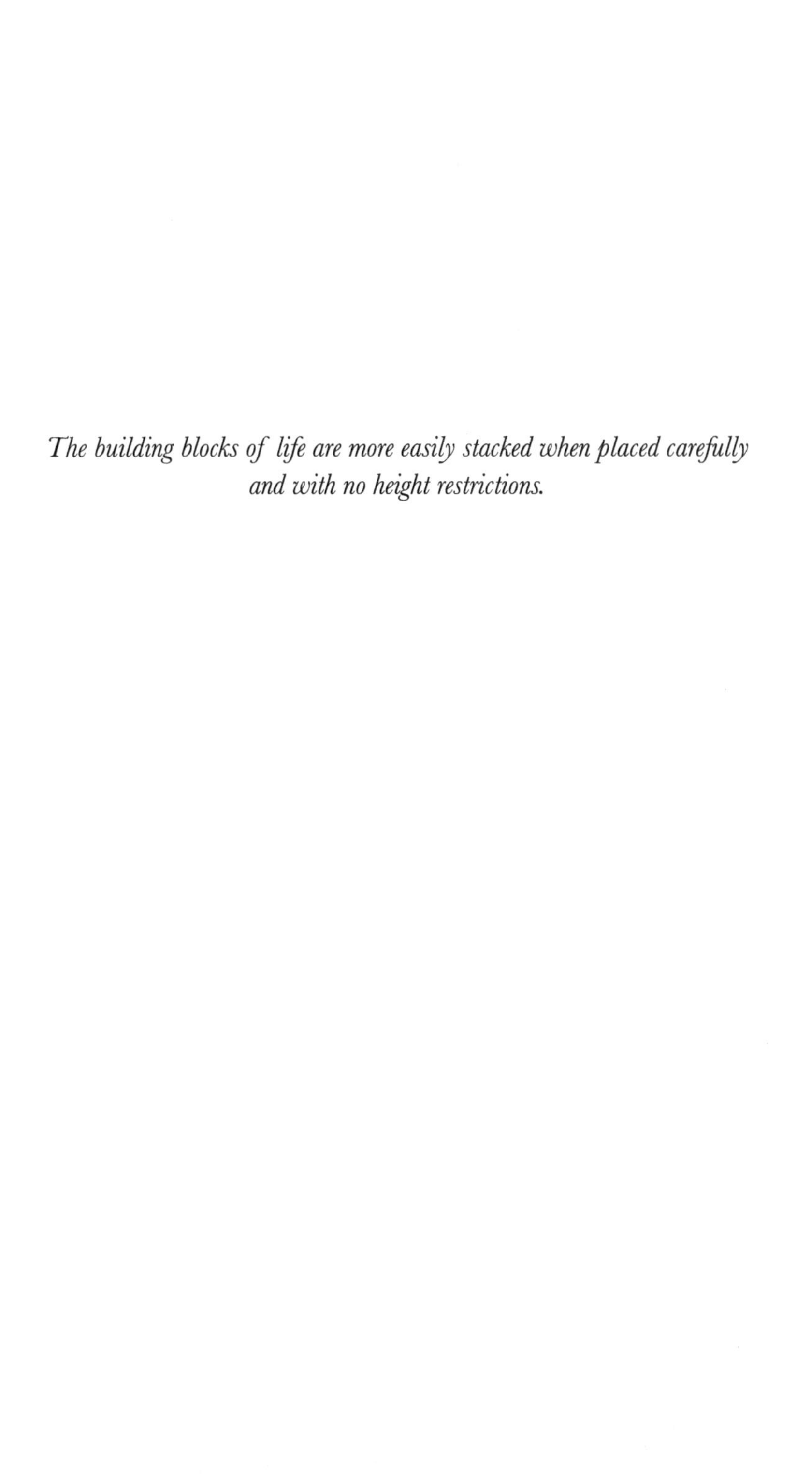

The building blocks of life are more easily stacked when placed carefully and with no height restrictions.

Prologue

Life, at least that part we pay attention to, contains a constantly changing series of challenging, yet controllable, circumstances cleverly disguised as opportunities. Some people choose to pursue their dreams, open to opportunity, happy to discard the past. Selecting a college versus joining the military, when to make a left turn, during a thunderous rain storm, in heavy traffic, or who to spend the rest of one's life with, are life-changing moments.

Whether we realize it at the time or not, each path we choose deserves thoughtful attention. Most people welcome life's challenges, according to Ted, my gray-haired, semi-stoned therapist, who sees right through me twice a month. Evidently, the average person constructs a comfort zone that provides protection from change. I never thought to build one of those zones. Maybe that's why I'm still single and in therapy.

My life has been one progressive step after another, until last year. All the chess pieces on the board of life were neatly arranged, ready for my next move, then all hell broke loose. The more I played the game, the worse the outcome. It was like the rules of the game had changed and no one told me. I didn't have time to question why the former rules of play no longer applied. What I had known and who I cared for took on a different look and feel. That rearrangement of my life came on suddenly like an evil ambush that had been carefully placed into a plan, titled:

Fate, written long ago. That development of events came out of the blue like a line drive foul ball nailing a fan looking at their program at the wrong time.

People that mattered most to me — family, friends, and business associates — who shared the dream, were also affected. My company, Blaine Manufacturing, had sales that exceeded projections. So, why did that foul ball target me? One explanation was that, somehow, I managed to upset the east coast mob and west coast law enforcement at the same time. The mob came after me, my company, and several of my friends, like a tidal wave bent on destruction. As a result, I had to find a way to escape, which was complicated by the fact that I had no protection from the authorities, since they were after me too. There was no way out, I had to disappear until the dust settled. Unfortunately, the most expedient modes of transportation weren't available. With time running out, a decision was made just in time.

Fortunately, a friend of mine and I were able to make a run for it. Our unexpected journey required two days of driving a long-haul rig over a thousand miles. A new experience that nearly killed both of us. My life was spared because of the actions of several brave women, among others, who put their lives on the line for me. Thanks to them, I survived with minor injuries and am back with a renewed spirit. And after close review, and months of rehabilitation, I'm returning, stronger, and with the determination to help others and return the favor if it takes a lifetime.

The remaining mob bastards that came after me have disappeared, which, I'm convinced, will affect my new strategic business plan. Wherever travel takes me, I will keep a more watchful eye out for them. Thankfully, I have a chance to prove myself. I've been called to action. My name is Rick Blaine and I plan to continue to succeed in life by following a new mantra: Welcome Success and Eliminate Evil.

Chapter 1

TANGIER, MOROCCO

Jamal the spice dealer, understood all too well the games being played among his competitors in the Grand Socco marketplace. Vendors throughout this enormous bazaar honored those who devoted their lives to selling merchandise, and if the opportunity presented itself, as it normally did, cheating tourists. Jamal considered it a game, one that he prided himself on playing very well.

If there were an all-time list of the most engaging vendors to have graced this marketplace, dating back centuries, Jamal's competitors would rank him among the most aggressive. Possibly the top five of all time. He would say the top three, and each of the other two would be family members, but everything here in the Grand Socco is negotiable.

Jamal operated a very profitable business, providing for his wife and family. Three boys, five girls, his mother and father, and one uncle on his wife's side all lived under five roofs that covered a beautifully constructed *dar.* Tan stucco covered the exterior, accented by red tiles that formed the roofs. If one stood on a mountain top and looked down across the land, they'd see these roofs matched most of the other dars in their neighborhood.

What separated Jamal's residence from the others were the ornate planters that outlined two balconies overlooking pedestrians walking along the narrow front street below. The street would be considered more of a wide alleyway by European standards. Only donkey-led carts and foot traffic managed to make their way past the thirty-meter-wide residence that had been constructed over time.

Jamal's home was the largest in the area, it had to be with all the people living there. And in order to maintain the dar, as well as his social status among thieves, Jamal remained open to new opportunities that would expand his business or provide additional income.

As a younger man, he served his country in the military and learned to use a computer — which in addition to a knife, extended the length of his long-range rifle.

Although Jamal detested violence, he had learned to kill in order to survive. Taking a life did not come easy for him, which didn't go unnoticed by his training officer. One night while Jamal slept in his bunk, two men surprised him. He suddenly awoke to a hand covering his face and a familiar voice whispering in his ear. While one man held him in place, Jamal's training officer, Qasim at-Tazi, explained the outcome if he didn't take a more aggressive stance toward the enemy. "What would happen to your family if you were to die in battle? Think about them when you aim the rifle or thrust the blade." The incident was over in minutes, but the thought of his family living without him remained.

Eventually, he fought the enemy as ordered, which grew more devious as his months of service dragged on. He passed the time by finding out as much about his opponents through the world of the internet as he could. His life, in the service to his country, became routine very quickly, however, he found new ways to profit for himself, using his mind to carefully guide his fingertips. Like magic, it came to him one night as he did a favor for his capitaine. Gathering high level, possibly top secret, information and selling it to the highest bidder or influential contact, as his capitaine revealed to his trusted corporal, created additional income.

"It's good for some, and not for others. Plain and simple. The difference is, those that need *good* information pay well, which is also *good* for me, so long as we keep our information gathering and selling to ourselves," said the capitaine, pausing in thought. "Can you keep a secret, Jamal?"

Jamal looked up into his capitaine's face, the man's dark beard neatly trimmed to within a few centimeters of his face. Jamal always wondered how he managed that procedure. What stood out more, on the face of the man he so respected, were his capitaine's steely gray eyes that appeared laser-like as they did then. Those eyes coerced many hard-core prisoners to confess.

Jamal never hesitated, knowing there would be consequences, imprisonment or death, if this venture were to be discovered. Those consequences were definitely a concern, but the confidence Jamal had in his capitaine equaled his own ability to uncover coded material to be sold. Buyers were not hard to find. Countries that despised Western culture and their evil tentacles, such as Israel, were willing purchasers. Consequently, he felt he had plenty of job security.

Six months later, the man he had grown to admire and collaborated with in a most devious, yet profitable scheme, was transferred out the unit. The news came suddenly leaving Jamal to fend for himself. His capitaine told him not to worry about his participation in their underhanded scheme. Even though he would not be able to work with him any longer due to his new assignment, the capitaine encouraged Jamal to consider expanding the operation. "You are very good at passing on secrets, corporal."

What now? Jamal thought as he watched his superior officer drive off for the last time. The capitaine had been the person behind the scenes, discovering new opportunities and engaging Jamal to take part in the lucrative, albeit, small time, operation. Jamal had a decision to make, whether to keep this pipeline of secretive information gathering going, or let it perish.

For nearly a month after his discharge he labored over the decision. On one hand, Jamal would soon take over his father's spice business, that was a given. But would it be enough income for a young man raising a family? As he readied himself to take over the spice business, the more covert life he had created, up to now, pulled at him like metal to a magnet. After a grueling few days of lost sleep and agonizing thinking, Jamal made a decision. He purchased "State of the Art" PC equipment required to continue gathering "Hidden" information. The purchase was an upgrade from what he'd been using in the military. It didn't take Jamal long to become proficient with the new software. He enjoyed the upgraded speed and accuracy of the process he now had set up in the below area of his Dar.

That was nearly thirty years ago, and although he continued to upgrade his equipment, Jamal never discarded the original PC, like a jeweler keeping a prized jewel.

This newer, faster technology allowed him access he never thought possible. But his original PC equipment, including floppy disks, never let him down. Occasionally, Jamal would head to his storage area, uncover the old equipment and plug it in just to make sure it remained operational. Watching the lights come to life, listening to the hum of the server fans, gave him a good feeling, adding to his confidence.

Even the client list his capitaine left behind remained useful. One such person who worked with MI-5 remained in contact, which resulted in a nice retainer for Jamal.

The dawn prayer, salat al-fajr, ended, and Jamal was on

his way to Cafe Tinjis for his first cafe au lait of the day. Dawn prayer, then caffeine, and back to his spice stand in time to wash the red brick sidewalk in front of his stall, lay out his spices, change into his multi-colored vest, and then slip out of his sandals and into red colored-pointed toe slippers. He carefully checked a small mirror attached to the back of the stall as he donned his red fez with blue piping. Jamal adjusted until he liked what he saw in the mirror, smiled and waited for the onslaught coming up from the harbor in the form of cruising tourists.

The day will be hot and humid, encouraging early visitations for items the public didn't know they *absolutely had to have.* Jamal puffed up his chest as his smile broadened with anticipation. He relished playing the game of *negotiation* with his customers, where they are allowed to win, so long as, in the end, the results provide him a modest income.

The sound of voices approaching the gates created a warm buzzing in his ears, the vibration of which reached all the way to his wallet. A group of excited visitors with a variety of languages are unified by their eagerness to spend. Here they come now. And with a broken toothed tobacco-stained smile he offered, "Welcome to Morocco, please, allow me to *spice* up your day."

§

SAN FRANCISCO INTERNATIONAL AIRPORT, SAN FRANCISCO, CALIFORNIA

The fog began to rise and burn off as people made their way through security. Belts off, shoes off, water bottles being thrown away or drained at the last minute by infrequent flyers.

Rick Blaine, innovator, CEO of a Silicon Valley high-tech manufacturing company, and proud owner of a newly refurbished vintage Porsche, stood polishing his sunglasses as he watched the ebb and flow of humanity shuttle past TSA agents like cattle wandering out to pasture on his family's farm in North Idaho. He made his way past restaurants, shops and bars, stopping to buy one of his favorite author's latest novels to read on the flight overseas. Grisham never disappointed and this one about freeing people from prison who were wrongly accused intrigued him. Rick was running late as usual and opted not to visit the Oceanic lounge, instead he headed straight to his gate in Terminal 1.

As he stowed the Grisham book in his backpack, Rick couldn't help but wonder if he made the purchase because of what happened to him a few months ago. He'd managed to survive a serious death-threat, turned murder charge. Although his rehabilitation took a little longer than he'd anticipated, it was time for him to move on with his life. The thought made him smile as he joined thousands of others appearing to do the same. He'd read, recently, that sixteen million visitors pass through this airport annually. Even though the number of visitors seemed high, he wondered what percentage were looking for adventure or at least being open to it.

He guessed most people that came face-to-face with death and recovered would consider *picking up where they left off.* Not Rick. His main focus in life now, beyond overseeing the successful management of his company, was to eliminate evil that came his way. Moving his life into that new gear felt invigorating and energizing. Near death experiences present new opportunities, evidently.

So many people had come together to help him a few months ago. Their actions deserved more than a thank you. The only way he could live with himself and remain creative was to listen and prepare to take action. Friends and colleagues, plus those he knew who were in trouble, would be the beneficiaries. Rick committed himself to be especially proactive in using his influence in the corporate world, a universe he knew well and where he enjoyed competing and succeeding. Rick couldn't help but wonder if the trip he was about to take would challenge this new commitment. His older sister, Jess, used to caution him to watch out for things he wished would happen, and instead spend more time making things happen. That thought has stuck with him since high school and continues to play a major part in the criteria he uses in making most of his wishes come true. Rick never believed in luck coming along at the right time. He couldn't wait for luck, he's a planner. *If you don't have a plan, one will be made for you.*

The original purpose of this overseas excursion was to generate new business for his company, Blaine Manufacturing, the largest producer of protective covers for digital hand-held devices in the United States. The trip would also fulfill a promise to meet with good friends and colleagues at Lamperson Services in London.

Winston Lamperson, and his son Ben, own an international information technology company that provides Blaine with various business services. The most notable service provided to date were sales leads. Rick adjusted his sitting position and shook his head slowly, side to side, stretching his neck muscles. A smile appeared as he thought about the Lampersons.

Their chance meeting was the result of an unfortunate incident. Two years ago, Rick saved Winston's life from choking on a crepe by performing the Heimlich maneuver at a trade show, a fact that continues to loom in the shadow of their relationship. Winston returned the favor by providing background information on a criminal element that was making Rick's life a living hell last year.

After that incident was neutralized, Winston and Ben invited Rick to join them in London after he recovered enough to travel. Rick and his team had intended to establish a presence in Europe once the company gained total distribution of its products in the United States. Now was as good a time as any. And according to the Lampersons, they could provide valuable distribution and marketing information to the, yet to be established, Euro-Blaine team.

But there was other information the Lampersons could provide that intrigued Rick even more. "We have it on good authority that the American gangster fellow, Mr. Castillino, who caused you so much trouble last year, has European connections as well," Ben Lamperson revealed to Rick earlier in the week.

Ben's call included two of Rick's most trusted associates: Brenda, Rick's former Executive Assistant, now Vice President of Administration, and Major Connors, Head of Production. Both Brenda and Major were instrumental in helping Rick escape his near tragic confrontation with Michael Castillino and members of his organization. Brenda maintained the communication between Blaine Manufacturing and Lamperson International with Ben as her main contact. Even Rick recognized he couldn't be everywhere at once, and Brenda Johnson was the only person he could totally trust to have his back.

The new information concerning the Castillinos had to be recognized and dealt with, which is why Rick had others on the call. He would take the next few weeks and split his time between work and play.

Rick's first stop will be in Milan, Italy, to spend a few days with Pete Reynolds, a former college roommate. The two men kept in contact, with Pete joining Rick and his family for Christmas eight years ago. "*Had it been that long ago?*" Rick asked Pete when they talked on the phone a few weeks ago. Pete heard about what happened to Rick, and immediately set plans in place to meet, in person, once Rick recovered.

He stood up to stretch his legs. Rick turned and put his hands on the back of the seat and began moving his legs in a downward dog fashion when a toddler came rushing up to him. Rick's head sank low to the point where he looked out underneath his right armpit at the child. "Hey little buddy." The boy laughed and ran back to his mother who welcomed the child with open arms. The little guy was obviously excited to be going on his first trip as he pointed at the "big bwue pwane!" while simultaneously smacking a window behind his seat.

Rick liked kids, especially his nieces and nephews. He observed the warm and loving interaction between parent and child, which was a good distraction, not only for Rick, but also for several hundred other passengers waiting to board. An announcement came over the speaker just as a familiar, foul odor emanated from the little boy's diaper. "Sorry folks. There will be a slight delay of approximately one hour," the announcer said as an apology, while Rick made his way to the bar as the little boy's mother headed to the restroom with the child.

Rick sat nursing a vodka tonic watching the airport bar's big screen television showcase the latest news. He rarely watched the evening news, but when he did, his interest quickly distilled into: who lied and who died. Today, the drink and the television viewing blended into a distraction that was more than welcome. After a few months of being highly sensitive to loud noises, he'd recovered from a concussion, cuts and bruises, and a left leg injury that had him laid up just as long. It felt good to feel better at the moment. Stories he watched on the news reminded him that he wanted to inject more excitement in his life. The exception, at least for now, would be romantic relationships, especially long-lasting ones — those would have to wait.

Included in Rick's recovery routine were two sessions with Ted, his therapist, last week. The man, described by Rick as his secret weapon, was also known for his ponytailed silver hair, shrewd wit, and hipster lifestyle. The look and feel of the man dated back to the seventies, which naturally included his occasional smoking of pot, in his office, during sessions. Those special meetings usually required a half hour of walking around the downtown area to relieve traces of the inevitable contact high and airing out before driving back to the office or home to his apartment in Tiburon.

Rick's smile grew as he took another sip of his drink and thought of the people he depended on most, which, of course, included Ted.

Brenda, Rick's former executive assistant was his rock. She was the main reason Blaine Manufacturing operated smoothly while he was away. In fact, she was the one person he trusted most, period. He offered her a Vice President position while he rehabbed recently, and she accepted with one condition. "Rick, I have to know what's going on at all times," Brenda said. "You can't keep anything from me or make decisions that affect the company without my knowledge." The comment took Rick aback for a moment. It didn't take more than a minute to realize that she was right. He agreed to the condition.

Brenda accepted responsibility and understood what it meant to work under extreme pressure, especially when it came to keeping track of her boss, Mister Blaine. For that reason, she maintained her status as Rick's chief liaison with Blaine Manufacturing. No one understood Rick's new mission in life of helping others better than Brenda. She also knew the threats. There were competitors in business, but Blaine was the leader in its category and she intended on keeping it that way. It was the newer, more sinister threat of the mob that had to be dealt with and she would address that on another level when the time came. Brenda had the ability to do so, as long as her boss kept his promise.

Rick admired Brenda. Admiration, from his perspective, came with a hefty monetary reward, making her one of the highest paid, unattached, executives in Silicon Valley. They led separate lives outside of work and both preferred it that way.

Rick's rehab included the recent loss in weight, fifteen pounds, due mostly to a new diet, suggested by surfing friends, Artie and Jillian. They're neighbors in Venice Beach, where Rick keeps his weekend condo. Who knew avocado had so much weight loss potential? These random thoughts made him laugh as he finished his drink and an avocado-laden salad.

Taking time to go overseas comes on the heels of Rick doing six weeks of physical therapy to regain body strength, suffering through a concussion, mending a few broken bones and catching up with his friends and family. His elderly mother was the only person in his life that didn't know how close he came to dying. As Rick healed, he directed his business team to put a master plan together, focusing on international markets, with the goal of expanding Blaine's distribution. Blaine Manufacturing learned from various mistakes that had happened in the past, domestically, and worked methodically to introduce new directives that would place Blaine products in Western Europe without jeopardizing sales at home. Brenda Johnson led this new and exciting thrust.

As Chief Executive, Rick worked more "hands on" in all facets of the company without micromanaging, which could be considered difficult to execute, unless you had the energy to sustain the effort. That's why it's taken him a few extra weeks of rehab to get back to where he left off. His key people understand how the Blaine system works, similar to the Steve Jobs model, only without all the drama. Rick had had other drama in his life to deal with, and putting the mob chase and shooting spree behind him had not been easy. Rick was ready to open new vistas for Blaine Manufacturing, and Europe was waiting.

The last decade of business required plenty of hard work, learning from mistakes, and expanding to meet demand. He'd converted his family's small seat cover business into one of the largest producers of protective covers for cell phones, laptops, iPads, tablets and computers in all colors and styles, and recently added new lines, beyond IT covers, like eyeglass covers, smart brief cases and wallets, with new additions either in development or on the production line.

Life, it seemed to Rick, created adventures that led to opportunities, or was it the other way around? In any case, the next two weeks in Italy and England promised to be exciting for the company and Rick personally.

The news ended on TV and a new announcement presented itself overhead: "Oceanic Flight 1406 for Milan is now ready for boarding at Gate 3B, all those in first class are welcome to board at this time."

Rick heard the call, settled his tab, left a nice tip, stood up, and made his way to the gate. As he was walking, Rick noticed a text with an itinerary change from Brenda. He'd check it on the plane before take-off.

§

BOSTON, MASSACHUSETTS

Lorretta Petrula sat at her desk in the back office of the Petrula Trucking Company. She'd just given specific instructions to Joey "the Rat" Arronotti, one of her most trusted lieutenants. Joey's and Lorretta's fathers grew up together. Joey had spent time in and out of juvenile detention for stealing cars and small-time burglaries. He had the reputation, early on, as a trouble maker. Later in life Lorretta's father asked her if she would consider hiring Joey to do odd jobs. He'd been struggling to go straight, but with his record, no one would hire him. Although he was strange-looking, with a long, rat-like nose and close-set beady eyes, Lorretta felt obligated to give the guy a chance, so she hired him. She quickly found out that Joey had another talent that no one, especially the cops, knew about. He enjoyed using a knife to defend himself. Joey may have been small in stature, but tall in being able to use his knife for a new purpose, eliminating people that crossed Lorretta.

Lorretta was not only the president of her father's trucking company she also ran one of the most influential crime syndicates in the country. The Rat was a trusted soldier, who understood that any deviation from exactly what Lorretta had instructed would result in his own body parts being spread across Boston's big, beautiful harbor. Enough said. And just for the record, she had a short list of the most hated people in her life and Rick Blaine's name held the top position, because of what he and his associates did to her beloved Michael Castillino.

It was now up to Joey, a devious little man with felony convictions to take care of Mr. Blaine, and that Lorretta found, for now at least, invaluable. When it came to value, Lorretta could smell it. And there was nothing more pressing to her right now than to follow Rick Blaine's every movement. She would spend her last dollar to make sure Mr. Blaine suffered from now unto eternity. Amen.

§

Oceanic Flight 1406 was an overnight flight bound for Milan, Italy. Rick laughed to himself as he settled in first class seat 4A. His thoughts focused on his best friend in college, Pete Reynolds. He looked forward to catching up. Time keeps on slipping, slipping, slipping, into the future. Thank you, Steve Miller. Rick settled in as he reminisced and listened to Miller's greatest hits on his headphones.

He and Pete were complete opposites. Pete was outgoing. He had the magic touch and found the girls to date, set agendas for partying, and instilled a study regimen that made all the difference for Rick, who admitted to being more "hands on" and "intuitive" rather than academically oriented. But, following Pete's lead, and with a strong family "get it done" work ethic, Rick was able to earn a business degree with honors.

Pete achieved what he considered his dream job in the United States Foreign Service. Although he remained single like Rick, and enjoyed his life in Italy, Pete recently shared a strong desire to settle down, but it was nearly impossible for a Foreign Service Officer like him to become attached because he was at the State Department's mercy: he went wherever and whenever Foggy Bottom wanted him to go.

From Milan, Rick would make his way to London, or that was his intention, until he reviewed Brenda's text, which read: "Winston would like you to consider a slight change in plans before arriving in London. Would you mind a quick trip to Tangier, Morocco first? Call him when you land. Be Safe. B."

Rick enjoyed flying at night — hanging with the stars. Learning about our galaxy came early thanks to Gramps, his Grandpa Blaine. Rick's grandparents lived close by, in North Idaho, and visited often when he was growing up. They had divided up the old homestead of three hundred acres, gifting Rick's parents forty acres when they were married. Rick and his siblings would often walk down the quarter mile trail to visit their grandparents when they were kids.

Whenever he was over there at night, Rick and Gramps would climb up to the roof where a special platform had been constructed just for viewing the stars. Rick's heart would race as they ventured up through the attic where Gramps stored his telescopes and star maps hung from the walls. The room held a certain magic for Rick as he anxiously followed his grandfather out onto the platform. With a steady hand, the old man would point up to the night sky and encourage his grandson to check out stars and constellations, and more importantly, learn their names. One of Gramp's favorite expressions was, "How can you thank your lucky stars if you don't know who they are?"

Once in a while they would take a hike up to another favorite stargazing location further up in the hills overlooking the valley that seemingly held the farm in the palm of its hand. Together, they would climb to the highest point where Rick would view the stars, and the moon in complete darkness. A full moon looked as though he could reach right out and touch it through a heavy old telescope his grandfather carried in an old canvas seed bag.

Rick thought of those times as the stewardess turned down the bright cabin lights, providing a better view as the more comforting blue atmosphere lights appeared above in the cabin. Cassiopeia, Andromeda, and Orion were his favorite fixed navigation points, not that he would see them tonight, but comforting to know these "celestial guideposts" were out there.

Those same *guiding lights* kept him company on clear warm nights sailing his boat, *Fore Sail*, on the lake in North Idaho. Rick enjoyed waiting with his friends for the International Space Station to pass over on special nights. His boat could comfortably accommodate eight guests looking into space, lounging from the cockpit in the stern to the deck on the bow.

Sailing silently as the night progressed, just last week they gathered in the cockpit with Rick, hugging each other under blankets to stay warm, trying not to spill their cocktails. Penny, the seaplane flying restaurateur, organized a small bon voyage party that included: Dave, her father; Jenny, a newcomer to the area who had helped Rick escape last year; Lannie, owner of Harbor Barber and Tavern, a favorite gathering place; and Butch, Penny's golden retriever.

It was a perfect night, made more special because Penny and friends secretly decorated *Fore Sail* with Christmas lights along the mast support stanchions, from stern to bow, as a sendoff surprise. The boat made for quite a show in June, generating cheers from the shore as the boat motored and sailed around the bay, close enough to converse with people along the shore. Hellos, good-byes and an occasional "Merry Christmas!" could be heard that night.

Rick wouldn't be as comfortable taking time to make this journey without the support of his "carefully crafted" management team. Everyone knew that when the boss was gone they had to be on, which happened more often now than ever. This didn't go unnoticed. *Wired Magazine* called his escapades into question, and so did Wall Street. The media labeled his company "the illusion of Silicon Valley success," mostly because Rick had multiple locations to manipulate on any given day. His headquarters and production facility were located in San Jose with sales offices in San Francisco, causing him to live in Tiburon, and get away to his weekend condo in Venice Beach.

One recent article in *Wired* jokingly stated that Rick spent a majority of time driving his vintage Porsche rather than working. They aptly named him the Top Executive Driver in Silicon Valley. He didn't mind the reputation; he liked the fact that he drove himself instead of most top executives who had chauffeurs and rode in limos.

His Porsche would be ready when he returned. It sustained damage after a crash along California's coastal Highway 1 a few months ago when Rick attempted to outrun the mob. While he survived, the car didn't.

This latest time away was doctor ordered. Rick had sustained a concussion while being chased by the mob. He had been accused of rape and murder by the authorities as he attempted to outsmart the mob all in one week. If it hadn't been for Penny and her seaplane, he wouldn't be here sitting in seat 4A. Thoughts of appreciation and anticipation encircled Rick, who leaned back, closed his eyes, and drifted off into sleep.

Rick's trip to England would be strictly business from a

Blaine perspective and an opportunity for him to share what he learned about the drug cartel that he had the misfortune of running into last year.

Winston Lamperson had a plan and Rick couldn't wait to hear what he had in mind. Rick knew Winston had high level connections throughout the British government, including Britain's goofy, wild-haired prime minister, members of the Royal Family, high ranking officials in Scotland Yard, MI5 and MI6, not to mention the chefs of some of the best restaurants in London. Rick also suspected that Winston had more on his mind than helping achieve European distribution for Blaine Manufacturing's products. Rick wondered if he could be of any real assistance to Winston in matters beyond their business relationship. His hesitance came, not because he wasn't capable, he was, this mood would show itself from time to time. At six foot two and nearly back to his normal weight of 195 pounds, Rick could handle himself. The thought gradually faded as Rick heard something, which snapped him awake.

Rick opened his eyes, and along with other passengers, watched the little boy bouncing across the aisle from him. His thoughts went to the bouncing and jostling he and others went through in the seaplane as they made their daring escape from the Columbia River a few months ago. Thanks to his friends, the unbelievable happened. Penny piloted the rescue mission that saved his and the lives of Jillian and Jenny, who managed to get Rick's semi-conscious lump onboard the seaplane, just in time. Thankfully, Penny is recovering from the shattered metal fragment wounds to her face. Her vision, slightly affected for now, has a full recovery prognosis.

The cabin returned to calm and Rick's thoughts began to shut down. He returned to sleep mode. The footrest came up, shoes off, as the seat back lowered to nearly horizontal. Blanket up tight. First class really paid off on these longer flights.

Further back in business class a man was also preparing to sleep. The short stocky traveler, dressed in black jeans, stuffed a black three quarter-length leather coat next to his grey fedora in the overhead bin. He smiled at the lady sitting across from him as he rubbed his bald head. Then raised his arms, which also lifted his black collared shirt, showing off a hairy belly. A big yawn graced the moment as he settled in, turning off his reading light, and quietly whispering a good night to Mister Blaine.

Chapter 2

Sleep normally overcame Rick, gradually, like a tidal wave approaching a beach at night. Once the flood hit its maximum height, it was all over — especially at 37,000 feet, racing across the sky at nearly six hundred miles per hour. And that particular night he dreamt of driving on a foggy California coastal highway being chased in his Porsche by the panther-like BMW. This particular dream looped more often on constant repeat. It didn't help that part of his update from Brenda, read just before reclining, included new facts about the people who had recently been trying to kill him. The participating members of the Castillino family were either dead, in jail or, in the case of one Michael Castillino, unable to be found.

The "unaccounted for" kept Rick's dreamscape in fast and furious mode. Ted had done his best to help alleviate the nightmares, during a phone call therapy session, last week. "Change your routine, oh captain of industry. Go away, to a different place if you can, and soon." Rick took comfort from his aging guru and decided then and there that this trip could be just what the doctor ordered. From a side curtain, the female flight attendant in first class watched as Rick reacted to the chase being played out in his head.

The engine hum gave way to a gentle "bong" sound followed by a welcomed Breakfast Service announcement. Rick had been awake for a half hour, going over some notes on his laptop. Number one on the list; stopping off to visit his college buddy, Peter Reynolds, in Milan.

He and Pete set all kinds of "non-athletic" records at the University of Idaho, which was ironic for Peter Isaiah Reynolds. A natural athlete, Peter was recruited out of Georgia to come and play football for the University of Idaho. He was one of only three black players to receive a full scholarship in his freshman year. Unfortunately, Peter sustained a career-changing injury to his knee in his first game, but decided to remain at the school. He and Rick met at the physical therapy center in Moscow's regional hospital. Rick was recovering from an ankle injury sustained on the farm while haying the previous August. They shared the same therapist and became fast-friends, walking together on campus to classes using crutches, then canes, which became swords on occasion. They, surprisingly shared a lot of the same interests, music, sports, telling jokes, and, therefore, became inseparable. From that day forward to graduation, Pete, who was a few inches taller, watched out for his new friend. During their four years together at the U of I they had the opportunity to visit each other's family home. The introductions Pete and Rick received at their respective holiday dinner tables turned the initial surprise visitor's moment into a warm welcome. Rick introduced Pete as his friend from Georgia who is the real reason his GPA is the highest it's ever been. And Peter, who, jokingly, warned Rick about the number of people who would be at his family's Christmas dinner table, introduced Rick as a classmate from the Northwest who still believes Santa Claus is a white man. Needless to say, both boys became men together, but not until they had their fun through various activities.

Some of those activities could be considered irrational or simply "Boys being boys" behavior. Their favorite activities included flag football, soccer, golf and a wide selection of odd contests between fraternities. Most memorable was "The annual peeing for distance contest," organized and managed the first two years, rather successfully, until a girls' sorority became involved — no one saw Pete's girlfriend, Sandra, take first place. Pete had a likeness for girls who were considered outstanding in their field. Needless to say, the event was forever cancelled after the third year.

Rick sat back in his seat and looked out the window of the aircraft and laughed to himself as he continued to reminisce. Participants were encouraged to sample various brews at selected pubs in downtown Moscow, Idaho. Golf carts and a bus, for the less able participants, were then lined up and everyone, including spectators, made their way to the nearby river. Suffice it to say, the actual "peeing" part of the event took place at nightfall on a secluded beach where buoys indicated the length of peeing distances. Flashlights, cellphones and the motor coach headlights helped to mark each attempt. Rick won the first year, Pete the second, and Sandy, in the last year of the event, won the Women's competition. Pete, as well as many of those gathered, were amazed at the girl's dexterity. Pete and Rick received a slap on the wrist by the University's Provost, partly because the man's daughter was a finalist in the Women's' competition. Pete and Rick were generally recognized by the faculty as good students academically, an achievement that normally fades over time. But their extracurricular reputations will most likely live on in perpetuity thanks to class reunions and a makeshift plaque nailed to a tree down by the river.

Oceanic Flight 1406 was on the last leg of their journey as the plane prepared to descend. Breakfast clean-up was in progress, customs forms were being passed out, as the target and his pursuer prepared to exit.

TANGIER, MOROCCO; GRAND SOCCO MARKETPLACE

The youngsters, boys and girls, ranging in age from twelve to six, gathered in their usual meeting spot, halfway between the Casablanca bazaar and the Grand Socco marketplace. All ten wore tattered street clothes, some with leather sandals, the rest barefoot. It was early, between morning prayer times. Each child anxiously awaiting their first delivery of hashish. If all went well, they would be back for more throughout the day.

Abbas, twelve in age, was much older in experience, proudly led his ragtag band of hashish dealers. Taller than the rest, he wore a loose-fitting knitted cap that he'd traded an Italian tourist a gram of hash for a few weeks ago. It sported the puma logo of an Italian soccer team and fit perfectly on the crown of his head.

Abbas passed out the last of their rations — bread and cheese he'd stolen the night before from a local restaurant. The food, left outside on a dining table, would have been thrown away as soon as the waiter cleared the table. His skills at finding rations were really tested during meals in the middle of the day around lunch time when the patrons happened to look away from their table.

He spoke softly to his gathered charges as he handed each of them even amounts of food. Their job was to infiltrate the crowd, pick a pocket or two, and when the opportunity presented itself, lure vacationing buyers into purchasing their tempting contraband. Primary targets among the tourists were young, single males or college students of both sexes, who had come over to Tangiers for a day trip from Tarifa, Spain, on the other side of the Strait of Gibraltar. Drunk or hungover military sailors and soldiers were also targeted and easy to find. No one expected kids this young to be dealing, which made the set up even more enticing and potentially successful. The sale of hash was just one part of Abbas' operation. Unknown to his customers, he worked with the local police to shake down tourists. After selling contraband to the tourists, the police would swoop in and take over. It was all part of a clever scheme to feed the wallets of the local police. The unsuspecting customers would be arrested, asked to show some identification, which would be returned after paying a hefty fine. The Grand Socco had a local reputation as the "Land of Golden Opportunity" by the local gendarmes. The patrol of local authorities ran the operation rather successfully, in conjunction with the little artful dodgers. The orphans were allowed to "pick" from pockets, handbags or tables, without worry of being arrested, so long as they created enough arresting revenue for the men in blue uniforms. It was a deceitful game played daily.

In a way, Abbas and his troupe conducted their own version of patrol in the Grand Socco. The hashish would be distributed carefully to the boys in the back alley behind the jail. Each young thief received six tubes, with three spliffs — a combination of hashish and tobacco — per tube, each valued at around $25 per tube. A good thief would be supplied more than once during the day. If, at the end of the day, the sale amount and the quantity of contraband didn't add up for some reason, punishments would be handed out in the form of beatings. Often, the police would play tricks on their ragtag scoundrels just to be mean. But, should one of Abbas's fellow orphans have a habitual issue with their superiors, the child would simply disappear.

"The sun rises to greet our faces and lift our spirits, so we go," Abbas proclaimed as he and the others walk from the alley, stepping over broken bottles and puddles of urine. Then, on his count of three, they disburse into a run as each member of this makeshift group merges into the crowded marketplace.

Jamal watched the youngsters run past, out of the corner

of his good eye, as he approached his first customers of the day. He spotted Abbas as he held out two bundles of coriander for the lady to judge. "You will find my coriander is more floral and citrusy, madam," Jamal boasted as Abbas ran past, saluting the spice dealer as he disappeared into the crowd.

The old man made the sale as he watched for the young man who had done some favors for him in the past. Jamal would be calling upon Abbas to help carry supplies to the stand this coming weekend. The adolescent thief with a good heart had to be careful not to offend the local police by spending time away from his appointed illegal duties. Jamal understood and met with the boy only when there were no visitors in the Grand Socco.

The young lad was smart and had the ability to avoid danger, at least up to that point. Jamal worried about the daily risks the street urchins faced, especially for the younger children. He despised the police for making a game out of crime. Just the same, he let his thoughts simmer, after all, it was a living and every dealer in the Grand Socco had to endure in order to survive.

§

The plane shuddered slightly. Rick heard a woman raising some concern with a flight attendant, who continued raising window shades and welcoming first-class passengers back from their night's sleep with coffee and juice. Rick checked his seat monitor to see where they were in the flight. It showed that the plane had less than an hour before landing. Outside, the weather was clear, which allowed everyone on the port side of the plane to see the Alps come into view. The lake country below looked as if a giant had stepped through the area revealing periodic bodies of water, footprints in the landscape. Lake Maggiore, bent around like a horseshoe met Lake Como to the east. Although this would be Rick's first experience in Italy, he had studied the area before leaving on vacation.

"Gorgeous," Rick said to himself as he ate from a bowl of fruit and added cream to a dark bold coffee.

"Buon giorno. Theesa ees your Capitan a speaking," said the plane's captain, speaking in stereotypical Italianized English. "We will be landing in Milano a few meenuts from now. Pleesa to sit now and buckle you upa. Buona giornata!"

As the plane began its descent through an intermittent cloud cover, Rick viewed red tiled roof terraces and vineyards, identifying Italian landmarks as the plane descended. The patterns made something click inside and he made a note to discuss a "patchwork" blend pattern for a future product design added to Blaine's new line of cell phone covers.

Deplaning went smoothly. Rick had one carry on, no checked luggage. Neither did the man in 34C dressed in fashionable black.

WE'RE AT THE FRONT ENTRANCE. RED ALFA ROMEO 4C, PILLAR 5. DON'T BRING MUCH LUGGAGE! read Pete's text.

We? thought Rick.

§

MILAN, ITALY; ARMANI HOTEL

Rick stepped out of the terminal at Milan Malpensa Airport and was hit immediately with the mid-morning Italian heat. Pete greeted Rick at on the sidewalk A tall attractive lady wearing dark glasses, stood smiling, next to Pete. Rick attempted to shake off the past 13 hours of flight as he returned his friend's welcome with a big bear hug.

"You haven't changed a bit Pete, in fact, you look younger," Rick half shouted through his smile. "Must be the shaved head – looks good. Why is it that black men look more handsome bald and white guys look like accountants?" The comment made the tall woman cover her mouth and Pete to howl with laughter. When Pete recovered from laughing, he grabbed Rick's arm.

"Hey buddy. One thing's for sure, you haven't lost your sense of humor, even though you've been through a lot. Thanks for making this stop. I want you to meet someone special," Pete whispered the last part as he reached for the lady's hand.

"Rick, this is Sese," Pete announced, motioning towards his companion.

Sese (say-say) had the appearance of an angel with a big smile. Tall and lean with dark hair and light brown complexion. She wore sandals, white shorts and an orange sleeveless top, oversized round sunglasses and a large straw hat.

Rick found himself in a hug fest with the two. He was glad he'd taken time to freshen up before deplaning. This was friendly Italy after all. They made their way to the car after the urging of a petite female security guard. As they walked, Rick took a call from Brenda. He excused himself, finished the call and made another. This time to Winston Lamperson.

"Rick, so glad to hear from you old boy. I understand you're in Milano," said Winston in his posh Oxbridge accent.

"Just landed, Winston. You needed to talk?"

"Yes. I won't keep you my friend. Hopefully, you're rested enough to render me some assistance."

"Anything. What's up?"

"I hope this won't spoil your plans, but could you make a day trip to Morocco sometime this week? Tangier to be exact."

Rick wasn't expecting or planning to have to leave Italy so quickly. "I...I," Rick stuttered, thrown completely off guard. "I'll see what arrangements can be made. But, yeah, sure, I'll check with my friend to see what they have planned and let you know right away. I'm only here for a few days."

"Good then," replied Winston directly, adding. "I'll wait to hear from you. In the meantime, you'll be sent more details about where to go and who to meet."

"No problem. Give Ben my best."

"Absolutely. My son is on the line with your Brenda as we speak. Have a good time with your friend and enjoy Milano."

They signed off with Rick wondering what Winston needed from someone in Morocco. From what Rick had heard from business colleagues, Morocco was a place that was interesting to visit, but a suspiciously complicated area to conduct business. He personally knew a firm from Silicon Valley that attempted to do so and lost their entire investment in a deal that nearly bankrupted the company. He'd wait to see what Winston had in mind.

It had been three years since Pete visited Rick in San Jose, while on business in nearby San Francisco. Rick had to admit that Pete and Sese made a handsome couple. It didn't take much imagination to see that Pete acted differently around her. But that was Pete's modus operandi with past relationships, falling so far in and down into the tunnel of love that he'd eventually crash and burn. Rick's first impression of Sese, however, was positive. She acted more mature than Pete's past loves, who tended to be younger and more immature. More of a lady that deserved to be treated like one. Good for Pete.

"Hey, glad you could join us, Rick," Pete jokingly stated as Rick caught up to their car.

"Sorry about that, business, no more calls. I'm all yours, Peter."

Pete suddenly went into tour guide mode. He'd been stationed here for over a year and, up until now, hadn't had the opportunity to show Milan and the surrounding area to any visitors. Serving as the U.S. government's consul in the

Lombardy region of Italy was a coveted assignment. Pete told Rick that he pinched himself every day, especially after meeting Sese, who would really be conducting their sightseeing during Rick's time there.

"Welcome to the second largest city in Italia, and the capital of Lombardy," Pete said as he shifted through the gears entering traffic. Rick relaxed in the back seat behind Sese. She turned and spoke in a soft tone through broken English asked, "There's so much to see, Rick (Reek). Do you have anything specific you'd like to do first?"

Rick blamed the flight for his hesitancy, but he found himself mesmerized for an instant, had that blank, deer in the headlights look. Pete noticed and laughed: "It's the Italian accent, am I right?"

"What?" asked Rick. "Ah, yes... beautiful. To answer your question, no, not really. I've never been here, but would like to know and see as much as possible."

"Peter and I want to suggest we eat first at VUN Andrea Aprea. One of our favorite restaurants, right in the heart of Milano."

"Food? Great, I'm ready."

"Good. It's open at 12:30 today. I will make a reservation," she offered with a big smile.

An odd sense of comfort came over Rick as she spoke. It could have been the tone of her voice or the unique blend of her Italian accent with English that allowed him to sit back and relax. It could have been the revelation of witnessing 900-year-old stone structures as she guided them through Milan, or simply the early onset feeling of jet lag slowly taking hold. Whatever was happening, Rick began to loosen up.

The trio continued through traffic where cars and trucks competed with scooters and pedestrians. The sound of the Vespas was so intense, it felt like they were driving through a beehive.

Pete decided to take a back street route that led, more conveniently, into the downtown area. Soon they were parking in what appeared to be a "preferred" area, although he couldn't really tell, everything, including the sign on the pole, being in Italian.

As they parked and exited the sleek four-passenger red and black Alfa Romeo, Pete, slightly taller at six foot two and a half inches, put both arms on Rick's shoulders and joked: "Hey, you sure you're ready to shake off the flight and do some sightseeing?"

Rick turned to face his friend, put his finger on his chest and said, "Only after we eat!"

Simultaneously, they both said, "God it's good to see you." The conversation gained momentum with more laughs as Sese joined in by wrapping both arms around her two companions.

The three of them walked ahead, arm in arm, Rick in the middle, through a huge mall that Sese referred to as a galleria. The place was encased in glass, as big as two football fields and framed by green iron ornamentations and beams. Fresh flowers, perfectly arranged in huge six-foot-tall white marble urns, stood tall, like artful sentinels, as the threesome made their way past upscale vendors, artists, and restaurants. For Rick, the experience featured a cacophony of sounds unlike anything he had ever heard. People speaking primarily in Italian and French dictated a high-level of melodic tones as floral scents overtook his sense of smell. There was more hustle and bustle than Dodger Stadium on game day, only more entertaining.

Even with all the distractions, they reached the restaurant in time to save their reservation. The iron ornamentation continued into what felt like a giant solarium. The floors were checkered black and white with tables of white linen and large eight-foot red ceramic urns with more multi-colored floral arrangements. According to Sese, she expected this restaurant would more than satisfy his hunger. "You have to remember that, here in Italy, we eat slowly and drink even slower. I hope you can stay awake for dessert."

Sese laughed at their conversation as the restaurant filled to capacity in no time. No wonder, Rick thought, as he watched the crowd and read through an English version of the menu. Rick caught his second wind as the first course service began. His meal of scallops with truffles and fruit salad was out of this world. Every sip of chardonnay complimented his lunch just as Pete said it would. His friend had turned into a gourmet, which was light years from the hot dogs and beer days at the U of I.

During lunch, Rick explained that he needed to make a short trip to Morocco in the next day or two. Pete stopped mid-bite and looked at his friend as if his hair was on fire. Sese looked down at her food. The conversation went into a lull for a few seconds until Pete offered:

"Sure, not a problem Rick. We do have some things planned, but we can carve out a day for you. Mind if I ask what's going on in Morocco that needs Blaine's attention?"

The entre of pasta in various forms came for each person. Plates began to pile up and wine continued to be poured. Rick found it difficult to keep his mind on the conversation.

"I'm doing a business colleague, the man I'm meeting in London, a favor."

"So, you have no idea who you're meeting or why?" asked Pete.

"I'll know more soon," Rick offered. "I, evidently, need a day to make it happen though."

Pete moved the pasta around in his plate, looked at Sese, who excused herself, and headed for the lady's room. Pete moved his chair closer so he could look directly at Rick.

"I'm going with you."

"What?" said Rick, taken aback. "Why?"

"Morocco might be fine for a tourist, but it isn't a place you go for business without knowing more than you know right now."

§

CARINI, SICILY; THE PETRULA COMPOUND

Michael Castillino escaped from the American authorities thanks to his trusted compatriot, Lorretta Petrula, who was the head of the family's business operations. It had all happened so fast: the chase, gunfights, his brother killed in front of him, and the escape in the belly of one of Lorretta's long-haul trailers. Michael attempted to find comfort in where he was at the moment, but a horrible cloud of disappointment settled around him, like a thick fog, and wouldn't leave.

He had failed his family terribly, in his mission to eliminate Rick Blaine from the face of the earth. And the next thing Michael knew, the family decided it would be best to send him away, like a bad boy being banished to his room. Only this room, the one he'd been pacing for the last few weeks, was located thousands of miles from his home in Boston. Lorretta had made all the necessary arrangements for his successful departure, while Michael's father made the living arrangements.

"You need to get your head together, Michael," Lorretta passed along after talking to Michael's father, who chose not to look at his son or hear any excuses. He wanted Michael out of his sight. Michael's brother, Tony, along with several trusted soldiers, were killed as a result of Michael's poor judgment.

"Look, you can take as long as you want. In Sicily, you'll be surrounded by Castillinos who care about your safety. Your cousins will treat you well, you're famiglia for God's sake, so take advantage of your time there and come back to us with new eyes," said Lorretta, who tried to be as benevolent as she could.

After all, she loved the man and hated to see him go. Those who knew her well were intimately aware that kindness, in any form, was rare at best. But her love for Michael overshadowed all his faults. Michael Castillino, the love of her life, would forever be hers. Lorretta also had another reason for living; she wanted Rick Blaine's head on a platter with his eyes removed and stuffed in his mouth, along with other parts of his body. When she announced this to the Made Men she reported to, it clearly demonstrated more of her real self. The side most of her associates recognized.

Lorretta considered accompanying Michael to Sicily so they could share some time together, but she had previous commitments to the family businesses. She enjoyed succeeding where only men had tread before her.

Petrula Trucking was the front for illegal operations all over the United States and parts of Canada and Mexico. And so long as the borders both north and south remained porous, the contraband would continue to flow. The transportation business required hands-on management, which was her second most productive skill in supervising a billion-dollar empire. Murder, and knowing how and when to incorporate it, being her first. Women in leadership positions that affected every facet of life were gaining momentum, which made Lorretta proud. But, in the Cosa Nostra, leaders wearing red nail polish and low-cut blouses to meetings were rare. No woman had ever risen to the level Loretta had attained.

She surrounded herself with protectors—lawyers, judges, politicians, assassins—all of whom helped to make her invisible to investigators representing authorities tracking down countless unsolved crimes. One such case involved the wealthy East Coast Harsten family. All five—husband, wife, and three children—disappeared on a Caribbean sailing vacation. Their sixty-foot yacht was found drifting off the southern Jamaican coast six months ago with no one aboard. The only possible clue, leading to a motive, was revealed after a reporter discovered a possible competitive angle related to fashion advertising on the side of her long-haul trucks. It happened to be a business Lorretta was interested in, and would fervently pursue, now that "Mr. Negative," as she preferred to call young Mr. Harsten, unfortunately disappeared. Lorretta made sure that the floral arrangement, sent to the family's memorial, overshadowed the rest.

Michael finally landed in the small city of Carini, outside of Palermo, Sicily. He'd spent the first week pacing his room in his stocking feet. He had to walk shoeless, as his Italian family had taken his stylish oxfords on purpose. They watched him closely. Their first priority was to make sure he didn't do harm to himself. They couldn't afford to have Michael die on their watch. Michael's girlfriend had a reputation that stretched all the way to Sicily.

When the second week rolled around, he was free to roam. He got his shoes back, sandals actually, and plenty of invitations to feel better about himself. His cousin, Rom, urged him to get out and meet people, his people —who wanted to ask him all kinds of questions about America, the Yankees and if he knew Silvester Stallone.

"How can you help yourself if you just stay cooped up inside?"

Each day, for weeks, Michael woke up sweating. His dreams replayed the final moments leading up to his brother's death. Tony meant more to him than he realized. That, plus the fact that he let his father down, jeopardizing his chances to take over the illegal empire his father had helped to build, caused a depression he found hard to shake.

Finally, after nearly a month, Michael agreed to leave the small house he'd been living in and meet with the parish priest about his near capture.

Michael, hesitant at first, began to open up to the priest. And after two other sessions he began to find comfort. Michael could face the deaths of his brother and men who he considered close associates through a renewed faith. He found it difficult at first, but not impossible, to let his brother and the others rest in peace. That renewed spirit led to making new friendships among his cousins and their friends, even attending Mass on Sundays. And for the next few weeks he came to realize the importance of his Famiglia in Italy.

Michael was used to watching over family, being the protector. His father had raised him to be responsible and he welcomed the opportunity.

He'd lost that job of protecting others, but, thanks to a renewed spirit, that would change. Michael did something he'd nearly forgotten over the years, he prayed, as his Sicilian relatives continued to watch over him. One question remained, however: How could he ever take over the leadership of the family business with the Blaine incident negatively affecting his reputation? The only answer he could come up with was to finish the job.

§

SILICON VALLEY, CA; BLAINE MANUFACTURING

Brenda Johnson found her new position as Head of Administration full of challenges. From Production to Human Resources, everyone needed answers in order for Blaine's record setting volume to keep flowing smoothly. Blaine's management team, of which Brenda was now a member, had nothing but compliments for the way she handled her new responsibilities. One area of responsibility that she insisted remain, was being Rick's main contact. For the past year and a half, and especially through his latest conflict with the mob and authorities, Brenda directed all efforts required to save his life.

After a full day of work, around 10:30 PM on the West Coast, Brenda made a conference call to Rick in Milan on a secure phone line at the request of Winston Lamperson.

"Brenda, Buon giorno. Oh, wait, I mean buona notte."

"Hi, Rick. Are you enjoying Milan?" The two continued to talk for a few minutes until Winston Lamperson came on the line. Brenda needed to know more about Rick's side trip to Morocco. She made notes as Winston spoke:

"Rick, I have a new enterprise that's grown since we last conversed. What primarily involved the continual bother of smuggling contraband across the Strait of Gibraltar between Spain and Morocco has now grown into a concern over terrorists threatening Great Britain's Royal Family. I have a man in Tangier, Jamal is his name, who fronts his operation as a spice dealer in a local marketplace, the Grand Socco. You'll text him and meet in a location away from his stall there in Tangiers. Once you've made contact, an envelope, containing recently obtained information will be passed it on to you. It contains two floppy disks and a rare coin that will be used for identification purposes. I know that seems odd, but it's a system that hasn't failed me for many years."

"Why me, Winston?" Rick asked. "Couldn't you have one of your people do this?"

"First of all, Rick, you are one of my people. A favorite. Someone I can trust. And most of all — no one would suspect you, a leader in your industry working as an operative." Winston stopped for a second as if congratulating himself for being so clever. He then continued, lowering his voice as he did so, sounding more official. "Besides, the information contained on those drives factor heavily into our next project together. The sooner we find out what's really going on here in London, the better it will be for us all my boy."

"Brenda?"

"I'm on it, Rick, you'll need flight reservations. Text me the particulars, now, and I'll work on arrangements immediately."

"By the way, Rick, to answer your earlier question, there's no problem having your friend, Peter Reynolds, tag along," Winston added. "As a State Department official, he's already well versed in secrecy and spy craft, and could be helpful."

Rick and Winston continued their conversation as Brenda made the arrangements. She also included Pete Reynolds, as per Rick's text. He didn't want Winston to know of Pete's concerns about Morocco, or that Rick couldn't handle his request himself.

Pete took vacation time while Rick was in Milan in order to catch up. This side trip would allow more time together; a side adventure. Pete felt the same and tried not to show any anxiety over this sudden change in travel plans.

Brenda came back on the line. "Gentlemen, I'm sorry to interrupt, but everything is booked. I'll send confirmation,"

Brenda's efficiency matched her concern for Rick's safety. There was no place for her to question the motives behind this change in travel, but she felt better knowing Rick wouldn't be making this part of the trip alone. Before the conversation ended, she had to ask Winston about the package.

"Floppy disks?" she asked, confused. "Winston, those haven't been used since the '90s."

"Yes, my dear, Brenda, you heard right," replied Winston, offering no further explanation. Brenda let the matter drop and she signed off.

§

MILAN, ITALY

After a cocktail in the rooftop bar with Pete and Sese, Rick found his room and collapsed on his hotel bed. Jet lag had hit him earlier, but it was a full day of sightseeing that finally did him in. They started at the Milan Cathedral, located just around the corner from the restaurant where they had lunch. Back through the Galleria Vittorio, that he admired on the way in, and then on to fountains, archways and beautiful gardens. Milan was a city of romance, much like Paris, only more fashionable with less art. He made a promise to himself that he would return with someone special one day. He looked forward to that and smiled as he rose from the bed, changed, turned off the lights, set his phone alarm for 6 AM and returned to sleep.

§

TANGIER, MOROCCO; GRAND SOCCO MARKETPLACE

Evening brought on darkness and the darker sky slowly suppressed any hope, like a gnarled finger pushing against silky lips signaling silence. Fear rises from behind, invisible, but nonetheless ever-present, causing one to shiver. Caution kicks in and makes one more aware of the shadows forming, lengthening, turning away, pointing and running from a full moon rising. A voice inside suggests it is time to shelter or risk survival in Tangier, especially if you're 12 years old. The games being played in this coastal town didn't stop at sundown with the final prayer sent off to Mecca.

Wide-eyed alley cats and hungry dogs with ribs showing, moved carefully between the few people who braved the night and those who preyed on them, the unseen. But Abbas promised Jamal he would do one last task before bedding down for the night. And a promise kept meant meat in the pan for the main meal tomorrow. The others would be pleased.

Carefully, the boy made his way down Octagrade, the lane

of eight turns. Being out past curfew meant pressing up against stucco walls, and bending at the waist, as his feet moved softly and quickly on hard packed sand worn down from stone over the centuries.

The leather pouch, supplied by Jamal, tucked safely inside his smock, felt smooth and comforting. Abbas thanked Allah that his way could be seen much better under the moon so big and bright. His day of running and begging took a toll on his young body, but he was up to the task laid out before him, while thinking of his young charges he called brothers and sisters. They weren't related by birth; instead, the children were bound by the job given to this troupe of unwanteds. So long as the orphans complied to the rules laid out by the police, they were all safe, Abbas convinced himself. There were times when even the police could get out of hand and rough the kids up, for playing soccer or sitting in the shade to cool themselves for more than a few minutes. Some would be offered a treat to go for a walk, only to return bruised and battered. Those were the "unfortunate" ones, the little or unhappy ones that wanted to go home or to have a home. If their behavior didn't change, they became expendable to the police. It was up to Abbas to keep them in line.

Unfortunate disappearances hadn't happened since Abbas took over leadership a few months ago. He made it his main prayer that he would keep those with him safe, so long as they listened and did as they were told. Tonight, everyone under his care enjoyed a safe sleep, he'd made sure of that before leaving. He pictured all ten of them laying on a fresh bed of straw, under the deck of a warehouse as he rounded the last of eight corners leading to the Rue Alaam address he'd been given by Jamal. Abbas chewed the last of his gum to keep his mouth from drying. His heart beat increased as he slowed his pace. Allah be with me tonight.

Abbas waited for the sign, as he hid under a canvas tarp as instructed. The tarp overhead covered oven wood used by a bakery nearby.

Abbas actually arrived earlier than he'd planned, so he settled in and watched the shadows for any sign of movement. His eyes began to droop, Abbas needed to stay awake and remain alert. As he shifted his position, a light appeared from a doorway next to the address marker he'd been given. It blinked three times. That's the sign, he thought. His young body ached as he began to rise from under the tarp. He stopped suddenly, frozen mid-stride. He couldn't see it, but something was crawling up his right leg. He knew what it might be so he moved slowly as he crouched and picked up a handful of sand. In one quick motion he threw the sand on his leg, mid-calf, as he rolled out from under the cover. The scorpion, nearly the size of his palm, shook the sand off in the moonlight and swiftly returned to its hiding place. Abbas went the other direction, hiding behind a large pot used to collect rainwater. He needed to catch his breath before pushing on.

Jamal's directions were specific: "Once you reach the porch, say: 'I am here, inshallah.' Repeat."

"I am here, inshallah," Abbas said in a slow and deliberate tone.

"Good. Then count to ten and knock three times on the door. Stand in front of the door. Understand?"

"Yes, sir," Abbas replied, repeating the directions carefully in his head.

"The door will open and you say: 'By Allah's grace, I'm here for the coin.

Jamal sent me.' This is very important. Repeat." Jamal repeated the line exactly as he was told.

"Once you have the coin in your possession, say: "Jamal thanks you. Allahu akbar.' Then step away and bring the coin to me without delay." Abbas made sure he said the second line clearly and with confidence.

"Good, good, boy," Jamal whispered as he patted the boy's head and hugged him before sending him away earlier in the evening.

Jamal watched as Abbas, walking straight and true, followed the same path of the sun as it, too, had disappeared from sight.

As Abbas approached the door, two men, who appeared to be arguing, came around the corner not far from where he stood frozen like a statue. The two men shuffled close to where he was standing, behind a small pillar. Someone shouted in Arabic from a small dar across the street for the men to go away. The men appeared to pay no attention to the shouted request and continued to argue. Less than a minute later, a stream of water came splashing down upon the men in the street. The water had a heavy scent. It smelled to Abbas like animal urine, but who knew? The men ran away, yelling curses as they went. It was all he could do to keep from laughing, even though this was no time for joking around.

Abbas knocked three times, stood back and waited. The arguing men's voices faded, giving way to the sound of a creaking door. The weathered wood appeared to be almost too heavy for the hinge that cried out, as the door continued to slowly open. Abbas squinted his eyes, attempting to find some light. He waited patiently, tapping his fingers on his legs as if encouraging them to stay alert in case he had to run for it. Floorboards began to creak as the face of an old woman or man, he couldn't tell, began to take shape.

Abbas lost all thought of what he was supposed to say. He swallowed hard, his gum was gone, he coughed once then stammered: "The coin for Ja... Jamal. I... I am Abbas."

The wrinkled face came forward, closer, with a smile. And when she spoke, he knew. "Here you are son, now go and may

Allah be with you. Yala," she commanded, using the Arabic word for go.

The coin felt warm as he carefully took it from the middle of her wrinkled palm. The old woman's hand was soft to the touch and comforting. He bowed quickly, turned and flew off the porch heading back the way he had come. It wasn't until he rounded the fifth of eight corners that he realized the coin was still in his hand. He stopped near a large urn and placed the coin in his pouch, fastened the strap and took off running again. He ran with abandon, faster than he ever thought he could, weaving in and out of the shadows, around corners, not caring if someone heard him, he became the wind.

§

CARINI, SICILY; THE PETRULA COMPOUND

The carefully worded note Michael read from Lorretta encouraged him. It had been sent by special courier, which made him feel better about being sent packing to Sicily. Michael opened the door to the small house he'd been held for his own protection, took a deep breath and sat on the top step and continued to read. He'd hated the place at first, but lately, he'd grown to appreciate the beautiful surroundings and what his Italian relatives were trying to do for him.

Lorretta had been careful when writing to Michael. She had many reasons for covering her tracks, which left deep scars on people that disagreed with her. She'd built a successful business enterprise into a billion-dollar empire by always looking forward — never back. For that reason, the note began with hopeful wishes for Michael and his relatives. She loved Michael and expressed her feelings for him. Before signing off, she included the kicker: The man you hate most is in your part of the world.

Milan to be exact. Trust your cousins and others to take care of him. I urge you to stay put and heal. I want you back in one piece, my love.

Michael felt a surge of energy begin to swell from deep inside. It was an old sinister rush of emotion that he'd felt on a more regular basis back when he made life and death decisions. A smile formed as Michael contemplated what he would do if he and Rick Blaine ever came face-to-face. His thoughts raced. In the end he would not comply with Lorretta's wishes to stay put. I've been here long enough. He would personally take care of that bastard.

Michael would not be treated as a patient any longer. He was never anyone who would wait until further notice. Her suggestion, as thoughtful as it was, didn't sit well with him. He was tired of being told what to do, where to go, how to act. This is bullshit.

Instead, he decided to finally say, yes, and go out and get drunk with his cousins. Why not raise a little hell? He'd been living in seclusion, under guard, long enough. The sky had fallen in on him, it was now time for Michael to push back.

§

MILAN, ITALY; MILAN MALPENSA AIRPORT

The flight to Morocco was on time. Rick and Pete were in the process of boarding when Rick's phone vibrated. The caller ID had a wild animal emoji — and for good reason. Rick walked over to a quiet corner of the terminal to take the call.

"Hey, Rick, how's your head?" Just hearing the man's voice brought on a sudden feeling of relief followed by a minor throbbing to his head. "Thanks for the reminder, Bear."

His real name was Bobby Hansen, a six-foot-four inch,

250-pound, badass private investigator that helped to save Rick's life a few months ago. Ralph Phillips, Blaine's corporate attorney, engaged Bear's services when the Castillino family was making Rick's life a living hell.

"Bear, sounds like you're driving."

"Yep," he said, pausing. "Just a sec, I'm pulling over. Just checked on your condo in Venice Beach. Jillian and Artie said to say hi." He paused again, "You know I've never been off your case."

Ralph agreed to expand Bear's security retainer to include Rick. Ralph's concern centered mostly around the fact that the Castillino family may not simply go away. Bear was more than pleased to have the additional duty, after all, Rick Blaine was not your average client. He led a very exciting life and Bear enjoyed tagging along. "What's up?"

"Turns out Ralph's suspicions were right on. Rick, you're being followed. One of my sources in Boston found out last night. We don't have any identification yet, but you're being shadowed by a man who's in with the Castillino clan."

"Someone followed me here to Italy from San Francisco? Are you kidding me?"

Rick's comment caused Pete to lean in on the conversation. Pete began to look around as he continued to eavesdrop, trying not to step on Rick's heels as their section was called to board.

"Yes. Mister whomever it is most likely following your every move. Sounds like you're boarding a plane. Look around, he's probably on that flight."

"Got it. Jesus."

"Watch your six. There could be a kill order out on you. Other than that, have a good time. Where are you headed?"

"A friend of mine and I are taking a side trip to Morocco."

"No shit? You really know how to take chances, I'll give you that, man. Stay close to your phone. I'll be in touch."

When the call ended, Rick looked at Pete. "Someone may be following me on this flight. Keep your eyes peeled for anyone who looks suspicious." Pete nodded as they hurried to catch up and board the plane.

Once they found their seats, both Rick and Pete looked around at the other passengers. Neither one knew exactly who to look for since Bear had no description to pass along. Turban-wearing men and women in general were automatically ruled out. Bear had suggested looking for a man who looked American/Italian, most likely sitting toward the back of the aircraft.

The flight to Tangier leveled off at cruising altitude. The ride was smooth on the older model Boeing 737-200. Pete couldn't hold back any longer.

"Question: Who are Bear and Ralph?"

"Ralph Phillips is our corporate attorney. He set me up with Bear, a private detective with twenty years of military service behind him. I owe my life to the guy. Okay, so someone

could be on my tail, which means they're on yours too. Bear suspects it's a guy, he'll text more details later." Pete looked at his friend then sat back. After taking a few seconds to look out the window, he sat back up.

"I'm going to the restroom in the back of the plane, checking seats along the way," Pete whispered as he unbuckled and slowly rose.

It was a long shot, identifying someone without a description, but it didn't hurt to try. Pete whispered to Rick upon his return. "If the bastard is on the plane, and we see him following us while we're in Tangier, we'll know." Pete raised his hands over his head and used the cargo bins for balance as he made his way along the aisle. An elderly lady looked up at him as he passed. Her smile revealed tobacco-stained teeth that appeared to be chewing on a substance Pete hoped was organic and healthy.

Two young people huddled together as if this would be the last time they'd ever see one another. A few others were catching up on sleep, while their neighbors wore headphones to drown out the engine noise. There were one or two suspicious looking characters that Pete glanced at before reaching the restroom. He only had to wait a short time before the door folded back and a lovely young lady appeared holding a baby. He stepped aside and let the mother and baby go past. As he entered the toilet he noticed a man, dressed all in black, talking to one of the flight attendants in the back galley. Pete made a mental note of the man and what he wore.

Pete had gone through various stages of training before becoming a foreign consul. The most important feature of their defensive exercises was to learn how to read people. The other was to be constantly watching your back when you're away from the embassy. Both of them were now on the alert.

As a diplomat, Pete was fortunate to be able to travel with a diplomatic pouch, which under international law is prohibited from being searched. Searching a diplomatic pouch would create an enormous scandal and could lead to foreign diplomats being expelled from the U.S. The pouch served Pete and Rick well, because it allowed him to carry a 9mm Glock 19 for protection. He was planning to act as tour guide/bodyguard, because of the area they were traveling to, while assuring Rick that he always traveled with a gun. Add the fact that Rick may be followed, and Pete's role took on even more significance. There I go again, Rick thought, putting friends in danger.

The flight time to Tangier from Milan was less than three hours. Pete explained that he and a military officer had taken the same flight a few months ago to meet with a local dignitary. Rick tried to pay attention to Pete's explanation, but his mind was on who might be following him.

After an uneventful flight at cruising altitude, the plane began descending with seats 6A and B on alert.

§

SILICON VALLEY, CA; BLAINE MANUFACTURING

Brenda's workload became more manageable with the hire of two new assistants. Her reduced workload allowed Brenda to focus on more administrative matters with Rick Blaine heading that list.

She sat in the sunshine of her new office that overlooked the new production facility. Her notes from that morning's management team meeting were being prioritized as instructed. She needed those for the administrative meeting later that afternoon.

Report after report reflected a positive vibe emanating throughout the building. Business was good and the main topic was how to expand production in anticipation of new international business. The team felt confident that Major Connors, Head of Production, would be able to meet increases in production up to fifty percent. The confidence came as a result of the completion of the new production facility on campus, plus the addition of new line equipment installed in a recently acquired warehouse, located a block away, previously owned by Apple.

Brenda kept Rick informed of every major occurrence as they happened. Day-to-day operations were another matter she could supervise. She was in the middle of preparing a report for Rick to review when one of her assistants buzzed.

"Miss Johnson, you have a call on line two, it's Ralph Phillips."

Brenda took the call even though it meant putting Rick's "Good news" report on hold.

Ralph explained what Bear had uncovered concerning Rick being followed. He urged Brenda to consider sending Bobby Hansen overseas, to meet up with Rick, and act as his bodyguard for the remainder of his trip. Brenda could tell that Ralph was beyond concerned and he had no other reliable resources in Europe.

"The Castillinos have to be behind this," Brenda responded in her calm, thoughtful manner. Before making the decision to send Bobby to Europe she wanted to check with Winston, first, to see if he knew of someone on the Continent capable of protecting Rick.

Ralph agreed, but asked that she not take too long in making the decision. He also wanted to make sure that Hansen Services, Bear's company, would be keeping an eye on Blaine Manufacturing. Brenda sat back in her chair after the call. She wondered what it would look like having Bear shadow Rick in London. The thought made her smile. A different feeling of relief came over her knowing that Bear, a superhero in her estimation, would be working behind the scenes to watch over Blaine Manufacturing in addition to their own security people.

The Castillinos were a big concern. Just thinking of them made her turn her chair and get back to work.

Chapter 3

SILICON VALLEY, CA; BLAINE MANUFACTURING

Brenda normally kept one desk light on in her office when she worked late. On that particular night her office atmosphere included two standing lamps and a large box-shaped chandelier. The additional lighting provided more than enough ambient light for a late-night meeting with Blaine's corporate attorney, Ralph Phillips. Brenda was more than concerned about Rick's safety, now that they'd discovered he was being followed. The dignified older counselor sat across from her, with his briefcase open next to his chair, and his laptop open on one corner of Brenda's desk. They were ready for Bear's call.

"Brenda, Ralph, let's talk Rick," greeted both of them as Bear came on the line.

They each felt the urgency for creating security for Rick. Blaine's namesake had convinced each of them that he could handle this trip on his own. Ralph didn't agree, at least not at first. He and Bear had to be talked into letting Rick go off on his own, believing the Lampersons would take care of security. But Rick, as he was known to do, went off his original plan and was now on his way to Morocco? That, when coupled with the new information of him being followed, didn't sit well with the three protectors.

As the conversation continued, the decision was made to have Bear meet with them, as soon as possible, in San Francisco. Bear agreed with the urgency, and said he would fly out from Tucson, Arizona in the morning, pointing out that he lived out of suitcase most of the time. He had an ongoing consulting contract with the border patrol in Nogales and could rearrange his schedule. After talking with Rick, his gut feeling was that Mr. Blaine had that bullseye on his back again. Bear prepared himself for whatever the group, which included Blaine's management team, required him to do.

The late-night meeting ended after forty-five minutes of heated discussion.

Brenda decided to call it a night instead of finishing the report she had started earlier. It could wait, security for Rick couldn't. She expected an overseas call from Winston any minute, and would take it on her cell. She heard the elevator bell ding as Ralph said his goodbyes and left. He would meet Brenda at his office in the morning, after he picked Bear up from the airport. Brenda looked at the clock, it was nearly midnight, she decided to call Winston.

"Oh, hello, Brenda, this is Ben, my father is on another line, may I be of assistance?" She had to take a breath, she didn't know why exactly, but she hadn't expected Ben to take the call. Could that be it or was she just tired? She didn't know, so she continued.

"Hello, Ben. I hope I'm not disturbing you, but we have a new development with Rick."

"You mean something more than his side trip to Morocco?"

Brenda went on to explain that Bear had received intel that someone connected to the Castillino family was following Rick. "Ralph and I are meeting with Bear in the morning, but in the meantime, we were hoping you had someone available to act as bodyguard for him in London for sure or sooner."

"Oh, dear, the Castillinos? Well, we need to get on this straight away. From what you're saying, he'll need protection immediately."

"Yes. Agreed. I just spoke to Ralph Phillips and he suggests we put Bear on it, but as you know, he'll have no authority overseas. Bear is willing to travel; however, I wonder if it wouldn't be more prudent to use someone there."

"That's good to know about your Bear fellow, Brenda. I'm on it. Father has several connections that work undercover. Bear and I will discuss the matter with my father as soon as he's off the line. I know it's late there. Will you be at this number within the hour?"

Brenda gave Ben her cell phone number. She would be leaving her office in a few minutes.

As Brenda made her way down the elevator, Jimmy the security guard texted her to let her know that he was waiting at the outside exit door.

Jimmy worked the swing shift for Blaine's security team. Since the incident with the Castillinos, Blaine increased its security for personnel and overall operations 24/7. Two additional guards were posted to walk the grounds at night with Jimmy. A force of ten guards worked security on Blaine's expanding campus, which now covered just over eight acres of real estate in the, very expensive, high-tech mecca known as Silicon Valley.

Thirty minutes later Winston's call from London appeared on Brenda's phone as she pulled into her condominium parking garage in Palo Alto.

"Hello, my love," Winston said. "Well, our Rick is a popular fellow these days. He can't even go to visit a friend overseas without looking over his shoulder."

Winston's attempt to bring levity into the matter was greeted with silence that required no further explanation. He quickly went on to explain that they had someone to help protect Rick in mind. A person equal to the merits of Mr. Bear named Sir Archibald Turlington, better known to MI5 and Scotland Yard as Archie.

"Archie is our man for the job and he is available. Only one problem, he's in Scotland at the moment, hunting birds. The only time of year the sport works for him, and his prey."

"What's next, Winston?"

"Flight arrangements are being made for the day after tomorrow. The quickest he can be here in London. We'll bring him up to speed and be ready when Rick arrives three days from now. It's the best I can do, Brenda."

"Fine," said Brenda, clearly annoyed. "I mean, that's great, Winston. Sorry about the rush, but we just found out. I'll have Rick call you when he's back in Milan."

"Get some rest, my dear. Rick will be fine. And as we both know, Rick is fortunate to have you, and he just happens to be the luckiest man alive."

§

TANGIER, MOROCCO; IBN BATTOUTA INTERNATIONAL AIRPORT

It was not yet midmorning and the air was already so humid you could taste it as Rick and Pete walked out of Tangier's Ibn Battouta International Airport. Pete hailed a cab, and asked Rick where they were going, which he then relayed to the driver. Pete had picked up workable French and Italian during his time at the Foreign Service Institute in northern Virginia, while preparing for his European assignment. Winston had given Rick directions to follow and a time to meet with a man named Jamal.

Rick checked his phone for the notes he made from his call with Winston. The driver wore a fez — a short, red cylindrical, peakless hat — and had a full beard. He looked at Rick through the rearview mirror as a car honked behind them. "Ah, found it. The Grand Socco Marketplace, driver."

Both men were hungry and asked to be dropped off near a cafe serving breakfast.

The cab driver nodded as if he knew just the place. For the next two and a half hours, Rick and Pete would eat, prepare for the meeting, and watch their backs. Pete felt even more obligated, even though he wasn't responsible for the two of them being there in Morocco, instead of on a beach in Italy.

Rick had instructions to meet his contact at noon, the hottest time of the day in that part of the world. Most vendors in the marketplace, because of the heat, shut down for prayer and a meal at that time. The restaurant, where they would meet Jamal, happened to be a short distance from a small park they walked to after breakfast. The park bordered the Grand Socco Marketplace, a tourist Mecca if ever one existed.

Someone else had the same feeling about the amount of people attracted to the Grand Socco. The Rat had a hard time keeping up with them, but managed to position himself across a roadway, behind a bush outcropping, within sight of Rick and his friend. Unfortunately, the Rat was busy throwing up. He did not enjoy the flight from Milan that morning after having his usual breakfast of eggs and sausage. He hated flying to begin with, but his target had been hard to follow, going from one venue to another like a kid at Disneyland. But this gig was too much to pass up, he needed the money to pay for his horse race betting obsession. The Rat also wanted to stay on Lorretta's good side. Who didn't? And who the hell was that guy with Rick Blaine? His lower back was giving him fits as he focused a small spotter's scope that had almost been confiscated before the flight. It took some fast talking in order to convince the gate agent that the Rat had eyesight issues and needed the scope to help find his way around.

The target and his friend were obviously buddies from what he overheard on the plane. This asshole added a new dimension to the mix. I shoulda taken Blaine out in San Fran when I had the chance. But he retched a third time disagreeing with himself and shaking his head for more than one reason. There were too many people around at the San Francisco Airport. I could be at the track right now betting the horses rather than puking in this God forsaken place.

His mission was simple; kill Rick Blaine. Lorretta preferred making it look like an accident or suicide. The fewer the inquiries the cleaner the kill. But, if that wasn't possible, and he had the opportunity, use any means possible to take him out, just get it done. Those were the last instructions Lorretta uttered before kicking him out of her office. The Rat wasn't exactly sure why Rick was here in Morocco, or for how long, but he felt the need to move quickly. He had to leave his gun behind because of airport security, and needed to purchase a knife for the job. Fortunately, in this land of high crime, weapon vendors were on nearly every street corner around here. The one he selected had a curved blade with an ornate ivory handle. Very cool. He would mail it home and give it to Lorretta as a present once the job was completed. The Rat rotated the knife around and around in his hand as he watched the target and his friend walk along the parkway.

§

CARINI, SICILY; THE PETRULA COMPOUND

The afternoon sunlight hit him like a two by four in the head. The last thing Michael remembered was being delivered to his small abode by three of his cousins. They were laughing at his inability to walk a straight line or sing along with them in Italian. The four of them had extended the Cafe Lava's Happy Hour, into the early morning hours, at Michael's request. The cousins were entrusted with Michael's safety, so they made sure he made it home and into his bed before leaving. Giovanni took care to pull off Michael's shoes and covered his cousin with a blanket as he exited the room. After closing the door, the three cousins walked off singing and laughing as they made their way down a winding path back into the village and more vino. A guard stood watching as they left. Lucky bastards.

Michael closed his eyes tight then opened them slightly, as he made his way from the bed with sheets that were now covered in dirt and grime. He tripped over an armchair as he headed to the bathroom, a ghost-like figure that had way too much to drink. Sitting on the toilet, head in his hands, he discovered that his feet were filthy. Where were his shoes? His balance was off and he bumped into the shower curtain, grabbing on to it for assistance, which didn't come. Instead, the curtain rod and Michael, ended up in the tub as if that was his original intention. He hit his head on the way down, which gave him an additional reason to hate the world even more.

A knock came to his door. "Cugino, are you alright in there?"

Michael, wrapped up like a caterpillar in a cocoon, pulled his head forward and managed to respond: "I'm fine. Be out soon."

An hour later, lunch awaited him on the covered porch of a beautiful stucco villa that sat in the middle of the family vineyard. Michael managed to find his way across from the caretaker's cottage, that he now shared, to the porch, thanks to his dark glasses and strong determination. He sat with his cousin, Mario, who greeted him with a big smile and a welcoming hug. Michael tried to return the smile, but failed miserably, paying more attention to his headache. Mario had a big toothy smile and a cell phone close by. He was in the midst of talking to Lorretta on the phone, which he then handed to Michael as he reached the top step.

"Mario tells me you two had some fun last night in Palermo," Lorretta uttered.

"Yep," Michael paused, trying not to retch. "A little too much I guess."

"Well, get your good-looking head together because I need you," she stated more emphatically.

"Keep talking," Michael could feel the concern in Lorretta's voice.

"It seems the Rat ran into trouble in Morocco. He's in jail," Lorretta added.

"What the hell is the Rat doing in Morocco?"

"Long story. For now, pack your bags, and ask Mario to join you in tracking Rick Blaine. You need to be in Milan right away. I'll send you details."

§

TANGIER, MOROCCO; MOHAMMAD V HOSPITAL

Rick and Pete looked across the room at the short little man who had just attacked them in the park. No sooner had they arrived near the fountain by the bench, and were about to sit and wait, when a man with a knife surprised them from behind. Actually, he didn't surprise Pete who spun the attacker around like a top, disarmed him, and choked him into submission.

Two local Moroccan policemen were on the scene almost immediately. They had been talking to two tourists on the other side of the fountain when they heard a man scream for help. At first, they didn't know who staged the attack, until Rick pointed to the short man being choked, dropping the knife. The man was taken into custody and Pete and Rick were asked to join the officers at the station.

"That little shit cut me, twice," Pete said as a female aid attended to his wound.

She was young, in her mid-twenties Rick suspected, light brown toned skin, wearing what appeared to be the Moroccan version of an EMT uniform. She had professionally stitched up a slice on Pete's right arm and was busy wrapping up the palm of his left hand. Rick excused himself to call Winston about the attack.

"Yes, I know, Jamal just contacted me. How are you and your friend?"

"We're fine, what about the drop?"

"Jamal is concerned," said Winston. "He will make other arrangements, which will delay us no doubt."

"That's not necessary. Look, we're here. Pete sustained some minor injuries, but he's good to go. Besides, if he's not, he can meet me at the airport if necessary. I can meet Jamal. What time works? We don't leave until eight tonight, five hours from now."

"I'll call him back and do my best to convince him to meet with you. I'll let you know. This is most unfortunate, but deeply appreciated, Rick, thank you."

Rick went back to where he left Pete and found him gone. The attacker had been taken back to what the officer called: The Cages. A guard came up and ushered Rick to a side room where three police officials sat at an interrogation table with Pete on one side, the officers on the other.

"Please sit, Mr. Blaine. I'm Capitane Alami, head of this precinct in Tangier. We'd like to ask some questions."

Before Rick sat down to be questioned, he sent Winston a quick text asking him not to call, but to text. He then entered the room with Pete for what he hoped would be a short session. Two hours later, with Pete ready to blow his top, Rick masterfully led him to the front door, hailing a cab as they went.

"Those bastards! Two hundred dollars!"

"It's only money, we're fortunate it wasn't more. Let's go. We have a new rendezvous time and place, and an hour to complete the transfer with Jamal."

§

TANGIER, MOROCCO; LE PETIT SOCCO MARKETPLACE

Jamal's wife and uncle took over the spice stall duty as requested. Jamal had a meeting to attend to, which no one questioned. Jamal paced himself as he slowly made his way down the Rue Es-Siaghine, known for silversmiths, cafes and bars. His pace was even and deliberate as if counting his steps as he went. He purposely didn't want to attract attention. His destination was an area called, Le Petit Socco. Located within the smaller marketplace was one of his favorite hideaways, a bar called Souk Dar (Little House).

The dark musty bar with a dirt floor became their new meeting location. Jamal insisted on it knowing the place would be mostly empty during early evening prayer. He sat in his favorite booth. Hidden in the back, in a dark corner, facing the wooden double doored entrance, perfect for what needed to be done. Jamal ordered a Torbo, his favorite mud-like coffee drink, and waited.

Pete and Rick walked from the opposite direction following instructions, sent earlier by Jamal, on Rick's phone, after giving him the good news that a meeting with Jamal was back on. The streets they walked through were so narrow both men could stretch out their arms and touch walls on either side as they strolled. Rick couldn't help but notice how clean the streets were, and Pete explained that the architecture was such that no windows faced the street, instead, all open areas, windows, patios, and gardens were located on the inside in courtyards that normally featured a water well. That kept the hot temperatures out and the comfort in, with the aid of ceiling fans. Smart.

They turned on Rue Es-Siaghine and found the meeting place. It took a minute or two for their eyes to adjust as they slowly entered the dark and musky bar. After the incident in the park, their alert antennae were in the up position. Jamal sat still, facing the door, keeping an eye on them. He studied their every move, an ex-military habit he called upon as he watched the men take their time. At first, he wanted to put the transfer off, because of the commotion these two Americans caused earlier in the day. Jamal did not favor Americans. He felt they were greedy capitalists always looking for deals at his stall. Winston convinced him otherwise, at least as far as these two men were concerned. "Jamal, you know me and I know Rick Blaine. He and his friend can be trusted." Winston also pointed out the fact that Rick, and his friend, were doing them a favor. Jamal agreed, but made a mental note to have Winston consider a favor he, Jamal, was considering for the future.

As the men made their way through the place, Jamal slowly rose to greet them as they approached. Once eye contact was made, it sent the wrong message to stay seated, unless your intention is to kill.

"As-salamu Alaykum," Jamal offered with a prayerful bow.

Pete scanned the place and then focused on the stranger, who blended into the background in front of him, and replied: "And Allah's peace be upon you, sir."

Jamal nodded and motioned toward the booth with his hand. Rick asked if he spoke English, causing Jamal to nod his head.

"My English is good to me, maybe not to you, sir." He paused, looking around. "We need to be quick."

Jamal then reached into his robe. Pete automatically moved his right hand to his back waistband. Jamal's movement caused both strangers to sit up, Pete with his hand to his waist where the gun rested, Rick ready to push the table at the stranger. Jamal watched their reaction and smiled, revealing tobacco-stained teeth surrounded by a full beard. Through the amber glow from a nearby table lamp, Jamal's eyes appeared to have gray steely points as his cheeks relaxed causing his lips to close.

Jamal raised his left hand in a reassuring gesture as he brought out a small leather pouch with his right. He carefully peeled back the flap to reveal a coin that appeared to be gold. Both men leaned forward to get a better glimpse of what appeared to be a rare piece. In a friendly gesture, Jamal moved it closer for a better view of the highly polished coin. "This is the ancient Roman coin our Winston is requesting. For centuries this has been the way. It serves as the key to opening the information located on the disks also located in this pouch."

Both men had questions, Jamal could see it on their faces. He held up both hands, signaling silence. "You will be wise to leave now and ask no more questions of me," Jamal smiled with a slight bow as he brought both hands back in the prayer position. He passed the pouch forward. Rick accepted the coin and noticed two grey and black, five and a quarter inch floppy discs in the pouch. He couldn't take his eyes off discs as he read their size and which way to insert them into the disk drive. Lines formed in his forehead as if to question the use of old technology. Jamal picked up on Rick's confusion. "Ah, yes, the discs," he whispered with a laugh as he leaned in a little closer. "They are ancient too, but they contain much needed information for my friend, Mr. Lamperson. One more thing," he paused, taking on a more serious tone. "Be ever watchful. I suspect your enemies look more like you, not me. If you know what I mean, sir." Jamal whispered as he took his last sip of coffee.

Rick suddenly felt a shiver as he looked into Jamal's eyes. He decided not to question the use of such outdated technology, and placed the coin back in the pouch, put the pouch in Pete's diplomatic bag, and nodded his head to Jamal. Pete's pouch was untouchable to authorities, because of Article 27 of the 1961 Vienna Convention on Diplomatic Relations, in which all nations agreed that diplomatic pouches "shall not be opened or detained" and that the person holding it "shall not be liable to any form of arrest or detention." This pouch, when combined with Pete's diplomatic passport gave them a level of security that Rick had not anticipated, but heartily welcomed at this point.

Fifteen minutes later they were on their way to the airport, with thirty minutes to go before take-off.

"What do you suppose Jamal meant by: For centuries this has been the way."

"Pete, I'm not sure, but it sounds more complicated than picking up a Federal Express package for a friend."

Pete reached under the seat ahead of him for his leather satchel. After unlocking the sturdy blue pouch with the words "Property of U.S. Consulate" emblazoned on it and unzipping it, he pulled the envelope that Jamal had handed them earlier. He studied the package, turning it over in his hands, then looked at Rick. "This envelope contains something that deserves more explanation, my friend."

Rick responded, both whispering back and forth. "Winston and Jamal have some kind of secretive system, that's all I need to know for the moment. That attacker, though, he was clearly after me and not this," Rick stated as he took the package back, squeezed it, and placed it in the satchel and looked directly at Pete. "You need to know that."

"Got it. Hope you're right," Pete responded looking pensive

as he turned to view the coastal landscape racing past the cab window.

They made their flight as the last call could be heard over the speaker. The return flight rode much smoother as shots of whiskey were served over friendlier skies. A welcomed relief as both men were completely exhausted. Just before landing, Pete turned and whispered: "Hey, whatever's going on in your life right now, I'm here for you, buddy."

Both men were busy catching up, going over old times at the University of Idaho when the sign for landing sounded like an unwanted alarm clock. Pete texted their ride, one of Pete's associates from his office, who waited at the curb on time.

Their original plan had Rick staying with Pete that night. But with Sese in the picture, the plan changed. Rick had no problem staying in the beautiful Italian hotel that provided a 270-degree view of Milan. Besides, Rick's friend needed some tender loving care that evening and the package they picked up would be kept in Pete's home safe until Rick left for London in two days. As the French would say, c'est la vie.

Pete dropped Rick off at the hotel so he could freshen up and join his hosts for a tour north to the lake district.

"Catch your second wind, Rick. We'll be around in an hour to pick you up."

Even though they'd had a long day, Pete decided that they would keep to their schedule, even though Rick would understand if his wounded bodyguard asked for a time out to be with Sese.

Both men were eager to pick up where they left off. Rick always wanted to see the Alps from the Italian perspective. He couldn't wait. After loading the car, they headed north to the town of Stresa on Lake Maggiore. The ride up through the countryside showcased the true Italian look of vineyards, villas and vistas that were unique to Italy. Pete had to slow down as they entered small towns along the way. That gave Rick a chance to see how the people of Italy lived away from the larger city of Milan. He found the more rural areas not only relaxing, but exact duplicates of all the paintings he'd seen in homes and museums. Colorful and intriguing.

An hour and a half later they arrived at their destination of Stresa where they planned to take a break as the sun began to set.

"Most of Lake Maggiore is in Italy with the upper quarter completely in Switzerland," Sese said as she pointed north toward the Alps that towered over the landscape. "This is the place where the locals caught Mussolini and his girlfriend during World War II. They were trying to escape up the westside road on the lake leading to Switzerland." Her voice lowered as she added, "One of my family's relatives, an uncle, was involved in that capture." The look on her face said it all. Sese's radiant features slowly changed from beauty to pride and back again. Pete looked at her as he downshifted and reduced speed. "Rick, you'll notice that everything around here slows down. You can't help but relax in this part of the world. There's a speed limit on the lake, thirty-five miles per hour, and no jet skis or wave runners allowed."

Sese continued to highlight the landscape as darkness came on. Her family owned a small villa on the lake, which she'd recently inherited from her parents, a gift for her achievements in modeling and the fashion business. The oldest of two, she helped raise her brother as they roamed throughout the region, learning to hunt, fish on and around the lake, and ski in the Alps. Her brother attended school in Florence and planned to graduate next year. Sese shared the villa with her family, including an uncle who lived in Germany. Sese and her brother worked out a schedule at the beginning of the year, and this was her time to bring friends for the next month.

The drive along the west side of the lake reminded Rick of what it must have been like to travel back in history along the same route. The roadway, although smooth to drive on, was narrow with large granite stones lining the water side, serving as an indigenous guard rail. The hillside opposite the lake included an even mixture of evergreen and deciduous trees of various heights that shot up the landscape like rockets launching skyward. Rick found himself straining to find the top of the hillside, pressing his face to the car window as Sese continued to explain the surroundings. "Here we are, Rick."

Pete turned into a driveway, half hidden by the landscape. A black wrought iron gate encased in granite greeted them as they turned down a graveled road that serpentined for another two hundred feet to the water's edge. The villa, artfully coated in cream colored stucco, showcased red tiles over the main doorway and all along the roof. The single car garage, located off to one side, looked more like an ornament as opposed to a refuge.

The trio unpacked in the driveway and made their way along a fragrant boxed hedge that ran for more than forty feet to the front door.

A large flagstone path led to a wooden pergola that hid the side entrance, which opened onto a kitchen to envy. High ceilings, Florentine tile everywhere, and a stone fireplace off a dining room, set the tone for the rest of the first floor. An enormous picture window, revealing blue water and slow-moving water craft, kept the viewer spellbound.

Rick noticed the unusual design of the long wooden boats with a large rudder in the stern and asked Sese what they were. "These are mostly water taxis and cargo haulers, but some owners also fished from them. They have a customized hull and keel so they can ride up on large granite stones at various launch and docking sites along the lake. This is a deep lake with very little beach. So, the boats have to dock or slide up on the stones."

Rick acknowledged her explanation by nodding, and continued to watch the boat traffic go past as if in a trance.

Pete suddenly snapped his fingers, which brought his friend out of the trance, and motioned for him to follow, as they headed to a guest room on the main floor. They walked into a smaller living room area that led out onto a screened-in porch with four large ceramic pots that were a portrait of colorful plants and flowers. Each pot showcased a wide variety of color schemes in paisley-like designs.

"Change into something more comfortable. We're going for a ride, on an old wooden sailboat. You're going to love it, Captain." Pete knew all about Rick's love for sailing, who had a beautiful sloop of his own anchored in North Idaho on Pend Oreille Lake.

Thirty minutes later, with help from his two-person crew, Rick found himself sailing under moderate wind on a lake that he'd only read about in the visitor's guidebook. The dusky sky had yet to reveal the evening stars. Rick favored evening sailing back home. He knew heaven was about to burst as the boat silently made its way out of a small cove and into the more open water. The familiar slow-motion relaxation gave each of them an opportunity to enjoy the moment. Rick stood at the helm watching Sese and Pete sitting together on the bow, feet dangling over the side, allowing the movement to take them away. The captain watching his crew.

After a few minutes they both returned to the stern where Rick maintained the heading he'd been given when they cast off. "We're coming up to our destination and will need to take the main down, Captain," Pete said as he headed for the main mast ready to undo the halyard from the cleat when Rick gave the word. Rick headed the boat into the wind and gave the command to reduce the main slightly.

They were a beam of their destination, about one hundred

yards from shore. Pete started the engine and took over as captain as they proceeded to motor toward Cannero Riviera, a castle/hotel on the water, a family favorite located two clicks from the villa by road. Sese had called ahead and reserved a spot along the restaurant's wooden dock with large stone pillars.

Dinner and cocktails were served by the owner and her daughter, while papa worked the kitchen as head chef. An older son served the table as Mima, the hostess, hugged Sese. A few patrons enjoyed their meals while other family members, children, could be heard playing outside. Rick sat making mental notes for his friends that ran a lake restaurant in North Idaho. The evening felt perfect as the whole experience seemed to shift into slow motion. He felt unbelievably safe here and relished this moment in time with Pete and Sese.

Pete kept watch on the room and his bandaged hand below the table. The wound was minor, and he didn't want to draw attention to it or them. Rick noticed Pete's surveillance mode. Pete had once told him that during his training to be a diplomat, he was told to enter a room, memorize and surveil everything he saw, and then was tested on what had been moved when he was sent back in. Of all the people that Rick felt safe with, Pete was high on the list. Catching a glimpse of Pete's bandaged hand, Rick also felt guilty for putting his friend in danger. He decided to change the mood.

"Let's raise a glass to friendship," Rick offered as he lifted a glass of a local red varietal he couldn't pronounce. "To friendship," Rick looked down as he paused for a few beats then added: "Both of you have been so generous with your time, I can't thank you enough. The last few months have been, well... tough for me. I needed this. Grazie and Cheers!"

The trio sailed back under starry skies, which gave Rick his opportunity to point out various celestial guideposts, a favorite hobby of his. Sese explained that the sun set earlier here because of the gigantic mountain range that watched over them. The Alps provided a continual supply of water that the trio had just enjoyed as they walked, arm-in-arm, along the dock that secured the boat. Night fell like a blanket being tossed over each person, as they sat in lounge chairs on the patio deck drinking warmed Grand Marnier. It was then that the most incredible thing happened. The lake shore lit up with fireworks accompanied by Italian music could be heard across the gentle waves. Sese leaned forward to explain. "I forgot to tell you two. We do fireworks every Friday here."

§

LONDON, UK; HEATHROW AIRPORT

"Archie," Winston called out as he stood waiting for his old friend. He had looked forward to picking the man up himself instead of sending the company limo and driver. Archie wasn't a limo type of person anyway. He'd rather ride all day in one of those conventional black English cabs, or on his black and gold vintage Triumph wearing his Guinness leathers with matching saddlebags flying in the breeze.

Sir Archibald Fredrick Turlington had the reputation of being his own man. At seventy years of age, and standing just over six feet tall, dressed in a black turtleneck sweater, gray cargo pants neatly tucked into military boots, sporting a shaved head, dark glasses and gray goatee, he had the appearance of a warrior. It was a look that supported his 40 years of military intelligence, spying for MI6, and hunting down criminals in service of MI5 and Scotland Yard as one of their most successful investigators. Those 40 years resulted in being knighted by the Queen. "Facing the Queen, as she held a sword pointed in my direction, was the most frightening and proudest moment of my life," Archie once told a BBC reporter.

Sir Archie, as he became known to his inner circle of friends, continued to live for adventure on his own terms, of course. Selecting when and how to serve the Queen, as a Private Investigator with a title, had been his second life since unofficially retiring two years ago.

"I can't just sit and do nothing. My mind is as sharp as ever, and I can take on any one who challenges me in hand-to-hand combat," he says with pride. "And those I can't, I'll out think the bastards."

Winston knew what had been quoted, recently, in the London Herald, was true, as he helped his friend carry his gear. Archie's reputation also included being able to put all the investigative puzzle pieces together, quickly, to create a solution. In Winston's mind, Archie continued to be unequaled. Being able to defend himself, having spent time with British and American Special Forces, made the man appear superhuman. Winston admired both attributes in the man, crediting the Brits with more mind power and the Yanks with more muscle, leading to better use of his intuitive skills. The combination gave Archie an uncanny ability to defend himself and to be ruthless on the offense. Pound for pound, Sir Archie was someone you wanted on your side, no matter how old he happened to be.

Archie credits a unique workout routine, going to the gym three times a week and the pub twice, not necessarily on the same days. The other two days he hunts birds, unless he's on a project, like now with Winston. In that case, no gym time. The pub, however, will always require a workout.

When they approached the airport transportation area, Archie asked: "So, which way to the car?"

"Oh, I'm afraid there is no car, my friend; we're taking the rail," Winston said, which brought a smile and a comment to his old friend's face.

"You know me too well, Winston."

They both had a good laugh over that, but it was true. Winston hardly ever drove in London anymore. The rail was efficient, relaxing, and ultimately faster. The public transit ride gave both men a chance to catch up, and before long, they were downtown. Archie normally packed light, backpack and a satchel. He had one additional bag that required a special permit. Winston knew about the weapons, and didn't need to ask what the custom-made canvas bag with rollers contained.

The rail-stop in Paddington left them a fair distance from Winston's office in Kensington. After hailing a cab, they were two gents sharing a good laugh about the new transport method they just shared as they made their way to Winston's building. Upon entering, Archie threw his load to the carpet and raced over to Ben's desk, surprising him with a choke hold. The two wrestled each other to the floor in front of several aghast employees who stood back and made room. The swiftness of Archie's maneuver caused a slight commotion in the office that managed to startle one new employee and a delivery person, each of whom watched with concern until Ben began laughing.

"Good to see you too, Uncle Archie," Ben said, red in the face, after picking himself up off the floor.

"Ben. Young man, oh how you've grown. Soon you'll be a giant. Love ya boy."

Ben and Archie weren't really related, but he and Ben's father went so far back that the kinship grew naturally over time. Ben had his heroes, beyond his father, Archie came next.

"Can you give me an hour or two before checking into your hotel, Archie?" Winston asked, hoping to move things right along as they entered his office.

"Of course, on one condition."

Winston looked at his old friend and smiled. "Scotch, 80 years or better. I have it right here. He opened a cabinet and brought out a decanter with two glasses.

"Condition met. Let's get on with it, Winston."

There were two urgent concerns to discuss. First, the matter of Rick Blaine. He pushed a file across the desk toward Archie with a half-poured drink balancing nicely on it. Archie opened the file and began leafing through the first few pages, taking a sip of pure gold. He knew the basics, which Winston had explained on the phone, but new information revealed that Rick continued to be followed. Rick would be in London in the morning to elaborate on what he knew regarding this recent development. The second concern could wait.

"For lack of a better term, Winston, let's call them," he paused, thinking. "Projects, alright?"

"Ah, surely, yes, of course old boy, projects they are."

Archie reached for the decanter, poured himself another, sat back in one of the two old brown leather chairs that faced Winston's large mahogany desk and listened. "Project One: Keep Rick Blaine safe while he visits Europe and the United Kingdom. Evidently, there was a miscue in Morocco yesterday, which involved a man who targeted Rick. That person, known as the Rat, remains incarcerated in a Moroccan jail at this time. But my instincts suggest the Castillinos will pick up where this guy left off."

"So, I'll meet Blaine tomorrow and we'll take it from there."

"Right, Archie. You'll like him straight away, I'm sure. Now for Project Two, a slightly more complicated situation because it, too, involves Mister Blaine once again."

"Honestly, does he go around looking for trouble?" Archie took a small sip as he kept reading through the file.

"No, no, no, you see, yesterday's confrontation," Winston paused. "Well, that one's on me. I'm afraid I put him in that situation only because he was in the right place at the right time, and there was no one else I could or would trust to make the transfer."

Archie looked up, "The transfer?"

"I'll explain in a minute."

"Yes, well then, Project Two." Winston's glass needed a refill and Archie accommodated. Winston then continued to explain that the transfer of two disks and a rare coin had to happen, time was of the essence.

"So, what's the significance of the disks and the coin?"

"The disks contain valuable information regarding the Royal Family. I'm afraid there's a plan in place to assassinate the Queen and possibly other members of her family."

Archie stopped mid-sip and took on a serious look. Winston's demeanor also changed suddenly as he continued. "You remember the Hatterson job in the late eighties?"

"Vaguely, remind me." Archie stood and walked to a side table where a platter of sandwiches, cheese slices, and fresh fruit had been left earlier. "Oh, by all means, forgive me, Archie, help yourself." He did so, as Winston kept going, moved to a white board on the wall and began to draw.

"Back before the internet, we used a rare coin to identify and verify a secret message that came from East Germany by carrier pigeon. The note referred to the coin and the year it was minted, stamped in Roman numerals, gave us a numerical sequence, which provided the key required to decrypt a previous message. And so on, for a series of thirteen messages, after that, the sequence changed. The concept had been used many times throughout the centuries, dating back to the Carthaginians; we just reprised it for that job. And it worked! Remember?"

"I do. And you reprised this ancient method, hoping to confuse the opposition. I get that too. But the use of the diskettes or floppies, as opposed to, what do you call the new finger-length sticks?"

"Thumb drives."

"No, these are off an old system. It took Ben two days to find the equipment we believe will read the Word Perfect format on Jamal's floppy disks. It's ingenious, really. The world has moved on from this antiquated technology—most people under 40 wouldn't even know what they were looking at—which makes it the perfect system to use. Imagine if someone out there wants to intercept our correspondence. Who would even to be able to open the message using Word Perfect of all software. This makes it virtually unreadable, except on ancient PC equipment, if you can even find some that still works!"

"Okay, so what's the connection between the coins and the disks?"

Winston drew as he spoke. "The coin is extremely old with Roman numerals imprinted on both sides. Each sequence is eight digits long, the emperor's mark is contained in the first four numerals, then the year. The passwords for each disk are those series of numbers, minus one for each number, zero is zero. Side one is read right to left and just the opposite for side two.

"How is each side designated, sides one and two, Winston?"

"The side with the emperor's head is side one," he replied, adding, "The disks can't be read without the coin." Winston had a worried look on his face as he completed his last statement.

"What's wrong?"

"I was just thinking of our contact in Morocco. May his Allah keep him and his family, safe."

§

MILAN, ITALY; DOWNTOWN

The sun rose gracefully against a cloudless sky as Mario drove the stolen Fiat sedan around the corner of his friend's body shop. He made his way through bumper-to-bumper traffic three kilometers to where Michael waited out front of his hotel with his carry-on. A rooster crowed in the far-off distance, it was early. The rooster announced the orange morning glow once again, causing Michael to stop and listen as he looked skyward through metal-framed sunglasses.

The car appeared next, stolen a few hours ago by a family member, was yet another example of small rides that didn't quite fit his six foot-three-inch frame. Michael appreciated Mario making transportation arrangements, and decided not to let on about his discomfort. Instead, he had a new concern, one that had to be answered.

"What's with the chickens? Here in the city?" Mario looked at his cousin as if he'd never seen him before. Up to this point, Michael's main concern involved timing and how long they needed to be in Milan. They had spent hours discussing the fact that the sooner he and his cousin took care of Blaine, the better. Milan's crime rate rivaled all other cities in Italy, especially in stolen cars and murders. Blaine's death would help Michael heal emotional wounds that tortured him on a daily basis. "Chickens? You're now concerned about chickens?" said Mario as he slammed the hatchback of the Fiat down hard, and re-entered the car on the driver's side. "I heard a rooster a few minutes ago. Can people own chickens in Milan?" Mario returned Michael's gaze. "Yes, cousin, they can. Since Jesus walked the earth, hens have been dropping eggs around here. Can we go now?" Michael nodded and grabbed onto the passenger strap above his head. "Testa di cazzo," Mario muttered under his breath as he drove off.

The plan to kill Blaine was simple: Aim and Shoot. Both Michael and his cousin, Mario, were excellent shots. If the moment presented itself, Michael might take a knife to the man as a second option.

Michael felt free, re-energized. He couldn't have stayed in Palermo much longer and couldn't wait to return to Boston and get on with his life. He preferred Boston over Italy and hoped to be on his way soon.

Mario had proven to be good company, about the same age, early forties, and about the same size, six-two, but huskier. It shocked Michael at first when Mario picked him up at the airport a couple of months ago; it was like looking in the mirror. Mario brought up the similarities first. "You could be me and I you, cousin." But looks were where the similarities stopped. Mario had an outgoing personality and considered himself a ladies' man. He had no vendetta against Mr. Blaine, but pledged to help his cousin carry out his mission. Life matters most where family is concerned. Blaine completely destroyed Michael's life and was the cause of Tony's death. Michael's brother meant the world to him, or so Mario was told. The story was not entirely true, Blaine didn't pull the trigger, but that didn't matter. Mario found Rick's hotel address thanks to a few hospitality connections. Because of the early morning hour, they were able to find a parking spot across the street. Michael remained in the car after sending his cousin inside Blaine's hotel to check the registry. Michael hated waiting, especially on a warm day in a capsule sized sedan, with poor air conditioning—a car sitting idling for hours was also bound to catch attention.

His handsome counterpart returned to the car after confirming that Blaine was a registered guest. But no room number could be given out, so they waited. But for how long? Michael closed his eyes and focused on Blaine making an appearance. Their car, parked behind an old war monument of a hero on a ragging horse, partially hid the small car. Michael slunk down as far as possible, pressing his knees into the dash as he trained binoculars on the hotel's front doors.

"Man, there are some gorgeous women in this city," observed

Michael. "Like the one with Blaine right now!" Michael smiled as he announced the discovery. "You see him?"

Across the street, Rick and Sese got out of Pete's car in front of the hotel.

"That's a yes, cousin."

"Mister I-have-to-have-my-morning-latte and this babe, are walking to a side patio. Looks like they might be waiting for someone. She has two drinks," Michael half whispered as he spoke under the binoculars perched carefully on his nose.

Sese met Rick, walked to a local espresso bar and ordered coffee drinks to go, including one for Pete. He would join them in a few minutes after finding a parking place.

"Mario. Go. Follow them, the tall lady with the guy in the khaki shorts with the blue shirt. Find a table close to them. We need to know what they're up to."

As Mario was leaving the car to make his way across the street, Pete walked up to the table. Michael watched as Mario, who was very good at spying on people, made his way across the busy street and up around the area where the two strangers sat with the target.

"We're going to miss you, Rick," Pete said as he took his first sip. "Any chance you can come back to Milan or wherever I end up within a year?"

Before Rick could respond, Sese reached out and touched Rick's hand.

"Yes, we hope you had a good time, and that you will return soon. Oh, and have a safe journey to London today," she softly stated.

Rick couldn't help but feel comforted by what they suggested. He'd always felt that Pete would find that someone, a soulmate, and from what he could tell, that connection had happened. Deep down he had the urge to say something, but thought better of it. Instead looked at both of them and raised his cup in a toast.

"Here's to you both. My time here has been too short, and you've made every moment count. I'd like to return and bring someone who would enjoy Italy as much as I have with you two. Just the four of us."

Mario overheard Sese's comment concerning London and texted Michael. He waited for a response. While Sese was talking to Rick, Pete noticed a reflection coming from the binoculars pointed in their direction. It happened again, coming from a small car parked across the street by the Garibaldi monument. Pete raised his cup, blocking the Fiat's view, looked at Rick and mouthed: We're being watched. Pete had been on alert the entire time Rick was around. In fact, being on alert had become natural to him since taking his post in Milan.

"I know I just sat down, but I have to find a restroom," Pete whispered as he then began a fake cough and excused himself from the table.

The Castillinos continued to monitor the table preparing to make their move. Mario was still there, and had just texted to ask Michael what he wanted to know how to proceed? Do you want me to kill him?

There was no way they could escape from this place, too much traffic for one, and too many witnesses for another. Michael texted Mario with that message just as someone knocked on the passenger side window. It was the guy who had been sitting with Rick and the woman.

"Hey, you lost or are you just looking for trouble, friend?" Pete shouted in Italian above the sound of the traffic.

Michael's immediate thought was that this guy was good, but who did he think he was? He admired the ballsy approach, even though the guy was pissing him off.

"If anyone is looking for trouble, friend, it's you," came in English from inside the car.

Pete's left hand was out of commission for a few days or he

would have asked the guy to step outside and have it out with him. He thought better of that and instead suggested: "Look, why don't you put the binoculars away and move out before I call the police."

Pete raised his phone up to make the call. "Okay, asshole, have it your way. I'm leaving."

With that, Pete made his way through horn-honking traffic and back to the table. In the meantime, Mario received a text to meet Michael around the corner. By the time Pete returned to the table he knew he would have to convince Rick that they were being watched. But for which reason? The Castillino affair and the Winston Moroccan situation, were both issues that now involved Rick. His friend's life was even more complicated than Pete imagined.

"So, what was that all about across the street?" Rick asked as Pete sat down.

"Rick, you're the man of the hour, but I'm not sure why. The guy across the street was very defensive, but moved the car right away. He was definitely watching us, you. I'm convinced of that."

"What did he look like?" Rick asked as he shifted his gaze around the area.

"Italian, very Italian and he spoke perfect English."

Rick immediately pulled up a photo on his phone and showed it to Pete.

"That's him. Who is he?"

"Michael Castillino."

Sese looked at Pete as he sat back in his chair. The concern for his friend was clearly evident on his face. There had to be a way for them to protect Rick and at the same time help him deliver his Moroccan package. Sese looked at Pete and whispered: "Cinque Terre."

§

TANGIER, MOROCCO; MUNICIPAL PRISON OF TANGIER

The Rat was in a bad state of mind. He and the prison cell were at odds and one of them had to go. No one noticed or even cared about his wounds, bruises mostly. His left shoulder was in never-ending pain from his arm being skillfully twisted as Pete took him to the ground. That guy I cut was good.

The Rat's mental state was tested even more by the smell emanating from the latrine he nearly fell into last night. The latrine, basically a disgusting hole in the ground, was positioned about three feet from where he now sat and stewed, made him want to vomit as he stared at a tray of what passed for food. The largest flies he had ever seen were enjoying his stay, and his food, much more than the Rat. Besides, they could come and go, those little bastards. The Rat found the only fulfilling thing about his rotten jail cell was that it gave him time to think about how to complete his job. He would kill Blaine as soon as they let him go. Unfortunately, the Rat's anger toward his situation couldn't begin to match the feelings of anger Lorretta had for him at the moment.

What the Rat didn't know was that Lorretta had been made immediately aware of his incarceration and why. As a result, plans were being made in his regard. A decision had been agreed to by her associates concerning the little rat's welfare. The Rat, according to the Castillino family, was a liability and quickly became expendable.

"He is a worthless piece of trash. The Rat is dead to me," Lorretta sighed as she added to the cigarette smoke in her office back in Boston.

§

TANGIER, MOROCCO; GRAND SOCCO MARKETPLACE

Jamal felt the celebration needed to include one more person. The day belonged to his son, Barre. "Ten is a very special age to be," Jamal proclaimed to all that would listen as he pitched his spices at the stall. Abbas listened to the big man while sweeping the ground in front of the stall, and would be joining the festivities. Barre met Abbas a few times in the market and looked up to the older boy. Jamal's wife objected at first, but Jamal convinced her to change her mind about the street orphan. He explained that Abbas did many favors for Jamal, and he felt an obligation to reward him in a special way.

Abbas risked his life the other night retrieving the coin as directed. He also helped around the stall, carrying heavy boxes and sometimes making deliveries. The young boy was much older than his years, and always appeared happy to oblige when it didn't interfere with his commitment to watch over his companions. That burden of responsibility impressed Jamal even more. Today would be a surprise for both his son and Abbas.

The party began with a meal that had taken Jamal's wife, grandmother and an aunt all day to prepare. Eleven trays were being passed around, while everyone sat on the floor with the birthday boy, dressed all in white, next to his father. Jamal was pleased with the festivities, but, as time passed, he began to worry. Abbas was late.

After the first course of soup had made the rounds, there was a knock on the door, interrupting the party. Jamal excused himself and with a smile, Abbas finally made it. He rushed to the door and opened it. Standing there was one of the smaller street urchins, Amir, who seemed distraught.

"Mr. Jamal, Mr. Jamal! Abbas sent me. The police have taken him away!" he said in Arabic.

"Thank you, Amir, take this and go, be safe." Jamal gave the boy a coin as he methodically closed the door, turned around, leaned against the heavy wood, inhaled and let out a sigh. He said a small prayer for Abbas with eyes closed. After a moment, he opened them slowly and returned to the celebration.

§

LONDON, UK; LAMPERSON HEADQUARTERS

This latest change in plans concerned Winston as Archie waited patiently for more details. All his life, Sir Archibald prepared for the worst, leaving others to hope for the best. He looked at Ben, sitting next to Winston, and asked: "Why Cinque Terre?"

The question circled the room as Ben looked at his father then back at Archie. Down the hall people could be heard talking, a door slammed. Archie sat waiting, like the two men he faced, anxiously awaiting the package Rick picked up in Morocco. It was Ben's job to keep track of Rick and stay in communication with him, as well as his company in the states. The question had an answer, but Benjamin didn't think the two older gentlemen looking at him were going to like it. So, it hung, like the fog outside, for a few more seconds.

"Rick's friends suggested he try and throw the Castillinos off his trail by diverting to Cinque Terre, a series of five small Italian fishing villages nestled along the coast to the north of Pisa."

Ben explained that Cinque Terre was located in the northwestern part of Italy, where the land reaches out like a witch's crooked finger toward France. Nestled along the coast were five small coastal fishing villages, each hanging onto cliffs facing the Ligurian Sea, as they have for centuries. The names of the five villages, running from north to south are: Monterosso al Mare, Vernazza, Corniglia, Manarola, and Riomaggiore.

"Okay, but I still don't understand why they would go there," said Archie. "It seems to be a random choice."

"Rick's friend from college, Peter Reynolds and his partner, Sese Gillaterri, apparently already had plans to vacation there once Rick left for London," Ben explained. "The three will be traveling together. Pete is an American Foreign Service Officer stationed as the U.S. Consul in Milan. He's also armed."

Ben's situation update included everything they needed to know, except one thing.

"Where are they now?" Archie inquired with a pensive look on his face.

He'd made time to be in London, with Winston, working to keep Rick safe, rather than sitting around waiting on his duff for the American who seems to relish throwing himself into trouble. Ben cleared his throat before responding.

"They've just boarded a train to La Spezia, scheduled to arrive in Cinque Terre at around 5 PM our time. From there they will change to the train that runs between the five villages, stopping in Vernazza, the fourth village in the line of five. They have a house booked for two weeks. I have the address," Ben said.

Winston began pacing the room. Rick's safety remained a high priority, but the information on those disks was a major concern, not only to Winston, but also the anti-terrorism group he supervised. The incident in Morocco was unfortunate, something that Winston could never have foreseen. Still, he needed to reassure Rick that what the Lampersons' had in mind could potentially place Blaine's products into the European market. But there was more to Winston's plan for Rick, much more.

Lamperson's conference room became as quiet as a library. Rain, beginning to fall outside, provided a rhythmic distraction. The light pitter-patter of drops quickly turned into waves slapping at the windows. Winston felt as though nature was telling him to make up his mind. Finally, he said, "We go where Rick goes. We can't wait. He needs protection and we need the disks."

§

PISA, ITALY; PISA CENTRALE

The train stopped as scheduled for twenty minutes in order to transfer passengers before moving on to La Spezia. The three travelers from Milan transferred to the coastal train and on to Vernazza, one of the more picturesque of the five villages comprising Cinque Terre. Vernazza is famous for its homes, painted in a variety of pastel colors, that cling to the side of hills surrounding the village. One snapshot had the appearance of a uniquely created Italian watercolor painting. Another hour and they'd be there.

"We'll have to come back sometime and tour the Leaning Tower of Pisa before it leans any further," Pete joked as they made the switch between trains. The top half of the tower could be seen from the train platform. It looked as if a giant had tossed it from afar only to have it stick in the ground like an ornate javelin.

"From this angle, it's hard to believe the structure hasn't fallen by now. Are those people walking on the upper floors? Hope it's still standing whenever I return to Italy," Rick commented. Sese mentioned that she and one of her sisters toured the tower two years earlier and found it somewhat challenging.

Their last train had open seating, so they decided to sit together in the upper section of car 609. The side window slid open easily to let in fresh air. The breeze felt good. Rick was nervous knowing he had Winston's package tucked away in his sturdy black nylon pack. Always on alert, Pete watched the passengers, checking for strangers with familiar looking faces, as Sese tried her best to keep the conversation going. "They say it is good luck to walk the tower while it's leaning." She paused, then asked, "Did you know that there are people who want to try and set it straight?"

Rick turned from looking out the window. "No kidding?" Rick said in amazement. Sese look at him and assured him, "Is true."

And so, the conversation starter got her wish. The three of them debated the possibility, and the necessity, of bringing the leaning tower of Pisa into a full upright position. The debate lasted until they reached their destination, about forty-five minutes later. The three were warned by a fellow passenger that the train transfer between the five villages would be quick. Some passengers were just riding the rails between towns for fun, others because they had to, leaving some residents of the area having no choice but to stand. Consequently, you had to be fast in order to survive the maelstrom that developed on the train station platform.

After three quick stops, the last being Corniglia, the middle village of the five, the sign for Vernazza appeared. This last stop took approximately five minutes. As they departed, so did Mario, who had been seated just three rows behind them. Mario made his way across the station's small platform and out into the open, keeping an eye on his three targets. He immediately texted Michael, who was driving the Fiat, to let him know of his arrival. Michael was about 60 kilometers out from Vernazza and would join Mario within the hour.

"Follow me," Sese shouted as she waved her hand up high like a tour guide. She led them off the platform, each with a carry on, in addition to Rick and Pete with backpacks, and down the stairs to the bustling village below. Neither Rick or Pete had been in the Ligurian region before, so it was up to Sese to show them the town of Vernazza, but not before they found where they were staying.

Vernazza has no car traffic within the city limits, the streets being too narrow, which makes it a true fishing village. The multi-colored houses hung gracefully off the hillsides surrounding the area in a semi-circle that faced the Mediterranean Sea. The town has a natural harbor that the Italian government had built up over the years, providing plenty of room for small boutique shops that attract visitors along the cobblestone main street. Boats moored on tidal anchors, moved back and forth with the sea's ebb and flow, waiting their return to fish outside the harbor.

The fishing boats lay on the sand when the tide is out, and float back to level with the bow facing out when the tide is in. A large outcropping of rock acts as a breakwater, keeping large waves from eroding the gorgeous landscape. The breakwater also allows boats the ability to exit outward into the sea more easily, and serves as the backbone of the small harbor. Looking at Vernazza from the sea, the entire area could easily be compared to a patchwork quilt. Each patch is represented by houses, buildings, vendor's tents, businesses and churches of various colors, mostly muted in washed-out pastels, all with weathered red tile roofs.

The town's population of around eight hundred, work around the constant flow of tourists that never seems to stop. The crowds, at times, outnumber the residents, but the residents don't mind. Tourism has become a vital part of their economy, allowing for less dependence on fishing revenue. As their mayor says: "If it weren't for us, tourists wouldn't be here, but if it weren't for tourists, chances are, neither would we."

Sese led Rick and Pete up through winding cobblestone streets that were, in some areas, less than ten feet wide. Every uphill step showcased doors of various colors with wrought iron numbers twisted around to form addresses. Customized planter boxes containing shrubs, flowers and the occasional assortment of garden herbs created a distinctive look for each. Italian music and conversation could be heard behind closed doors as the three passed by at a steady pace. Large stone steps led them, and up, and around to their eventual destination. Sese seemed to be the only one of the three not breathing heavily when, at last, she turned around and shared some good news:

"Here we are boys!"

Chapter 4

SILICON VALLEY, CA; BLAINE MANUFACTURING

Brenda, Ralph, and Bear sat in the conference room eating lunch awaiting Winston's call from London. There had been a change in plans, causing Rick and friends to move on together to a place in northwestern Italy called: Cinque Terre.

"I've heard of it, the Italian Riviera on the Mediterranean Sea," Brenda said as she walked to the picture window after pouring her tea. She stood there for a few minutes, smiling slightly, in a thoughtful trance, as the call came in.

"Hello, everyone. And who exactly do we have, Brenda?" Winston asked.

"Hi, Winston, good to hear your voice. I have Ralph and Bear with me."

"Good, good. Joining me is Archie Turlington, whose resume I emailed earlier. Let's begin, shall we? Time being of the essence." They greeted one another and got right to it. Bear shared his concerns about the near miss by the Castillinos in Milan, forcing Rick to change plans and move in another direction.

"Do you think Pete Reynolds can provide enough protection for Rick?" Bear asked.

"This is Archie. At this point we have to assume no. Don't get me wrong, Reynolds has been extremely helpful up to this point, but he, in fact, they, will need more support. I'll be watching Rick's back. I'm leaving in an hour for his location."

"Let me say in addition that this whole mess is my fault. Rick wouldn't be in this predicament if it hadn't been for me asking a favor," Winston admitted.

Ralph spoke up: "No one's pointing fingers, Winston, but we have to know that Rick will receive full protection. The Castillinos' intentions are serious. That guy in Morocco had a knife and was ready to kill."

Their conversation continued for another thirty minutes. Bear and Archie had a productive exchange of back and forth discussing strategic options, finally settling on Archie taking the lead and keeping Bear informed via text message, as the plan turned into a more active state.

Bear had one more question that was bothering him: "Hey, Winston, what's in the package?"

"Excuse me? You mean what Rick picked up in Morocco? Well, that package contains information that one of our operatives gathered on our behalf regarding a job we're currently working here in London. I'm afraid I can't reveal anything more. I hope you understand."

Each person at Blaine had a look of concern on their faces. Bear spoke next: "I don't mean to tell you what to do, but if I were you, I'd get that package out of Rick's hands fast, he has enough to deal with on the Castillino front, agree?"

"Roger that, Bear. I'll be in touch," Winston added with a serious tone.

Ben and Archie left on Winston's private jet exactly one hour later. They landed in Genoa City Airport, about 70 miles north of Cinque Terre. From there they arranged for a boat, avoiding the train, enabling them to work on their own schedule, which included blending in with the locals as much as possible as they sailed south to Vernazza.

§

VERNAZZA, ITALY

Rick, Pete and Sese sat together around a beautiful inlaid stone dining table looking out to the sea from the house that Sese and Pete rented, thinking it would be a romantic vacation, just for the two of them. Those plans changed of course. Life with Rick was proving to be ever changing and very exciting.

"Okay, so this Archie person is on his way and you're going to hand over the package, correct?" Pete inquired, sounding relieved and skeptical.

§

VERNAZZA, ITALY; VERNAZZA HARBOR

Michael and Mario were cooped up in a tiny fisherman's shed near the beach close to the main pier. It happened to be the only location Mario could find to stay overnight. The place reeked of fish guts, motor oil, cigarette smoke and sweat. Mario didn't mind helping his cousin, but playing the waiting game made him nervous. He hadn't planned on coming all this way to sit idly by in this stinking hell hole. Mario preferred to be anywhere, but in this god-forsaken hut. Michael insisted on remaining out of sight during daylight hours and away from the crowds of tourists.

"What now, cugino?" Mario asked as he did a half hour ago. He couldn't help but wonder how deep family, or the feeling of helping a family member, had to go. Is there some point at which one could say enough is enough and leave?

"For the last time, I'd prefer darkness for cover and Rick, preferably by himself, at the same time. If we do this right, we'll be in Palermo before his body is discovered."

Normally, Michael's frustrations bubbled up from the inside like a slowly building volcano ready to erupt. That led to mistakes, miscues, and miserable heartaches. No more mistakes. This time would be different.

Mario smiled as Michael brought his hand to the back of his cousin's neck, bringing the younger man's head forward to Michael's shoulder.

"You're a good man, Mario. I need you to be with me on this. Tell you what, you help me take care of Blaine and I'll arrange for you to come stay in Boston with our family there. You will work for me, and we'll go to a Red Sox game, if that interests you."

The comment brought tears to Mario's eyes. He nodded his approval and sat back down, feeling better about what they were about to do.

Michael could feel the change that came from deep inside. He still had the urge to kill and make money the only way he knew. But the voices that drove his earlier life had quieted since his brother's death. Michael now took more time to think things out. Impulsive behavior could no longer be counted on. It was almost like he had a conscience to answer to, so he had to come up with a more agreeable method of working with his associates, like Mario.

"Hey, Mario, let's get a pizza. Would you be willing to go into town and order one?" The distance was less than a mile round trip. Michael handed him the money with a pat on the arm. "Be careful, and think pepperoni." Mario explained that American style pizza was pretty rare in Italy, but said he'd try. He then wiped sweat from his brow, picked up his backpack, stood up from the bench he'd been sitting behind, walked to the door, peaked out, and was off. Michael noticed a coastal fog forming as a boat horn sounded. "The captain of that ship is concerned about coming too close to shore," he whispered to himself. "Good luck, captain, I hope you find your way."

As Michael watched his cousin make the turn up the slope to the breakwater he had one more thought that came out in a whisper. "Better enjoy the next twenty-four hours, Blaine. Because they'll be your last."

§

VERNAZZA, ITALY; THE NEXT MORNING NORTH OF VERNAZZA HARBOR

Further north, the boat captain stood in the pilot house of the forty-foot cruiser, Jenny, assuring Ben that the coastal fog would work to their advantage tonight. He knew the rocky shore like the back of his hand, and the fog would allow them a blanket of cover as they entered the Vernazza harbor.

"We have another hour before landing in Vernazza. By then, the sun will be ready to rise," the captain said as he checked for the last coastal marker buoy.

The morning fog slowly revealed calm seas as gulls gracefully glided in and out of Ben's vision, disappearing upward with the early thermals. The stone encrusted harbor had a ghostly feel thanks to the intermittent fog layers. Ben suddenly had chills as he stood ready to carry out their plan. The captain, true to his word, off-loaded Ben and Archie into a dingy that motored them closer to the harbor and onto the granite seawall, right on schedule. The boat slowly made its way out to sea once the dingy and crew were back onboard. The sky brightened, turning light blue under an uplifting blanket of fog.

Rick checked his phone for an expected text from Ben. It read: "WE ARE HERE. MAKING OUR WAY TO CHURCH ON PIER. MEET INSIDE FRONT DOORS IN 30."

Rick, Pete and Sese left fifteen minutes later for the church rendezvous. Rick spent the early morning hours reading about Sir Archibald Turlington from information written and sent to him by Winston. Sir Archibald grew up in Cambridge, the son of Baron and Lady Turlington, and second cousin to the Queen. He went to school at Eaton with Charles, the Queen's oldest, where the two became close friends and had kept in contact over the years.

Archie began his service as a second lieutenant, but quickly decided that law enforcement, in service to the Queen, would be his ultimate calling. At Eaton, he used to look out for Charles, as others tended to pick on him behind the scenes away from his normal security. Archie took it upon himself to learn more than books or teachers could ever explain. He had very good instincts, learning how to study people and what to glean from their movements and the look on their faces. Once he decided to act, it was all over. He approached academics and athletics with mutual enthusiasm. Archie developed a mantra that remains with him to this day: Anticipate in Order to Participate. He credited the ability to anticipate as the one attribute that kept him alive through military service and other more clandestine services, that he'd been sworn to keep secret. He relished, with great joy, anticipating and thus defeating evil.

Married and divorced, two children, a girl and a boy, both grown and married, and two grandchildren. The boy lives in Canada with his family, and the girl is a news reporter for the BBC in London.

Archie prided himself on being an avid hunter, mostly game birds, and a pool shark, a self-proclaimed King of the Eight Ball, with his mates at an exclusive club, The Parliament, on Pall Mall, near the Oxford-Cambridge Club. When he's at home in the country he reads biographies mostly. If you ask, he will say that he'll never retire, and that, to be remembered as a productive member of the Royal Family, is his only wish.

§

VERNAZZA, ITALY

Sese walked ahead as Rick and Pete made their way behind her, dodging the early arrival of tourists and watching their backs for suspicious characters. Locating the church, with its five-story bell tower rising at one end, was easy. The sacred structure bordered the north end of the harbor, just off the main pier. Sese secretly hoped the three of them appeared to be tourists going to church. They were five minutes from meeting up with Ben and a mystery man named Sir Archie.

They walked up the front steps, made of old stones, weathered over centuries, smoothed by wind and a salty sea. As they grew closer, organ music could be heard with a choir that began to sing. No sooner had the singing begun, it stopped.

"There must be choir practice this morning," Pete said as the trio moved through the twelve-foot-high front wooden doors and into the church, passing a bronze covered cornerstone as they entered. The inscription on stone marker outside the church read:

Santa Margherita di Antiochia Church
Roman Catholic Est. 1318

Their whispers echoed off large granite stone columns, four feet in diameter, twenty feet high, supporting large arches that rose higher, supporting several domes dotting a fifty-foot ceiling. Darker shades inside slowly lightened as the early eastern sun began to peek over the surrounding hillside and through multi-colored stained-glass windows.

While the three waited patiently, Rick read from a leaflet inviting tourists to services daily and on Sunday. An early service had just ended and a few stragglers, who had been lighting some prayer candles, left the narthex. Beautifully decorated wooden front doors creaked slowly after allowing their exit. One of the doors stopped before closing and two gray forms, outlined by a backlit sun, walked through. Both had the appearance of arch angels coming down from above.

The stream of light disappeared as Ben Lamperson came forward, removing his knit cap, leading an older man, both dressed in dark, sea worthy, Gore-Tex gear. Stepping forward, Ben smiled as he reached out to shake Rick's hand, and said, "Rick, you don't know how good it is to see you, my friend. Father sends his best." They shook hands and Ben added as he turned back around, "And this is Sir Archibald Turlington."

The older gent behind him stepped forward, and with a slight smile greeted them, "Call me Archie." He was slightly taller than Rick, with a robust build, and steely colored eyes that caught your attention right away. Archie shook himself as he removed his cap that revealed gray hair with a matching goatee.

"We need to keep moving, people, time and daylight are not on our side," Archie stated with urgency in his voice.

The five of them walked to a side alcove where Rick removed the package and handed it to Ben. Young Lamperson opened the seal, looked inside, smiled, then raised his head with a look of relief. "Thanks for doing this, Rick. I'll take it from here and say my goodbyes. Archie will bring you up to speed on what we've discussed. He's been updated as to your status, Rick, and knows little about your friends here, but I'm sure you can fill in those blanks. Good luck. Oh, just so you know, you'll be taking a different route home—Archie will explain."

With that, Ben turned and quickly retraced his steps out the front and disappeared with the package safely in hand.

"They still need you in London, Rick, but for now, we — you and I — will deal with the people tracking you. The Castillinos, I believe?" Archie said as he stepped closer to Rick, pulling out a cigarette case. "I suppose even Catholics frown on smoking in church, let's step outside," Archie chuckled to himself as the four of them moved through the ancient narthex toward the front of the church and back down the stone steps near a twenty-foot-high seawall.

The seawall delivered on its promise of protection from erosion. Rick heard the crashing before he noticed as waves struck the centuries-old stones, sending a mist over the top of the wall. Beyond the wall, he watched Ben jump onto an awaiting boat with the top secret package. Rick wondered, as the boat made its way out past the jetty, what fate awaited him in London. He snapped out of his thought when Pete called his name.

This morning, as they collected themselves under the canopy of a large shade tree, overlooking the harbor, Archie gave a warning: "I'm convinced that we're dealing with a psychopath, a Mr. Michael Castillino to be exact. As you know all too well, he has more than a vendetta against you, Rick. From what I've read, it's his reputation that he's struggling to revive as well. He's been shamed, by you and all you stand for, right?"

Rick agreed as Archie continued to lead the discussion, asking questions of Rick and Pete, pertaining to the attack in Morocco, and the confrontation in the courtyard in Milan.

Looking at Pete, Archie asked: "So, you believe there could be two people, maybe more, following you, is that right?"

Sese explained that she had noticed a dark-haired man sitting close to them in Milan. "He was sitting without a drink, just watching his phone and appeared to be eavesdropping."

"I noticed him, too," said Pete, adding, "as I walked back after approaching the man in the car."

Archie sat looking at the two of them, and studying a small book of notes as Pete continued: "It had to be the same guy I recognized sitting close in Milan. Yes, he nearly ran off the train here in Vernazza, yesterday."

"No sign of the other man, the one we believe is Castillino, on the train, yesterday?"

Archie listened intently, watching their eyes as words were said, faces wrinkled. He knew when suspects told the truth, and didn't worry about lies, results always depended on the truth, no matter how long it took. Archie believed Pete, who was still nursing his wounds and most likely wouldn't have any reason to lie. It became clear to Archie, Pete was here to help, along with his girlfriend.

After a few puffs from his cigarette, and standing up to look around while the three waited for a response, Archie spoke: "Okay, here's what we do. First thing this afternoon, Rick, you and your friends need to get away from the harbor area. This is exactly where they'll be looking for you." Archie stopped and glanced up at the terraced cliff face towering above the small village, and all the pieces suddenly locked into place. He turned to them, blew out another puff, pointed at the cliff and said, "You need to go for a hike."

§

TANGIER, MOROCCO; MUNICIPAL PRISON OF TANGIERS

Nights in a Moroccan jail were much worse than days for the Rat who shook, head to toe, from the cold and fear. He didn't feel sick to his stomach, rather, he was tired of being in this god - for - saken, rodent and bug infested cell. His straw mat on a concrete floor was not enough protection against the mysterious crawling creatures that invaded, freely, from everywhere, like the intermittent human wails that came and went. He did his best to fight the pests, which led to sleep deprivation and major paranoia. He couldn't remember exactly how long he'd been locked up. Days? Weeks? Judging from his facial hair it had been more than a week. Somebody do something.

Just when the Rat was beginning to settle down, he heard the rattling of keys. It was late, very late, no reason to hear anyone doing anything at this time of night. What the hell? The lock to his cell turned and two large men entered. No words were said. Suddenly he was lifted up and shoved against the wall. The smaller man put up a fight, but soon was rendered helpless with a severe punch to the gut. The Rat's breath left him, taking with it his spirit to resist.

Later that morning, a jailer discovered the body of the American thug. It hung suspiciously from an overhead pipe that ran the length of the cell. He had no reason to know that this method of death had been used many times before to end a life. The body swayed a little as the jailer poked at it with his night stick. Limp, dirty, and beginning to smell, the hanging body quickly became a magnet for the flies the little man had fought for days. The jailer watched as the insects' revenge played out in front of him.

It had been determined by investigators, that Joey the Rat somehow managed to climb or jump straight up nine feet, wrap his own belt around the pipe, secure it, stick his head through the loop, all while hanging with one hand, five feet off the floor.

The man obviously couldn't take being incarcerated. No

one questioned how this suicide could possibly have happened. A short man hung himself in a room with a tall ceiling, people had more important things to do. How unfortunate. The death certificate provided to the U.S. Government read: Death by suicide. Later that night the jailer in charge of the Rat's block, ate his favorite dish in a local cafe. He had on a black leather jacket that nearly fit. No one asked where he got it—no one cared.

§

LONDON, UK; LAMPERSON HEADQUARTERS

After sailing south and on to Pisa, Ben flew direct to London aboard Lamperson International's private jet. Upon landing at London City Airport, he raced to the office with Jamal's package. What a rush. He looked forward to the day when he could tell his grandchildren about cruising at night, in the fog, listening to a boat captain relate one near death experience after another.

Once Ben shook off the previous night's experience, he immediately began the process of retrieving the information on both floppy disks. He would report his findings only to his father, who decided to take two days leave in Edinburgh, Scotland, supposedly fulfilling a pre-planned reunion with friends, including a round of golf. You never knew with him.

No one else knew about Winston's special project that he reluctantly left behind with Ben. It would be in good hands, but the manner in which his Tunisian contact came upon the information, captivated his every thought.

Jamal had uncovered, intercepted really, a communication between two factions: One in the Middle East, with a sophisticated Iranian encryption that he immediately recognized, and another in northern Africa, possibly Tunisia, which had a less complicated encryption system. Once he deciphered the first few paragraphs of the Iranian message, he contacted Winston. Immediate decisions were made, leaving it up to Ben and his associates to decipher the second message.

From what the three—Winston, Ben and Jamal—could ascertain early on, this appeared to be a plot that involved the British Royal Family. At first, no one knew exactly what or who was being targeted, but it was understood that some kind of action on the part of the British government needed to be taken, and soon.

The first matter at hand, however, was to make sure that the five communications received so far, each building on the same threat, were credible. Ben worked with several contacts in North Africa to cross reference the communications, plus Jamal's most recent intelligence, which pinpointed targets, time, and possible location for an event of a "catastrophic" nature. He also found a puzzling link to a German source called: Reign.

Ben needed a minimum of two days to decrypt the message because of the antiquated nature of the disks; at most a week. He'd depend on others to assist, beginning with Jamal in Morocco and involving one or two others located in London. Once someone new is recruited into this situation, it will be understood that they can't leave the premises until the project is declared over. That could take weeks.

The average citizen only heard about the underworld's clandestine activities on the nightly news after a catastrophe struck or was alleviated. Once Ben and his team confirmed the suspected magnitude of the content with each other, the proper authorities would be notified. That would be the most challenging part of all, because, in this matter especially, who do you trust? That's the world of the Lampersons and their associates. A world that now invited Rick Blaine to join.

§

EDINBURGH, SCOTLAND; FERRY'S RESTAURANT

Winston was in Scotland, but not to meet with relatives or to play golf as previously communicated. There were more important matters to address. He arranged for two meetings on his first day there. The first was with an old trusted friend retired from Interpol, an international organization that connected police all over the world. One international location his friend was most familiar happened to be: North Africa.

They met at Ferry's Restaurant near downtown, across from the opera house, a block from Carrick Knowe Parkway. James Slaughter, his real name, worked in the British Foreign Service primarily. He and Winston labored over several projects in the mid-eighties, eventually setting the tone for the Berlin Wall to come tumbling down. Their main focus wasn't targeted on that experience, but on keeping the spy network they created intact. It was relentless in causing the Russians one problem after another, especially across northern Africa.

"The fish and chips are superb my friend, you might give them a go," Winston suggested.

James made his selection and they took their meals outside to an umbrella covered patio. He knew his friend well, and had the feeling Winston was involved in something of utmost importance.

"We have a possible tragedy in our midst, James," Winston stated in a serious tone that surprised his old friend. James hadn't seen that look in years.

"By 'we', I take you to mean the entire British realm," James surmised. "Or is this meal tainted with something that will kill the both of us and we need to speed up the conversation?"

Winston nearly spit his drink across the table. The man was funny, this time to a sad end, because if what Winston suspected was true, the Royal Family was in the crosshairs of some very sophisticated terrorists.

James apologized, slightly, for his comment once he found out what Winston had to discuss. He wanted to know if James still had connections in Africa that could substantiate what he and Ben suspected. Ben had called earlier and then sent an analysis in a coded format to Winston, which outlined the following: Terrorists from the Middle East were connecting with some faction of operatives in or near Morocco. Their plan was to kill Queen Elizabeth and Prince William at the Royal Ascot Race in June of this year. It was one of the only times these two Royals were together in one location, at an event, outside and away from London. Each element was critical to their plot to make a statement, most importantly, while everyone gathered for the sole purpose of enjoying themselves. Terrorists always appear to enjoy the yin and yang of relaxing entertainment becoming tragedy. Waiting on your response.

"Elizabeth and William, the present and the future. Interesting," James reasoned.

"Yes, my guess is that those targets would affect a full range of British citizens, from young to old, as well as send a message that they can do anything to anyone at any time," Winston replied as he sat back and wiped his mouth with a napkin.

"It makes sense they would pick that time and place, but why? I mean, do they say exactly what their motive is, according to some decree?" James asked mid bite.

"We haven't seen everything as yet, there's likely more, but no, there seems to be a general feeling that eliminating these key members of the Royal Family will send a terrifying ripple through the Empire and around the world," Winston's speech pattern was breaking up toward the end of his comment. Both men agreed that there was no way the races would be canceled, the races had to go on. It wasn't in the British DNA to give into a threat, they would deal with it.

Winston added: "I have one more concern, James."

"What's that?"

"We believe there are operatives on the inside, in the British Parliament assisting the effort," said Winston. "Consequently, I'm not sure who we can hand this off to. We only have a few weeks before the event."

"Who do you suspect or is that up for discussion at this point?"

"With you, yes," Winston paused. "Someone close to the Queen is all I can tell you at this point."

§

LONDON, UK; LAMPERSON'S HEADQUARTERS

Winston decided not to create a large team to work on this project. Ben agreed. The fewer people involved the better at this time.

Ben contacted Jamal to make sure he stayed on point and to let them know of any new internet activity. Now that they knew an assassination attempt was in place, the clock of responsibility was ticking: Who knew what when?

§

LONDON, UK; 10 DOWNING STREET

Jonas Hammersmith, the Home Secretary, left the Prime Minister's office with a full brief case. The files he transported contained the Queen's confirmed schedule for the next quarter. This time of year, she spent most of her days inside Buckingham Palace approving and signing various communiques that frequented her daily life. From the day she had the crown placed on her head, Elizabeth enjoyed being Queen. Her mother used to say that Elizabeth was born to be a leader, and she was right. Elizabeth managed to raise a family and perform all the tasks that were asked of her to do according to those who managed the affairs of the Royals.

The Firm, as it was known, insisted on constant communication, reviewing, signing, scheduling appearances, all of which were organized by Elizabeth's personal secretary.

Phillip's passing created a sudden surge in communications. All eyes were on the aging Queen, hoping to witness her every reaction. The need to respond to the public increased to the point where other members of the family were called upon to support the Royal lineage by granting interviews and corresponding on behalf of the Palace. Still, the Queen, with the Home Secretary close at hand, supervised every detail. He suddenly had more top priorities than projected for this time of year, which put a great deal of stress on him and his staff. Added to the list would be the expectations for Phillip's funeral, outlined in his will that the Queen insisted on adhering to, down to the last detail. That last detail was a specially designed, electric, Land Rover, designed by Phillip himself. The vehicle served as his "Carriage of Choice" in the funeral procession.

Hammersmith and his staff found themselves dealing with more requests than time allowed. One thing after another kept adding up, to the point where it all became overwhelming. When a secure email arrived from MI5 headquarters announcing the investigation of a terrorism plot targeting the Royal Family, it just about blew the top off his limo. "For God's Sake, what's going to happen next, the whole damn island going to sink into the North Sea?" Hammersmith thought to himself as the limo driver headed to the other side of London for a lunch meeting with the Minister of Justice.

The Home Secretary had plenty of time to ponder this last email and answer a few calls, once he settled down. He may send a text, he wasn't sure, his head spun just trying to think. Maybe he should call MI5 for clarification. He had two phones he used, one for business, the other for more personal reasons.

One of the most powerful men in the UK, he dreaded the drive across town at any time of day, heavy traffic, street repairs and stupid drivers, added to his frustration. Like now. All that, coupled with the fact that the day, unusually warm for this time of year, was made even warmer when traffic came to a standstill.

Two transit buses came to a stop, one on either side of his limo. Hammersmith sat back, eyes closed, sweating. The air conditioning had to be turned down, because he nearly died of pneumonia having it up so high last week. Wiping the sweat from his brow required the removal of his glasses. Every movement agonizingly manipulated.

Herman Kruger, Hammersmith's assistant, sat facing the man he used to idolize. Kruger had become the punching bag for the secretary in the last year, and he hated every minute he spent with the man, like now. Sitting and watching Hammersmith in his confused state made Kruger want to leap from the limo.

Just as Hammersmith began to quiet down, Herman's phone vibrated. He checked his phone, and what he read caused him to sit up. This caught Hammersmith's attention. "What is it, Herman?" Kruger had to think fast. He couldn't possibly tell the Home Secretary what he had just read. Hammersmith hurried to replace his glasses after wiping them clean. In the process of replacing the glasses, he poked himself in the eye. "Damnit!" he exclaimed. Kruger just sat back, while slowly replacing his phone, carefully, into his breast pocket. The message he read moments ago, kept repeating in his head: A "Field Operative" in Germany discovered a possible effort to intercept the new directive from headquarters. The operative said that it was not necessarily a concern, these things can happen randomly, but not normally by the method used in this instance. Software security had a difficult time identifying the equipment being used, processing was slow, tedious. More on this to follow.

§

TANGIER, MOROCCO; GRAND SOCCO MARKETPLACE

Jamal continued to watch his computer screen. Things weren't right. The access he had been tapping into suddenly stopped. Sweat began to pour down his face as he reached for a towel that lay next to his tea. He glanced at the time: 1 AM. He had to do something, and fast. "What is happening?" he whispered to himself as he clicked aggressively on the keyboard. He had been denied access while following clandestine activity before, but never in real time, like now. He had to be careful in shutting his equipment down and backing off the internet the way he went on—slow and deliberate. He couldn't afford to cause suspicion and would monitor the situation closely. His chair squeaked as he sat back and removed his glasses. He'd been at it since his wife went to bed three hours earlier. Jamal made a note of the incident on his phone, he had to alert Ben Lamperson. As he completed sending the message, he heard a knocking sound on the wall behind him. It came from the outside alleyway. Who could it be this late at night? Jamal reached for a curved knife with an eight-inch blade. The knife had a dual purpose, it was kept at home for defense and on his person when shopping or gutting fish at the market. His movements were slow as he crept toward the back door of his dar. He heard footsteps and then a louder sound as if someone threw a bag on the ground. He opened the door, knife at the ready, and found Abbas lying prostrate in the dirt.

Chapter 5

CINQUE TERRE, ITALY

For centuries, access between the five small coastal communities, known collectively as Cinque Terre, was limited to the sea and an ancient Roman road that served as the only land connection between the villages. The path became more usable when Roman engineers, under Caesar's direction, added large stone steps and small bridges in order to appease tax collectors. Modern day hikers found the path to be challenging as it twisted up and down small hills past gorgeous breathtaking Mediterranean vistas. In 1870, the Italian government built a railroad line from Pisa to Spezia near the coast, just south of the five villages. Once that line went into service, the citizens of each village could travel between villages in a matter of minutes. The railroad also created an additional income source: tourism.

The apartment Sese and Pete rented looked out over the tiny fishing village of Vernazza and the Ligurian Sea beyond. The view had an amazing view that flowed from south to northeast for 270-degrees. When Archie walked out on the small veranda taking in the entire experience, he stopped and raised both arms high overhead, as if he just witnessed a revelation. "This is a most spectacular view. It reminds me of... of a...." Archie drifted of, staring in amazement.

"Of an Italian painting?" Sese chimed in. Her interjecting thought made the elder man laugh until tears appeared.

"Precisely, my dear." Archie explained that he did favor Italian artists, but this perspective would be difficult to replicate, even for an old master.

The morning gradually warmed the slate flagstone of the veranda with seagulls competing for airspace as they called to one another overhead. Coffee and local pastries were served from a large wooden tray that Sese carried from the kitchen. The calm surroundings disregarded the serious nature of what had to be discussed.

Pete and Sese sat at a white wrought iron table facing Rick and Archie. A slight breeze helped to create a fragrant environment as the foursome went over a plan to stop Michael Castillino.

"The man has a vendetta against you, Mr. Blaine, and from what I read on his background, he won't stop until you're dead." Archie stated the obvious, but he felt he needed to declare why he was here and the reality of what could happen. He wasn't the bullshitting around type; there was no time for mincing words. "And that's why I'd like to tackle this with just you and Pete. Sese, we can't thank you enough for helping Mr. Blaine up to this point, but I think we can take it from here." Pete didn't see this coming and looked down in embarrassment.

Sese, however, stood up from the table and walked over behind Archie's chair. "May I see your weapon, sir?" Archie looked puzzled as he handed her his gun. "This is a Glock 17, pretty standard for the British military, but I prefer the more compact 19 myself." As she said this, Sese proceeded to take the weapon apart. Pete smiled, completely self-satisfied, while Rick and Archie had a shocked look on their faces. When

Sese proceeded to reassemble the weapon, Archie erupted in applause: "Well done, my dear!"

"You won't have to worry about me hiking with you today, Rick, I can handle myself." Pete then explained to Rick and Archie that he first met Sese when he landed in Rome two years ago. He was headed to the American Embassy to meet with State Department officials who gave him his first assignment. "Sese headed up my security team of three people." Sese explained that her family, especially her mother, grandmama, and two aunts, wanted her to pursue modeling because of her natural beauty and poise. They had no idea she wanted to be in law enforcement until she enrolled in it as her major in university. She then spent two years in active military service and was transferred into Agnzia Informazioni e Sicurezza (AISE), Italy's foreign intelligence service. "I'm no longer assigned to guard mister Reynolds here, but I remain involved in foreign intelligence work."

Pete looked up at Rick. "Sorry I hadn't told you before, it's just that we've been on the dead run…." He trailed off. Rick needed no more convincing about Sese's qualifications to be of assistance regarding the Castillinos.

They finished planning their strategy over breakfast. Each person agreed that Michael Castillino posed a threat, and after two failed attempts, one in Morocco and one in Milan, he was likely planning to strike in Cinque Terre. Archie shared, once again, how the Lampersons felt this situation needed to be dealt with, immediately. "In order to put this matter to rest, we have to draw Castillino out." Archie's voice took on a very serious tone.

§

VERNAZZA, ITALY

Down and around a multitude of stone steps, not far from Archie's planning meeting, Michael and Mario sat outside a bakery at a small bistro table sipping espresso near Vernazza's main town square. Their table, strategically located in the shadow of the railroad trestle, provided Michael with a perfect view of the main street. Mario had learned from the barista that everyone had to use this street to go anywhere in Vernazza, including Blaine and his friends.

Thoughts of his family, Mario's willingness to help, and Lorretta's best wishes, rotated nonstop in Michael's head. He needed to focus. They'd slept under a tarp that hung over a stack of lumber, two blocks away, last night. The tarp afforded a much better atmosphere than the stinking hut they'd found refuge in yesterday. Michael's patience, a virtue almost non-existent in him, had been put to the test. Waiting around for Blaine and his friends to come out of the shadows was driving him crazy. They were running out of cash and needed to take care of Blaine once and for all.

One cup became two. Michael already felt jittery and knew from experience that he dare not have a third. Mario looked up after checking his text messages. "Michael, we have two more cousins joining us. They're on the train from Corniglia and will be arriving shortly." Michael smiled at Mario, placed a hand on his shoulder and nodded, then whispered. "Famiglia, cousin, famiglia." After about a half hour, due largely to the haphazard train schedule, Michael's two cousins walked down the stairs from the train platform. They spotted Michael and Mario, walked over, said hello, sat down and order shots of espresso. "What's the plan?" asked Gino.

As the four men huddled together with Michael leading the conversation, the baker from nearby stopped in for his morning coffee. As he stood waiting he couldn't help but notice the four men in the corner. He could tell they were not tourists as he overheard their conversation – in Italian. The more he heard the more he felt threatened by their very presence. These men had to be Cosa Nostra. He couldn't leave and found himself shuffling back even further into a corner, nervous, trying to drink his coffee – listening. He nearly choked on his second sip when he heard a man describe how they were going to kill three hikers on the trail that very day. The baker knew what he needed to do as he exited the front door.

Just as Michael began to speak, Blaine and his two companions slowly came into view, dressed in hiking gear and walking down the bustling, narrow cobblestone street, which was packed with small shops, cafés, grocers and small restaurants on both sides. "That's them!" he uttered excitedly. Michael knew little about the area, but all morning he had watched people dressed in hiking gear going down the steep hill towards the harbor or up towards the train station. As the hikers came closer, Michael stepped into a shop to ensure he wasn't spotted, while Mario, Gino and his brother Vinny sat drinking espresso, assuming they were unrecognized.

Once the hikers passed, Michael rushed out. "Okay, Mario and I are going to follow them on their hike." He then turned to his cousins, "you two hop on the train and head to Monterosso and circle back."

Gino cut his cousin off. "That won't work, cugino; the next train is in an hour."

A flash of anger briefly crossed Michael's face, but he let it go. "Damnit. Okay, grab some water and come with us."

An hour later, the trio had made some good progress as they appeared to be out for a day hike. The morning sun began to shine over the tops of the trees that seemed to rise higher and higher the further they walked. Their hike between Vernazza and the most northern village, Monterosso al Mare, would normally take two and a half hours if they followed the path to the end. Sese and Pete turned out to be good company on the hike. After a full kilometer on the trail, they would become separated at a designated point where Archie would be waiting according to plan.

Sese and Pete would move ahead on the path, just out of sight, and Rick would fall behind, creating a vulnerable situation. Archie would keep eyes on Rick as he observed from the underbrush, and maintaining communication through ear buds. Archie provided the latest in two-way communication devices.

Monitoring the area behind Rick, for anyone matching Michael or Mario Castillino's description, was Archie's responsibility. He remarked to himself of how closely the two men resembled one another, Michael was taller, however, with shorter hair. They were cousins, but they could easily be brothers.

Archie checked in with the trio once he was in position ahead. "Rick, can you read me? Over."

"Roger. Loud and clear, Archie," came Rick's voice through the Bluetooth earbuds.

He did the same with Sese and Pete as the three hikers made their way toward him. Archie had chosen this location from the map Sese showed him the evening before. He sat perched on a branch in a stand of giant pine trees that overlooked a switchback turn in the hiking path. Up to this point, the path was a relatively easy to follow, except for the steep incline leading out of the town that gave the hikers an impressive view of the quaint town. The hikers then had to cross an ancient stone bridge that led to a steep rise with huge granite steps, constructed by slaves under the direction of Roman soldiers centuries before. It was the perfect place for Rick to fall behind as Sese and Pete disappeared up the steps and beyond. Archie would be able to see a wide expanse of the trail from his position, and anyone on the trail for 100 meters in both directions.

Michael gathered his band of cousins together near the start of the hiking trail overlooking the train station. He waited for the train to leave the train station and the lead engine's whistle to stop before talking.

"The mark, Mr. Blaine, is on the trail heading to Monterosso al Mare. We have plenty of time to catch up if we move fast. He's with two others. All three must not return, is that understood?" Each of the three men nodding their heads were killers in their own right. What they were about to do was in keeping with the Castillino family tradition of brotherhood. They didn't, necessarily, have to know what the mark did, they just needed to know what needed to be done.

Michael smiled as he brought them all together in a hug, holding his large hands out and around the backs of each of their heads. "Gino, you and your brother take the point, Mario and I will follow. Let's go."

Archie's iPhone's "Find Your Friends" application allowed him to track Rick's every move. Reception was surprisingly good, so he was confident he could maintain a safe distance from Rick without being seen.

The hiking terrain accommodated villagers traveling between the five small enclaves, over many centuries. Since the advent of the railroad in the nineteenth century, the main trail was turned over to the average hiker, with an occasional steep incline that eventually led to a more meandering decline. Along the way, people of all ages, including children, would pass one another on the ancient path.

The trio made good time, even though they were on an ever-watchful hike. Archie patiently awaited the three who were about a quarter mile out. Dressed in camo gear, he blended in nicely to the surrounding area from his forested vantage point.

Settling into the shadows, he laid in wait for them to pass, and after checking for followers, his plan was to follow the Castillinos as Rick dropped back.

The trail demonstrated the uniqueness of the landscape as it cut naturally through the terrain. Numerous hills with small hillside gardens located closer to Vernazza. Further on, patches of olive vines dotted the landscape in perfect rows, each growing area leading back to the path. Below the path was the Ligurian Sea in all its splendor. Under normal conditions, visitors took their time to hike, stopping to take pictures at every other bend, due to the incredible viewpoints.

The trio experienced a serpentine trail that started inward, away from the sea at first, then turned, as if changing its mind, out along the coastline edge, which grew in drama as the snake-like pathway rose up, accommodated by more Roman stone steps with smaller treads, matching smaller foot sizes of the time. Cliffside, facing the sea, rose two to three hundred feet from a rocky coastline as it towered over the railroad tracks running between the five villages. For those who enjoyed the outdoors, it was worth every step.

"Here comes Dorothy with the Scarecrow and the Tin Man," Archie jokingly whispered to himself as he slowly focused the spotter's scope.

§

LONDON, UK; MINISTRY OF JUSTICE

His driver opened the limo's backdoor for the Home Secretary. "It's about bloody time. I'm late, thanks to you. I need water," the stuffy career politician shouted as he left the car in a huff.

The Minister of Justice sat patiently with his team, the regional head of Interpol, and a plate of cold cuts, in the MJ's conference room. Tea had to be served for the second time and polite conversation became less so as the room grew quiet. The meeting was thirty minutes late. The MJ muttered something about England's chances in the World Cup when the conference room door flew open, a smallish female secretary, whose job it was to introduce the guests as they arrived, hung onto the door handle in desperation as if she were being catapulted to her seat.

"Out of the way! Good day everyone, your patience is appreciated. Next time I'll use a helicopter."

The HS had the reputation of making late appearances, he thrived on attention, and nearly always caused a commotion. But today was different, he didn't want to be here, plus the limo ride gave him a headache that began to throb as if his head was a bass drum. Half stumbling into the room, he tossed his briefcase onto the end position of the table, knocking his name card to the floor, and causing a few water glasses to slosh. Someone at the table mumbled as another reached to retrieve the name card.

"Does he know he'd have to land his chopper at Heathrow, 20 miles away?"

The HS heard some mumbling, noticed people snickering. He hated not knowing what had been said, in his presence, and responded: "What was that?"

The Minister of Justice jumped in: "Helicopter, Minister Hammersmith. We have no way of landing around here." People around the table either smiled or looked down at their phones, shoes or each other. One fellow blew his nose as the HS cleared his throat, adjusted his tie, and came back with:

"It was a joke, people. Ha ha. Now, let's begin, shall we?"

The purpose of the meeting, which would last longer than most people felt necessary, into the night, was to construct a final security framework around the Royal Ascot weekend in June.

"As you all know the Queen has asked my office to coordinate the Royal Family's appearances at the Ascot Races this year. There will be eighteen races in all, but the June event is the largest and most prestigious. The Queen and Charles's first born, William, and his family, Kate and the children, will attend for the first time. Everyone attending will be excited to see the Queen since the Ascot Races were a particular favorite of Prince Phillip's, now that he's gone, these days...," the HS's voice trailed off as he checked his notes.

"Question, sir?" came from a young lady in the front.

"I'm taking questions after my comments, wait or leave," the HS directed.

What an ass.

Each person around the conference table had an opinion of the man, to whom they strained painfully to pay attention to, as he droned on for the next two and a half hours. The HS let it be known that his assistant, not he, would take questions, as he needed to be on his way. His assistant would be arriving in approximately thirty minutes.

Finally, as the HS made his way to the awaiting limo, the thought that he would ever be challenged like that just made him even more angry. He was the key administrator to the Queen for God's sakes; "Don't they know who I am?" Buffoons, all of them. After all, he was Jonas Hammersmith, Home Secretary.

Jonas Hammersmith emigrated to Great Britain, with his family, from Central Europe. His parents instilled a deep belief in the Monarchy from his early childhood. A large picture of Queen Elizabeth hung in their tiny living room apartment in Brixton, below it, a smaller framed piece outlining their undying pledge of loyalty. Jonas would sit transfixed by the regal stern-like look that emanated from the face of the special woman known as; Her Majesty the Queen.

His family life was difficult, with a demanding father and

a secretive alcoholic mother. She passed away when he turned thirteen, a day lodged in his mind, because he happened to find her lying on the kitchen floor, passed out and barely breathing. He held her hand as she slowly slipped away with a final exhale. There was no mistaking the familiar vapors of the sweet poison of vodka as he pulled away from her face.

From that point on, Jonas was driven, by his father, to understand that education meant everything. "You will make something of yourself, Jonas, make this family proud, unlike your mother, God rest her soul." Academic achievement came out of nowhere. Jonas excelled at all subjects, beyond his grade level, setting an almost unachievable standard for his two younger siblings. As his academic accolades gained in number, from certificates to trophies, his father continued to push, until Jonas rose to the top of his class, becoming Valedictorian.

While attending college in his junior year, a friend invited him to a lecture regarding the British Royal Family. What had intended to be an informative speech, provided by a noted authority on the Royals, quickly turned into a heated debate. It was the first time he had ever witnessed anyone question the justification for Queen Elizabeth's reign. Jonas had always assumed that the majority of British citizenry were more than happy to pay taxes as well as homage. But the point about the expense to the taxpayers, especially as the country suffered through tough economic times, never left him.

The speaker left the stage, surrounded by guards, as others took his place. One of the first to speak was a student in the same class as the future HS. Jonas couldn't believe what had just been said. That day, that meeting, changed his life forever. From that day forward he would defend the Queen and her family with his life if need be.

Hammersmith left college with high honors, becoming Valedictorian, with degrees in economics and political science.

He studied law where he earned an additional degree, which propelled him through the ranks of public service to the prideful position he now held as Home Secretary.

§

CINQUE TERRE, ITALY; HEADING NORTH BETWEEN VERNAZZA AND MONTEROSSO

The view became even more breathtaking as the threesome made their way along the trail. The path had narrowed as indicated on their map, just wide enough for hikers to pass each other along the way. Light sandy soil covered hidden pea gravel size stones that could cause one to slip if they weren't paying complete attention. The dirt path descended in a meandering zig-zag, causing the hikers to look directly at one another in a passing fashion that became humorous at one point, taking their minds off the current situation for just a moment. The path eventually straightened to reveal a small stone bridge that led to steps ascending up a hill that afforded a quick look back over Vernazza as they pressed on.

"As I look around, I can't help but take in the view. But I keep losing my footing, this place is very distracting," Pete said as he caught himself from slipping for the third time.

Rick and Sese were now leading the way as they passed by the unseen watchful eyes of Archie's spotter's scope. He had taken a circuitous route that didn't involve the heavily used trail. He liked this spot and wished he could remain longer, but that was not an option. The small village of Vernazza had its charm, which he found comforting. Archie shook his head, he hadn't had much sleep in the last twenty-four hours. He sat up, repositioned himself and that's when he noticed movement coming along the trail behind.

Archie raised the spotter's scope slowly and waited until four men came closer into view. "These are no ordinary hikers," he whispered to himself. He glanced back over his shoulder. The men appeared, just as Pete disappeared up ahead. Almost like clockwork, the oncoming men had his complete attention as Rick, now in last place, still in full view, made his way up and over the rise behind Archie.

On any given day it would be difficult at best to distinguish one of these four men from another. They all looked like they could be related. Archie matched the photograph of Michael Castillino on his phone with each of the men as they came his direction. "That could be the Castillino fellow, no the eyes are wrong." Raising the scope to get a better view of the two that followed behind, he found his man. Clear as day, there he was, Michael Castillino, talking to his slightly shorter companion. "What have you four in mind today, huh, gents?" A smile appeared, then turned quickly into a more serious look as the scope went back into his pack and the elder warrior morphed from observer into hunter and disappeared into the brush.

The chase was on and Archie contacted Rick to let him know. Sese and Pete went into defense mode as they slowed their pace watching for Rick.

The late morning sun was hot, as Michael and his crew hiked rapidly up the steep path. Taking a second to wipe away some sweat, Michael looked up and smiled. "There, up ahead, that's him," he said, pointing to a person beginning to crest the ridge about a quarter mile in front of them. "That's the outfit he was wearing."

"Wait, where are his companions?" Mario remembered the attractive blond woman and the Black man, who confronted Michael in Milan. "There's no hurry, cousins, he's ours now," Gino observed confidently as he patted Michael's back. The sudden rush of confidence helped them to pick up their pace.

The forest grove was the perfect place for a predator to prowl after prey. It happens every day in nature, and in this part of the world, between the five villages, it takes place off the trail. But not today, because survival of the fittest will happen on the trail, and soon.

A trap would be set, but the question is: who would be the target? That was yet to be seen, as the sun continued to rise, the sea relentlessly crashed against the shoreline below, as the prey appeared to quicken their step.

"Scurry along now, keep moving, time is of the essence boys, the sooner the better," Archie muttered to himself as the men hurried past his location.

The seasoned veteran dismounted from his perch, silently slipping through the brush, making his way along the trail, circling around behind the men, and more importantly, the man he believed to be Michael Castillino. He moved like a cat, low, leaning forward, careful not to turn an ankle, as he anticipated his next move. Archie checked his six, routine in these matters, as he cut his own, undetectable, path.

Up until now, he had given the situation a fifty-fifty chance that the mob would continue to hound Mr. Blaine. Unlike the Soviets, who prefer to work alone, making the chase less complicated, this Castillino fellow brought company. A trait that the Germans re-invented in modern times: intimidation.

Up ahead Sese led the trio, having hiked the path before, at a steady pace, alert to oncoming strangers, especially those not dressed in hiking attire. Their plan anticipated the possibility that they could be surrounded at any time. She welcomed Pete's offer to serve as bait in order to lure those who most likely were chasing Rick. Pete originally suggested she go ahead to Monterosso al Mare and wait for them. But she insisted on joining the hike, and besides, she knew this area better than anyone involved.

Rick and Pete positioned themselves, one behind the other, both of them challenged a bit to stay ten paces behind Sese, talking about nothing in particular, as a distraction, and doing their best to keep watch. Each one waited for Archie to call with an update. Rick and Pete traded a 1.5 liter bottle of water back and forth as the trail meandered out toward the sea. Almost on cue, the undergrowth faded away and a majestic view opened up, highlighting an enormous expanse of turquoise blue water under a two-toned blue sky dotted with puffs of white clouds. It cast a refreshing feeling over the tense hikers.

A dozen fishing trawlers and two large cargo ships could be seen making their way through the relatively calm waters. The view became so overwhelming as the three approached a lookout, Rick suggested they return to this very spot, once they took care of matters at hand. Sese smiled, took a drink of her own water, and started to move on then stopped, smiled, turned around with her phone out, and ordered the two men to stop.

"Magnificent. And now we have proof, with you two as witnesses."

Sese was in the process of replacing her phone when a voice came from ahead on the trail. "Hello there."

An elderly couple and their small dog, made their way toward the trio. Both of them looked as though they were knowledgeable hikers out for the day going the opposite direction.

"It's good to see people enjoying the trail as much as we do. Are you from this area?"

Pete looked at Rick and both of them turned to Sese, who happened to be petting the little dog being held by the woman. "That's Grover. He likes you." Talking to the dog, Sese offered, "I wish we could visit Grover, but we are pressed for time."

"We're the Bishops, Gladys and Fredrick; we're from Ontario, Canada. We've hiked this trail, more than once, in the ten years we've been coming here."

"Are there any side trails you could take from this point?" asked Sese. She was concerned about the Bishop's safety, as were Rick and Pete. According to Archie's latest text, the Castillino group was not far behind.

"Yes, as a matter of fact there are two. Very scenic, but they take a little longer, why?" Sese looked deep into Mrs. Bishop's eyes and said with intense sincerity: "I think today would be a good time to choose one of those routes." The Bishops recognized something was wrong, looked at one another, and, without another word, turned around and moved swiftly back down the trail. As they did, Mrs. Bishop looked back at Sese.

"Be careful, dear, and thank you. We'll be staying in Vernazza with friends. Adieu."

The two seniors defied their ages as they sprinted off, walking sticks in hand, quickly disappearing into the trees and bushes covering the interior landscape. They were out of sight, but Grover could be heard barking, happy to be on his way.

Rick used his phone to video their departure, cataloging the experience, just in case their identification was needed in the future. Archie's voice sounded in their ears.

"Castillino is behind you—approximately a quarter of a mile. Stay alert, the man and his mates are armed. Move out to our designated location, now, and wait for my signal."

They picked up the pace with Sese leading the way. The location Archie referred to had to be close. The map showed it less than 100 meters ahead. Sese had suggested the interior open area, away from the tourist viewpoints along the sea overlooks, which dotted along the shoreline.

The trail led them past a cave set back from an overlook built close to the edge. They knew to look for it or would have passed by without even noticing. The Bishop's had mentioned the cave with an iron gate in passing.

"We didn't enter through the gate, our dog wouldn't go near

the place. So we decided not to investigate," Mr. Bishop's gesture sounded more like a warning to Sese as she watched them leave.

As the trio raced past the cave, an eerie feeling came over Rick. It reminded him of a time last year, when he drove fast down California's 101, while being chased. That flashback almost threw him off his pace. He shook it off, regained his focus. Rick wanted nothing more than to eliminate being chased by darkness.

Michael pushed ahead of the two cousins he'd never met before today. Mario kept up, checking his automatic handgun, trying not to run into Michael as he replaced the gun in his waistband, at the small of his back. The men were ready. For what, they didn't really know. The only thing for sure, united among the cousins, was that their American relative, and his brother, had been harmed. And it was up to them to set things straight. Each man had been taught that there was a finality in death, beyond the spiritual. Once that has been achieved, no questions will be asked or answered.

Archie slipped past a mound that looked as if it had an iron gate. A hideout of some sort, probably used by the Germans or Italian forces during WWII. He stopped to listen and catch his breath. He'd just witnessed two people with a dog that surprised him as he made his way through the forest. He didn't expect to see anyone since the trail the people used was not on the map. Spotter's scope in hand, he found the four men making their way, to his three, up the trail.

Rick confirmed with Archie that they found the location where they'd plan to make their stand against the Castillinos. Archie related that he had the Castillinos in sight. They were approximately fifteen minutes from the target location, although two of the men had stopped to piss against a tree.

Sese moved quickly into the brush to take cover while Pete and Rick stood and talked by one of the visitor information kiosks. The plan was for Sese to cover them as Archie made his move and surprised the men by engaging them from behind. Both Rick and Pete were armed and ready to take cover should the Castillinos begin firing, which is what they expected.

Archie made his way up against one of the taller, wider pine trees in the forest as the four men passed. Archie could hear one man, he assumed to be Michael, giving orders. "They should be up ahead. "Gino, you and Vinny scout ahead while we check our ammo. The map shows a visitor's stop not too far ahead. Be careful not to alert them."

The men took off at a fast pace. Each packed a two-way radio. Vinny had a hand gun, Gino his favorite knife that he preferred to use. Very personal, which made the hunt more exciting for him. Gino was the more dangerous of all of the cousins, according to Mario. He liked to cut and disfigure, but his ability to throw the knife with accuracy also made him a valuable asset. Michael had no idea that Lorretta had specifically ordered Mario to find these two men. She knew of their reputations and wanted this confrontation to be the final moment that Rick Blaine would ever see the light of day.

Archie caught the men's scent before seeing them on the trail. He watched the two scouts proceed forward on the trail at a fast pace. Archie replaced his scope and began to move off the boulder next to the tree when an animal bolted close by, causing him to lose his balance. Archie ended up taking a tumble down in between two fallen trees and out of sight.

The faster pace that Sese set, worked in perfect rhythm with Rick's heartbeat. He had to ask himself if he needed more cardio training or more confidence in their ability to challenge the Castillino force.

The air temperature in the grove cooled as the trio awaited the Castillinos. Neither Rick nor Pete had anything to say. Wind in the trees made cracking noises, the only sounds heard at the moment. The wait reminded Pete of battles that had been fought in this region over the centuries. He'd read stories of how the Romans fought to gain ground and later to defend it. How the soldiers must have felt, waiting for the fight to begin. Like he felt now.

Further back on the trail, Frederick Bishop suddenly stopped. Gladys turned to him, "What's the matter, Freddy?"

"There's something odd going on with those three hikers, I think they're in trouble. You go on ahead, I'm going to catch up and see if they're alright," he said. Gladys would have nothing to do with leaving her husband of 40 years, on the trail alone. Especially if there was trouble of some kind.

"Absolutely not, Frederick, we're going with you."

And off they went, using a back way through the woods, with Grover sniffing out the old trail. Gladys trusted her husband's instincts. One time two years ago they rescued some tourists from Greece during a terrible thunder storm. They had wandered off the trail and ended up lost and scared. Frederick, somehow, knew to follow the tourists' footprints after noticing a lone shoe in the brush. After the rescue, Gladys and Frederick met their friends in Vernazza, because the Bishops had a great story to tell.

Archie felt as though he'd been swallowed up by Mother Earth. Laying flat on his back, in near darkness, he did a quick assessment of his body and what he'd been carrying. No broken bones, no equipment lost, but his right ankle hurt like bloody hell. "A sprain. Better than a break, but still. Damn." Some animal must have spent some time recently near where he laid. The ground around him smelled like wet dog hair. He wasn't going to stick around and argue with the beast. There was no time to dwell on misfortune. He found a long branch and snapped it off. Then carefully began to make his way back up the side of one of the fallen trees. Broken off branches and heavy bark provide sufficient hand holds as he pushed away from his support branch. He stopped briefly to catch his breath before proceeding upward. He had to hurry. The pain surprised him as he attempted to stifle a shout. With one last loud gasp, he reached the top of the wooden crevasse he'd fallen into.

Michael heard something and stopped on the trail, holding Mario with one hand. "Did you hear that?" They both listened for a few seconds, nothing. "What did you hear?" asked Mario, "someone shouting?"

Michael turned his head around, eyebrows furrowed, scanning.

"I didn't hear anything. It was probably a hiker," Gino added.

"No witnesses, let's go," shouted Michael with some uncertainty.

Archie used another tree branch for support as he made his way toward the rendezvous point.

Frederick grabbed Grover and covered his mouth before he could bark. Gladys took the dog as her husband signaled with his hands to lower themselves in the bushes.

§

LONDON, UK; LAMPERSON HEADQUARTERS

Ben led the small group consisting of two technicians from MI5 and one other person from Lamperson International. They were located in the Special Services Lab (SSL), working together on several hidden messages on the floppy disks that had arrived from Morocco.

According to Winston's instructions, they used the Roman numerals from the first coin to open the first disk, which required a few tries. After a few concerning minutes, the screen came alive with the first message: THE REIGN WILL DECIDE WHO LIVES AND WHO DIES.

The second disk confirmed the date and place to be the Royal Ascot Races in June. There were more blanks to fill in, but for now, there was enough information to alert the Home Secretary's office. Ben contacted his father and they met in Winston's office. There were some parts of the new information that Ben wanted to share privately with his father.

"What is it, Benjamin?"

Winston could tell his son, whose intuitive skills he highly respected, had more on his mind than what happened in the SSL earlier. Winston hoped there wouldn't be any further details more devastating than a conspiracy to kill members of the Royal Family.

"Father, there's more information than what was revealed in the meeting today." Winston remained calm as he took another sip of tea. "Aye, go ahead, lad."

"There were two references I found last night in preparation for today's meeting. You weren't available to discuss the importance, so I held them back. You trust me, right?" Ben said, looking very serious.

"You know that all information needs to be turned over eventually. I trust you've thought this through."

"I realize the Home Secretary's office comes next, but take a look at this."

Ben reached into his briefcase and pulled out two copies of the translation he worked on last night. Neither of these pieces were seen at the meeting today. Both transcriptions had the same reference, a cell phone number, which was new in the sequence. But, that wasn't the problem, it was the notation: H2S2 that concerned Ben. "What do you think it means?" he asked.

Ben's worried look caused his father to reach forward, taking the sheet in his hands, then suggesting, "I've seen messages similar to this one. Not recently, but back in the day." Winston's voice trailed off as if he reminisced for a minute. He looked up at his son, who was nibbling on a sandwich—Ben hadn't eaten for hours.

"It's a code referring to a person or place based on where the image is placed on the page."

Many times in the business of decoding you run into a signature or mark that points to certain operatives. It was eventually decided that whoever was behind this plot to kill the Queen and her grandson, William, could be considered old school.

"This mark reminds me of a similar post-World War II correspondence we reviewed from Casablanca," Winston offered. "In August 1944, the Vichy government was collapsing, and its officials were either surrendering to the Allies or being shot. The Germans were in retreat and factions of the Nazi regime were attempting to find safe shelter in South America. Most of those who remained were tracked down and killed or repurposed—all of us, even the Soviets, found good use for these technocratic Germans. Aye, they took the Yanks to the moon! But we knew many of those bastards had escaped. So, my mindset was that of a younger man and wanted to track them all down in order to deliver justice, but we knew the cold war was coming. The Soviets had taken an unimaginable beating, losing 60 million civilians alone, but they now occupied more than half of Europe. So, it was no surprise when the iron curtain descended upon Europe—there was no way Stalin was going to give up what he had paid for with so much Russian blood. We let up on one chase, and turned our attention to the curtain, made of iron, that was slowly being closed."

Ben suddenly felt the pressure of having to make critical decisions that could change the course of history. Like the time when his father worked with the Allied forces during WWII, Ben now played a significant part of a process that held the future in their hands. He looked at his father and back at the information contained in the folder in front of them.

"What about this mark: HMIISCII?" Ben asked.

"Is this the only time it was used?" Winston responded.

"No. Here are two more correspondences with the same mark off to the side in the identical spot." Ben pointed to the locations on the sheet.

Winston stood and walked to the picture window, showcasing gray clouds and fog rolling in over the roadway. The mist reminded him of a subtle invasion, made to look like an everyday occurrence to everyday citizens. Something needed to be done by more knowledgeable sources, and fast. This plot, whatever the plan, must be contained. But first, they had to uncover the source.

"We need to know if HMIISCII is an inside contact. My gut feeling is that it is. That's why you kept this from the others, correct?"

"Yes."

"Then we wait to turn the information over. You have twenty-four hours, Ben, go."

§

CINQUE TERRE, ITALY; HEADING NORTH BETWEEN VERNAZZA AND MONTEROSSO

Archie heard what he thought was a dog behind him. As he reached for his revolver, a gentle voice greeted him. "Hello, there. Woah, took a bit of a tumble, eh? Are you hurt?" Archie turned back and couldn't believe his eyes. A man and a woman, holding a dog, were there in the forest with him. At first, he thought he was hallucinating. "I'm sorry, but what, in the bloody hell, are you two doing here?" Frederick, eyeing the pistol in the man's hand, rapidly explained, as best he could under the circumstances, what he felt about the hikers. "Sorry, mate. I am in pain, and, yes, you're right, those hikers are my responsibility and I can't move, my ankle you see." With that, Gladys, a retired nurse, handed Grover to Freddy and went into action. She broke off a piece of Archie's walking stick and with the help of a strap she removed from her back pack, made a walking brace for Archie. She also gave him some ibuprofen. "That should help control the swelling." Archie felt immediate relief. He also knew he had to go. "Thank you, kind people, now leave while I continue on."

"Sorry, no, you're not going anywhere without some help," said Gladys. She wasn't having any of Archie's nonsense.

Frederick helped Archie back to his feet and nearly jumped out of his skin as the first shots rang out.

Michael felt no remorse for taking action against the two people helping Blaine. They were aiding the target and that could not be tolerated. The Castillino bunch were attempting to outflank the hikers. Vinny and Gino had arrived first, with Vinny firing the first shots, which didn't sit well with Michael. He'd told them to hold back, and only fire if the three targets moved on before he got there. Gino just smiled, happy to see some action.

Michael radioed Gino to hold his position, on the left flank, and for Vinny to stop firing from the right, as Mario and Michael came on the scene. Pete had returned fire, but no one, on either side, had been hit so far.

"Hey, Mister Blaine, or should I call you Rick?" There was no answer, so Michael continued. "You shouldn't have included your friends in your private matters." Michael waited a second. "Rick? Can you hear me? This is between us, remember?" Still no answer. "Your death is in retribution for my brother, and my associates. Their blood is on your hands."

Sese and Pete were spread out behind Rick. The trio formed a triangle in the bushes with Rick on the point closest to the open square. Rick had insisted on the arrangement. Sese covered the left side, Pete right. Each had a boulder for a shield, except for Rick who had a garbage can and an information kiosk between him and the voice.

"Why don't you come out, Rick, and we'll let your friends go. There's no reason for additional bloodshed, is there?"

Rick knew the answer. Castillino felt he had nine lives and could not be killed. The line had been drawn and the first one to cross it would be killed. Rick was not about to make that mistake. He decided, instead, to remain silent and see what developed. His heart raced, palms sweated, as he waited along with his friends.

Michael signaled Gino to make the first move. Gino pulled his knife and began to slink toward Sese's position. It surprised him when she went out on the flank by herself. He knew where she hid, behind the large gray boulder with moss covering one side. He moved like a leopard, camouflaged in tan and green hunting gear. The predator came closer to his prey with every step. No sound now, other than some birds in the trees. Just a few more steps. Gino charged in behind the boulder, but there was no one there. The two rounds that hit Gino in the chest came so suddenly that he never had time to react. The impact sent him falling backwards. Vinny started shooting again, setting off a wild series of shots, coming from all positions. Michael sent Mario out on the left flank to check on Gino, and took a number of shots to cover him while he moved into position.

Pete watched as Sese removed a knife and handgun from the man she'd just killed. He started to shout to see if she was okay, but had to dive for cover as shots came toward his head. Pieces of rock flew all around him. When he looked back, Sese was gone. Pete inched his way along the forest floor, attempting to find better protection. He guessed that there were three men left, so we had them outnumbered. He had to move out further to try and get a better position on the man who'd been firing at him. Where was Rick?

Fortunately, there were no early morning hikers on the trail coming from the north. Rick was relieved, hoping no one, like the Bishops, would get in the way. He had to put a stop to this madness. Pete alerted everyone to his next move, and Rick responded by moving out, heading toward Sese's last position, leaving the middle open. The smell of gunfire hung in the air as people on both sides changed positions, stalking one another.

Mario signaled to Michael that Gino was dead. When Michael realized what had happened his confidence turned into rage. He could no longer contain himself. He hated Blaine now more than ever. The others didn't matter, he wanted Rick Blaine dead, now.

"Hey, Blaine, Michael Castillino here. Let's you and me end this. Tell your friends to back off and meet me in the middle of the crossroads where we can settle this man to man."

Rick froze in place, crouching down behind a brown sign board with gold letters that welcomed all tourists to one of the most beautiful places on earth. He could tell he was close to Castillino's position. Rick could almost hear the man breathing hard as he spoke.

Michael slowly stood up with his hands up in the air. His dark complexion featured a perfect smile that normally put strangers at ease. Those that knew Michael, however, knew otherwise. Mario watched as his cousin made his way out into the open. Vinny couldn't believe his eyes. This move had not been discussed as an option. Vinny didn't know Michael, as well as the others, and thought the man was off his nut.

"So, Blaine. Are you going to let your friends put their lives on the line, trying to save you, like the first time we met? Hey, Mister Blaine, I'm waiting."

Rick came out from behind the sign with his hands in the air. He knew this moment might come. This very action, like two gunfighters in an old western movie, facing one another, had been a recurring daydream. Pete watched, not really surprised by his friend's action. Pete had his gun trained on Castillino, while watching for any sign of Sese.

"If I said it was good to see you again, Blaine, I'd be lying."

"One of your many attributes I'm sure." Rick sounded confident, ready to take on whatever came next. He, too, was ready to end this.

Both men put their hands down at the same time. Each looking directly into the eyes of the other. Rick's focus went from Michael's face to his right hand, which began to twitch. Sweat poured down the face of the man who looked ready to kill. Rick's shooting practice with Major Connors and Bear would hopefully pay off. Connors, Blaine's Production Chief and former military officer, made sure Rick knew how to fire a weapon after last year's encounter with the Castillino gang.

"Tell you what, Blane. I'll count to three and then we draw. How's that?"

Rick knew he had seconds based on what he and Connors had discussed. Castillino was not to be trusted. "And if you get an open shot at the sonofabitch, take it." He could hear Connors's rant ringing in his ears.

"Sounds way too complicated." As soon as Rick finished his sentence, Michael began to draw his pistol from behind his back. Rick reacted instantly and rolled to his side as he took a shot at Michael, hitting him squarely in the chest. Michael responded with a shot of his own, but missed. He kept firing as he went down to his knees. Mario saw Michael go down, and emerged from cover like a spewing volcano firing madly as he traded shots with Pete.

Vinny glanced over in time to see Michael's lifeless form fall forward. He didn't care much for his American relative, and in that moment realized he had to switch from attack to survival mode. Vinny had just begun to look for a way out when he noticed movement out of the corner of his eye. It was the young lady he and Gino had been tracking and she was making her way toward the center of the crossroads.

As Sese moved swiftly through the underbrush, head down, gun up, she bent down to check the identification of the man she'd killed earlier. She lowered her gun as she retrieved the man's wallet, safely tucking it away, when Vinny jumped on her from behind, sending her gun flying. Together, they rolled across into the clearing. That action caused Rick to stand up as he called Sese's name. A shot rang out, it missed Rick as he charged back into the brush and out of sight.

The shot came from Mario who had left himself open for a split second. Pete took dead aim and shot. The bullet struck Mario in the forehead. He fell back into a large clump of thorny bushes, but it didn't matter. Mario was beyond feeling pain at that point.

Vinny straddled Sese, who by now, lay totally exhausted, the fight drained out of her. Vinny smiled at his captive as he pulled Gino's knife from his belt. He'd retrieved the old blade from his dead cousin's body minutes before while in pursuit. Sese began gasping for breath. She felt helpless lying beneath two hundred pounds of her sweaty knife wielding attacker. He leaned close to Sese's face.

"You killed my cousin and now I'm going to do some killing of my own."

From out of nowhere came a fast-moving ball of fur. The small dog latched onto the man's knife hand, shaking its head side to side, tearing into his skin. Sese found new energy and seized upon the opportunity that Grover created. Sese pushed Vinny off, and started to roll away, as Vinny freed himself and began to run after her. Grover barked and lunged back at the attacker, trying to defend Sese.

Suddenly, a red dot appeared on the back of Vinny's head just as he raised his knife to throw it at Sese. Before he could make the throw, the front portion of his forehead blew open, ending the man's ability to ever throw a knife — or live — again. The shot had come from a police marksman who had arrived just in time.

The Bishop's stood with Archie as Sese, Pete and Rick entered the middle of the information area as a small contingent of police officers joined them. They had responded to a call made to law enforcement in Monterosso asking for help. The group of six made their way from the northern village just in time to witness the attack and help in the end.

Sese hugged her new furry friend, who was busy licking her face.

Archie spoke first. "I believe Castillino is still alive, but not for long. The other three are dead, correct?" Rick nodded as he bent over Michael Castillino who was gasping for air and trying to say something.

"You, you are as good as dead, Blaine."

"You said that before, remember? Besides, you don't look so good, Michael. I don't think you'll be doing anymore killing."

The dying man, finding it hard to breathe and talk, took one last breath and spoke. "She… will find… a… way." The air left Michael Castillino's lungs as he spoke his last words and then rolled to one side.

Pete, standing alongside Rick, asked: "Who do you think he was talking about?"

"I'm not sure, but we'll need to find out." Rick, certain there would be repercussions, knew it was just a matter of time. This matter wasn't over, unfortunately. He would ask the Lampersons to check it out further when he arrived in London.

"We have three dead in the woods and their leader, here." Sese had her military enforcer voice on, which did not match her physical attraction. "I've provided the local authorities with our information, they will take our statements later.

In the meantime, allow me to re-introduce our new friends." Sese stepped forward before Archie could speak. "Gladys, Frederick, and my new pal, Grover." The look of surprise on Archie's face could not be replicated. Finally, he spoke: "If it weren't for these two," he stopped, pausing to look down at Grover. "Excuse me, little chap, I mean three…. I wouldn't have made it here in time to shoot the man who attacked you, my dear Sese." As it turned out, Archie was the only one wounded, which was self-inflicted. He managed to severely sprain his ankle, which only slightly delayed his departure for London with Rick.

§

SILICON VALLEY, CA; BLAINE MANUFACTURING

Brenda walked the halls of Blaine Manufacturing nearly every morning. She likened it to making hospital rounds. She enjoyed making it part of her morning ritual, plus, it added to her ten thousand steps a day. Rick always questioned the reasoning behind setting an exact number to the appropriate number of steps a person should take a day. Before he left for Europe, he was leaving his office around 3 in the afternoon. Brenda casually asked Rick where he was off to and he answered, "Heading home I'm almost at ten thousand steps for the day. Bye." In reality he was heading to the gym to work out, but that was Rick, having fun with the moment.

Rick had become popular in the media, especially in the local news, and Brenda wanted to be able to answer any questions from her employees on a daily basis. She shared her employee conversations with Rick. He wanted to know how they felt, and appreciated Brenda's attention to that particular detail. He told her once that listening to employees, and what they felt, was a positive addition to his decision making. For the most part, it also confirmed his belief that others shared his dream.

She liked to take his thought one step further into the creative realm. Each step Brenda took, from the parking garage in the basement to the executive offices on the sixth floor, represented the progress she would make that day. Voices, sharing unrecognizable points of view as she passed by, were creative echoes that helped to produce unique products.

As she exited the stairway door, heading back to her office, her cell phone rang. Bear's call would be one of many that day, but this one made her heart race. She listened as Bear relayed what Archie reported about Rick's confrontation with Castillino and his gang in Cinque Terre. "Is Rick hurt?" she asked anxiously.

"No, he and his two companions are fine, but it was a battle. Castillino didn't go easy. He and three of his associates were killed." Bear told her about Archie's sprained ankle, and explained that he and Rick were on their way to London after being interviewed by the local authorities. The pause that followed allowed Brenda time to catch her breath. "Brenda."

"Sorry, I just walked up some stairs and had to catch my breath. This is crazy."

Brenda thanked Bear and immediately called Ralph Phillips. But before she could connect with Ralph, Rick's caller ID showed up on her phone. She immediately took the call instead:

"Rick. Where are you?"

"On Winston's private jet with Archie. Castillino is dead."

"Bear just told me."

Their conversation stopped suddenly. Brenda knew Rick had something bothering him. "What is it, Rick?" She heard him clear his throat and take a drink before answering. "Brenda, we, Blaine Manufacturing I mean, need to beef up security." He went on to explain what he and Archie had been discussing on the plane. "Archie feels the Castillinos aren't going to let up just because Michael is dead. In fact, they may expand their hatred for me to my company, which puts everyone at Blaine in jeopardy."

Brenda assured him that she would personally see to it that they double their security force in San Jose and make sure all their people are made aware of the situation. Rick agreed and added, "I'll send you some ideas that Archie and I have discussed."

The conversation shifted to Rick's next assignment: working with Winston in London. A new plan would be put in motion for Rick to follow. He would be seeking new distribution for Blaine products, but that activity, true in one sense, would also serve as a cover for Winston's urgent matter, whatever that meant.

"Let me know what your new schedule is so we can be of assistance," Brenda said as she motioned to one of her assistants to sit and close the door.

§

MONTEROSSO AL MARE, ITALY, COMANDO STAZIONE

Rick and Archie spent several hours with the local authorities, explaining what had happened along the trail. The death of Michael Castillino and three others was a big deal in Cinque Terre, but it was determined that he was the leader of a group of gangsters, determined to bring harm to people along the trail. Gladys and Frederick told the officers they feared for their lives, and credited Rick and his friends with defusing the situation. One witness, a baker in Vernazza, reported overhearing the man he later identified as Michael Castillino, meeting with three other men behind his store, the day before the incident. Although he didn't hear what they were discussing, he had the feeling they were up to no good.

"He had the look of a crazy person, wild, out of control," the baker told police.

Archie and Rick were free to go, after leaving their contact information. Both he and Rick were then driven to a local airport to catch a commuter flight to Milan where Winston's plane waited to fly them on to London.

Rick's friends, Pete and Sese stayed behind and finished their time in Vernazza before returning to Milan. As Rick prepared to leave, Pete asked:

"So, you'll be in London for the next two weeks?

"Yes. Winston and Brenda have a full slate of meetings set up. Then home."

"Try, just try and stay out of trouble my friend," Pete said as Sese gave Rick a big hug.

"Both of you are invited to visit California whenever you can make time. Let's not allow the years to pass again, alright?"

§

TANGIER, MOROCCO; GRAND SOCCO MARKETPLACE

Abbas awoke in a bed, which was very unusual. What happened and where was he? Abbas had trouble focusing. He must still be dreaming. The room had a lamp, but he couldn't reach it. Night or day, he couldn't tell. He wiped his eyes and tried to sit up. As his vision improved, he noticed a person in a chair alongside the bed. The person must be asleep. Who could it be and where am I? The orange glow of the oil lamp slowly revealed, Jamal. Although his throat felt rough when he swallowed, Abbas moved his lips and spoke. Nothing came out at first, so he tried again.

"Jamal?"

His voice sounded small to him, like one of the children. And it hurt to speak. Why? The old man didn't move, but it was his friend, the man who ran the spice stall and gave him food and money to buy food to share. Abbas was hungry, his stomach told him so. But Abbas, and his group, the children that followed him, who depended on him, were used to empty stomachs, going without, begging. His thoughts went to them as each face came clearer to him in his mind. The children.

He had to get up and go to them. Abbas began to move away from the oversized pillow. He slowly rose and shifted into a sitting position, as he did, the pain in his ribs was almost unbearable. Abbas cried out.

"Abbas, you are awake"

Jamal rushed to the bed and gradually, slowly, helped to

lower Abbas back down. The man, aided by his wife, had been taking care of the boy, since he was discovered in the alley, next to their dar, three nights ago.

"Let me tend to the boy, you go Jamal. Go. You need your rest," his wife insisted as she lifted the boy's head to feed him some broth.

Jamal and Abbas now stared at one another. "What happened?" The boy asked.

"You need to eat something. But drink this first." Jamal took over holding the boy's head as he spooned a tincture made up by his wife, from a bowl by the bed. Jamal felt the boy's head, his fever was gone. The young one, after taking some broth, then drifted off to sleep. After spending many late-night hours worrying about Abbas, Jamal was finally able to relax. Fever and bruises were treatable, but why? Why was Abbas attacked? And what about the others? Jamal hadn't seen any of the children that hung around with Abbas. Jamal would find out. He would have to be careful about asking too many questions, but he had to have answers, and he did have his connections.

§

BOSTON, MA; PETRULA TRUCKING COMPANY HEADQUARTERS

Lorretta Petrula sat in her office after hiring a new warehouse supervisor. After interviewing several candidates, she had settled on a woman who already worked for her, Carmella Margolis. The thirty-seven year-old, with one felony conviction, had previously worked the docks in New York as a Teamster. She started working for Petrula Trucking as a long-haul delivery driver two years ago. Divorced, no kids, a self-proclaimed Kenny Chesney groupie, and a rabid NASCAR fan. The deciding factor came when Lorretta asked her: "Why would you want to supervise a warehouse?"

Carmella's answer: "Because, as you are well aware, it's a man's world out there. And there's nothing I'd like better than to tell the men around here what to do and where to shove it."

Just as Carmella was leaving to take her first shift as supervisor, a call came in for Lorretta from Palermo. She knew something wasn't right before she picked up the receiver. Michael had promised to return her call last week. That never happened, but Michael didn't seem himself, more nervous than usual, from the day he found out Rick Blaine's whereabouts.

The caller, one of Michael's uncles, related the bad news: "Michael is dead. He lies in a morgue in the Cinque Terre region, murdered, along with my son, Mario, and two others."

"That stupid fool," Lorretta whispered to herself.

Carmella could see that Lorretta, who normally showed little emotion, had tears forming, as she held the receiver out in front of her. The new supervisor didn't know what to do, so she just stood there watching, as her boss hung up the phone, wiped her eyes with a tissue then blew into it. When Lorretta noticed Carmella standing in the doorway, she shouted.

"What? Go!"

Carmella swiftly closed the door and left. She'd made her way to the top of the metal stairway that dropped two floors to the main level of the warehouse, when Lorretta's office door opened.

"Come back, Carmella. I have an idea I want to discuss with you, now."

Chapter 6

LONDON, UK; LAMPERSON INTERNATIONAL HEADQUARTERS

"Brenda, it's me."

"Rick, where are you?"

"London. Archie and I made it early this morning. Did I call too late?"

"No, I'm just finishing up on some details for you that Ben requested for tomorrow."

The two of them caught up on some business details that required Rick's approval. Production of new products, the new production facility ramp-up, and the new security arrangements led a discussion that lasted just over an hour. Rick signed off with the promise that he would get plenty of sleep later that night, before tackling his new assignment in London tomorrow.

Rick and Ben met briefly after the phone call. He let Ben know that the final list of Blaine products for foreign distribution would be ready within the hour.

"How's our Brenda doing? Bet she was glad to hear from you."

Rick nodded his head as he kept looking at Ben. He could hear it in Ben's voice, confirming Rick's suspicions about just how much interest Ben had in Brenda, beyond business. The two of them had been carefully coordinating details, regarding Rick in his travels, for the last week, but, in reality, they've been communicating, back and forth, for months. He wondered, hoped really, that their discussions had developed into something more personal.

"What is it, Rick? Why are you staring at me like that?" Ben smiled as he asked.

"Oh, nothing. Guess I'm just tired." Brenda deserved to have someone like Ben in her life, but Rick was no matchmaker. He could hardly put his own personal life together, let alone Brenda and Ben's.

Ben patted Rick on the back as the two walked down the hall heading for the elevator. Once inside the elevator, Rick looked over at Ben and asked if he'd ever consider moving part of their operation to the United States. The doors opened and Ben suggested they continue that conversation over beers sometime. They walked into the meeting room together, a few minutes late, where Winston, Archie and Ben's assistant, Eli, were waiting.

"Good morning, you two, Rick, meet Eli Ortanguthalamatrimonula," Winston stated proudly.

"He prefers, Eli O," Winston continued, as he leafed through papers in front of him. Rick reached out his hand to shake, as Eli did the same.

"It's an honor Mr. Blaine."

Eli's background began with a tragic story, related later by Ben, about the man's family.

A monsoon wiped out his village in southern Thailand, leaving him orphaned and homeless at the age of eight. He managed to survive, thanks to a bright wit, and a superior intelligence. After spending four years in the Thai military, he worked as an interpreter for the foreign service, where he met Archie.

Ben handed out two sheets of information, as Archie lit a cigar and raised the window he was sitting next to, in time to send his first cloud of smoke outside. Everyone who knew Sir Archie understood his need, addiction really, for cigars. The cigar didn't bother Rick, he actually liked the smell. Archie continued to sit at the window, making notes.

Winston stood and walked to a large white board that ran the width of the conference room. He picked up a black marker and wrote: The Reign. He closed the top of the marker and placed it back on the desk. After clearing his throat, he turned and spoke.

"Eli and Archie worked together recently on a case in Scotland. That case led to where we are today in this room. That's why I've asked Eli to join us and, having said that, Eli, why don't you lead the discussion."

Eli stood and walked to the board. He was small in stature, five foot seven, Rick guessed. He placed his iPad on a stand next to the whiteboard, looked around the room as he took a sip of water and began. His voice took over the room immediately, with a smooth bravado, that captured everyone's attention immediately.

"There appears to be a new terrorist group operating in Great Britain. The communications we've intercepted are signed by The Reign. Its mission, according to the information we gathered in Scotland, is to kill members of the Royal Family. And in doing so, spark a national uprising."

He continued for another twenty minutes, outlining how he and Sir Archie were able to find a safe house operation located outside of Edinburgh, thanks to the diligent efforts of agents in France and North Africa. Eli continued: "New information out of Morocco links The Reign with a new effort to cause harm to two members of the Royal Family, namely, Queen Elizabeth and her grandson, William, the Duke of Cambridge. We feel this could be the beginning of multiple terrorist events modeled on the ten months during the "Reign of Terror" during the bloody height of the French Revolution in 1793-94."

Rick sat there knowing he was to play a role in helping to interfere and, hopefully, breakup, this terrorist plot. The more details Eli explained the more nervous Rick became. Winston had discussed with Rick how the introduction of Blaine Manufacturing's products could be used as a cover for the British authorities, attempting to infiltrate the Reign's network of spies. The more Eli explained, the more interested Rick became. He had no idea how involved The Reign were in the British government and how little time they had to thwart the terrorists' plans. Time was of the essence. Rick had a question: "Why the Queen and William?"

Eli was quick to answer: "Ah, yes, good question. They represent the legacy of the crown and the future of the Royal Family, if there is to be one. We should also note that the upcoming Royal Ascot Race in June is definitely the target event for eliminating them both."

Ben relieved Eli at the board and immediately began writing the coded messages, two of four, on the board. He explained how the messages were intercepted. It had to be understood by each of them, how old technology, not only provided the intercept, but also helped to slow down the possibility of the conspirators finding out just how much the authorities knew. "This method of cryptic deception is not new. In fact, it's been used, to one degree or another, for the past 2,500 years."

He held what looked like a coin in his fingers as if he were about to do the rolling between the fingers trick, before passing the ancient piece around the room. Ben drew on the whiteboard as, one by one, each man checked the coin over. To a person, each one thought the ancient piece was in remarkably good shape.

"To be clear, our contact intercepted normal conversation and translated it into our coding process. Each Roman numeral and letter corresponds with a letter in our alphabet, eventually, not directly." Ben went on to explain that that indirect sequence is what separated this code from others. Both sides of the coin contained important information that our contact in Morocco, working with dated processing equipment, originated. Jamal has worked with my father for over forty years in an effort to combat international terrorism efforts. I've mentioned his name, because he finally had to come forward recently when he met with Rick and Pete. Jamal decided to expose his identity, because of the importance of the information he discovered. He understands his exposure could put the lives of he and his family in jeopardy. One more thing. It is vitally important that Jamal's identity never leave this room if our efforts, now, and in the future, are to be successful."

Ben quickly scanned the faces of those in attendance, shuffled papers in front of him, and moved on. "Let's begin." He aimed his laser pointer at each of the numerals and their translated code.

ROMAN NUM. CVLVIVXXVPVII
Translated code: HXSX6X10XQX2

ROMAN NUM. IIVOVXXVIVQVC
Translated code: 2XWX10X6XSXH

The room sat silent while Winston stood and walked up to the board. Eli and another analyst had worked through the night decoding the Roman numerals into two messages. Ben, who summarized the findings, stood off to the side as Winston spoke: "Some of you may think this system to be archaic, but it's worked for thousands of years. And Jamal and I have used it for the last forty years. The coin decoding is unique and easy to decipher from our side, we created it. That code unlocks these disks and that's when the fun begins, or rather, began for Ben and Eli. Both men have a respectable knowledge of codes coming out of the north African region. They used that knowledge to decode what Jamal found in Morocco and transferred onto these rather antiquated disks."

Winston held the disks up as if he'd just found two missing puzzle pieces and then continued. "It's our belief that the two messages reinforce each other, and are, in fact, the same. So far, we've determined that terrorists are planning to assassinate the Queen and Prince William, based on what you see here, plus, what MI5 just sent us this morning. A phone conversation that originated between two cell towers was recorded for the fourth time in the last week, while moving between 10 Downing and Parliament. According to our findings, as of this minute, we have less than two weeks, three tops, to figure this out."

Winston moved away as Ben explained what he wrote on the whiteboard:

LOCATION: ASCOT RACE
DATE: 6 JUNE, 2020
TARGETS: THE QUEEN AND THE DUKE OF CORNWALL
SOURCE: THE REIGN (Top Foreign Suspect)
INSIDE SOURCE: TBD

"Our top priority is to identify the inside source. That person or persons are the break in the dam of classified information pertaining to the Royal Family. We believe this clandestine planning has gone on for some time. High ranking officials may be involved. This is where you come in, Rick."

§

ENGLISH CHANNEL, EUROSTAR, PARIS TO LONDON

Herman Kruger pulled the blanket up to his chin as he huddled in a corner seat staring out the viewless window. The reflection looked longingly back at him, as the high-speed train dove under the English Channel. Hum, hum, bum, bum, click, click. The paper in his breast pocket radiated warmth, like one of those warm stones they lay on your back during a massage. He knew he had held onto the message too long. Time was a precious commodity at this point, which made him sweat more, as he listened to the sound of the train. Hum, hum, bum, bum, click, click. He'd been celebrating after a conference in Paris, and one thing led to another. Excuses, excuses. His life depended on how the "leader" would react to what he had in his briefcase.

"How stupid of me," Herman intended to say that to himself, but those sitting close by looked over at him. One older woman smiled, as she continued to knit.

He'd been under surveillance, hand-picked by the leader, when he was on holiday in Germany, visiting family. Herman didn't know it at the time of course. It wasn't his good looks or vibrant personality that made him such a good choice. In fact, his being chosen was just the opposite. At barely five foot eight inches tall, weighing in at just under two hundred pounds, balding and sporting a thin mustache, Herman made the perfect spy, or so he told himself. Herman admitted to being plain and ordinary in every way; a person who never catches a second glance, and blends into the background. "No good looks on this guy," he muttered to himself, lost in thought.

"Excuse me?" The knitting lady uttered, startling Herman for the second time.

"Oh? No, nothing, I'm just, I'm just, talking to myself." He smiled, but Herman Kruger knew the reason for his being drafted into a spy network went beyond good looks and a strong demeanor, way beyond. Herman ended up being targeted by a radical terrorist organization because he worked in the Home Secretary's office.

Herman sat forward in his seat and reflected on the day he was selected. He likened it to being chosen, like the kid on the school grounds, standing with other kids the same age, waiting to be picked to play a sport. He'd always ended up taken last or not at all back then, but in this case, Herman was numero uno! A satisfied reflection looked back as he cast a glance out toward the nonexistent view through the train's window as the Eurostar continued under the channel.

It happened late last year. The sleeting rain had turned to snow and London ended up being blanketed by a unifying layer of pearly white, that slowed life down for a few days. Herman enjoyed being thrown off his monotonous routine of creating correspondence on behalf of the Home Secretary to the general public, one of his many dutiful attributes. Herman was an intricate cog in a rather large wheel of never-ending letters, invitations, emails, and more recently, social media. His work was important, that's why he was hired, selected over a long list of applicants. But the work gave him occasional eye strain, which led to debilitating migraines. On that snowy day, Herman headed to lunch, repeating his new mantra; I'm doing important work for the Queen.

As he crunched his way over plowed and unplowed granite sidewalks, he kept thinking of what the Home Secretary would do if he, Herman Kruger, took another job. What would happen to the whole department if he just suddenly left? Of course, he had no idea, as he trudged through blinding snow to lunch, just how much his life would change from the mundane into the extraordinary.

Only a few more steps and he would be at his favorite place, Kavar's Deli. But when he rounded the last corner a sign on the door read: CLOSED. The Middle Eastern delicatessen he frequented had closed, because of the snow conditions. Other people gathered close by were also disappointed by the closure. That's when he overheard someone on the street mention a small cafe that remained open around the corner. It turned out to be further off the beaten track than he was led to believe, closer to the Thames. His lunch hour went fast enough, Herman didn't mind walking in the snow, but he had to find the place soon or head back without eating. He hated the thought. Finally, he found the place, after slip-sliding his way down an extremely slippery sidewalk.

The Little Prince Cafe was nearly full as Herman stomped the snow off his feet, removed his hat, and sat at a two-top in a corner by himself. The ham on rye sandwich with chips sounded good, so he ordered right away while sipping a welcomed cup of herbal tea while watching the river boats pass by. He wondered if the boats needed to be driven differently in the snow, and quickly came up with his own answer, no, of course not.

The service was very good, he would be sure to compliment the server on his way out. He'd just taken a second bite, when a stranger asked if he could sit with him. The place was crowded, and with seating at a premium, he nodded with a full mouth. "Yes. Of course. Please, sit."

The man held a bowl of soup and appeared to have a German accent. The bearded gentleman introduced himself:

"I'm Fritz, and you are Herman, am I correct in that assessment?"

Hearing his name nearly caused Herman to choke on the bite he'd just taken. He showed what he'd been chewing, as his mouth remained open, accompanying a look of surprise on his rounded face.

"Please, don't let me disturb you, are you alright? Please, finish chewing. Enjoy your sandwich." The smile from the man looked forced.

"It can't taste as good as the one you normally order, at the deli, further back on your regular route," Fritz whispered as he kept eye contact while, simultaneously, dipping his spoon in a bowl of beef and barley soup.

The rest of his lunch hour was spent listening to a man who offered Herman an opportunity to serve in what Fritz called: the Cause. As Herman sat and listened to what the man professed to be the only way the UK was to survive, he wondered how he, Herman, fit into this stranger's narrative. After all, Herman believed in his ancestry that spawned generations of strong loyal Germans. It wasn't until the sandwich and soup were gone and tea refilled, twice, that the real essence of what the man needed revealed itself.

"Your connection to the Home Secretary and his office would be considered vital to the Cause, Herman. You are important to us. We need people like you to stand up and believe in a movement that will eventually reign over this country. The Royal hand that waves back at the people today is not the future, we, the Reign, are the future of this great nation. Do you understand?"

Herman sat there thinking, not moving, except for his napkin to his lips, more out of reflex than need. He had thoughts, where did they go? He had to give this man an answer. His life flashed before him as he felt his face warm. The clock was ticking as his stomach began to churn. Finally.

"What is it you need me to do?"

The man stood, smiled through thin lips, retrieved his coat, scarf and hat from the hook adjacent to the table and leaning down in the direction of Herman's right ear, whispered: "I take that as a positive comment, Herr Kruger. I will be in touch. For now, please understand that you are not to discuss what's been said here. Is that understood?"

Herman nodded.

"Good. I would hate to have to find anyone else to replace you. That would mean you'd never see another snowy London day, Herman."

The man left as quietly as he came, while Herman barely made it in time to throw up in the restroom.

§

LONDON, UK; LAMPERSON INTERNATIONAL HEADQUARTERS

"Rick, we need to put your IWP to work immediately."

"Come again?"

Winston smiled at the look on Rick's face. "Sorry, your International Work Plan. We work with acronyms around here. I was hoping we could give you more time to formulate a more comprehensive plan, but time is of the essence."

Rick understood, of course, as the two men sat alone in Lamperson's huge conference room. For all intents and purposes, Rick was to make it known that his only interest in being in Great Britain was to establish new business relationships on behalf of his company. Blaine Manufacturing was his baby and a very successful supplier to the high-tech world. Selling came naturally to Rick, it was the more clandestine activity, which hid behind the approach, that would take some nurturing. The question was, would Rick be up to the task?

"I understand, Winston. I'm ready."

"Expansion is what you're concerned with, and, hopefully, that will happen, eventually. Discovery of a mole, and how much they know, will help us in preventing an attack on the Royal Family. That's what we're after."

Rick had his sales team prepare a list of British contacts before he left. It was much shorter than Winston's, which they now merged together. The new contact list amounted to eighty-five valid business prospects. Added to that number were people who worked as the Queen's administrative support in Kensington Palace and the Home Secretary's Office. After reviewing the list, Winston decided that, any one out of ten people helped to plan the Queen's every move on a daily basis.

Rick made the last-minute decision to leave members of Blaine's sales team behind. Instead, Rick would be using the services of two staff members from the Lamperson company to assist him. This operation had serious underpinnings, and he didn't want to put Blaine employees in harm's way. Besides, Winston's people would have a better handle on how to make appointments and set the most aggressive business schedule he'd ever witnessed.

Brenda monitored their work and made any necessary adjustments regarding the Blaine business side of the operation. Rick would be wearing two hats, one as a businessman, the other would be more like a detective. The added thrill of finding a mole, while lining up new business contacts, presented a new set of larger butterflies.

When he considered the fact that Winston had come up with the idea, he realized how much confidence the old Brit had in him, which made Rick feel better about the whole scheme. Self-doubt would just have to take a back seat for now. He needed to focus on splitting his time between selecting potential contacts that could eventually become customers, and those who may turn out to be terrorists.

Rick was ready. Within an hour after meeting with Winston, contacts and appointments were being scheduled. His next five days were filling up with the following week close behind. The clock was ticking.

§

WESTMINSTER, LONDON, UK; THE HOME OFFICE

The Home Secretary had had a busy day. He threw his keys into the dish on his desk and briefcase underneath simultaneously. Hammersmith's meeting with the Prime Minister hadn't gone as well as he expected. The whole affair appeared to be some kind of set up. Some type of surprise attack, made to embarrass him in front of subordinates. Hammersmith was upset and close to writing a scathing report, specifically naming the Prime Minister as having had a hand in shaming Great Britain's Home Secretary. The audacity.

After giving his valet the night off, he decided to pour a scotch and soda before taking another breath. The tie disappeared, shoes off. He opened the slider leading out onto a deck that looked out over west London as the sun set. He saluted the diminishing light as the dots of street lamps revealed various avenues.

He'd been drinking more lately, so what? The alcohol had cost him both marriages, not entirely his problem. He knew that, but his dedication went beyond marriage and that required some numbing at times, like now. It would have been the same if they'd had children. They would have just gotten in the way. His mission in life was to serve those who feel less fortunate, partly due to the attention, and funds, provided to the Royals. He had to admit that he relished every moment he spent with the Queen. He'd come to understand the pressure she had to endure. Why she put up with the Firm that surrounded her was beyond comprehension. It was only a matter of time before the whole idea of royal lineage, dating back centuries, would be compromised. Jonas wondered to himself if he could support an effort to make it happen in his lifetime. He'd be out of a job he enjoyed, mostly working with the Queen. It was the rest of the crowd he couldn't stand.

After the third drink it was bedtime. The city lights began to dance in hypnotic circles beyond the window pane. He fell deep into the nighttime abyss.

"Sir, sir, I'm sorry to wake you, but it's time."

The Home Secretary's valet had been trying to wake the honorable gentleman for nearly an hour. Breakfast was out of the question, Hammersmith had meetings and a schedule to keep.

"I'm, I'm not feeling well this morning Edward, please go away and have my office cancel my appointments for the day."

"I forwarded that message earlier, sir, but you have some very important people on your schedule. One such person is Sir Archie and a guest from the United States, a gentleman by the name of Rick Blaine."

"Bloody hell, I totally forgot. Lay out my suit and run the shower, and bring some Nurofen, hurry!"

Sir Archibald knew immediately that he and Rick had been snubbed when they entered the Home Secretary's office. His absence would be duly noted. Archie didn't like the man who seemed to enjoy the reputation of being the world's biggest prick. Since they were made to wait, a man named Herman ushered into a waiting area adorned with portraits of long-forgotten royals and political leaders and served them tea and an assortment of sweets. The man took a few minutes to explain his duties as Chief Assistant to the Home Secretary, which included being in charge of the daily office schedule among other duties that were quickly forgotten.

"He said to give you his apologies, Sir Archibald, and of course you sir, what did you say your name was?"

"Rick Blaine, Blaine Manufacturing."

"Yes, of course. You're a colleague of Winston Lamperson, correct?"

"Yes. Winston's company is a vendor to mine in the United States. His company is helping to introduce our products to prospects here in the United Kingdom."

Herman's cell phone suddenly buzzed and he left the room, explaining that he was going to meet the Home Secretary as he arrived. Archie looked at Rick as Herman left the room. He rolled his eyes as if making some kind of unkind comment.

"What?" Rick was smiling. One thing Rick found interesting about Sir Archie, he didn't hold back any criticism for people he found to be phony or of unusual character. Herman, evidently, fell into that category. A moment later the small meeting room door opened and Herman reappeared, holding the door open as the Home Secretary made an awkward appearance.

Archie interrupted Herman and made the introductions instead. "Rick Blaine meet Jonas Hammersmith, Home Secretary."

Hammersmith threw his coat and hat at Herman, who stood straight with arms out like a human coat rack. "Herman, be so kind as to bring tea, immediately." Hammersmith then glanced at Rick, and added, "Oh, and a white Americano for our American friend."

Herman bowed slightly as he left the meeting room, trying not to look the least bit disturbed as his superior excused his lateness by blaming others, including Herman.

Hammersmith was now behind schedule and Herman

would hear about it for the rest of the day. As Herman made his way through his office door, heading for the mailroom two floors below, his eyeglasses felt funny on his nose. The glasses were a new and very expensive pair from the Italian designer: Illesteva. He wasn't usually an extravagant spender, but when it came to eyewear, the sky was the limit. An adjustment was needed. Unfortunately, he chose the wrong moment to look down to remove them as he rounded a corner. Papers flew up in the air, almost in slow motion, as the woman Herman ran into, fell in a twisting motion, like a ballerina trying to regain her balance. An embarrassing moment for both of them, but mostly for Herman, who was already viewed by some as a number one klutz.

There he sat, stunned, with his glasses dangling off his right ear. Red faced, and embarrassed, he quickly placed them on his face, before helping to pick up several pieces of paper, strewn across the floor. The woman he ran into, who worked in security, stood, straightened her dress, and thanked Herman as she rushed off.

Herman stood there alone in the hallway feeling like an awkward failure. He couldn't think fast enough to say something comforting, Herman smiled and weekly waved at her before she disappeared around the corner.

Rather than take the elevator back to his office, he walked the stairs, choosing to be alone for the moment. Herman's legs felt like two dead weights as his shuffle became more prominent step after step. The worn carpet, leading to his office, made him feel even more worn out. He raised his gaze as he neared his office. After slamming the door, he sat in his office chair, facing the wall, focusing on the ubiquitous picture of the Queen distributed to each office.

As the regal woman's image went from hazy to clear, Herman's mind did the same. It was as if he came up for air, after being submerged for an ungodly amount of time. Realization of the problem, weighing him down, suddenly made him smile. The glasses weren't the problem. The small bald-headed, overweight man had been given twenty-four hours to make a decision that would definitely affect his life as he knew it. No more thinking, worrying or losing sleep. He would do as they asked. He would join the cause and become a warrior.

Herman finished his day feeling much better. He caught himself smiling, which was not like him and completely outside the protocol for his stature as an assistant to the Home Secretary. The stranger had been very convincing. He admired people who believed so strongly in what they were doing, they would die defending it.

Everything on his desk was placed in an orderly fashion. Herman now placed the Queen's updated schedule on top. It included the times and dates of the Ascot Races, and the Queen's involvement. He would make several copies for tonight's meeting. He thought it curious that the group he would be meeting with tonight, requested the Queen's Ascot Races schedule. They must be race fans, he whispered to himself as he carefully packed his briefcase. What the group did with the information he provided, would be of no significance to him. He was determined to become a warrior among warriors, dedicated to the future of the empire. God knows the United Kingdom could use some positive changes. He hoped to learn more about that at tonight's meeting.

Before he left for the day, he double checked the place and time for the meeting. Even though the location was unfamiliar to him, that just made this more of an exciting journey.

He could hear the Home Secretary's voice from behind closed doors. The man's attitude remained the same, not only was he loud, he was an ass. Herman couldn't wait for the gathering tonight. Fritz intimated that attendance was mandatory if Herman was to join the effort. Herman left his office with his head held high.

§

Rick proceeded to go through the week moving from one meeting to another. Although he was used to selling his company's products, he'd never attempted to do it at this pace, or in a foreign country. The whole experience seemed surreal. Archie suggested beginning with the Home Secretary because Hammersmith had the reputation of being a piece of work, but the man had connections, which created new referrals and opened doors.

The length of the meetings varied, but on average they lasted an hour, which pleased the young American capitalist with a pleasant personality, a view that was shared after comments made to Archie and Winston by various government officials and business owners. Blaine Manufacturing's portfolio was well-received as Rick watched for anyone who made him uncomfortable or who might make odd comments that appeared to be unpatriotic to the UK.

Jamal walked quickly along the wall of stalls in the marketplace. He had a half hour before the tourists arrived and needed answers to questions. He wanted to know who attacked Abbas and why? Aromas from the various food vendors he passed tempted his senses, as he rounded a corner that showcased large hanging carpets. His friend and fellow vendor, Yanti, stood before him. A towering figure of a man, handsome and hairless, he welcomed Jamal with open arms. "Jamal, give me a minute. I have to hang one more carpet and then I am yours." The man continued to hang his most precious and unique woven beauties.

"Ah, bless be to Allah, it is my friend, Jamal," came a shout as Yanti stepped off a ladder with a long carpet hook in hand.

"Bless be to Allah, Yanti."

"You have a look of concern, my old friend, are you in need of something more than one of these fine carpets of mine?"

Jamal asked his friend if they could talk behind his stall, in Yanti's storehouse, where he kept his inventory on display ready for sale for tour groups that regularly come through the market. Yanti put his hook away as they made their way through a large wooden door into the cooler space. The room had to be kept dark, with curtains drawn. "No one buys a faded or disfigured carpet," Yanti always said.

Once they settled, Jamal explained what happened to Abbas and that he, thanks to Allah, was recovering in Jamal's dar.

The facial expression on Yanti's face changed to anger as he looked down after Jamal spoke. Jamal could tell that his old friend knew something. Yanti looked up, took a deep breath, and pulled his seat closer to Jamal.

"Abbas and two other boys were fooling around, three days ago, in that open field where all the kids play. They found a soccer ball, it was the end of the day, they were having fun."

Yanti sat in an oval shaped chair with a multi-colored pad, as he told of what happened next. The police were not pleased that the boys took an early break from their appointed duties to sell drugs. Yanti stopped to take a drink that had been served by one of his twin daughters. He was clearly upset. After a few seconds he continued. "Two officials hit the boys with clubs and hauled them off. The other boy escaped."

"Amir?"

"Yes."

Jamal and Yanti both served in the military. Each man knew what it was like to fight and kill if necessary. Jamal had that "Kill Look" on his face. He wanted the names of the two officers who carried out the beating. Yanti stopped talking, stood, and bent down to his friend. He reached over and held Jamal's shoulders, looking him straight in the face.

"What are you going to do, old man, have them arrested?"

§

LONDON, UK; BAKERLOO LINE – DESTINATION: EDGEWARE ROAD

The air felt heavier as Herman walked up and out into unfamiliar territory. He had never been in the City of Westminister. He'd taken the Tube, as instructed, in order to reach the designated stop far beyond his more familiar Piccadilly and Central line exits. The directions he'd been given were specific, he liked knowing details and expectations. But that didn't change his level of concern as he headed for an address on Edgeware Road. Herman pulled the note from his front pocket and re-read the last part, under a street lamp. Two more blocks.

Rain continued as he folded his umbrella and started up the tented stairway. The steps led to large lime-colored doors that matched the color of the tent cover. He stood still on the top step listening to the rain as it beat out a rhythm overhead. He also stopped to catch his breath. The evening's journey reminded him that he needed to exercise more. The apartment building had a call plaque, with all 20 residents listed. He pushed the call button for Smythe, flat 9.

Once inside, he placed his folded umbrella under his arm, stomped his feet, and proceeded down a dimly lit hallway with green walls that ran along a checkered black and white floor. The place reminded him of one of those older refurbished hotels he'd read about. Herman stepped into the lift and pushed the button for the second floor. Nothing. He pushed it again and the caged compartment began to rise with a lurch nearly knocking him over. The short ride was a bit unsettling with all the shaking and rattling. When the noisy ascent finally ended, Herman needed the strength of two men to slide the cage door open. A few minutes later he found flat 9. Herman slowed his pace as he approached the door, knowing he could turn and run, it wasn't too late. But he didn't. Instead, he lifted his head with a new confidence as the knuckles on his hand rapped at the door.

The peep hole slid open, surprising Herman. The metal piece was the same color as the door. An eye appeared as the voice of a woman asked his name.

"Kruger."

There was conversation emanating from behind the door in unison with her voice assuring Herman that this would only take a minute. His brain began to engage the idea of running, when suddenly, the door opened.

"Come in."

The young woman stepped to the side as a man greeted him. It was not Fritz, the man who first contacted him in the small cafe downtown. Herman never thought to imagine anyone else being there to greet him. For the past few weeks, he had communicated only with Fritz, who convinced him to cooperate, and meet with the group. There had to be others involved. He had to be mad to think Fritz acted alone.

Herman began to sweat. Internally, he blamed his sudden impulsive behavior on being bored with his job, but it really was more than that. In the last few days he had several run-ins with his boss, the Home Secretary. The man so highly regarded and revered by those who didn't have to work with him. Herman finally and absolutely determined he hated the man's guts. But was that enough to become a spy or, worse yet, a terrorist? At that time, the question took a few minutes to quit playing over and over in his head. When the disturbing thought finally stopped, he was standing in his underwear, staring straight into his bathroom mirror. He'd had two pints at the White Horse

Pub, around the corner that night after work. He told himself he deserved it, and he did. As he looked in the mirror he answered his spy question with a resounding: Yes!

"Are you alright, Mister Kruger?" The man who stood before him had a look of concern."

"Yes, yes of course. It was a long ride getting here."

The man smiled and said he understood, it was a horrible night to be out after all.

The hallway led to a room that was mostly dark with the exception of two orange-colored lamps. The lamps made his trip to an awaiting chair possible. Carefully sitting down on the chair with no arms, he noticed the legs and then shoes of others sitting and waiting. No one spoke. Herman forced himself to sit back, arms crossed, studying the half-lit room, trying to take it all in, in spite of the poor lighting. There were three monitors aligned in a semi-circle facing a laptop. The electronic devices were sitting on a large dining room table, within sight of everyone in the living room.

People shuffled in their seats, in front of a wood burning fireplace, as if they were waiting to be called upon. Two men were standing, talking quietly to one another, until one of the men broke away to add another log on the fire. Herman noticed two of them were speaking German and strained to translate what was being said. Someone, the leader, was expected at any moment. Herman closed his eyes in order to concentrate. One time Hammersmith walked into his office after Herman had closed his eyes in order to focus on a problem, and ended up being accused of sleeping on the job. The minimal conversation in the room dissipated as Herman opened his eyes. A few uncomfortable moments went by, someone coughed, breaking the silence, followed by the sound of keys rattling in the door.

Two men greeted Fritz, Herman's contact, as he walked in carrying a leather briefcase and pulling a piece of carry-on luggage. The meeting started promptly at 7:00PM as Fritz turned the monitors on, immediately displaying details outlining the proposed assassination of the Queen and her grandson. Everyone was glued to the screens. Fritz went right into his presentation, carefully relating the importance of the audience's attention.

Nearly an hour and a half later, Herman found himself swimming in sweat. He tried not to look too closely at the others in attendance as he pulled his briefcase closer to his side. Each person had something to offer; social media disruptors, drivers, munitions experts, security force supervisors, sharpshooters, and information gatherers. Herman belonged to the last group. According to Fritz's introduction of Herman, "Our newest warrior supplies us with a most critical piece to our elaborate puzzle." Applause came for the unsuspecting government servant turned terrorist. Herman continued to sit, but he felt a wave of energy rush through his body. All of sudden the sweat didn't matter as much as the faces smiling back at him. One fellow, sitting across from him, rose and proceeded to shake his hand.

With introductions complete, first names only, a young woman, named Bess, who had been introduced first, stood and began to speak once again. Her voice had a soothing rhythm to it. She looked right at Herman from her position, straight across the room from him, as she spoke. Blond hair with blue streaks, at least that's what it looked like. An odd choice in hair color for a spy he thought. Spies and terrorists are the same, right? Should spies stand out or should they look like me? he thought to himself. Everyone in here had to be a spy. He wondered if the other attendees felt the same way. Bess had suggestions for contaminating the food and water supply used at the event. Great. Just give me a heads up on that one. Wait, did she just say, event?

What event? Herman thought he'd made the comment to himself, but people sitting close, including Bess, suddenly looked at him. Fritz, laughing as if to himself, quickly explained that Herman was new to the movement and then added:

"Herman, several months ago, we were looking at several 'event' options. A happening that would clearly send a message to the British people. That message would be all about change. You and I discussed "Change" at lunch, remember? The monarchy has to go. The British Isles will forever be viewed as old and behind the times, until that happens. But the most important consideration of all is allowing money that currently goes to the royals, millions of pounds annually, be redirected to the people of this crumbling nation. We are here tonight planning to complete our mission. We will mount a successful attack on the Royal Family. The decision to focus on one place had to be kept secret, until tonight. I'm sure you understand. Bess was made aware this morning, you and two others gathered here tonight, are finding out for the first time. Bess, why don't you tell them more.

All eyes went from Herman back to Bess as she continued.

"We will be targeting the Queen Mother and her grandson, William, at the Ascot Races, three months from now. The date depends on which, of all the races, they choose to attend."

Bess's thoughtful explanation was diametrically opposed to the information that she shared. Herman couldn't help but notice an increase in tension in the room. When Bess finished, Fritz asked Herman to speak. The information pertaining to the Home Secretary's schedule was passed around along with the Queen's timeline for her Royal engagements for the next six months. The Ascot Races were the highlight of that schedule.

§

BOSTON, MASSACHUSETTS; PETRULA TRUCKING COMPANY HEADQUARTERS

Lorretta did not mourn well. Especially for someone she found to be a romantic pain in the ass. The one person she'd considered the "Love of her life" had been murdered in northwestern Italy.

"What the hell, Michael?" she yelled as she threw her glass of scotch against the office wall. She'd been drinking more since hearing about the ambush debacle in Cinque Terre a few days ago. The bottle of scotch, nearly empty now, exemplified her emotions, draining slowly down, down, creating an unpleasant reminder of what it used to be like, seeing him enter a room. Tears never came easily, but she couldn't hold them back, and that made her even madder.

"Someone is going to suffer for this," spit from her lips as she slowly slipped down the wall, finally settling on the floor, legs splayed out in a V. Lorretta sat there like a drunk party goer, mascara running, mumbling to herself, wanting more scotch. After a few minutes, she slid further down the wall, until her head landed softly, on the thick, furry, white throw rug covering the wooden surface.

Laying there, looking sideways through mohair threads, Loretta focused on the glow of her bedroom fireplace. Flames danced up and down the sideways grate, mesmerizing her alcohol-laden brain. The flames' movement grew larger as she pulled her way closer to the fire. The further she went the warmer she became, until she was close enough to touch the marble hearth. Sweat began to form, her makeup ran to catch up with her mascara. Even in her altered state she knew what she had to do to the person responsible for her loss. Lorretta began to laugh uncontrollably. She had to sit up and move away from the fire. She rose to a standing position with the help of the arm of a chair. Steady as she goes. Lorretta made her way to the slider next to her bed. Facing out, hands above her head on the glass, she screamed, loud and strong: "Rick Blaine must burn."

§

LONDON, UK; CLARENCE HOUSE

Rick tried not to show his nervousness as they rode through the gates leading up to the prince's residence. He couldn't believe they were about to meet with the man who would one day be King of the United Kingdom, if the Royal lineage remained intact. This meeting had always been considered a possibility on Rick's schedule, but one phone call from Sir Archie was all it took. Sir Archie, Winston and Rick rode together in Winston's limo, going over some final thoughts in preparation for a meeting Rick thought would never happen.

"He's a regular guy, Rick, you'll like him," Archie calmly stated as a guard came forward to open their side door.

"Archie, as much as I'm impressed with Charles's demeanor, we need to walk away with a commitment to help." Winston's point had a direct and serious tone.

After their time together in Italy, Rick had to wonder how far Archie would go in securing the prince's commitment to cooperate. The old boy had a way of getting what he wanted.

Precautions dictated certain procedures, as the three visitors stood outside the limo straightening themselves. The day had a brisk, early spring-like feel to it. The sun broke through a perfectly trimmed hedge that ran the length of the driveway. Rick admired the immaculate landscaping as they were led to a side entrance.

Each man picked up the pace as they were, quickly and efficiently, led to the security area before continuing their journey further into Clarence House, home of the Prince of Wales and his wife, Camilla, the Duchess of Cornwall. The beauty of the place wasn't revealed until they turned a corner and entered the reception area, referred to as the Morning Room. Sunlight filtered in from high horizontal windows and down to a large, oval shaped, oriental carpet that ran nearly wall to wall. Large bookcases lined the room. A crystal chandelier hung over a round walnut table in the center of the room, where the prince stood waiting.

Charles smiled as the old warrior led the trio forward. Archie held out his hand when they entered. Rick stood back, waiting his turn, surprised by the way they greeted one another.

"It's been too long, Archie, how are you?"

"Too long indeed, Charles. I'm fine, but the last five years have added a few pounds."

"And look who you've decided to run with, Winston! Good to see you, old chap." The last time the two men worked together, at a favorite charity, supporting war veterans, they raised a record amount.

"Your Royal Highness, please meet our guest and one of my clients, Mr. Rick Blaine." Winston had the look of a proud father as he waved Rick forward.

Rick didn't know whether to bow, shake or shit his pants. Instead, he waited for their host to make the first move. Charles reached out with his left arm and grabbed Rick's shoulder as he thrust his right hand into Rick's.

"A pleasure Mister Blaine. I was just reading about your company. Winston sent me a link to your website. Very impressive. Tell you what, let's retire to a more suitable meeting room."

The four men were never alone. Two guards in plain clothes kept watch from a nearby hallway, while the four sat around a low rectangular table, that Rick guessed, could have been hundreds of years old. The chairs were surprisingly comfortable for their age, and Charles turned out to be a very gracious host. Within a matter of minutes, Sir Archie took over the conversation and cut right to the chase.

"Charles, we have it on good authority that a subversive plot by a group named, The Reign, plans on harming members of the Royal Family at the Ascot Races this year."

Their meeting went longer than planned. Charles sat forward in his chair, completely consumed by the information Archie and Winston provided.

Rick's part in the investigation became a key point that had to be carefully explained. Rick would become a decoy, which Charles thought was clever, but wondered if they had time to find the spy and confirm the plot. It didn't take long before he pledged his support to connect Rick with high-level officials and industry contacts, as suggested by Archie. Charles headed up a Treasury council dedicated to creating a robust British economy. That connection provided the prince with immediate access to a select number of business contacts that would take an outsider like Rick, weeks to schedule on his own.

Archie raised the question of canceling the races this coming June. After all, there have been times when it needed to be done, like World Wars I and II. But Charles demurred: "There has been too much preparation already completed, besides, my Mum lives for the races. They are part of her and vice versa. I doubt canceling would ever be considered even by the government. That would be giving in to terrorism—would it not?"

When the meeting ended and the men were back in the limo, Winston made a call. Ben had to know that Charles would personally send a list of new contacts for Rick to add to his schedule. These were people who would be unable to delay or postpone a meeting because of Charles's involvement. Winston appreciated the prince's immediate participation. Sir Archie just smiled as he sat up in his seat and looked out the limo window. He too appreciated the time they'd spent with Charles. The more he thought about the times he and Charles ran around at Cambridge, on the athletic field, and in the pubs, the more he understood. Charles always made time to help his friends. Most of his classmates treated him as an untouchable, but not Archie. Down deep, Charles needed to show how his abilities made a difference, not his title. Either way, it made Archie smile.

"You seem quite pleased, Archibald," Winston nudged his friend as he served each man with a glass of his proprietary brand of Scotch Whiskey.

Archie accepted the drink, but didn't respond immediately. Instead, he continued to look out the window. Deep in thought, he took a sip, then looked, first at his friend, then at Rick, as if carefully forming a response. "I'll be pleased when we catch the bastards."

§

TANGIER, MOROCCO; GRAND SOCCO MARKETPLACE

Jamal and his long-time friend and competitor, Yanti, met for coffee early, after morning prayers. They gathered in Yanti's residence, located near the Grand Socco. Jamal felt comfortable in Yanti's presence and appreciated his host's willingness to avenge what happened to Abbas. The dar's interior design showcased the most colorful rugs in all kinds of configurations, round being the most prominent. The elaborate furnishings, highlighted by beautiful ceiling and wall tiles, made sense to anyone invited to his home. After all, Yanti had been in the business of selling rugs of all styles forever—mostly to tourists.

"Many of my finest offerings have been sent around the world," Yanti would often boast. And who would disagree with the man, who stands over six feet tall with steel-gray eyes and a foot-long beard to match.

Yanti and Jamal sat on cushions that ringed a small round table in the middle of a small room that overlooked a multi-colored flagstone garden patio. The mood in the room began on a somber note, but quickly turned hopeful as the two men talked about their options. Revenge, as it turned out, was not as easy to plan as first thought. Yanti served dark, thick, Ethiopian coffee and spoke as he poured. He favored this particular blend and served it only when he needed to find more energy, and when close friends came by.

"So, my dear man, you want to seek revenge on the officials that hurt that young street urchin, Abbas."

"Yes. And Abbas is not one of those troublesome youth that steal from us. He's a very responsible young man."

Yanti nodded slowly. He could see that his friend became upset when defending Abbas. Jamal seemed to behave more like a father or grandfather. Upset and ready to act at any cost. The two men had had enough of the corrupt police force allowing such behavior, especially in dealing with children. Years ago, Jamal wouldn't have cared as much. Back then his attention focused on building his business and didn't wish to bring any notice to him, or his family, by complaining about the strange matters that surrounded the police. Both Jamal and Yanti had too many improprieties, caused by the local police, in the intervening years.

Most officers had served in the military, which paid better wages. Police officers traditionally dealt with long hours for much less pay, and found it harder to make ends meet. Therefore, they either developed additional revenue streams or quit the force to find other work. Jamal did. He understood what the officers faced, and had no problem with them making money on the side, even if it was illegal. What bothered him were the police taking out their frustrations on children like Abbas. The beatings had to stop. Jamal would no longer look the other way, and he wanted his friend, Yanti, to join in his effort.

Yanti rose from his cushion to make a point regarding the matter, when a rapid series of knocks rattled his front door. He quietly excused himself and hurried to answer the door. Jamal could not hear what was being said and finished his coffee as he waited patiently. When Yanti returned, he had a big grin on his face.

"I have the names of the two men who beat Abbas."

§

LONDON, UK; WESTMINSTER

There were five major business districts in London: the city, Westminster, Canary Wharf, Camden & Islington and Lambeth & Southwark. So far, Rick had visited contacts in each of the first four areas. Lambeth & Southwark came next. The meetings had progressed better than Rick had expected. Although he was exhausted, Rick had made good business connections that he would pass on to his sales team. It was his more undercover work that concerned him. He was naturally less familiar with clandestine responsibilities, but they captivated him. He just hoped that the few names he'd suspected proved to be of use.

Rick looked in the hotel bathroom mirror. The man brushing his teeth looked tired, and truly exhausted. He'd met with all kinds of officials and business leaders, most of which were genuinely interested in his business. His watch read 10 PM. He decided to relax in his Park Plaza hotel room near

Westminster Bridge. Shoes off, a glass of French red on standby, as he devoured a Caesar salad that had just been delivered by room service. He flipped through some notes, separating business responses from spy work.

He'd been given names of suspected individuals that were on MI5 and Scotland Yard's highly confidential Watch List. Rick knew that most of the people he met with were legitimate business contacts, along with a few on the government's watch list. During his meetings with those with suspected behaviors, he would allow the conversation to drift into politics. Rick would play the part of the unknowing, albeit successful, American who had a curious nature. Winston's hope was that someone would take a liking to Rick and share their concerns about the government or more importantly, the royals.

Rick compiled a short list of three suspects, two women, one man, since he began four days ago. Each person had problems with the way the country was being run by the current Prime Minister, but no one had a specific issue with the Royal Family. Most contacts thought the royals were good for business, tourism especially. His timeline of two weeks ran in tandem with undercover work being conducted by Scotland Yard.

"Uncovering terrorist activities is more in my line of work than yours, Rick," Winston mentioned earlier in the day, when he dropped Rick off. Then he added: "I can't help but feel there's someone flying under the radar, so to speak, someone new to the game."

Tomorrow will be another day. His schedule included members of parliament, members of Prince Charles' new economic development group , and contacts on the Blaine list. The Home Secretary and members of his staff would also be attending the economic development meeting. Rick's last duty of the day was to call Brenda and check in, which he did before hitting the sheets.

Chapter 7

TANGIER, MOROCCO; GRAND SOCCO MARKETPLACE

Now that Jamal and Yanti had the identity of the two officers, they moved ahead with plans to seek justice for the boys. They'd had enough of the beatings, which were becoming too frequent in and around the Grand Socco Marketplace.

The officers, who had been identified, had nicknames. Yello stood tall and lean. He formerly served in the Army and enjoyed being in charge of the law. Yello suffered from a serious case of jaundice, thus the nickname. The orphans that ran wild in the Grand Socco would try to stay out of his way, because he drank on the job. He carried a flask as well as his weapons. From the time his shift started at seven in the evening, he would drink and become more and more agitated. People close to him knew he drank on the job, however, no one made the effort to monitor his behavior.

The other officer involved had a reputation for grabbing and holding on tight to offenders of the law. He preferred to be called, the Claw. He had three fingers on his non-shooting hand, his left. The Claw held onto a grenade too long during the war to overthrow Ghaddafi several years ago. He wore his hand like a badge of honor that could squeeze a person's neck until they passed out. If he ever grabbed a person out of a crowd they knew it. The Claw enjoyed watching the eyes of the person being arrested, as they turned watery, nearly popping out of their head. Jamal had seen first-hand what damage these two could do to a child.

Yanti had a contact inside the police headquarters who let it be known that both Yello and the Claw were not held in high esteem with their colleagues. The two had the reputation for slacking off and blaming others for problems they tended to cause. The contact emphasized how much she disliked them and said she would do anything to help teach them a lesson. If something had to be done, it came down to Yanti and Jamal to come up with the appropriate punishment.

Yanti was excited about the prospect of inflicting revenge. "Hang them upside down for multiple days in the desert!"

"How about stripping them down, tying them up and smearing them with fish guts, then hanging them upside down in the desert," Jamal countered.

Both men looked at one another, smiled, and laughed. Whatever they decided had to be enough to teach the men a lesson, but not kill them. And, they had to know why they were being punished. They thought about various other means of retribution and the more they thought about teaching them a lesson, the more creative they became.

§

LONDON, UK; ACTON TOWN

The rain stabbing his face felt like a necessary penance as he walked slowly to the subway station. Herman let the hurt wash him clean, while picking up his pace. Guilt followed him around like an extra shadow. He dealt with it every day, especially at work, and now he'd brought on more, creating an even larger shadow. The impact of what he had just done by turning over top secret contact information, and the private daily schedule for the Queen and her family, gradually slowed his pace and made the subway ride nearly unbearable. When he reached his flat, he collapsed on the entry floor as if he'd been shot. Herman passed out for a time; he didn't know how long. When he came to, he couldn't stop thinking about the bloody meeting.

His fellow conspirators congratulated him for his courage. He thanked them at the time and became caught up in the excitement of the moment, grateful for their support, but inside he was terrified.

The leader told everyone that without Herman, their effort would have been made much more difficult. It wasn't until he heard about the plans to assassinate both the Queen and Prince William that the meaning of what he'd just done began to sink in, causing a nauseous feeling in his stomach. He headed for the bathroom and made it just in time to throw up. Once, twice and then nothing. And there he knelt with his head hanging over the toilet rim feeling, what? He sat back against the wall, feet straight out ahead, one shoe off. He sat there for a few minutes, asking the same question over and over, "What have I done?"

As Herman then laid on the floor, he began to cry over his betrayal. He'd just committed the most heinous crime a government employee could ever consider: treason. He, Herman Kruger, would become an accessory to a terrible crime, possibly the most devious act perpetrated against the Royal Family in modern times. "Oh, God, what have I done?" He whispered to himself with a breath that would kill. How ironic.

The next day, as he sat on the subway, facing two teens making out, which always made Herman wonder, how can they do that in public? He locked his gaze on the window as the subway roared into the tunnel, sucking them further and further into blackness. The movement of the subway car on the track as it raced through an unrecognizable view gave Herman an out-of-body feeling. Within seconds he began to shake in his seat as he envisioned the rail car spiraling downward. The shaking increased as strange noises began to blurt from his mouth, causing people around him some concern. With eyes closed, Herman started to chant: "No, I can't, no I won't, no not that."

The subway car suddenly came out of the dark and into bright sunlight. Herman suddenly stopped shaking and open his eyes. He caught the look of terror on a few faces looking back at him. They just as quickly turned away. One lady looked back and smiled as she adjusted her dark glasses on her face.

His breathing came fast on the inhale. Herman's eyes began to water as a feeling of hatred turned to fear quicker than the next stop. Yes, he was on his way to work, but the emotion building inside became more evident the closer he came to exiting. All of a sudden, he realized what had manifested inside, the reality of what he had done collided with what he now needed to do. He worried about how his actions would affect his family, mother, father and two siblings. Although they were basically estranged from him, he hated to think that they would suffer as a result of his behavior. His commitment to the Reign was burning a hole in his brain. He couldn't let go of the regret. The more Herman thought about what the terrorist group could do to the Royal Family, to the heart and soul of Great Britain, the more his head ached and his stomach churned.

"I'm impossibly stupid," he admitted out loud. "Damn." When he looked up, the two people who'd been making out, stopped, and were now looking at him. She smiled before looking back at her boyfriend. Both acted as if they were going to respond to his "stupid" remark, but turned their heads instead. Herman's behavior must have been more entertaining than concerning.

He decided to walk and got off two stops earlier than normal. Walking usually did the trick, but as he attempted to engage his legs he felt nauseous. That feeling of being incredibly stupid overcame him — he had to do something to shake the shadow, but what?

§

LONDON, UK; THE HOME OFFICE

Rick sat in the Home Secretary's office foyer waiting for his assistant, Herman, to arrive. Hammersmith was out for the day, but Rick, at Winston's request, had some follow-up questions that involved the secretary's list of contacts. He had it all worked out in his mind. Rick would cleverly mask his questions by reinforcing the need to pitch the benefits of Blaine products. By doing so, he would be able to quickly discern the most critical connections. Rick had uncanny intuitive skills when it came to judging people. In this case, determining who enjoyed their work, country, and the Royal Family, and who didn't. It all depended on the conversation.

Rick heard Herman fumbling in the foyer before he entered the office area. Even the young lady who'd greeted Rick a few minutes earlier turned her head toward the door. Suddenly, there came a fumbling of hands followed by a push with a foot, as the young, heavy-set man entered, looking disheveled and more than a little flustered.

"Deloris, we have to do something about that damnable knob—it's sticking again."

"Yes, yes, sir," came her response as she accepted his coat and scarf, swiftly without eye-contact, as if in a rage.

"Oh, hello, Mr. Blaine, is it?" The man had red, twitchy, eyes as he pulled out a chair for Rick to sit, and offered, "Please, sit."

They sat in Herman's office staring at one another for a moment before Hammersmith's assistant looked down at his notes, shuffled a few pages, mumbling as he sought to discover what it was he needed to find.

"Ah, yes. The Home Secretary asked me to take this meeting with the avid hope I'll be able to answer any questions you have regarding business connections? Is that right, Mr. Blaine?"

Rick smiled before answering. The nervous vibe bouncing off the man seated across from him could not have been more apparent. Winston mentioned that the Home Secretary's office had more to do with details that involved scheduling and organizing anything related to the royals. If there were to be any diversion from the oath sworn to by every government employee, important information could be revealed that would put the Royal Family in jeopardy. "What has that got to do with distributing your products, Mr. Blaine?" Herman asked.

"Nothing. I just wanted to clarify what your office's responsibility was to the Queen and her family, that's all. Truth be told, Herman, I enjoy the monarchy and learning all I can about it. I'm excited to meet someone that plays such an important role in the Queen's life."

Herman appeared to be distracted as Rick proceeded to move right into the merits of allowing Blaine's product line into the British distribution system. His sales pitch began with the features and benefits of the covers produced specifically to protect all kinds of electronic equipment. "It's like what you do for the Royal Family, Mr. Kruger."

Rick clearly saw that the statement hit Kruger like a ton of bricks. Herman couldn't respond right away, so Rick continued to explain how his product line begins and ends with protection of those items Brits use every day, including devices

Prince Charles uses, who had pointed out some his favorites. The last selling point caused a noticeable twitch in Herman's left eye. Rick's non-verbal communication training, a skill he demanded each of his selling agents be proficient in, went on alert. Herman's eyes went wide, his smile had long faded, and he coughed. Each a sign that something else was going on in the man's head. But what? Rick scribbled a note: Protection of the Royals, British populace, showing signs of discomfort when Prince Charles's name came up.

The meeting ended a few minutes later, with each man going their own way as if the building were on fire. Rick left the building and hailed a black cab back to Winston's office with a final list of suspicious people, three to be exact, with one at the top of the list, Herman Kruger. Herman hurried off so fast he forgot to close his office door and turn off the lights, a regimented routine he demanded from others.

"Herman? Where are you going?" the receptionist called after him as he walked past her without speaking and abruptly left the building.

He didn't remember the 30-minute trip to his flat. Herman had trouble clearing his head. He had no one to talk to about his situation and the pressure, oh the pressure he felt. Falling into cool sheets, completely naked, in total darkness, felt better. The last thing he remembered was wondering where his gun was and if it were loaded. The pistol was a family heirloom handed down from his grandfather's WWII years of service. A German Lugar – and it functioned perfectly.

§

TANGIER, MOROCCO; GRAND SOCCO MARKETPLACE

Moroccan mornings, normally, set the tone for the number of visitors who would spend the day shopping the Grand Socco. That day had been unusually mild for the time of year, so the flocks of tourists came and stayed longer. Later, as the sun began to descend, amber highlights from a dusty sunset, created a beautiful memory as night prepared to take over. The stars weren't ready to make an appearance, when Yello and Claw stepped out of the field office and onto the thoroughfare, still jammed with tourists.

They stuck together like glue as they walked their favorite patrol route, same as always, that evening. Watching the rich tourists, overweight and loud as they made their way through the Grand Socco, searching for that rare treasure to take back home with them. A desert relic that they would relish for years to come. The two men laughed at the fools before them as Claw twirled his nightstick and Yello whistled at a pretty girl, flirting with his broken, tobacco- stained teeth. The two officers felt on top of their game in their small, warped, world of intimidation and loose morals. The saying: "It takes one to know one" was never truer than with these two arrogant officials of the law.

"Most people make me sick," Claw said as he lumbered along smoking a stubby, foul- smelling cigar. It was a trademark of his. Yello would often joke to his comrade, saying that they probably would catch more criminals, but they always seemed to smell the two crime fighters coming, alerting the thieves to run, before they could be caught.

After turning corner number forty-two, they came upon two young women who worked in the lower Petite Socco, a smaller marketplace located on the outskirts of the larger Grand Socco. "Hey, ladies, we need to see some identification." The inevitable groping that followed would only take a few minutes, if the girls were lucky. The two officers enjoyed giving the locals a hard time, especially the street urchins, because they had no recourse.

No reasonable citizen of Tangier ever fought back against the local authority. It was a given that police were untouchable, and they had no problem touching the pretty locals

The men continued their pace, then picked it up a bit when one of the young girls looked back and, together, they began to walk faster. The evening darkness fell fast around them as the two officers gained ground. Yello called out: "Stop, stop or we will shoot." The two young women, scared, not knowing what to expect, stopped just about on the spot that Jamal had pointed out to them earlier. Claw, in his most official voice, asked them to turn around. And then around again. It was a game they played. When the order came for them to kneel down on the ground facing the men, two giant nets came from above, covering the two men. A heavy web of hemp-woven rope ensnared the men, knocking them to the ground. When they looked up, the girls were gone, replaced by four hooded individuals, two armed with tasers.

"What the…" Yello started to say before they were both tased. Claw nearly swallowed his cigar as both men struggled, gurgled, trying to call out, but no attempt made sense through their spitting as their heads hit the ground like two soccer balls being kicked back and forth.

Yello came to first, asking for his partner in a whisper. He was in total blackness. "Claw, Claw, you out there?" His ears were ringing. He hesitated, listening for a response. Instead, he heard the faint familiar tones coming from a radio. Music. Loud, then louder. The two men had been blind folded, and placed on cold ground with their hands secured behind their backs. The music trailed off as Claw came awake with a swift kick to his stomach. A man's voice told them not to say a word, but to listen. After a few minutes Claw couldn't take it anymore and spoke up: "You can't do this... you will be prosecuted... someone will be looking for us…."

"You have another four hours on your shift tonight, most of that time relaxing with the ladies or mistreating others. That provides us with more than enough time to explain what will happen to both of you if you ever touch another woman or child, beyond your duty to serve the community. We know what you did to that young boy a few weeks ago, behind the Marketplace Bistro dumpster. You left him for dead, but he did not die."

"He is just one of our drug sellers, you can't," complained Claw.

"Silence!" the voice demanded as a swift kick struck Claw in the abdomen. "We know who pushes those children to do what they do, and who benefits from their drug selling you idiot."

A moment later the men began to rise from the floor as if by some mysterious force. Two pulleys were activated by two men with help from four others who volunteered to assist, so long as their identities were not revealed. The straps around their ankles began to tighten as the blood rushed to their heads. Neither officer spoke, instead they just hung there, like two sides of beef in the meat market. Only, these two tenderloins had to be wondering what would happen next.

And then it did.

A tap against each of their heads, it didn't hurt at first. Not until the attackers measured the exact distance between the heads and the bats being used. The hits became more frequent, coming from all angles, on all parts of the officers' bodies. Two pools of blood slowly formed on the ground beneath them. The beating went on for a few minutes, each man grunting and groaning as they spun in rapid fashion to music now turned up louder to mask their screams. This technique was not new to the men — it was one they used many times while interrogating suspects.

And then nothing. Both men were still conscious as they

were lowered back to the hard surface of the floor. It was then that Yanti, in a disguised voice, whispered the following: "You are scum, we all know it. However, we believe you will change your behavior and do the job you were hired to do. Because if you don't, you will die a slow horrible death over a fire pit."

Yanti kicked each man in the crotch, which made them react with gasps and violent twitching, then leaned forward and loudly whispered as his spital spread freely, "We will castrate each of you first before roasting you beyond recognition, if you ever touch another woman or child." As he said this, he reached down and nearly crushed their testicles. Yello called out to Allah; the Claw screamed profanities and begged them to stop.

Jamal and Yanti left the two with the others. They were pleased with themselves and the fact that they had finally taken action against this evil pair. They would be watching to see how this action would affect the rest of the force.

There would be another hour of raising and lowering Claw and Yello, beating them from the neck up to their feet. Jamal reminded his co-conspirators not to cut or bruise the two vermin above the neck. "We wouldn't want their commanding officer upset in any way." His comment brought laughter from his hooded friends.

Broken ribs and bruises would eventually heal. Recovery would also slow these two down for a few weeks. For now, Jamal hoped that would be enough to set these two on a better course, one that would keep the children safe. This night of action set a precedent, one that Jamal was ready to keep in play should the need arise in the future. Time would tell. Reprisals were a possibility, but Jamal and Yanti were not that worried. Each officer had a reputation to protect, which meant more to them than anything, including their own families.

§

LONDON, UK; ACTON TOWN

The flowered wallpaper in Herman's bedroom withered and died. But, within seconds, came back to life, only in a new color arrangement. His entire body buzzed in concert with his ears ringing like chimes. He'd promised himself not to take more than one pill, but one didn't seem to ease his discomfort. He'd called his office to say he wouldn't be returning today, or possibly tomorrow. He wasn't feeling much at that moment, but he definitely wasn't feeling well enough to work, or walk, or breathe for that matter. If he had pain, it would be a different matter. No, this was more of a gnawing discomfort that kept him from eating, sleeping, even thinking clearly. He had to do something to alleviate the anxiety. He had to make one more call: to Fritz. Herman had to let him know that a mistake had been made and he, Herman Kruger, would no longer be participating in their cause. Herman hoped this would not come as a surprise to the leader, but he could not live with himself. He had to move on. To where? He didn't know for sure, but it sure as hell wasn't with a bunch of terrorists.

Hopefully, the information Herman furnished would be enough to satisfy the group and they would let him go back to his life as it was before. It wasn't a perfect life, but it was better than what he dealt with now.

Herman's call went to voicemail. He explained to Fritz what he'd written down carefully a few minutes before. His voice didn't exactly sound like his own, he found that somewhat odd. It must be the pills. How many had he taken? When he ended the call, Herman went directly back to bed in the room with the ever-changing wallpaper. He hoped that would be the last time he'd have to worry about his wallpaper, or his job, or the terrible mistake he'd made in working with Fritz and his cause.

A half hour later a tall blond-haired woman, dressed in a black leather jump suit, stepped out of the subway entrance a block from Herman's flat. Mara worked for Fritz and was a dedicated follower of the Reign. She had been called to duty by Fritz a half hour earlier, where she left the bunker under the Overground in Brixton for the ride to her target's apartment. Mara headed up the Elimination Squad. She had proven herself over the years, while in service to an east German splinter group dedicated to white supremacy. She acted as an escort to top government officials, and had the looks and enjoyed the pleasure she attained from her work.

Her job was to bed her dates, either to thank them for their support, or kill them. Her resume attracted the leadership of the Reign, and now here she stood, waiting in a slight drizzle of rain, having just left the subway entrance two blocks from her target's location. She walked carefully past a mother pushing a child in a baby carriage. The mother was trying to adjust the hood over the child as the rain increased in intensity. Mara took pity on the situation and helped the mother to fasten the top of the contraption. "Those buttons are so hard to fasten," she mused. The mother agreed, thanking the stranger for her help. Normally, she would refrain from being noticed while on a job.

As she approached the apartment building, Mara stopped. Opting to wait a few minutes for a small group of people to leave the building, before she proceeded further. Once the group passed, she entered the old-stone structure, checking for cameras, which, to her surprise, did not exist. London had the reputation of having more security cameras per square mile than any other place on earth.

The stairway leading up to Herman's flat had a mosaic of gold marbled specks in the tread. Mara liked the speckled touch, it made finding steps much easier. She made a mental note to write about it in her journal that evening as she passed the fourth, heading to the fifth floor, and her destination. Black leather gloves came out and slipped over her hands in an easy rhythm, as she'd done many times before. Food smells were in the air, causing her stomach to feel emptier. She had skipped lunch, preferring to remain light on her feet.

Besides, dinner time was fast approaching and Mara knew Herman would be home, based on a phone message. Duty before dinner.

A gentle knock on the door, and once more, both attempts to no avail. The lock's tumbler gave a final click and Mara was inside the flat within seconds. She walked carefully along the entry hallway. Checking the kitchen, living room, as she moved on to the closed door at the end of the hall, the bedroom. She placed her left hand up on the door and turned the handle of the door with her right. There he was lying in his bed, asleep, snoring, dead to the world. She'd met Herman at the meeting a few days earlier. Poor soul, Mara thought. Herman had become a reluctant recruit. In cases such as his, death had to come as a relief, but there was no way to tell for sure. One could only imagine. C'est la vie, as the French like to suggest.

She reached into her jacket and pulled out a calling card, placed it on the dresser. The black on white business-sized card read: There's No Denying the Reign.

§

LONDON, UK; LAMPERSON INTERNATIONAL HEADQUARTERS

An hour earlier, Rick paced back and forth in Winston's office. Of the three people on his list of prospective suspects,

Herman Kruger, stood out. Sir Archie sat in a leather chair, reading over information sent by secure courier from Scotland Yard. He noticed Rick pacing and stopped reading. "What's up, old boy?" Rick didn't know how to begin, so he blurted out: "I think I know who the spy is, Archie."

Archie sensed his frustration and asked Rick to sit. Archie listened for the next few minutes as Rick explained himself. Rick quickly eliminated the first two people on his list, an older man who worked with Prince Charles, and a middle-aged woman who worked in public relations. Both people had families of their own and each was proud to have a history of public service. They also had great eye contact. Herman, the Home Secretary's assistant, was the most logical person to become an informant. Archie disagreed, with respect, at first. He'd just read reports, leading him to believe that the other two candidates were more likely because of their access to the royals. Rick countered with the fact that while that was true, Herman had access to everything that controlled the royals, beginning with handling their daily communications and ending with managing their schedules. This placed him in a perfect position to gain access to important information, while still flying under the radar.

Rick looked at Archie with an expression that Archie had seen before in Cinque Terre. That did it. Archie, convinced enough to consider Rick's rationale, changed his opinion. "Let's surprise the man and make an unscheduled office call, now," Archie said as they prepared to leave.

§

LONDON, UK; THE HOME OFFICE

About a half hour later, Rick and Archie arrived at the Home Office and asked to speak with Herman.

"Mr. Kruger called in sick today. I can schedule an appointment, if you like, sir," said the receptionist. Archie and Rick looked at one another and excused themselves before the receptionist could finish her sentence. "She said that he was ill and wouldn't be in for the rest of the day and possibly the next," Rick recapped as their driver slowly worked his way through the evening traffic, heading for Herman's address. "Well, Mr. Blaine, your sixth sense about this matter appears to be working. I believe you've missed your calling, my new friend."

Rick smiled at Archie. For some reason, the older gentleman reminded him of his father. Rick missed his dad, who'd passed away unexpectedly when Rick was a teenager. The man always encouraged his son to think before acting. Rick's dad could also pick out a phony a mile away. Maybe that's what Rick felt now, a phony, namely, Herman. They had to find out more. Rick had been given the man's address when he suggested he send Herman a cowhide cover for his phone.

§

LONDON, UK; ACTON TOWN

They found Herman's building, a solid stone structure that looked more like a bank, because of the brass trim and ornamentation around the windows. A large six-foot hedgerow covered most of the lower-level exterior leading to a canopied entrance. They were greeted in the lobby by a friendly janitor who recognized the famous British patriot. "You're him!" Archie flashed a smile and patted the man on the shoulder as they proceeded to the fifth floor. The elevator, ancient by modern standards, worked remarkably well with minor creaks and groans as they gained altitude. They were here in an attempt to gain some insight from Herman, but Rick had an odd feeling about the situation.

Archie's knock did not produce a response. Another red flag. If Herman was home, they were going to talk with him. If he wasn't, they were going to enter the flat and check the place out. Rick stood by as Archie picked at the lock.

The flat was dark. Archie flipped a switch. They figured no one was in the place, so they quickly moved from room to room and eventually down the hallway.

"What was that?" Archie whispered as he put his index finger to his lips. He continued: "Sounded like a window rattling."

Archie pulled a revolver from his shoulder holster and pushed gently on the bedroom door. The smell of sickness hung in the air as Archie scanned the room. No pictures on the walls, dresser with top drawer open, a pair of underwear hanging out. One slipper by the bed, one foot hanging out over the edge from under the covers. There in the bed the form of a person. The room was semi lit and cool. One of the windows in the room had been raised. Rick pulled back the drapes to allow in more light.

And there in the bed lay Herman Kruger, facing the window. Eyes open, mouth moving, no words could be heard, but Herman looked intent as he attempted to speak. Rick moved closer to the bed, while Archie climbed out of the window, a possible escape route. Rick tilted his head closer, trying to hear Herman. Moving closer the words started to make sense.

"I'm so sorry, so sorry, I don't know why," Herman uttered and then passed out.

Archie came back from the window, off the fire escape. He walked across the room as Rick stood from the bed.

"What's this?" Archie showed Rick the business card he found on the dresser then placed it in a plastic bag.

Upon closer inspection of the place, the two men found a bottle of tranquilizers in the bathroom, half full.

Archie noticed that Herman's breathing had slowed and then stopped. Rick checked his pulse and told Archie to call for an ambulance. Both men took turns administering CPR as they waited for the ambulance to arrive. Herman responded right away to the chest compressions. Weak gurgling sounds gave way to a cough and then a deep breath. Herman's bloodshot eyes opened as he attempted to see who called his name. He winced from the newly cracked ribs.

With Herman conscious, Rick began to look around the room, while Archie monitored Herman. To his surprise, Rick discovered that Herman was a fan of jazz and blues and classic film noir movies. His library of both turned out to be very impressive. Rick returned a Don Shirley Trio album to a neatly labeled filing system, as Archie called for him. "Rick, you're right, we can't lose this guy."

"He knows something, Archie. He's sorry for something. We need to know what."

"We also need to know who was just here, Rick."

Rick came back into the room, walked up to Herman, and checked his pulse again, it had gone from very weak to nearly normal by the time the ambulance arrived. Archie left to help guide the ambulance crew. Within minutes, people could be heard coming along the outer hallway. Herman looked scared. "You're going to be okay, Herman," Rick uttered as he adjusted the man's pillow.

Herman looked surprised to see Rick. "How did you…? What happened to me?" Herman started to tell Rick something as Archie led the EMT's into the bedroom. Whatever Herman wanted to say would have to wait, while an oxygen mask was carefully placed across his face. "Let's go, Rick. There's nothing more we can do here."

Herman, passed out on the gurney, and one other person, were jammed into the small elevator. His last thoughts of why Rick and Sir Archie were at his bedside, slipped away like the person who escaped the room earlier.

Archie suggested they walk the perimeter of the apartment building before leaving, and motioned to Rick. "Rick, you go to the right and I'll meet you around back. Look for footprints, clothing, anything that might have been discarded." He told Rick that he saw someone moving quickly, down the alley, behind the building, from Herman's fire escape. Herman's visitor had to exit quickly, so they may have left more than a calling card in the process. "This person could lead us to the rest."

Both men took their time hoping to find something. Rick walked while looking down and almost ran into the escape ladder, connected to the exterior metal stairway used for emergencies. He called for Archie who was busy going through a blue garbage can. The bottom ladder was an extension and retracted when pulled. It had not been pulled and remained in the down position. "Don't touch the ladder," yelled Archie. "I will have it dusted for prints."

Once the technicians from Scotland Yard arrived, the two men hurried to an awaiting car. Rick received a text from Ben Lamperson, and sat back in the seat. Ben's text read: "Rick, contact me immediately. We have a lead on your suspect, Herman Kruger. He's now a person of interest."

Rick returned the text, letting Ben know what had happened at Kruger's flat and that they were on their way. Archie made sure that an officer would be posted at Herman's side, until Archie arrived at the hospital after dropping Rick off.

Herman was immediately taken into one of London's major trauma rooms at the Royal London Hospital. Archie called ahead to make sure that Kruger would be isolated from the public and that security for the man was in place.

Sir Archie arrived about a half hour later and met immediately with the attending physician. Herman was in a stable, but guarded condition. A toxicology report would be forthcoming, but the doctor said that she believed the patient had been given a strong dose of opiates. She had given him Naloxone, an opiate blocker. "We are monitoring the patient's vital organs, especially his kidneys, and bringing his body temperature down at this time." His prognosis was good; Herman would survive.

Archie decided to remain at Herman's side until a security plan was in place. He would check with Winston to make sure Mr. Kruger would be protected, until he could be interviewed.

§

LONDON, UK; LAMPERSON INTERNATIONAL

Back at Lamperson's offices, Rick held up the plastic bag Archie had handed him before leaving for the hospital. "We found this business card on the dresser in Kruger's bedroom." He handed the bag to Ben, who checked it out before handing it off to his father, sitting next to him. Winston said, "Whoever left this intended to kill Mr. Kruger, but why?" Ben had a folder sitting in front of him. It contained everything he had gathered on the terrorist organization known as the Reign.

The three men proceeded to go over the information for the next two hours. The conference room white boards were filled with names of known foreign nationals who were suspected in recent bombings and assassinations, credited to the German-based terrorist organization labeled: The Reign. "There's no denying the Reign," Rick whispered to himself, feeling a chill as he did so. He felt a connection to Herman Kruger that wouldn't rest. "I'm going to visit Kruger," Rick told Winston. "I'll be in touch."

The chance that a print might be sitting on the calling card was slight, but that wasn't the point - whoever left through the window had one thing in mind, killing Herman. Rick knew they were close to finding a spy, maybe two. They had no time to waste.

Chapter 8

SILICON VALLEY, CA; BLAINE MANUFACTURING

Brenda promised herself that tonight she'd meet friends for drinks instead of burning the midnight oil at work.

It had been nearly a month since Rick left for Italy and, so far, things were going according to plan at Blaine. Sales continued to rise at a steady eight percent, production, especially for new items in the Outdoor Living category, managed to keep pace with orders. And the management team, from eight departments, had not presented any problems that couldn't be quickly addressed to this point. Public Relations kept asking for a new international business report, which had to be delayed until Mr. Blaine's return. Brenda instructed the PR team to look for domestic topics until she gave the green light. Only Brenda and Ralph Phillips knew the real reason for the secrecy.

Ms. Brenda Johnson enjoyed working at Blaine Manufacturing. The creative covers and accessories she helped to energize the tech world, filled a void she could only dream of satisfying. The addition of tracking Rick's exploits overseas, kept her adrenalin level surging.

Settling into her new position as Vice President of

Administration fit comfortably, like the two new summer dresses she'd ordered from Nordstrom recently.

Blaine Manufacturing wasn't without its challenges, however, especially when its Chief Executive was busy overseas attempting to garner new business, while assisting in efforts to rid the world of terrorism. Brenda smiled as she thought of Rick's new assignment.

Ben Lamperson had been Brenda's last call of the day. He'd brought her up to speed on what transpired in the last twenty-four hours, regarding Rick and Sir Archie. She would never have put those two together when she first joined the company two years ago. But, having observed Rick's behavior, since the events of last year, she understood why he felt the need to help the Lampersons. He seemed to favor older, former soldiers, who knew how to handle a gun, like Major Connors. Could these men be a replacement for Rick's father that he lost years ago?

She smiled as she thought about what Ben had said about Rick, being convinced that he was on the trail of a spy. And he was somehow involved with a British government official that ended up in the hospital, which was all over the news. The situation sounded very dramatic and clandestine, which worried Brenda. But she had to trust Rick to make good decisions there, while she worked to do the same at Blaine. She waved to Jimmy, head of security, as she left out of the main floor back entrance, heading to the parking garage. Brenda couldn't wait to find out more from Rick himself. She'd been tied to her desk for the last two weeks, putting in fourteen-hour days. After a phone call with one of her siblings, who would be coming to San Francisco in a few weeks, she decided to have some fun. Tonight, after putting them off for some time, she would be catching up with friends as she quickened her pace to her car.

Brenda came from a very frugal mid-western family. She was very careful with her own money. When she first arrived in San Francisco, nearly 6 years ago, she lived with her aunt because she couldn't afford a place of her own. Eventually, she found Blaine Manufacturing, eventually settling into the position of Rick's executive assistant. It didn't take her long to prove herself, rising quickly through the ranks becoming one of Rick's most trusted colleagues. Her girlfriends always teased her that Rick would be perfect for her, but while she cared deeply about Rick, he simply wasn't her type. That's why their relationship has always been strictly platonic—Rick always felt like an older brother to her. Being careful with expenses turned out to be one of her best attributes. But on occasion, however, she was known to splurge. Her new Tesla, after a two-day learning curve on how to drive in near total silence, was proof. The head of Blaine's creative department referred to her new purchase as Brenda's Stealthmobile.

After Brenda's recent promotion, she purchased a Tesla model Y SUV with an added battery package, extending her mileage capability. She admitted that Rick talked her into the additional expense, in case she allowed him to take a test drive. God only knew where he might end up. Of course, she would have access to his vintage Porsche while he was gone. Her sleek new ride awaited her arrival, gleaming bright red in her private parking space.

As Brenda drove along Blaine's serpentine exit lane, a pair of binoculars caught sight of her in her new ride. A husky man whispered to himself something about Teslas as he adjusted the focus. The heavily bearded man, dressed in black, reclined comfortably as he scanned from the front seat of a black SUV, parked outside the Blaine campus. Tattooed fingers flexed as the binoculars slid slowly from the onlooker's face, but he continued to turn his gaze as Brenda passed by. "Nice." Both vehicles' occupants were left unaware of the real significance of the moment.

"Charlie, let's move out, I've seen enough of the place." The command came from the rear seat where Lorretta Petrula sat comfortably in leather seats, nursing a freshly poured scotch and water. Lorretta was in the early stages of a new mission, coordinated, for now, from the back seat of a black SUV. She and she alone would be in charge of making sure Rick Blaine, and his company, would suffer for the loss of her man. Michael's death would be avenged soon.

§

BALLATER, UK; BALMORAL CASTLE GROUNDS

The Queen of the United Kingdom, having spent over seventy years on the throne, enjoyed her private time with her children and grandchildren. All through her reign as queen, her top priority was to serve the British people and her subjects around the world, up to now. In the last ten years it had become more evident that the world was not responding to anything remotely associated with reason. The walls of the world had been closing in on her and she could feel it. Since her husband's death, she had been feeling more anxious, which led to more time with family, wherever they lived.

It was clear to everyone around her that she had a special place in her heart for family, especially her great grandchildren. The portrait session being conducted by a renowned artist had been carefully thought out for that reason. Keeping the Queen poised, while children squirmed and became more restless, as the waiting time dragged on, became an enormous challenge. A digital photograph would be taken and that image would serve as the source for the oil painting, unlike so many previous sessions, where the family had to sit for hours at a time over months of painstaking smiles and poses. Phillip would be going out of his mind by now. Thank God for technology.

No sooner had the Queen finished her thought, when doors began to open behind her. The photographer/artist looked up and suggested a ten-minute recess. Cheers could be heard from the children as they were escorted from the room by nannies standing at the ready. Elizabeth was surprised to see Sir Archibald entering the room. She remembered the man who befriended Charles when they were classmates, and again when she knighted him for his service to the UK. More importantly, he was a favorite of her husband. Phillip and Archie would hunt together in Scotland, ending their day by cleaning guns and trading stories.

It seemed odd to her that Archie would be here in this room at this time. The monarch, who'd reigned over the nation for so long had more than intuition going for her, she had a great sense of urgency. She felt in her bones that something of great importance had entered the room. Decades of moments like this dictated that she smile as he bent to take her hand. "Your Royal Majesty, I need to speak to you in private."

§

TANGIER, MOROCCO; GRAND SOCCO MARKETPLACE

Thousands of miles and a couple of continents away, a young boy was enjoying life with a new family. Abbas healed, at least physically faster than everyone had expected. It could have been all the love and attention he received in addition to his bandages and medicine. His mental state was a work in progress, thought Jamal proudly, as he watched the young man fill the spice rack. Jamal complimented the boy on his hard work.

"Sukaran, baba." Abbas said this without looking up. For

Jamal, hearing Abbas say the words, "Thank you, father," meant the world. He and his wife still mourned the loss of their only son, Isaac, who died suddenly from a respiratory ailment two years ago. Isaac would have been fourteen, two years older than Abbas. Both Jamal and his new apprentice were delighted at how naturally the two made the transition from a former life into this new set of circumstances. Secretly though, Abbas knew that something must have happened between Jamal and the authorities that allowed him and the other street urchins like him, more freedom, at least for now. Abbas hoped it would last forever and that the ones he protected would find a better life as he did.

"Here they come, Abbas, have you completed your work?" The boy nodded. Jamal referred to the tourists that were entering the Grand Socco Marketplace. He knew that Abbas had finished all the chores he'd been given. His question was meant to sing out praise across the stalls to alert everyone, not just Abbas, that the day was about to begin. But for Jamal it was yet a new day of beginnings for him and Abbas.

§

LONDON, UK; ROYAL LONDON HOSPITAL

Rick made his way down the hospital corridor as directed by the guards that Sir Archie had put in place to protect the recovering suspect. The hallway had arrows painted on the walls, directing visitors to various departments. Oncology was red; Pediatrics blue; Surgery was yellow. Rick knew there would be no colored arrow for where he was going as he walked past the surgery waiting area where concerned faces looked up in anticipation. He nodded to the onlookers and picked up his pace.

Rick had a sudden flashback, remembering a time when his friend, Artie, had required surgery after a surfing accident. Rick and another friend, Jillian, waited together for several hours in the hospital waiting room until the orthopedist came to tell them that Artie was in recovery, joking with the nurses. The thought made Rick smile as he was led through a series of green colored metal doors.

Before entering the last door, which he imagined led to the suspect's room, a helmeted stocky military-type security guard stopped Rick. "Oi, this is a secure area, chum," he said with a thick Birmingham accent.

"I'm Rick Blane, I've been cleared to see Mr. Kruger." Rick handed the guard his ID.

"A yank, eh?" The guard checked the ID against a list on a nearby clipboard, nodded, and motioned Rick forward. He patted Rick down – standard procedure – no expression. The door opened and Rick entered a very sterile room with one bed, no windows, and a very scared young-looking man staring back at him. Rick made his way to the bed. As he did so, he introduced himself and remained standing at the foot of the bed.

"Hey, I know you," Herman Kruger's voice was a bit garbled and hard to hear. He cleared his throat, "You're Rick Blaine." The door suddenly opened and the guard allowed an orderly to bring in a chair. Rick thanked the man and sat down closer to the foot of the bed. Rick pulled out a folder from his backpack. He read through some notes that Winston had provided. Both Winston and Archie had to be convinced, but in the end, felt it would be better if Rick interviewed Kruger. They needed more information and Rick had a feeling that he and Herman had a connection.

"You're looking better than the last time I saw you." Herman looked back at Rick and his eyes began to water. He tried to sit up. Rick stood and walked around to the head of the bed and added a pillow behind Herman. "Thanks."

Rick sat back down.

"You saved my life," said Herman. The comment surprised Rick and before he could respond, Herman continued. "No one, especially a stranger, has ever done anything like that for me. I'm invisible most of the time."

Rick put his notes aside and listened to a very sad young man let go and tell a stranger his life story. How he grew up in a loving family, the middle child of five. His two older brothers were star athletes and could do no wrong. His two younger sisters were twins and smart. Herman was stuck in the middle, a place that was overlooked by his mother and father in favor of the others. It was as if life itself was a ball that his family kept tossing back and forth over his head as he tried in vain to grab and hold on to any chance of recognition for himself. As a result, Herman created a life of his own. Singular, secluded, and for the most part happy to share the name Kruger, as he set out on a course of his own. He decided to go to school in the UK, which didn't seem to bother his preoccupied family. He'd remained a bachelor and now in his early forties was resolute in his commitment to remain single.

It didn't take Herman long to complete his life story, bittersweet and sad. He, and the man he helped save, were not that far apart in age. Rick sat there processing what he'd just heard. He looked at Herman laying there as if he were suspended in a spider's web unable to free himself from the bedsheets and the turmoil facing his adopted country. Rick understood how this man could easily have been manipulated. His feelings of disbelief that someone could actually do something like this were shifting. Lowering his voice, he asked his next question in a more nurturing tone.

"Herman, let's talk about the Reign."

They spoke for another hour with Herman fading in and out. Herman's demeanor became more and more relaxed as he explained how the Reign found him that snowy day in London. Rick listened, recording Herman's every word as he continued with how he supplied them with classified scheduling information, the daily operation of managing the Royal family, and most importantly, the Ascot racing schedule.

A knock at the door interrupted their discourse. A nurse excused herself and came into the room with the guard. "Medication time." Rick took a quick break and stepped outside a for some fresh air. It was nearing eight and rain was falling from the night sky. He couldn't believe he'd been there for over three hours. Having no windows helps one to lose a sense of time, he thought to himself as he scanned the lights of the city. The guard, dressed in a more military-type uniform, AR-15 style rifle pointed down, green camo, helmet and dark glasses, came out onto the metal platform joining Rick. He offered a cigarette pulled from a pack in his sleeve, which Rick declined. "Changing of the guard, mate. You can go back now." Rick thanked the guard and shook the rain from his jacket as he re-entered the hospital. When he reached Herman's room Sir Archie was there to greet him.

"There you are. The nurse said you stepped out for a minute."

Rick watched as Archie made his way around Herman's bed up close to the headboard. Herman's eyes tracked the man, who looked as if he was going to do him harm, the entire way. "Don't worry you little shit, I'm not going to hurt your worthless, treasonous ass." Herman jerked his head back to look at Rick. His face distorted into a scared and confused glare.

"Archie. I want to show you something." Archie turned to look at Rick.

"Outside." Rick motioned with his head toward the door.

The two men left and stood in the hall. Rick could tell Archie was ready to hit someone, preferably someone else.

"Archie, let me talk to Herman, alone."

"Why? I'm not going to kill the little pissant bastard. I only want to talk to him, we haven't much time, Rick."

"He and I have connected. You joining us right now may be," he paused for a second, "too much."

It was everything the man could do to hold his tongue, Rick could tell. "I won't be long, maybe another hour. Herman has to rest soon."

"Well, we mustn't disturb the little traitor's rest now, should we?"

Rick looked down and back up again at the man he'd come to admire. In that short time Archie's mood changed. This wasn't his first interrogation and he clearly understood Rick's point. A smile forced itself across the older man's face.

"Go ahead. Get what you can, but remember, he's not your friend and the clock is ticking, Rick."

With that Archie turned and left.

§

SILICON VALLEY, CA

Lorretta paced through thick soft white carpet in her California hotel suite. Being on the West Coast threw her off a bit. The people here tended to be healthier and smiled way too much. Very different from living on the East Coast in Boston, her home and refuge. To her, California was a place where people pretended to be who they were. Californians could never survive back east after years of yoga, smoothies, and sunshine. She cradled her cell phone on one shoulder, lighting a cigarette as she headed for the bottle of scotch her assistant had just dropped off.

Lorretta became the head of the entire family operation

when Michael Castillino died. Petrula Trucking happened to be the main cog in a large underworld operation that included the continental United States, Canada, Sicily and soon, South America. Not one lieutenant in the small army her father, and Michael's father, constructed as part of the French Connection heroin trade back in the fifties, contested her elevation to the top. She would go down in the silent society as the first woman to take the helm. She considered the men beneath her as managers, and she— more than a Boss—had become the Godmother and CEO. For her, it was the only way to change the former Men Only management style of their Italian-American family. That and the fact that she would personally slit the throat of any person who voted against her.

Lorretta developed a list of priorities intended to improve the operation. Top spot on that list belonged to Rick Blaine and his elimination from the face of the earth. She would strike first at his company. Lorretta had the means, opportunity, and motive. "Ready or not, here I come."

The scotch made the mood she began to fall into so much better. Her masseuse would arrive soon and stay if she felt like having company. Lights down, music from the Rat Pack up, just a little. The saxophone rhythm behind Dean Martin's vocal made her dance in a circle, one way, and then the other. More scotch. A gentle knock on the door interrupted her musical moment. Lorretta felt good as she floated toward the door. It was now time to feel better.

§

BALLATER, UK; BALMORAL CASTLE GROUNDS

The Queen drove her Land Rover over the deeply rutted roads, something she'd done a thousand times before. Back roads in Scotland can be that way, especially at a higher speed when attempting to challenge the guard detail. Sir Archie hung on as the two enjoyed the ride along the Queen's favorite landscape. "You say that the terrorists are supposedly targeting me and my grandson, William?" Archie took a few seconds to answer as the four-wheeled vehicle made its way through a creek bed, bouncing the pair up, slightly, off their seats. "Yes, yesss, Your Royal Ma... Majesty. We are very concerned. They seem bent on ripping the very fabric of the British Empire to shreds."

The Queen shifted down a gear, looked at Archie with raised an eyebrow, "Archie, you and I both know that you can call me Lilybet, especially when driving through mud puddles!" Her eyes sparkled as she laughed along with her passenger as the Land Rover responded without hesitation to being down - shifted into third gear.

The Queen rounded a muddy corner causing the clay infused dirt to splatter, rather loudly, at one side of the vehicle. "We're almost there, Archie," she said with a chuckle. The Queen noticed Archie had switched to bracing himself with two hands, one in the stirrup that hung from the roof, and one against the dashboard.

As they came up over a rise in the road, Her Royal Majesty noticed the support team of six, waiting at the camp next to a helicopter. "Well, jolly good for them, Archie. But it's not fair, is it?" Archie smiled, guessing what the Queen was about to say. "I mean, you may have guessed by now that I took the long way. I so enjoy driving, even if it causes you to hang on for dear life, Archie." Their laughter continued as people, some with concerned looks on their faces, came to greet the monarch and her friend.

A meeting had been hastily scheduled in this remote location for a reason. The Queen already scheduled some vacation time away at Balmoral. Archie went along for the ride, so to speak.

His participation was last minute, and the Queen enjoyed the spontaneity of it all.

The meeting's main purpose was to decide whether it would be appropriate to cancel the Ascot Races at this late date. In a little more than a month the festivities would begin.

The Queen took Sir Archie's arm as they marched together through the mud toward a scenic lodge, on what the Queen thought was a most glorious day.

Chapter 9

LONDON, UK; LAMPERSON INTERNATIONAL HEADQUARTERS

Winston sat up as Archie walked through the door of the Lamperson conference room. The honorable man had that look of determination on his face that Winston had seen years ago when, together, they put away one of the most sinister IRA leaders in all of Ireland.

"So, how is Elizabeth, Archie?" asked Winston.

"She's fine, it's The Firm that drives me crazy, Winston."

Winston knew all too well what it meant to deal with the Queen's group of advisors. A bunch of overseers that act slowly with their own best interests in mind, not that of the British people. Or so it seemed.

"Her Royal Majesty wants to put herself in harm's way, along with her grandson, William, in order to help us."

The room went silent for a minute. Traffic sounds along Kensington High Street could be heard six floors up as the two men paced around a mahogany conference table in the large space. Winston stopped at the white board and began to draw a bullseye. "That's it, Archie." Still facing the board and continuing to draw even more rapidly, he turned, putting the top back on the felt marker. "She and William make these races the most exciting of all times. They encourage more participation than ever. The Ascot Races will become the highlight of the year!" Archie looked at his old friend as if he had a third eye.

"Winston, I'm in agreement with keeping the races on track, and not changing the schedule, but putting the Royal Family in harm's way like that? I'm not sure that's wise."

Winston asked his friend to sit while he explained. "Don't you see? The bigger we make the event the more the Reign will feel comfortable moving forward with its plans."

"But their plans are to kill the Queen and William, Winston. Do we have enough information on the terrorists to root them out in time to avoid a disaster?" asked Archie.

"Ben has new information that, I believe, may answer that question. I've asked him to join us in a few minutes to explain."

The three men waited patiently for Rick, who'd called to say he had to make a stop first, after talking with Herman. The Home Secretary's man finally broke down and told Rick where to find documents linking the Reign to what was about to happen at the Ascot Races.

"It's been over an hour, where is Rick?" Archie asked as he looked out one of the large conference room windows. Something was wrong, Archie could feel it. Lunch arrived and the men sat there eating and waiting.

§

LONDON, UK; ACTON TOWN

Rick normally enjoyed the ride in a London black cab. Watching for various landmarks and the oddity of riding on the wrong side of the road created its own sense of excitement. His focus was different on this ride, however, as he headed back to Herman's apartment building. Rick was on the hunt for copies of secret documents Herman had photographed during one of the three Reign meetings he attended two months earlier. "I had to do something to ensure my safety," he told Rick. Unfortunately, what Herman didn't realize was that the documents would never have saved him; the Reign intended to kill off most of its spy network, including Herman, all along. In the end, it would never have mattered one way or the other, which meant Herman remained a target. For that reason, Rick contacted Archie who doubled the security for Herman at the hospital. Archie hesitated when Rick offered to locate the documents himself and bring them to the meeting later that morning. Archie reluctantly gave him the go ahead and Rick was off the line and on his way. The Yankee was determined, Archie had to give him that.

Rick kept going over his conversation with Herman in his head as the cab made its way through traffic. The smiling face that Herman remembered staring down at him as he lay in his bed the day before. "I'm sure she injected me with something, or was in the process when you interrupted her." Herman described how the woman's face started to melt into a grotesque figure that kept coming closer and closer before suddenly disappearing.

"You saved my life. Be careful Mr. Blaine, these are not nice people." All Rick could think about, as the cab pulled up in front of Herman's apartment building, were Herman's last words, as he prepared to exit the cab.

Rick asked the driver to wait as he gathered his things. The driver told him he would leave the meter running, but Rick would have to hand over a credit card as collateral. The man had the look of an unshaven Mel Gibson wearing a dark knitted cap, chewing gum and smiling through tobacco-stained teeth. He looked honest enough, so Rick handed him his credit card and left. The cab driver watched with interest as Rick made his way along the sidewalk.

The stairway leading to the basement of the apartment building was located around the back of the 17th century structure. Rickety wooden steps, in need of serious repair, caused Rick to nearly lose his balance and catch himself, as he made his way down the cobweb infested stairway. Light was at a premium and Rick had to use his phone flashlight to find the door lock, which seemed to defy any attempt to be discovered. He blew dust off the lock, pulled out a key chain, and inserted the key. He worked the key into the lock, as he did so, there was a slight rubbing sensation against his right calf muscle. Distracted all of sudden, he dropped the key into blackness. As Rick searched for the key, two green eyes stared back, mewing as they disappeared. Flashing the light downward revealed a large black cat sauntering off as if upset by his presence. Rick reached down searching for the key, which caught the attention of the feline who now seemed to want to help. After a minute of patting the wooden planking, the cat backed off, bored with the hunt. Seconds later, Rick found the key. He could feel time ticking away as he quickly reinserted the key and, thankfully, heard the lock snap open. The door was stuck, and required a slight nudge in order to open, followed by an extended creaking sound. His phone's light illuminated more cobwebs as he cleared his way by waving his hand before him. Rick had to wonder how often residents visited this place.

The room was rectangular with stone walls that provided the backdrop for six cyclone-fence cages, each with a number. Herman's was number six, located at the far end. The cage required a second key on Herman's key chain. That lock easily released and Rick worked his way past a bicycle, a set of four tires, a row of neatly labeled boxes, and a workout set of weights that looked long forgotten.

Rick hunted for a brown leather briefcase, which he found tucked in behind the last row of boxes, just as Herman had directed. He opened the case and quickly inspected the papers inside. Page after page of meticulous handwriting described what was contained in three folders. Each folder had a title: Meeting Notes, Schedule, and Contacts. Rick felt a smile come on as he confirmed that this was the information Herman had gathered. As he began to exit, Rick heard the cab's horn. The driver said he'd give him five minutes, after the horn blast, to return. Rick stumbled slightly as he retraced his steps, closing the cage, ducking under a large sewer pipe that hung low across the room, heading for the outside. The door was now stuck open, which required some muscle to close properly. Rick carefully took two steps at a time as he ran for the cab.

§

SILICON VALLEY, CA; BLAINE MANUFACTURING

Brenda took a call from Bobby Hansen a.k.a. Bear. Bobby, a combat war vet turned private detective, helped to keep Rick safe when he was being followed by the mafia last year. Bobby and Rick became close. The former Vet helped Rick in his rehabilitation by teaching him self-defense techniques and how to shoot a gun. Bear is his unofficial "nickname" because of his size: Well over six feet tall and weighing in around two-fifty. His exact measurements are his own business and no one questions him about them.

Bear remained on retainer with Blaine Manufacturing while Rick was in Europe. His primary job required checking in with Brenda and providing her with an exterior security update. Blaine Manufacturing has always had an internal security force that checked the campus buildings, including the two parking garages, alleyways, and perimeter 24/7. Bear came with his own private force of three ex-military professionals, and several contract personnel, who worked, under his supervision, on several projects. Blaine being the largest.

"Brenda, have you heard from Rick since Castillino was killed?"

"Yes. Why?"

"Word on the street is that the Castillino family is planning some kind of action against Blaine Manufacturing. I have my men ready. I just need your permission to engage."

"Bear, if you think we need to pay more attention to the matter then let's do it."

"That's all I needed to know. Check with you in a few days. In the meantime, use my emergency line, we'll be close."

§

LONDON, UK; ACTON TOWN

The cabbie's wait time approached five minutes. He'd blasted the horn twice, that should have provided the gent with enough notice. The driver had a responsibility and a job to perform. He went from scanning the street front and back to glancing back and forth, from the apartment house to his watch. He started to reach for the parking brake when he noticed a figure running in his direction. It was the Yank. God these people can be insufferable. The American slipped slightly and almost lost his footing as he entered the vehicle. The satchel he carried, caught in the door as he tried in vain to close it. A few pulls and tugs and one more hearty pull and Rick was inside. Then, finally, a closing of the door.

"Sorry to make you wait."

"Not a problem, mate. Where to now?"

The driver radioed his situation and drove swiftly back toward Covent Garden, his destination near the London School of Economics. Rick called Ben to let him know he had the package and that he was on the way. As Rick hung up, he noticed the cabbie looking up into his rearview mirror, more than once. A worried look came across the driver's face as the driver then changed his gaze and shot a look at Rick that made him ask,

"Is something the matter?" Rick's impulse was to look over his shoulder, through the back window of the black cab, which he did, not wanting to see what he was looking for.

"Are you with anyone? Because we're being followed." The cab driver, an older fellow, said matter-of-factly. He seemed to be familiar with such happenings. While Rick was in Herman's building, he had noticed a car parked down the road with someone sitting inside. Normally, a parked car wouldn't catch his attention, but people didn't usually sit idling for that long. It was when the car pulled out after them that he knew something was amiss.

Rick looked out the rear window and spotted the car too. "Anything you can do to lose them? Can you do something about it?"

"Not a problem, guv. Tighten your seat belt."

The cab driver took on a different persona as he reached across and opened the glove box, pulling out a holster with a revolver. The driver noticed Rick's stare in the rearview mirror. "It's loaded. Sit lower in the seat and to one side if you would, I'll get you there." The second he finished his sentence the cab's back window exploded into pieces, sending shards of glass all around the cab. The cabbie accelerated and made a sharp left turn sending Rick higher in his seat to the right and swiftly back down, as pieces of safety glass rolled with him. Rick's mind went to a similar chase situation that happened in the States. The same feeling of having someone else driving, makes the escape feel even more dangerous. Although he'd rather be in control, there was nothing he could do about it.

The cab continued to make swift turns and drove down alleyways that appeared to be too small for a couple of bicyclists riding side by side. The cab stopped suddenly mid-alley, reversed and backed into a small alcove. Tall buildings blotted out the sun. They sat quietly, in complete darkness. A spot of sunlight made its way into the alley, like a visitor entering the wrong room and needing directions. It was their only reference to where they had come. The driver turned and asked if Rick was alright. "Yes, I'm fine. How long do we wait?"

The driver didn't answer right away and then: "I'm listening for screeching tires." Rick held his breath and remained quiet. "We're good." The driver started the cab and they were off once again.

From Rick's vantage point, which came from below the side windows as he laid on shattered glass, provided views of London he'd never witnessed before. A few more twists and turns, some through foul smelling back alleyways, thanks to the broken back window, revealed more sunlight as the cab began to pick up speed. The Thames River appeared out of nowhere, on their left, when the cab turned onto a main avenue. Rick began to relax, even though the driver remained vigilant. Rick knew they were close to his destination.

Within minutes the cab pulled up in front of the Lamperson Headquarters. "Are you sure you're alright, sir? Sorry about all the bobbing and weaving, but it comes at no additional cost." Rick found the unexpected humor a relief. Although he appreciated the man's proficient driving technique more and shared his feelings with the driver. As Rick went to pay the fare, the man interrupted him. "Oh, right, here's your card. Maybe next time, Mr. Blaine. Sir Archie only hires the best my friend. The ride is on him." Rick just looked at the man who was now smiling and tipping his cap. "And as for the horn honking, well…Archie said not to let you out of me sight for too long. If you hadn't appeared when you did, I would have gone in to find you." Rick smiled, closed the door and tapped the top of the cab as before it disappeared into traffic.

§

"You fool, we lost them!" Fritz beat his hands against the dashboard of the car, causing one of the vent controls to snap off. The driver had never seen him so incensed. Fritz sat for a long minute, drool coming from his nose and mouth, trying to get his breath back. The terrorist leader looked out of control as he stuffed the gun and silencer into its case and back under the front seat. Fritz took a deep breath, wiped his face with his sleeve and looked at his driver, Ernst, as they sat facing a three-way stop within sight of the London Bridge. The BMW 730i turned out to be no match for the Hackney cab, especially with a more seasoned driver piloting the black escape vehicle. "Don't just sit there, go!"

Ernst hurriedly exited the car in order to pull part of a bale of straw from under the front bumper. The straw came from a public market area they had been forced to drive through. Fritz, meanwhile, texted his most trusted lieutenant, Mara, to see if she had any new information regarding her quest to find Herman. Mara headed up the Reign's Elimination Squad. She immediately returned Fritz's text from the laundry room of the hospital: JUST DEPLOYED TWO OF OUR OWN DISGUISED AS NURSES. WE WILL FIND HIM.

The Reign knew the authorities were on to them and, therefore, had to be more cognizant of how they managed the Ascot assault on the royals moving forward. There was no turning back as far as the leaders of the movement were concerned. In spite of Fritz's efforts to control access to sensitive materials, or more importantly, who knew what, information had leaked out as the Ascot event neared.

For that reason, the decision was made to focus on finding and eliminating Herman Kruger. The Reign would have to be on their guard if they were to be successful. That meant keeping only those operatives that have worked with them in the past, people they knew and trusted. Herman, and those newer followers like him, were considered expendable and would be hunted down by the Elimination Squad.

The BMW made its way over the Thames and back into Brixton off the A23. Fritz had lost count of the trips he'd made over the last four years, back and forth, on this same route over the Thames. They were headed to the Reign's secret headquarters, a warehouse located near Brockwell Park. The location was perfect for storing supplies and equipment. It also housed the leadership team whose task it was to pull off the most heinous crime since the murder of King Richard III in 1485.

The ride back may have been disappointing, but the cause was not. Fritz reached over and patted his driver on the shoulder and assured him that he had done his best, chasing the cabbie. "They were just lucky this time, Ernst. We will be victorious in the end. Those who oppose us will suffer greater pain than we feel now."

The driver smiled back, knowing how Fritz could change moods as often as he changed his shirts. The car slowed as the driver turned off Dulwich Road, simultaneously activating the remote that controlled one of three camouflaged garage doors located out of sight from the main road. The warehouse itself sat off the beaten track with the back of the building built into a hillside, making it possible for the Reign to secretly excavate out and down into the earth. The burrowing allowed them to build a complex of additional rooms and an intelligence center hidden from potential intrusion. Any first-time visitor invited into the inner sanctum would think they were entering a giant cave, as opposed to a building. The entire interior was painted in various shades of brown meant to reduce the amount of light reflected to the outside. Even the giant windows, formerly used for light and ventilation, were painted over. Large amber colored fixtures dotted the ceiling, providing just enough light to maneuver safely. As the car entered the darkened bay, Fritz received a text from Mara: KRUGER IS ON THE MOVE. WE ARE IN PURSUIT. WILL ADVISE SOON.

§

LONDON, UK; LAMPERSON INTERNATIONAL HEADQUARTERS

Rick burst into the Lamperson conference room, causing all conversation to come to a complete stop. "There you are my boy, satchel in hand and a spring in your step."

Winston Lamperson looked relieved as he ushered Rick to a chair, while carefully placing Herman's briefcase on the conference room table. "Sit down and fill us in while you eat." Ben, Archie and Winston had notes strewn from one end of the conference room table to the other, plus schematic drawings on the whiteboard, adjacent to the head table. Even though Rick had just been through a harrowing experience, he mentally shifted into high gear and spent time going through the meticulous notes Herman had made concerning the Reign and their plans.

He suggested to Archie that Herman be moved from his current location to a safer place while he recovered. "And by the way, your cab driver was a welcome surprise." Archie smiled as he continued to look down at the notes Rick had given him. "We call him Captain because of his military service rank. Only a few people know his name. The Captain has been called upon to make unruly people disappear. Only the best for you Mr. Blaine." Archie looked up as he continued.

"Normally, I would say that jail should be the only consideration for Kruger, but based on what I'm seeing here I'm not so sure that would be prudent. We don't know how far the Reign's influence extends into the dregs of our society. Locking him up might be sending him to his doom. He might as well have a target painted on his bald head. Someone obviously wanted him dead and we need him as a material witness." Archie continued to look through papers as he passed what he reviewed along to the others. After a few minutes, he rose and left the room to arrange for Herman's transfer to a safe house.

Three hours later, Ben and Rick identified thirty individuals who, like Herman, were recruited into the Reign network within the last eighteen months. The recruits had one purpose: provide the most current information on the Royals, the Ascot Races, and security.

Winston Lamperson began making contacts within the secret service community he'd been a part of for nearly fifty years.

§

LONDON, UK; ROYAL LONDON HOSPITAL

The injection that Herman received came close to shutting down one kidney and doing the same to the other, nearly killing him. His head spun as he tried to focus on the person or people who were moving around him. The transport gurney that Herman had been hastily tucked into, like an infant unable to move its arms, slammed the back wall of the freight elevator. Herman could hear some mumbling between his transporters as the floor seemingly moved away. The mumbles became more audible as those around him prepared to exit as the elevator stopped. The next moment felt like being shot out of a cannon. The gurney moved rapidly across rough concrete causing the castor wheels to vibrate and spin. Voices, now echoed, shouted orders to be on the alert as the race with the gurney continued.

Up ahead, two masquerading nurses, trained assassins, leveled their handguns at the oncoming force surrounding the gurney. The noise in the cavernous underground parking garage made it hard to hear. The first shot came from one of the nurse assassins, the next eight shots riddled both nurses' bodies, four each. Two in the head and two in the heart. One military officer had gone down in front of the gurney, causing it to slide sideways and nearly tip. The side rails held the patient in, but Herman experienced a moment of weightlessness before slamming back down into his cocoon-like state. The gunfire, which was loud and startling, ended almost as soon as it began. The shouting lasted longer as agents, sent by Sir Archie, ran to where the nurses had been hiding. "We were almost too late, Sir." The team of six special agents had been tracking the two women for nearly an hour before the shooting. The captain and his team of five were given the coordinates of the transport team and managed to thwart the parking garage ambush. Unfortunately, one of the transport team had been wounded severely and was taken immediately into surgery.

The captain called Archie to give him an update and to let him know that the special agents were following the transport team to the secret location. A few minutes later an ambulance exited the hospital parking garage. From the outside, the white van with green trimmings and the word AMBULANCE, printed backwards in black bold letters across the front, looked like any other emergency vehicle that frequented the hospital campus. But the van contained Herman Kruger, a former government employee currently being treated as a traitor turned witness. If he remained alive, he would become one of the most hated individuals in the land. But he couldn't die because the British government needed him, and his collection of secret data, in order to apprehend and prosecute those who were bent on terrorizing life for the British people.

Consequently, Herman would be taken to a safe house. Location unknown or known only to a select few. He would continue his convalescence there until needed. In the meantime, the clock continued to tick and both the terrorists and their pursuers grew anxious. Tension mounted on both sides and Rick Blaine found himself in an ever-increasing pressure cooker of international proportions.

Chapter 10

LONDON, UK; THE REIGN COMPOUND

Fritz walked slowly from the car as Ernst drove the BMW into its special parking space next to two other smaller BMW's, six ATVs and a dozen motorcycles. The car had sustained some minor damage, which would require a new overall body color change, a realignment, and some body work. The changes would be made within 24 hours because all vehicles would be needed in order to carry out their mission.

He checked his phone to see if Mara had left a message. Nothing. He looked up as he walked, wondering how and where they may be moving Kruger. He knew there was something about Kruger that he didn't trust. The meek and less social ones didn't always make the best recruits. Fritz had plenty of experience from his days in the East German Secret Service known as Stasi. The meekest were the weakest and the more vulnerable tended to be more intimidated, like Herman. But unlike him, the majority of Fritz's recruits were given years of training. This particular operation did not provide him with enough time to complete the education necessary to make soldiers out those selected to provide important information to the Cause.

Fritz was the frontline leader of all that needed to come together in time for the Ascot Races. But that didn't make him the superior officer in charge. That duty fell onto the shoulders of one, Kurt Miemke. Miemke was short in stature, just under five foot ten inches tall. Slick black hair, with a small mustache, medium build, single and full of fury. His followers, who were scattered across middle European countries, proclaimed him to be a natural leader, like his great uncle, Adolf Hitler. The man, now in his seventies, walked with a slight limp due to an assault during a political protest when he was in his thirties. As Supreme Leader of the Reign, a name he created as an insult to all royalty, Miemke was relentless. There were those who agreed with his case against royal leadership, especially in Great Britain. But they did not always agree with his terrorist solutions. Miemke's feelings ran deeper, however. When it came to the British, he not only hated the royals, he also had a great dislike for the British people in general. After all, they were responsible for the death of his great uncle, and the down-casting of his family as a result. He had devoted his life to raining down retribution on those that ruined his family.

Miemke resided in a bunker apartment in the warehouse on Dulwich Road. Fritz was on his way to meet with the man who would not be pleased to hear what he was about to report. Fritz knew the man would pat the military pants he wore with his leather-handled whip as he listened carefully to every word. The Supreme Leader would stride back and forth, often with one hand behind his back (a move he adopted after watching his great uncle speak), nodding as he listened. When Fritz would finish and wait for questions, the man would smile and look at him, not saying a word at first. And then all hell would blast suddenly from his mouth. Spittle would be slung across the room, hitting anyone in its wake. Eardrums would be challenged and bladders would be loosened to the point of some in attendance, embarrassing themselves. That kind of response was rare, but it did happen, as it would on that day. The Supreme Leader was not pleased that information relating to their operation managed to reach the authorities, and that a target had also managed to slip through their fingers. "This will come back to haunt us," Miemke blurted out. "Unless, you take action now!"

When the man finished he sat back down, refusing to look at Fritz or any one of the dozen or so leaders who were in attendance. Fritz decided not to ask what the man meant by "now". Did he want to attack sooner than the Ascot Races? It was too late to put a new plan together. The races were preparing to begin their multiple-week experience. The latest word from Buckingham Palace was that the Queen and her family were making their annual appearance next week. Fritz read over this latest report as the Supreme Leader continued his unwelcomed, but not unexpected, rant.

Fritz ushered Miemke into a smaller meeting room, away from the group of followers who had begun to slow down and gather around, out of respect for their two leaders. Fritz grew concerned about the mental stability of the man he'd considered to be brains behind the Cause.

The two men had met at a conference ten years ago in Prague. The Nazi movement had disguised the symposium within an old Slovakian festival celebrating the change of season, from winter to spring. There were entertainers of all kinds — musicians, singers and dancers on a big open stage surrounded by vendor booths, and a beer garden with food and more alcoholic beverages. Miemke was a featured speaker in a large white tent set up for the event. His speech was sold out, but Fritz, and few of his friends, sympathetic to underpinnings of white supremacy, felt an obligation to attend. Of those in attendance that day, only Fritz and about a dozen others, stayed behind to visit with Miemke and purchase a copy of his most recent book:

The Cause. From that moment forward Fritz understood what it meant to be committed. None of his close friends decided to dedicate their lives to the resurgence of Nazi hatred, or the man who looked and sounded like his great uncle, Adolf Hitler.

Miemke quickly brought Fritz, Ernst, and a few others waiting for an autograph that day, into his inner sanctum. The years went by quickly and the number of loyal followers grew. Kurt took great pride in knowing that Fritz, who had been elevated to number two status with the Reign, was his most trusted follower. Fritz was like a son, an offspring that appeared to be more of a miracle than if he'd actually fathered him.

As Fritz proceeded to settle his leader down with a glass of water and two Thoridazine antipsychotic pills that would alter Kurt's disposition into a more relaxed mood. Eventually, Miemke would forget he had had another episode. As the Supreme Leader's face became more relaxed, Fritz's head nodded with a reassuring smile, masking a troubling thought. Fritz knew a change in plans had to be made. The Cause he'd been following for some time was in jeopardy if Miemke continued to spiral out of control as he did today. His beloved leader's outlandish outbursts had become more frequent of late. Fritz witnessed that day, and not for the first time, the look of concern on the faces of the most trusted warriors, working feverishly behind the scenes, here in the bunkered warehouse. If time and terror were to remain on their side, Fritz had to take control. He knew that Miemke could no longer be counted on to lead.

§

LONDON, UK; LAMPERSON INTERNATIONAL HEADQUARTERS

The five days of festivities at the Royal Ascot Races were about to begin. Rick had been away for almost a month, and was longing to return home. He'd been keeping in touch with Brenda, who had settled nicely into her new position. According to her latest information, business was at an all-time high. Brenda shared her concern that Rick might have put himself in a more dangerous position personally by offering to aid his favored business associates, Lamperson International, in their quest to uncover a terrorist plot.

Brenda decided she better keep her focus on Blaine Manufacturing, rather than wedge herself between Rick and the Lampersons. Too bad. The fact was, she'd grown rather fond of Ben Lamperson. He seemed to be a gentleman and an extremely intelligent man who also happened to be single and attractive. Brenda, dedicated to her work first, never really took the time to "play the field" like some of her friends. But she found Ben Lamperson handsome and respectful, having met him last year when he and his father ventured to the states to visit Blaine Manufacturing's offices. She liked a man who stood tall and could carry on a reasonable conversation about more than one subject, had a sense of humor, and dressed well. It didn't hurt that he had the most sensual, posh British accent. She smiled at the thought of Ben calling earlier to give her an update on Rick's status.

The target event, the Royal Ascot Races, were a few days away and Rick appeared to be in the midst of final preparations for dealing with the terrorists' threat. Herman's notes were instrumental in allowing the Lamperson team to develop a comprehensive battle plan. The Queen, along with her family, including William, would be making a royal appearance this coming Saturday. The Queen would be expected to make remarks prior to the first race of the day scheduled to begin at noon. "We have seventy-two hours to finalize and implement all the details in this document, gentlemen, Winston declared."

Winston held up the twenty pages of stapled material that contained directives for each of the three major security forces, working behind the scenes. Sir Archie spoke to the MI5 and Scotland Yard directives, Ben outlined what to expect from the secret militia force that had been assembled. That group was comprised of former Special Forces officers, who had trained either with the British Special Air Service (SAS), the Israeli Sayeret (Special Forces) or Mista'arvim (Counter-Terrorism force), or the U.S. Navy Seals, Delta Force, or the Army Rangers. Each unit of the three groups worked under Winston or Archie's direction. Rick sat back as the weight of the undertaking finally hit him. Granted, he was tired having worked without much sleep in the last forty-eight hours.

Rick looked around the conference room as both Archie and Winston finished and asked for final questions or comments. Ben, sitting directly across from Rick, looked up from his notes and smiled at Rick. "I feel as tired as you look my American friend." Rick nodded back at Ben. "I'm honored to be here, Ben. But, I feel as though there's nothing more I can do to help."

Winston rose from his seat and walked around the table to sit next to Rick. "I hope you don't feel as though we're leaving you in the dust, Rick. What you've done for us is more than I could have expected. I, we, can't thank you enough." Rick had the look of admiration on his face as he turned toward the man who he considered to be more of a mentor or father figure.

Winston reached out and touched Rick on the shoulder. "There is one more thing, but it will have to wait until we sort this terrorist plot out. Can you stay here with us for a few more days?"

Rick nodded his head as the four men rose and left the room they'd been meeting in for the last five hours. Rick headed back to his hotel while Winston, Archie and Ben each met with approximately a hundred authorized security officers from various law enforcement agencies, delegating their agreed upon actions. They had three days to find and capture the terrorists before they could complete their threat against the Royal Family. The clock was ticking faster than ever.

When Rick reached his room, he noticed the red message button blinking on the room phone. There was a message from Ben. "Rick get some much-deserved rest and then consider a new request. It comes from Herman Kruger. He would like to talk with you once more. Tomorrow if possible. Call me and I'll make arrangements."

§

SILICON VALLEY, CA, SAN JOSE LUXURY HOTEL

Sitting on her hotel balcony, sipping a glass of ice-cold rosé, Lorretta realized for the first time that she actually enjoyed being on the West Coast. She didn't like the reason she had to be there, but the lovely weather and the sites appealed to her flamboyant nature. Lorretta found it easier than expected to run her business from the west, something she had never previously considered. As a result, she decided to move into a temporary location not far from Blaine Manufacturing. The property lease typically rented for more than she paid. Lorretta was very good at negotiation. The paperwork gave her the option for another three years. That would be more than enough time to do what needed to be done. And when she succeeded, she may choose to stick around to see how things played out with the aftermath of the Blaine destruction.

Lorretta continued to monitor the Blaine campus with a small crew of highly skilled observers. Her goal, for now, was to take time to devise a plan of action that would ultimately destroy the facility and Blaine's future along with it. And with any luck, Rick Blaine would be caught up in the destruction. She would wait until his return, which she also had on her monitor. Each night as she saluted the beautiful sunset along the coast, sometimes from a secret location in Golden Gate Park near the Observatory, she'd smile a toast. "For you my dear Michael. I will complete what you set out to do, only this time, I will make it happen you poor fool." Her driver would supply the wine, champagne or scotch, whatever her desire—even sex later in her suite; it was up to her.

§

LONDON, UK; UNDISCLOSED LOCATION

Four members of Winston's special security force drove Rick to a safe house where Herman Kruger had been relocated. The rain had stopped and the sun was just beginning to rise in the east. The reflection on the Thames as the black bulletproof Escalade cruised over the river, reflected tones of orange and blue. Rick had never seen those shades together. All of a sudden, he had feelings of melancholy as the driver slowed for waiting traffic. A saying that his father used often came to mind. "Remember, Rick, whatever you don't deal with, even if it scares you, will ultimately deal with you." Rick fondly recalled his dad telling him that when he played football in high school. Rick filled in for the starting quarterback when the poor guy sustained an injury. Rick had always wanted to take charge of the team, but was hesitant, thus he ended up being the back up. He then had to face his fears against their team's number one rival when the starter went down. The memory was a good one because he took charge and finished the game in the second half. Even though they lost, Rick gained respect for himself and that of his father, which was the most important thing at the time.

When the driver pulled off the main drag in New Cross, the American passenger was transferred to an awaiting car. That ride, a military vehicle of some sort, headed into an area that appeared to be off the beaten track and more industrial. Whatever he was riding in appeared to have a loose suspension, allowing the transport to account for every dip, hole, and unevenness in the road. Thankfully, the ride didn't last long and no sooner had Rick found a way to use the overhead passenger handles for balance, the vehicle unexpectedly turned into a garage.

Everything went black as the vehicle slowed to allow the door to rise as they entered. The back door of the vehicle slowly opened and Rick was hurriedly escorted into a dimly lit hallway by two men, one on each arm. "Sir, a few more steps and we'll be there." The hall, painted in what appeared to be a dull green, was wide enough to allow the three men to walk side by side. Actually, the three moved in a fast-paced syncopated rhythm with Rick slightly swinging in between the two others in an opposing motion. Rick felt as though he was being escorted into a bad dream.

The men stopped a few moments later. Rick's head was on a swivel as he attempted to gain focus. He jerked his head back and looked directly at a spot on the wall with a red dot below. A security camera watched as they made their way toward a fast approaching, steel door. Off to the side was an illuminated wall plate with numbers. One of the men punched in a code, the red light started flashing under the camera. The door slid open to reveal two more soldiers and a woman dressed in a blue business suit with a white blouse.

"Good morning, Mr. Blaine. I'm Lucile Saunders, a business associate of Sir Archibald Turlington. Welcome to one of our Safe Houses."

Lucile had brunette hair that she wore in a tight bun. She stood taller than her petite frame, because of her high-laced black military boots, which Rick thought was an odd accessory. She looked to be about 50 as she sported a slight smile, most likely because she questioned, like the soldiers around her, what reason would this Yankee want with their prisoner.

Lucile appeared to be all business, letting Rick know that not many people, outside the military assigned to duty, are ever allowed inside one of their hideaways. After a brief conversation, Rick was ushered into a more comfortable waiting area for a 15 minute wait. His cell phone had to be shut off, part of the rules, no phone calls in or out while on the premises. Understandable and yet Rick felt as if he'd never been this disconnected from life. The place reminded him of a morgue without the smell, or a funeral home, both waiting in anticipation of what may come through the door next.

Rick's discomfort became more apparent as he began to pace the room, but he had to see Herman. because Herman had asked to see him, but Rick also wanted to see how the guy was doing. He couldn't help but feel sorry for him, alone and confused, not knowing what might happen to him at any minute. Everybody hated him.

Lucile came into the waiting area and escorted Rick, along with two guards, to Herman's room. "We have to make sure no one is concealing any weapons, Mr. Blaine, would you mind stepping in front of the screen." It was similar to one used at airports that showed your skeletal structure. Fortunately, Rick had no weapons to speak of and he was allowed the final steps into Herman's room.

Herman looked better than the last time Rick saw him and he told the young prisoner so. "Thank you for coming so soon, Rick. I hope you don't mind if I call you by your first name." Rick found the man somewhat engaging, which was a surprise.

It seemed as though the weight of the world had been lifted off his shoulders for some reason, which also came as a surprise. "I'm feeling better each day. I look forward to when I can...." Herman hesitated as a blank stare came over him suddenly.

Rick took the opportunity to ask what the group at Lamperson Headquarters most wanted to know: Where is the Reign staging? But that question would have to wait. "Herman, can you hear me?"

Herman seemed to snap awake even though his eyes were open. He sat up as he answered. "Yes, yes of course."

"Good, good. As you can see, you are currently under the protection of the British government. What you need to know is that you may be asked to be a material witness against the Reign."

Herman's eyes began to gather more focus. His brow wrinkled slightly and his lips parted into a smile showing perfect teeth.

For the next hour Herman shared as much as he knew about the Reign. His reasoning behind joining the Cause paled in comparison to the loyalty he felt for the Royal Family. It wasn't the job, working for the Home Secretary the last four years, that bolstered his feelings. In fact, he hated his job, but that never changed the good feelings he had for the Royal Family, especially the Queen. After some soul searching, since being hospitalized, Herman decided that his German ancestry would be rewarded more positively if he were to make up for his indiscretion and share all he could about the Reign. They were after him, and it was time to fight back. "I want to do the right thing, Rick."

Herman knew of a few others who may also testify, if it came to that. Based on what he knew and had been able to steal out from under the distracted coordinators guiding the misguided, he was an open book.

All Herman knew about any headquarter operation was

a reference that Fritz made during a meeting some weeks ago. "He shared with a few of us, who stayed after most everyone left. I'm not sure whether Fritz was feeling euphoric or what, but he did ask that we not share what he was about to say. He talked about London's special place known as the crossroads. It's where people from all over the world have come to stay."

Herman went on to say that Fritz shared more about the Reign settling in that place, devoid of any royal connection. It became apparent to Herman that Fritz was talking about a large facility, but did not elaborate. As they left the meeting, Fritz and Herman rode together on the subway. Thinking back on it, Herman felt that it was Fritz's way of gaining his respect. Fritz continued to keep a friendly conversation going, as they rode the line together. Herman's destination happened to be close to Piccadilly Circus and he said his goodbyes as he exited. Fritz continued southward towards Brixton.

Rick didn't hesitate to make the call the second he cleared the safe house. Whether Herman realized it or not, in Rick's mind, Brixton had to be where the Reign's headquarters was located. Ben answered after three rings. "Brixton? Are you sure?" Rick assured Ben that Herman's contact didn't provide a specific location, but he mentioned a warehouse and Brixton three or four times during a subway ride they took together a month ago.

When Rick returned to Lamperson Headquarters, he asked to see Winston. The elder Lamperson was on a call with the Home Secretary—who was aghast to learn of Herman's treachery—but allowed Rick to enter and sit while he ended his conversation, which did not appear to be going well. Winston looked up after ringing off and placing the phone slowly back in the cradle. "The Royal Palace is adamant about having the Queen attend the Ascot Races. There's no dissuading them."

Rick sat in silence as he looked at the man who added some new age wrinkles in the last few weeks. "Rick, my boy. How did it go with Kruger?" Rick noted how easily Winston could shift gears and go from deep concern to being inquisitive in the blink of an eye.

Rick shared what he knew about the warehouse and Brixton. "Ben is on it and should have details for you and Sir Archie within the hour." Rick hesitated before speaking again. Winston picked up on the moment.

"What is it, Rick?"

The minute Winston asked the question he knew the answer, but he let Rick respond. "Winston, it's time for me to leave. There's not much more I can do to help you. And God knows you've provided Blaine Manufacturing with more business contacts than our sales group would have imagined."

Winston stood and walked around the desk. He pulled another chair over and sat facing Rick. "You have done a great service to our country, Rick. And we're pleased at the possibilities that exist here for your company. Of course, it's time for you to leave." Winston hesitated before continuing. "Before you do, I want you to consider one more favor as you pack your bags."

Chapter 11

LAMPERSON HEADQUARTERS, LONDON

Ben, working with Sir Archie's main contact, stationed in South London's Lambeth Borough, began researching warehouses throughout the Brixton area. The contact was given a few clues to go on, but responded positively, suggesting it would only be a matter of hours before she'd report back. Agent Angela Salisbury knew where most of the major buildings and industrial structures, like warehouses, existed in her domain. Besides some small-scale industrial projects built under the Overground rail lines, like breweries, bakeries, and bespoke clothing manufacturing, this part of London was more commercial and residential than industrial. Agent Salisbury and two colleagues worked feverishly, combing through real estate records, building permits, and business licenses that pertained to any warehouse operation located in Brixton. Salisbury's small office had become a whirlwind of activity with comments being shouted freely. "Here, mark this address down," "Check this out," "Where's the list?" Time was of the essence as they isolated in on the most likely candidates.

Salisbury's reputation for analyzing, planning and executing, preceded her throughout the British Isles. The attractive, dark haired, martial arts champion, attributed her tenacity to her upbringing. Her Haitian father taught her early on how to survive after escaping into a better life himself. Her British mother, whose heritage was buried deep into the English realm, taught her to always have an opinion and a better than good reason to fight. Her British husband shared a love she never knew she could have. He also shared her passion for law enforcement as a detective with Scotland Yard. At 38 years of age, Angela was the youngest senior agent in MI5's legion of professionals.

§

TANGIER, MOROCCO; GRAND SOCCO MARKETPLACE

Jamal hurried to answer his private line. It was early and the encrypted satellite phone was stationed close to the bed where his wife slept. Thank goodness she was a sound sleeper. "Hello, hello, Winston?" Jamal had given the man he most admired, beyond his father and Allah, a proposition to consider and had been waiting for an answer.

Since Abbas had come to live with Jamal and his family, the boy had shown signs of unbelievable aptitude and intelligence. The young man had not only fit into Jamal's family as if he were a son, working daily at the spice stand in the Grand Socco, helping with chores around the dar, and watching over Jamal's other children, including nephews and nieces.

It had only been a few weeks since Abbas was found unconscious in the alley nearby. His recovery was miraculous to say the least. These thoughts lingered like the smoke from his pipe as Jamal sat with his wife and watched the stars appear in a clear night sky. "You are thinking, old man," she whispered sweetly. "I can tell by your eyes. They are looking out, but not seeing. Am I right, my dear Jamal? Jamal?" He heard her the second time. Slowly, he placed his pipe in the stand and reached over for her hand, raised it up and kissed it. She was right. His weathered fist felt good against her soft skin.

Jamal shared what he'd been thinking about Abbas. The boy was not like the others. He had a sense about him that grew stronger every day. Given the chance, he could be more in life than Jamal could ever offer. And so, it came to him that night, an idea that just might work.

Jamal contacted Winston the next day concerning his idea about Abbas. Winston assured him that he would help. Jamal, feeling better about life after that call, then kissed his wife and proceeded to dress and leave for work.

§

SILICON VALLEY, CA; BLAINE MANUFACTURING

Billy arrived at Blaine Manufacturing's Security Office a few minutes earlier than usual. As Chief of Security, it was his job to check all monitors with Carlos, who sat drinking his last cup of coffee, six in all, having just come off the night shift. "We had to intercept some late-night party goers at 2AM who thought our entryway led to a public parking garage. Other than escorting employees to their vehicles, it was a pretty quiet night, Chief."

Billy took great pride in the twenty-six person patrol force he managed. The group had grown substantially over the last three years. Together with Major Connors, Production Vice President and former Special Forces Commander, the two men mapped out a strong and loyal security organization made up of former military soldiers and law enforcement officers looking for a different direction in life.

Blaine offered more than the average security job with strong benefits and higher pay. In return, the twelve men and fourteen women selected to keep the Blaine campus and its employees safe, were expected to do more than walk the route. It was Billy's responsibility to make sure this part of the Blaine corporate culture worked seamlessly.

Carlos no sooner closed his locker, getting ready to leave, when Billy called him back into the monitor room. "Take a look at this." Billy pointed to a black Cadillac SUV on one of the screens, recorded an hour earlier. "How long has that Cadillac been there?"

"I'm not sure," said Carlos, irritated with himself for not spotting it earlier.

Billy opened two more location screens from around the same time. As he worked his way through the footage, Billy noted that the same SUV appeared to park across from the Blaine campus at three different locations from 4 to 6 AM. "Someone is watching us, Carlos."

Carlos looked down at the floor then back up to face Billy. He felt bad that he hadn't caught the strange behavior. "I might be paranoid, but let's be on alert for the black SUV and see if we can get a license plate number and ID the driver, okay?" Carlos agreed and stayed another hour going over footage from the day before to see if the vehicle showed up again, then filed another report.

Billy left a message for the other monitor observers about the SUV. He would bring up the incident later in the afternoon in their group meeting.

The Chief of Security had a bad feeling about his discovery. He then placed a call to the one man he knew was also out there in the shadows ready to help, Bobby Johnson.

§

LONDON, UK; THE WAREHOUSE

Kurt awoke from a deep sleep. The subterranean room was pitch black, he liked it that way, but he had to move. Moving slowly through his small, windowless, quarters in the warehouse, he took his time searching for the light switch. Even in his groggy state he was able to find the damn thing, but not before stubbing the big toe on his right foot. Damn again. The light overhead cast a low amber tone over his bed where he'd fallen into a deep and grateful sleep. Lately, the voices in his head had become more numerous, almost unnerving at times, keeping him up later and later at night. He turned on the bedside lamp. More light added the chance of more attention paid to listening. Ah, here they came, the voices. "What? I don't understand." He listened for a response. "But Fritz is a comrade, my most trusted of all of them. No, I can't. I, what? Please don't make me do it."

Three floors above, final plans were coming together. Fritz held a meeting of his lead team. He had intended on having Kurt involved, but thought the better of it based on their last conversation, which wasn't a normal discussion, but rather a nonsensical, spittle-flinging rant by the one man who created the Cause. Fritz could not allow Kurt to come between him and the successful completion of the Reign's mission to destroy the Royal Family and those who blindly favored them.

The plan called for three compartmentalized groups designated by color to keep it simple. Red, Black and Blue. The groups were kept separated from one another in case of capture. If one group was caught they would not be able to expose the total plan, only their portion of it. The Red Group was mostly comprised of radicalized former infantry soldiers who had joined neo-Nazi organizations in Germany. They were directed to cause a wider distraction away from the races by setting off bombs in remote parts of London, just prior to the time of attack at the Ascot Races. Then, as the authorities responded, the Black Group, who will have blended into the race-going crowd, would set off flashbangs, smoke bombs and tear gas canisters that had all been buried on the race grounds months before to create pandemonium, and draw away the security forces protecting the Queen and her family. Finally, the Blue Group— a smaller unit made up of four operatives: two former special force snipers and their spotters—were assigned to kill selected members of the Royal Family amid the chaos.

There were no questions when Fritz finished summarizing the final plan to each team separately. The look of a successful leader crossed his face as his small army of terrorists disbursed. There was very little chatter as the 30 trusted souls headed for their segregated sleeping quarters as directed. Fritz wanted them to get a good rest before executing the most fateful assassinations in history. It was late afternoon, and except for some final preparations with weapons and explosive ordinance, the warehouse became a quiet sanctuary. That was about to change.

§

LONDON, UK; EN ROUTE TO LONDON CITY AIRPORT

Rick said his good-byes as he headed to the airport on one more special mission prior to leaving for the United States and home. Winston's secretary coordinated with Brenda. Together, they made special arrangements for Rick's trip home. He would begin his journey by flying out of London on the Lamperson private jet, a new Gulfstream that accommodated twelve passengers comfortably.

His destination brought back memories of only a short time ago, although it seemed like months instead of a few days. Rick found it hard to believe just how much had happened in his life since leaving California and his very regimented lifestyle. As the driver made the final turn into the private aviation facilities at Heathrow, Rick knew he was about to depart London a changed man. What he didn't know was what to expect from friends, family and his business associates, except for the Lampersons, especially Winston. This whole trip had been one of discovery thanks to the old Brit.

"Right this way Mister Blaine." Rick made his way through the newly remodeled airport, which reminded him of a science fiction spaceport. Everything was chrome and glass with marble floors and high ceilings. Rick didn't know what to expect as he walked into the large concourse, but it was nice to be led through such an overpowering rotunda. A young woman guided him to the tarmac. He excused himself to use the facilities before taking off. Once he returned they walked in bright sunlight to the gleaming, white with blue trim, aircraft. Rick was the only passenger and decided to sit at a small conference table during the flight. The young woman that escorted him onto the plane turned as she exited. "Enjoy your trip to Tunisia, Mister Blaine."

§

MI5 HEADQUARTERS, LONDON

Agent Salisbury met with her staff after dinner. They had been working on locating suspected warehouse locations. After just a few hours, they singled out three locations that were known to have been recently purchased or rented in the last year. Each facility was located in Brixton, and most importantly, one in particular, near a large park, was hidden from the main thoroughfares. "This one, we need to put eyes on this place, now." The place she referred to happened to be a short distance off of Dulwich Road.

§

LONDON, UK; THE REIGN COMPOUND

Miemke didn't like what Fritz suggested. Speeding up the timetable, because the British authorities were on to us, was absurd. Kurt could feel the reins slowly slipping away through his fingers. That, combined with the voices, was driving him mad. He took more Thoridazine pills. Soon they would take hold. He looked in his mirror over the dresser, who was that person? He suddenly realized he was morphing into a creature he didn't recognize.

Seeking to find a way to rid himself of the evil voices that grew stronger with each waking minute, he dressed and made his way up the stairway to the main floor of the warehouse. As he rose to the top of the stairs the voices inside his head gave way to Fritz's familiar deep-throated pentameter.

Fritz was in the midst of rallying the troops, delivering a message, no, his change in plan. Yes, he agreed with the voice, this was treason and needed to be dealt with immediately. Kurt looked around, he had to hide from what was being said. Fritz was moving too fast, his new plan could easily fail, and at the same time he was creating a coup. "Yesterday most of you witnessed Kurt Miemke breaking down. It's not unusual to assume that the man has had a tremendous weight thrown upon his shoulders for the past few years. It's unfortunate that just as we are culminating our plans to rid the world of royal authoritarian rule, his mind has become compromised. I want you to know that his situation will not deter our plans. The future is ours to take, and we will not be denied." The crowd of followers applauded and cheered at Fritz's last expression.

The voices began again, this time in earnest. Kurt put his hands over his ears, partly to cancel out what was being said by Fritz, and partly to shield the evil message he was now receiving inside his head.

In Kurt's mind, eliminating the royals was the beginning of change. The fall of the British Empire came next. But it would never happen using Fritz's plan, so it will not happen at all.

When the group dispersed and the main floor was basically empty, Kurt came out of hiding. He was very good at evading people, it was in the blood. He had backed himself into a closet, formerly used to keep the mops and brooms of past owners of the large structure. "I too have created a plan," he thought to himself, "A new idea, one that keeps ringing in my ears and does not need any approval. I see, now, that there is no other way to make a statement for my Cause."

§

LONDON, UK; BROCKWELL PARK

Outside the warehouse, off of Dulwich Road, a small force of a dozen heavily-armed MI5 counter-terrorism officers in full gear —helmets, protective field jackets, automatic rifles and night vision goggles – clustered in two groups in Brockwell Park, waited for Agent Salisbury's signal. Crawling on his belly through a grove of trees, a scout dressed in all black rounded the top of a mound and leveled his sniper rifle with an infrared FLIR scope attached at the structure. At first glance, the building appeared to be a vacant, with plywood boards blocking a clear view.

"Leader A this is Seeker, over," said the scout into his hands-free field radio.

"Seeker, this is Leader A, update?"

"I've got a full visual of the target. There are two guards patrolling on the west side. They appear armed but can't confirm. No other patrols. My FLIR scope shows a half dozen bogies inside, two on the top floor and four subterranean. I have a small visual through an open vent. Have eyes on vehicles and ordinance. There are rows of canisters that appear to be explosive devices, rocket launchers, and AK-47s, all stacked and ready for action."

The scout's report confirmed Salisbury's suspicions, beyond a shadow of doubt. "We found them."

"Hold your position, Seeker. Wait for further instructions, over."

"Roger."

§

LONDON, UK; LAMPERSON INTERNATIONAL HEADQUARTERS

Sir Archie received a call from one of his former Scotland Yard colleagues. The man had just been contacted by Agent Salisbury, who was on scene in Brixton. "Archie, they've surrounded the suspected headquarters of the Reign."

Winston hadn't witnessed movement like that from Sir Archie in a long time. The man was out the door, on his phone, yelling instructions. The team on the scene was to wait for any further action, until Archie arrived.

§

LONDON, UK; THE REIGN COMPOUND

Kurt followed the random flashes of voices that were now directing his actions. He understood how to attach the timing mechanisms to each of the six bombs he'd selected. After all, his background in the military service to his homeland was in explosive ordinance. One after another, the forty-pound canisters were placed strategically, one in each corner of the main level and two on the floor below, while everyone slept. The effort nearly did him in.

The second subterranean floor was where raw materials for bombs and munitions were kept. "Soon, this would be an exciting place, sparks and flames shooting in every direction," the voice whispered convincingly, as Kurt made his way to the firearms section. He armed himself with two automatic rifles and two hand guns, rounds of ammunition went into a backpack, along with grenades. Kurt didn't realize, of course, that the Seeker was watching his movements carefully.

"I'm not sure what exactly is going on inside, sir. It looks as if one person is gearing up, perhaps to launch an attack," said Seeker, adding, "Not sure how many others are involved, but except for a roaming guard, no one else seems to be moving inside."

Angela had to make a decision. She suspected that the terrorists found out about their presence on the outside and were preparing to fight, but it was odd that no one else was moving inside. A lone wolf? She ordered the Seeker to keep watch.

Sir Archie had called and said he was at least fifteen minutes away, directing a "lights only, no sirens" column of additional officers, ordinance and weapons. She decided to hold their position. It didn't appear there was any other way in or out, which was true, but they wouldn't sneak past Seeker's FLIR scope.

In a short amount of time, Kurt managed to turn the warehouse into a seismic bunker of explosives. He was sweating, out of breath, smiling as he sat on a stool by the side garage doors. One of the guards came in through a side door and saw Kurt sitting and talking to nobody that could be seen. The man thought it was strange to see anyone up this time of night, especially their Supreme Leader.

"Sir?" said the guard in an attempt to get his attention, but startled him instead.

Suddenly, Kurt swung one of his rifles around, ready to begin firing at one of his own. The thought made him smile, which, in turn, grew into a deep discharge of laughter. The guard froze for a few seconds, taking in the abnormal behavior of the leader.

The guard, dressed in a black one-piece Reign uniform with orange piping, carefully moved his right hand toward a remote panic button on his waistband.

Kurt had begun to twist and turn in place, still laughing until he saw the hand movement of the guard. "Stop now, or that will be your last effort!" Kurt shouted as he busily wiped his mouth, freeing it from the spital build-up that had been erupting.

Three things happened fast: First, an internal alarm system went off. It consisted of flashing lights and a low buzzing sound that ran throughout the building. Second, Kurt fired the rifle straight at the guard's chest, killing him instantly. Third, a second guard came running up the stairs into the room, only to be shot and killed.

Fritz ran up to Kurt, armed with a handgun. Kurt turned to face his most trusted follower. "You're not going to take this away from me!" he hollered as he gestured up and outward with his arms as if praising the place. "This is mine and will never be yours, Fritz."

Fritz slowly laid his gun on the floor, then stood back up, raising both hands into the air as he did so. A half-dozen or so followers stood waiting for orders. Each person held a steady aim at the Supreme Leader as he began to laugh once again. In his crazed state he looked around scanning the ground. In his hurry to confront the guards, he lost his remote detonator. The air in the large open space held a heavy scent of sweaty confusion. Fritz saw an opportunity and grabbed the man before he could do any more damage. The two men struggled until others helped to subdue Kurt, who now flew into a rage, causing the men to take him down to the concrete floor. As he laid there, sniffing dirt and tasting the pebbles matted into the oily surface, he spotted the remote, laying under a metal rack.

Sir Archie arrived at the growing Brockwell Park staging area with his small force made up of six special forces soldiers and six agents. The additional agents and officers were instructed to deploy along the west and southern perimeter, basically sealing off the warehouse facility's escape route. He turned to Agent Salisbury, "Bring me up-to-speed."

Agent Salisbury nodded to Leader A, who quickly explained, "Sir, we heard gunfire a few minutes ago at 1:30, coming from inside. We prepared for an attack, but that was not the case. There were shouts, but then nothing. We're not sure what's happening, sir, but our scout reported some sort of confrontation just occurred."

Archie thanked him.

"Hold your position for now and wait for further instructions," said Agent Salisbury.

Sir Archie signaled for his men to follow him.

Meanwhile, Ben sent out an alert to the local police authority. The alert was part of the community plan of action that would be put into motion wherever the Reign's headquarters happened to be located. Brixton citizens within a 2 kilometer radius of the warehouse, received a warning from officers as they rushed through the streets, ordering people to shelter in place and to stay off the streets. Roadblocks were set up by the police, who were now officially engaged in the late-night effort.

The small force, led by Sir Archie, spread out as they neared the garage doors on the west side of the building. A buzzing alarm could be heard, coming from inside.

Archie signaled for the men to drop to the ground as he and two soldiers continued along the side of the building until they came to an oversized entry door, adjacent to the first garage door. He had no idea what was going on inside and wondered why they'd been able to come this far without engagement. The three men hid behind four large, forty-four gallon drums stacked by the entry door. Archie radioed their position to Leader A, who waited for further instructions.

Inside the warehouse, time stopped. The two dozen members of the Reign's active force stood completely still, some trading glances back and forth, each with wrinkled brows and looks of concern. Fritz smelled fear and hated his old friend for whatever he was going through. He could not allow indecision to take hold, not now, not ever. The Reign had come too far to have its plans fall apart at this point. He pulled Kurt up, the older man's hands zip tied in front of him for his protection. Kurt could not stand, so his limp frame was held to a kneeling position on the floor. Hands gripped firmly on Kurt's collar and bending down close to the man's ear, Fritz whispered loud enough to be heard by those standing close by. Fritz spit furiously as he spoke. "I gave you every opportunity to lead. You have betrayed us."

Fritz tossed the man backward, landing hard against the floor. "Take him away and lock him in the storage room." The supreme leader resembled a rag doll as two men raised him up from the floor and headed to the storage area. As the trio passed by a large row of metal racks, Kurt collapsed to the floor.

Before his escorts could pick him back up, Kurt rolled to his stomach and snatched the remote detonator out from under the rack. He may have been having a mental breakdown, but remained focused enough to retrieve the remote. The guards were distracted by the response from those gathered around and didn't notice the quick grab. Keeping his hands closed, Kurt looked back over his shoulder as his followers now gathered around Fritz. The fallen leader knew what he had to do. He couldn't remember exactly how many C4 plugs he'd been able to attach to the pile of munitions neatly lined up in the middle of the warehouse. Six? Eight? It didn't matter. They were all wirelessly connected to the little remote he now held.

Once they locked him in the storage room, Kurt sat in somber silence contemplating his next move.

Chapter 12

LONDON, UK; THE REIGN COMPOUND

Sir Archie had to make a decision, and fast. He radioed Leader A who had officers in place on the perimeter. "Angela we're going in. We'll need you to move up and cover us. You make your advance once we open the garage doors, got it?"

"Roger that, sir," came her response. For Angela, this situation was different from the day-to-day street crime she'd become more accustomed to since joining law enforcement. When it came to dealing with terrorism, she would depend on the crash course she'd taken in MI5 training.

Archie urged her to think of terrorism as less of a crime and more of a war. "This will be a battle," he shared a few minutes earlier. Even though there hadn't been enough time for intel on exactly how many enemy soldiers or how much ordinance they controlled, their mission was a go. She watched in admiration, as Sir Archie prepared his men for battle. It was no wonder to her that the man adjusting the strap on his helmet was so revered. Archie's smaller group would be taking the lead with Leader A's contingent following.

Archie signaled his small force to move out, with a raised hand that suddenly thrust forward and down. Two men led the way, smashing through the side door next to the larger garage door with a battering ram.

Inside, the Reign members were caught completely off guard, as they had been distracted by the Supreme Leader's unexpected attack on its members. This meant the sophisticated surveillance system had been abandoned because the threat appeared to be internal. The timing couldn't have been worse for them.

As Archie's armor-laden men poured in through the door, covering one another with their weapons, shots rang out from two guards standing close by the door, hitting the first agent's Kevlar jacket in the chest, and sending him backwards to the ground. Wincing from pain, he managed to crawl to the side out of harm's way. Gunfire filled the air, scattering Reign followers as Archie's men returned fire. Two of the terrorists made their way to an elevated platform, with high-powered sniper rifles, in order to improve their firing position. The attacking troops below were too busy to notice as each sniper took aim. Each man was able to get off a shot, killing one soldier fighting next to Archie. Before either sniper could take another shot both were hit, first one then the other, with shots coming from behind. Seeker had the advantage on both snipers, which caused a tired smile to form as he collapsed his tripod and improved his position as ordered.

One of the attacking officers located the garage door control panel and pushed the green button. The door began to rise, signaling to the awaiting contingent to move out.

Fritz and two of his men were returning fire when something else caught his eye. One of the garage doors began to move upward. He grabbed a backpack that contained several rounds of ammunition, several hand grenades, and a handgun, and ran to one of the parked BMW's. The keys were in the ignition. After starting the car, he pushed the garage opener for the third bay, which faced straight out of the warehouse at a 90 degree angle to the door that was now completely open. The BMW accelerated out of the garage at a high rate of speed, narrowly eluding shots being fired from Archie's force. Once outside, Fritz turned onto a side road, rather than take the main driveway.

"Go, go from all positions," came the order from Leader A. Approximately fifty officers rushed forward from the front and two sides. Inside, the Reign followers did what they had been trained to do, fight to the last. The firefight grew in intensity as the Reign spread throughout the main floor of the warehouse.

Inside the storage room, Kurt rose to his feet the instant the firing began. We're under attack. Thoughts raced through his head like lightning flashes. Thunderbolts were careening back and forth as the relentless popping sounds of gunfire echoed over and over. He'd dropped the remote when he stood and put his ear to the storage room door. Retracing his steps, he picked the remote off the earthen floor. With tears forming in his tired eyes, he straightened his left arm out at a 45-degree angle and saluted the small window near the top of the storage room wall. Without any remorse, Kurt pushed the button activating the remote.

The explosion that came next blew out and up through the warehouse's main floor. Everything and everyone within the blast zone of a half a mile was affected, mostly by incineration and pieces of shrapnel. Sir Archibald Turlington and the twelve soldiers that accompanied him were feared lost because of their location at the time of the blast. Agent Salisbury and the fifty officers assigned to her, suffered a number of casualties due to flying debris from the concussion from the blast. "It was as if the warehouse became a rocket blasting off into outer space," a reporter stationed behind the outer perimeter was later quoted as saying.

§

LONDON, UK; LAMPERSON INTERNATIONAL HEADQUARTERS

Shortly after the news of the blast reached the Lamperson headquarters, Ben took a call on his mobile phone.

"This is Agent Salisbury. I'm not sure what caused the blast, Ben. We had no warning that this would happen."

Ben listened as an unbelievable tension filled his office. When Angela finished with her update, he asked. "Have you heard from Archie?"

The agent waited a few seconds, gathering herself before speaking. "We are not able to get close enough to the blast site to locate him or any of his men at this time. We fear the worst, Ben, because of the enormous amount of destruction involved."

Ben knew he had to contact his father immediately, and that Winston would want to go to the site of the explosion.

Chapter 13

TANGIER, MOROCCO; IBN BATTOUTA INTERNATIONAL AIRPORT

The city of London, witness to more than one cataclysmic event throughout the centuries, had one more to add to the list. The Reign's base of operations warehouse in Brixton created a 25 foot wide crater. The terror threat from the Reign appeared to be over as the amount of dead and wounded field agents, police and special forces continued to rise. The number of unaccounted for officers became a priority with Sir Archibald Turlington topping the list.

The terror threat had been kept secret from the public until now (with the exception of raising the terror threat color code up one level), which became top news when reporters discovered and exposed the direct threat the plot had to the Royal Family. BBC News reported the number of killed terrorists at twenty-three, which matched the master list provided by Herman Kruger. When interviewed by an investigative reporter, Herman could hardly contain himself as he broke down on live television. "I-I could have been there, in that warehouse with them. Oh God, what have I done?" The media spin on the matter portrayed the former public servant as a guilty hero of sorts. Eventually, Herman Kruger would be tried and convicted of treason. His sentence of twenty years seemed too harsh to those who questioned the funding of the monarchy. The media suggested that his conviction would be appealed, which made the story linger on the nightly news and in the tabloids.

Rick read about the Brixton explosion on his phone while waiting in the airport terminal in Tangier, Morocco. His thoughts went immediately to the man who taught him so much in such a short period of time. He had come to admire the older gentleman with the Scottish accent. Sir Archie had become a mentor to Rick in the last few weeks, as well as, helping to save his life in Italy. Rick wished he could have had one more conversation with the man who extended his knowledge base on how to use a service weapon and a knife. He looked up from his phone as he remembered one of the last things Archie told him: As you engage your future, watch your back. Rick contemplated those words as he waited. This last-minute detour to Tangier had come as another Winston surprise, but once he understood why, Rick was more than happy to help. After all, he was on his way home, and that felt good as he scanned the terminal perimeter, front and back. According to Winston, Jamal and a young boy, named Abbas, would be arriving soon.

§

TANGIER, MOROCCO; GRAND SOCCO MARKETPLACE

Abbas pushed back the covers earlier than usual that morning. Since joining Jamal's family, he'd been allowed to sleep in, helping him heal and recuperate. Abbas had decided that he felt much stronger and didn't need the extra sleep. Besides, his stomach growled; he couldn't wait to have breakfast, which was also a good sign.

It had been nearly a month since Abbas had been attacked. If it hadn't been for the old woman who found him lying in the gutter, he wouldn't have been able to make his way to Jamal's home that night. That was the second time she had touched his life. The first time was when she placed the roman coin in his hand, on that dark night, which seemed so long ago. "I have been watching you child, you are special, I'm here to help." She'd told him the night of the brutal attack.

Abbas dressed and hurried down the stairs heading to the now familiar kitchen where Jamal's coffee aroma tempted non-users like himself.

The old man had asked him a curious question the evening before, and the thought still lingered in his head as he skipped through the hall, putting one sandal on and then the other. Jamal wanted to know if the boy could live anywhere in the world, where would he go? Jamal followed the question up with what, if anything, Abbas knew about America? The boy, having watched visitors come to the Grand Socco, judged foreign countries by how tourists treated one another. By far, the Spanish and the Asians were very respectful. The British and the Germans were more serious, but the Americans definitely had more fun. He remembered a time when two American teenage boys invited him to play in an impromptu game of soccer, one day, when he was working at the spice stand with Jamal. With the old man's permission and a wide smile, Abbas joined the boys and played in a field nearby, for nearly an hour, under Jamal's watchful eye.

Abbas did not consider Jamal's questions serious, until he saw the faces of Jamal and his family. He slowed his pace as he entered the kitchen where Jamal, his wife, and their older daughter stood waiting. Jamal spoke as Abbas stopped in the doorway. "Good morning, Abbas. Please sit down, we have some good news for you.

Rick received an email from Brenda as he waited for Jamal's arrival at the terminal. He had relocated himself to a small area near the main entrance, so he could get a better view of the area. The email from Brenda was in response to the one he'd sent earlier. It was Brenda's birthday and Rick wanted her to know that he felt even better about leaving his company in the capable hands of a, now, older woman. The response he received came in the form of a laughing emoji and one sentence: "It is said that age and wisdom grace women more naturally than men—I agree."

She also mentioned the bouquet of flowers he'd sent in a follow-up email, which also had an attachment of a meeting agenda due to happen the second day after he arrived home. Rick smiled as he read her email. He was about to open the attachment when he noticed two people, a man he recognized, Jamal, walking with a young man.

"Meester Blaine, good to see you again," said Jamal with a smile.

After a brief introduction, the three of them walked through the main terminal to the general aviation wing where the Lamperson private jet sat waiting. The two pilots had just finished breakfast and headed to the plane when they saw Rick. The flight plan called for them to fly to Lisbon where Rick and Abbas would then catch a Delta flight that would take them straight to San Francisco.

Ben Lamperson made the arrangements and cleared them with Brenda. The two of them had been working closely together to make sure Rick and Abbas would have no issues while traveling together. That included obtaining a special clearance for Abbas, who would travel under a special visa allowing him to enter the United States under the veil of an alien looking for asylum. Abbas would eventually connect with Jamal's brother-in-law in Los Angeles.

Abbas, who was used to being in much more control of his life, having taken care of his fellow tribe of artful dodgers in the Grand Socco, now found himself becoming a passenger in life—literally—at least for the time being.

Abbas welcomed the new adventure as he and Rick began their journey north to Lisbon aboard a sleek jet aircraft. It was a first for the former orphan of the tourist-infested sanctuary, as Jamal referred to all the children that ran through the Grand Socco with no family connections. For Abbas, that life with the others had been slowly fading since Jamal and his wife took him in and treated him as one of their own. But no matter where he would end up in life, those young ones that once depended on Abbas, remained with him. Etched in his heart, their faces clear and bright. They were part of him, a part that he would build on as he faced a future that seemed to be fast approaching. That feeling continued as the plane he was buckled into began to taxi down the tarmac.

§

LONDON, UK; LAMPERSON INTERNATIONAL HEADQUARTERS

Sitting in his London office going over the details of what had happened two nights before in Brixton, Ben received confirmation on his mobile that Rick and Abbas were taking off. He couldn't believe what had happened to Archie and the two dozen other officers that were killed that night—vaporized in the massive blast. The terror threat from the Reign had yet to be fully analyzed, while authorities methodically dug their way through the wreckage of the warehouse, hoping to find more evidence related to the terrorist group.

So far, they'd been able to identify three people of interest: Kurt Miemke, a known white supremacist leader with a criminal history; a white male whose burned body was found inside a car he'd been driving; and a German national named Fritz Waller, who Herman had identified as his recruiter and possibly one of the Reign's leaders—he had escaped from a British jail several years ago with two other inmates.

Winston remained in London, working with British authorities to ensure that the Royal Family was safely guarded during the follow-up investigation. He dropped all other business in lieu of making plans regarding Sir Archie's funeral. A meeting would be scheduled in the coming days with the Queen, who wanted to be personally involved. Winston called each of Archie's three children, all of whom were married and living in various parts of Scotland. He eventually contacted their mother, who divorced Archie a decade ago. The two had grown apart, but remained on friendly terms. Archie had nothing but praise for the woman he called a saint.

§

TANGIER IBN BATTOUTA AIRPORT – GENERAL AVIATION TERMINAL

Rick sat across from a young man he didn't know, checking the flight plan that will take them from Morocco to Portugal and on to San Francisco their final destination. The adolescent was dressed in tan khakis, white tennis shoes, a blue tee with a blue hoodie. His complexion was not as dark as Jamal's, more of a light tan, about the same shade as the new pair of pants he wore. Rick's young charge was excited about being on a plane for the first time. He had always seen planes flying low over the Strait of Gibraltar as they approached Tangier's airport, but he had never dreamed of being up close to one, let alone on one. Abbas imagined that he had just walked into a beautiful cave-like room. The scent of leather blended with food smells as both overtook the heavy odor of jet fuel. White leather seats, soft and comfortable, were trimmed in gold that extended throughout the cabin that was also lined in dark wood. The lighting came from above with the push of a button. The boy showed signs of bewilderment when he pressed another button causing a light to go on at the sound of a ping and an onboard steward to approach and ask if there was anything he could get for him. Abbas returned the man's smile, but was at a loss as to what to do next, so Rick leaned over and asked for a lunch of mixed fruits, meats and cheeses.

Winston had assured Rick that Jamal saw great potential in Abbas and had put himself on the line to help the young lad. Winston also mentioned that Jamal was such a critical link in the chain of espionage that he had developed over the years, so he owed him greatly. Helping out with Abbas was the least he could do for a trusted friend.

"So, Abbas, how old are you?"

"Twelve in years, sir," Abbas replied in clear English. His blond hair led Rick to believe that Abbas was mixed, which only added to his handsome features.

Rick became more interested in the favored orphan boy who had helped somehow in Jamal's scheme to code the disks sent to London.

By the time the plane was on final approach for landing in Madrid, Abbas had answered one question after another, between long looks out the port side window. He couldn't get enough of seeing the Atlantic Ocean from such a height. Rick traded seats with Abbas, half way through the flight, so that

Abbas could look out the starboard side of the plane, allowing him to see the incredible landscape with mountains, rivers and cities along their route.

"Your English is very good, Abbas."

Before Rick could ask how he learned the language Abbas added, "I know seven languages, sir, mostly because of talking to tourists." From an early age, Abbas, admitted that he had been hustling American and British tourists, which had given him a good grasp of the English language, among others. He had to find a way to engage the public or die of starvation. Rick nodded his head and sat back, allowing Abbas to continue to look out his new window to a world that was becoming larger by the second. Above the hum of the engines, there was silence in the cabin while the two passengers contemplated the ride.

Abbas broke the silence with a question. "Mister Blaine, may I ask what it is that you do?" Rick explained his role in Blaine Manufacturing and the fact that he was on a business trip, doing a favor for a friend who knew Jamal. The multi-lingual guest sat back after Rick finished. He had a smile on his face as if he had an idea to share. "What is it, Abbas?"

"Mister Blaine, I know two things from what you just said. One, your name is the same as the company you work for, so you must be very important. Two, you also had something to do with the information that Jamal sent to his friend in London. I hear things and keep them in my mind." Abbas's smile widened as he watched the plane begin to descend further toward landing in Lisbon.

§

SILICON VALLEY, CA; BLAINE MANUFACTURING

Brenda busied herself, finishing details on plans the whole company prepared for Rick's return. All of a sudden it was as if she had a million things to do before he arrived on campus in two days.

The plan was for Rick to come into San Francisco tomorrow morning, rest up and come in the following day. Her "to do" list would have to wait for at least an hour. She intended to celebrate her birthday with some friends at lunch. As she exited her office, which had become a floral shop with none other than six beautiful arrangements, the scent from the flowers was almost overwhelming. She stopped for an instant next to two of the largest floral gifts, one from Rick the other from Ben Lamperson. Of all of the bouquets, Ben's was the largest. White roses competed with big blue hydrangeas that stood proudly together in a beautiful cut crystal vase.

She waved to her assistant while exiting gracefully with her usual big smile. Birthdays were always a big deal at Blaine and Brenda was known to be a surprise instigator. So, when the elevator doors opened to Major Connors and two members of the management team holding huge bouquets of blue balloons, her favorite color, she was more pleased than surprised. "What is going on?" she asked with one hand covering her mouth.

Brenda laughed as she entered past more balloons than an elevator should be able to hold. On the way down to the first floor, she had to laugh with the others as they sang their rendition of Happy Birthday, which included Major's deep, deep baritone voice. "That was awesome, everyone. Thank you, again." She gave Major Connors a hug as she left for the parking garage. Brenda didn't expect a balloon-holding entourage, but that's what she received, all the way to her car.

§

SOMEWHERE OVER THE ATLANTIC

Abbas could not believe the size of the aircraft he and Rick were enjoying. Rick always rode in business class, so Abbas had the royal treatment the entire way. The size of the private jet Abbas and Rick had taken to Lisbon seemed huge, so when he saw the Boeing 787 Dreamliner he stared at it in stunned silence. This plane felt bigger than the Grand Socco's main mosque.

As luck would have it, one of the stewards was from North Africa. The man enjoyed the fact that Abbas understood his dialect and was able to converse with him without skipping a beat. "Your son is very good with language." Both Rick and Abbas quietly laughed at the steward's comment, raised their shoulders upward at the same time, tilted their heads left and right and high-fived each other. The man had moved along, so there was no correcting his understandable mistake. Rick thought it best just let it go. He looked over at Abbas, stretched out completely with his feet under the blanket fast asleep. The steward had helped him figure out his sleeping arrangement. They were both exhausted and soon the hum of the engines overtook all conversations as the Boeing 787 slipped through the starry, starry night.

§

SILICON VALLEY, CA; BLAINE MANUFACTURING

Bobby "the Bear" Hansen met with his surveillance crew regarding Blaine Manufacturing. One of his newest recruits, a young, former Marine, asked if he could speak in private. The two met at a Starbucks located a block away from Bear's office in a small industrial park on the outskirts of San Jose.

After ordering, the two sat at a bistro table near the restroom in the back. "What's up, Jimmy?" Bear asked, sensing something was wrong.

James Sandrow explained that he had a girlfriend who worked at Blaine. "She said that some of the women employees have noticed a black SUV parked close to the campus on several occasions. The driver appears to be taking pictures or using binoculars to watch people on the Blaine campus."

Bear asked Jimmy for his girlfriend's name and made a call to set up a meeting that day. Before they left, Jimmy had one more thing to add: "One of the Blaine employees said they thought the driver had a passenger in the backseat."

The two men made their way back to Hansen Investigations. It was still early, seven a.m., and Jimmy headed to his apartment after working the night shift, Bear sent a message to Brenda and Ralph Phillips. "We need to extend surveillance hours at Blaine. Will conference call. What time works for you two?"

Bear had taken his 6x6 Patriot Jeep Camper in for a maintenance check and had been using Rick's vintage Porsche for the last two days. He had an hour to be in Sonoma for an appointment, normally an hour and half drive. Bear smiled and placed his dark glasses over his black skull cap then fired up the Porsche. He brought the seat all the way back in order to fit into Rick's Ride and Pride, as Bear liked to call it. The 1975 turbo driven, Army green 911 kissed the wall of a tunnel earlier in the year, resulting in some serious frontend repair. Bear supervised the rebuild at Rick's request. "The man knows his machines and I'd like him to take care of mine." Bear came through for Rick, so Rick made the car available to him any time he needed a ride. The big man wasted no time hitting I-5 and making his way north, making his appointment with a few minutes to spare.

§

SILICON VALLEY, CA

Lorretta wasn't getting the answers she needed - so she drank. Drinking had become her second obsession, Rick Blaine being the first. She wanted the man to suffer as she had, because of Michael's death. The soldiers she'd put in place to devise a plan of action that would take out Blaine Manufacturing had failed her. In her mind, the plan was simple, BLOW THE PLACE UP! One of her most trusted people, Enzo, a former lover and MMA fighter, had come to try and settle her down.

"Signora, we will soon have an idea for you to consider regarding Rick Blaine and his company. We've only been working on this for two weeks, we need to make sure no trace of blame can reach back to you or your company. That takes time. Give us a few more days, I assure you, the man will suffer."

Lorretta enjoyed the moment with the tall, muscular Enzo and his tattoos. She relaxed, listening to his soft Italian accent. It was the voice that attracted her to him the first time, before Michael. Blah, blah, blah, what was he saying? It didn't matter. Still dressed in her pajamas, she started walking toward the dark curly haired man who appeared to be backing away. It's a curse I have with men. It wasn't as if he hadn't seen her dressed like this before, the woman looked sexy in whatever she wore.

Enzo began to get aroused and thought it best to leave before he embarrassed himself. He raised his arms overhead in order to put his jacket on when Lorretta made her final approach and landed her right hand on his crotch, looking him straight in the eyes. She smiled, erasing all thoughts of Michael and Rick Blaine, at least for the moment. Enzo was here in front of her and so strong and getting stronger. Lorretta took his hand and led him to her bedroom where she would make sure they both felt some relief.

§

SAN FRANCISCO, CA; SAN FRANCISCO INTERNATIONAL AIRPORT

Rick and Abbas made their way from the plane, the boy with his backpack securely fastened, including the chest strap. He made sure all the pockets were zipped tight, because the backpack contained everything he owned, even a pair of old sandals. The sandals were a reminder of a life he thought he would live in forever. Thoughts of his former life soon dissipated as they entered the main terminal in San Francisco.

Abbas found himself being jostled back and forth in a river of people rushing to and from various locations called; "Gates." He looked back over his shoulder as Rick checked his phone for messages. Abbas wanted to make sure he didn't lose sight of Rick and drown in the mass of people. They headed toward the baggage area after going through customs. Rick urged Abbas to be careful on the moving stairway. Suddenly they were on the first step of the escalator moving down, exhilarating for the boy from the tourist-infested market who looked back and smiled at Rick as they descended.

Outside, Bear pulled up in his recently serviced Jeep 6x6, causing heads to turn and cars to head out or pull up to make room. "That is one awesome machine," one curb attendant exclaimed as Bear opened the back, preparing for his passengers. Bear smiled at the man as he checked his phone for a message from Rick. "We're in line at customs, should be out in 10."

A man with a pony tail, a Hawaiian shirt, and sandals walked up and asked Bear how many miles to the gallon he got for the rig. Bear could tell from the man's posture he was about to get a lecture, so he looked at the man with dead eyes and told him he didn't care and neither should anyone else. The annoying man looked determined to continue the conversation, but just then, Bear heard Rick call his name. Thank goodness, Bear thought as he smiled and walked towards Rick and his young companion.

"So, you finally bought something that fit!" said Rick, laughing as he and Bear hugged.

"Who's this?" Bear pointed at Abbas with a big smile. Rick introduced his companion who seemed to be among a gathering group of admirers beginning to assemble around the monster Jeep. "We better get out of here before I have to start giving tours of my new rig, here."

Bear loaded the two suitcases as Abbas and Rick made their way up and into the ride.

"Strap in kid," said Bear as he shifted the Jeep into gear.

Abbas looked at the man called Bear, who returned the boy's frightened look with a smile, and did as he was told. The strap was a little more complicated from the one he used on the plane, he managed to snap the buckle and they were off.

Brenda had forwarded an email to Bear that Rick had sent regarding his young companion. "So, Abbas, do you have family in America?"

The young man could hardly sit still in the backseat, moving his head back and forth from side window to side window. "Yes, yes, I have a sponsor family living in Los Angeles."

Rick explained that Jamal, a man he'd come to know in Morocco, had relatives who immigrated from Tunisia five years earlier. "Jamal's sister and husband have three children, Abbas's new family." There was more discussion about plans to have Abbas attend school, but for now he would be spending a few days in San Jose then driving down to Venice Beach with Rick.

Abbas's senses were on overload. There was so much happening in his life all of sudden, beginning with jet aircraft and currently the Jeep ride. Abbas just recently became proficient at driving an ox cart; he'd never ridden in an automobile, let alone an oversized one that appeared to be flying over the road.

Bear decided to take a more scenic route from the airport. Abbas enjoyed the sights. He couldn't believe all the water surrounding San Francisco. When they reached the Golden Gate Bridge Abbas nearly lost his breath as they made their way across to the other side and ending up in Tiburon at Rick's apartment. He had never seen a structure like this before and wondered if a bridge would ever be built across the 8-mile-wide Straits of Gibraltar to connect Morocco to Spain.

Both Rick and Abbas were tired from the trip and crashed after Bear dropped them off at Rick's apartment. The next day Rick and Abbas woke up early due to jet lag and walked the main street in Sausalito. They ate breakfast at one of Rick's favorite oceanside restaurants that looked out over San Francisco Bay. Rick acted as a tour guide and the young man soaked up all that Rick was telling him about the history of the area. After explaining their schedule for the next few days, which included a tour of the Blaine campus and a drive down the coast to Rick's condo in Venice Beach, Abbas had a comment. "You, sir, have many dars to keep track of, is that so?" Rick laughed and nodded his head, knowing that a dar was a house where Abbas came from. "I hope to someday have a dar of my own."

Rick looked at the boy as their plates were being cleared and suggested: "Well, California has plenty of dars to choose from, I believe you'll do just fine."

Rick watched Abbas with admiration. The boy, who would be a teenager soon, seemed to absorb and remember everything he was told. He put his hand on Abbas's shoulder as they left the restaurant. "Let's go this way, I want to show you the harbor."

Even though Rick was anxious to catch up with everyone at Blaine, he enjoyed his time with Abbas. After spending the morning sightseeing and shopping, primarily for clothes for Abbas, Rick called Brenda and asked her to move his company meeting to the following day. He explained that he needed more time before returning, which Brenda understood completely.

"Is Abbas still with you or has he been turned over to his sponsor family?" She asked knowing that her boss was probably having a good time showing the boy around.

"Oh, ah, no. He's still with me. I'm going to, ah, contact them just before we drive down to Venice Beach on Friday. We'll be in tomorrow to say hi. Are you going to be around in the afternoon?"

Before Brenda could answer yes, she could hear a young man's voice in the background urging Rick to hurry up. It was obvious the two were taking the Alcatraz harbor tour cruise by the time Rick ended the call.

§

SILICON VALLEY, CA; BLAINE MANUFACTURING

Brenda sat for a moment, after the call, and wondered what it would be like for Abbas to suddenly find himself in a completely different part of the world. She couldn't imagine what was going through his mind at that moment, but she knew one thing, he was with someone who would make the experience exciting. She left her office heading to the boardroom and a production meeting. She couldn't shake the feeling that Abbas wasn't the only person aboard that flight whose life was changing.

Chapter 14

SILICON VALLEY, CA; BLAINE MANUFACTURING

Rick and Abbas entered the serpentine drive of the Blaine Manufacturing campus around 1:30 PM in a very special ride. Of all the vehicles that Abbas had been buckled into in the last four days, Rick's vintage Porsche had to be the most exciting. Small and powerful, the car moved the young man along the roadway like nothing he had felt before. "These are buildings that belong to you, sir?"

Rick nodded his head as they pulled up to the guard gate. "Hello, Mister Blaine, welcome back, sir." The guard was new and recognized Rick by the badge he presented. Still it was impressive enough for Abbas to hear confirmation that this place really did belong to the man driving next to him. He even had his own police!

The elevator voice came out of nowhere, causing Abbas to look up and around and then to Rick—who smiled watching the boy's bewilderment—for an explanation. After a few binging sounds, the voice announced the sixth floor as the doors opened to marble floors and a lobby entrance outlined in glass and metal. Letters spelling out the name Blaine Manufacturing were on the wall above a long wooden bar and a young lady began to stand as they walked up. "Mister, Blaine. Welcome back!"

Rick returned the greeting as a woman came out of a large glassed-in office. She walked slowly and looked very important to Abbas. He stood back as she approached. Her smile revealed a perfect row of white teeth, which was hard to come by in Tunisia. She opened her arms to give Rick a big hug. "Brenda, it's good to be back."

So, this was the Brenda that Rick spoke with yesterday.

Brenda turned her attention to Abbas. "And you must be Abbas. I've heard good things about you, young man."

Abbas could feel his face throbbing, a new feeling. He wanted to say something, but couldn't. What would he say to such a nice and beautiful lady? He stood a little closer to Rick, who reached around and placed an arm on his shoulder as the two were ushered into Brenda's office. Abbas appreciated the added support Rick gave him as his legs had suddenly forgotten what they were intended to do.

"Check out the flowers. Did someone have a birthday recently?" Rick was kidding of course; he'd sent flowers for Brenda's big day. There were two bouquets that stood out and were placed directly behind Brenda's desk, one slightly larger than the other. Brenda noticed Rick checking out the tags. "Thank you for the flowers, you really didn't have to with all you had going on, Rick."

Rick turned from the larger bouquet with a quizzical look on his face. "Oh, the large one over there, that's from Ben, Lamperson." Brenda's face suddenly reddened. With a big grin, Rick couldn't help himself but tease her: "Ben? That's great, Brenda. When did this happen?"

"You're getting ahead of yourself, mister. We're just friends."

Rick could feel the vibe from where he was standing, but saved any further comment for another time when they were alone. Rick would have fun talking with Ben about flowers.

They had a young visitor who required some special attention. Abbas had wandered off while Brenda was quickly catching Rick up on some important matters. He stood looking out over the newly expanded footprint of Blaine Manufacturing's campus. The place had expanded from two to six buildings over the last decade, but Abbas didn't know that and Rick didn't focus on the ten-year history of Blaine. Rick pointed out the two new buildings that were near completion before he went on his trip just over a month ago. Now that construction had been completed, the campus included new greenbelt walkways, two fountains, and a large employee gathering area for lunch and breaktime. Around the side of the new production building, an employee climbing wall had been constructed. It had a specially designed frame that allowed for climbers to be safely belayed while ascending and descending up to forty feet. Abbas remained mesmerized while watching two climbers scaling the wall. Continuing to look out the window, he asked Rick: "Are they trying to escape?"

His comment, serious as it was, made both Brenda and Rick chuckle at the boy's innocence. Brenda explained that the wall was for employee recreation. She then added; "It was his idea, not mine," pointing at Rick, who looked at the boy and shrugged his shoulders.

"Would you like to try it, Abbas?" The boy's eyes lit up at the idea. Brenda stepped forward, arms folded, facing the boy. "Why don't we keep your feet on the ground for now. She looked at Rick and said that Billy, the chief of security and father of six, was going to take Abbas for a tour while she and Rick met for a briefing; she needed to cover some agenda items that would be discussed at tomorrow's company meeting.

Billy greeted Abbas at the front desk. As the two entered the elevator, Abbas asked if they could go out to watch the people on the climbing wall. His second question was in regard to the lady who lived in the moving room, the voice. Jimmy looked back at Rick, who simply raised his shoulders as if he didn't know what the kid was talking about. Brenda pressed her lips tight, trying her best not to laugh as rolled her eyes, looking up at the ceiling, as she led Rick into his office.

§

SAN JOSE, CALIFORNIA

Two tanker trucks moved silently down I-680 like two silver colored snakes with black heads slithering through the night. Their final destination yet to be revealed, but for the time being they enter the newly constructed Petrula Trucking warehouse property. The site became available after a small auto freight company was convinced to merge with Petrula Trucking after a hastily arranged meeting with Lorretta Petrula and several of her lieutenants three weeks ago.

Lorretta received the confirmation text just before midnight. She'd been waiting anxiously. "We're one step closer," she whispered to herself. Tanker trucks were not normally part of her inventory, but Lorretta Petrula had a special assignment for these particular rigs.

Midnight was her favorite time of day. She had dismissed Enzo hours ago. Good boy she thought as she lit another cigarette and poured a double scotch. She walked out onto her condo's veranda wearing a see-through negligee with a soft white feathery boa wrapped around her neck. The cool breeze against her body made her tingle. The scotch warmed her just enough to remain standing by the iron railing as she enjoyed the lights piercing the darkness. Although she missed her home in Boston, she had a special feeling for the west coast now. Lorretta was on a mission, one that would end soon enough. As she stood admiring the view, she couldn't help but think of him, Michael. "I will always love you," she murmured into her glass of scotch.

§

SILICON VALLEY, CA; BLAINE MANUFACTURING

The next morning, Brenda sat looking out over the newly constructed production facility as she sipped her latte. Thoughts of how much time Rick put into perfecting the coating process and how much that hard work contributes to Blaine's business, made her feel proud. It took several years, but Blaine Manufacturing's team of scientists and engineers developed a proprietary blend of highly flammable liquid used in the coating process of various products. They were first used on pads and covers that served as protection for a number of electronic devices: Laptops, computers, cellphones and image projectors. Once Blaine expanded their product offerings to include specialty designed backpacks, wallets, and panniers for bicycles, an idea that Rick developed with his production team in the last year, the volume of chemical coatings increased. Blaine's new product line had become a favorite with the outdoor enthusiasts, a new market for the company.

Tanker trucks carrying these coating chemicals were now making frequent stops at Blaine. So much so, that the new production facility had an extended driveway constructed to speed up the safe delivery with the addition of a separate guard gate, and three additional supervisors watching over the process.

Lorretta and Enzo sat in the back of the black SUV as it drove past the new Blaine production facility. The SUV was headed for a parking lot a block away where they could sit and watch as the two new Petrula Trucking tanker trucks made their way into the new complex at Blaine. Lorretta smiled while peering through a small pair of binoculars as her trucks took their turn at delivering, flawless and dependable. She snacked on some sushi take out – it was lunch time and they planned to be there a good part of an hour.

Petrula Trucking had just received approval as a licensed carrier. They monitored the rehearsal run for the double-trailered rigs as they moved along the drive, heading to the transfer port. Enzo timed the movement of the trucks from the guard gate to actual unloading of the fuel. Lorretta watched the man as he meticulously made notes as the trucks completed their deliveries. He looked up and smiled as she turned and looked at the two trucks as they drove off. Lorretta whispered toward the SUV window, "Too bad those new, very expensive, beautiful trucks will be blown to pieces next week."

She was referring to both of their new investments. An expense her father, and his group, would've never allowed. Her plan—Enzo's really—was to have both rigs pull up to the transport disbursement areas at the same time next week, just as they did today. Both drivers would leave their vehicles, as per usual, and connect the hoses, under Blaine supervision, in order to initiate the off-loading process, which normally took thirty to forty minutes. The drivers would immediately set the two bombs to detonate on command, each located in the cab behind the driver's seat. Both bombs contained enough C-4 to blow each rig apart, which would also trigger the explosion of the fuel being off loaded. The C-4 had to be installed properly in each container in order for the blast direction to do its job. If the blast went straight up and forward there was a chance that the chemical tanks would not ignite. The blast flow had to move backward and out, which caused Enzo some sleepless nights. He had gone over the diagram of the bomb more than once, and had three days to finalize his detonation plan.

In that time, he would check the bomb container's wiring connections, install them in the trucks, and set the remote control for detonation. He wanted to drive the second truck, but Lorretta would have none of it. "Find someone else, pretty boy. Your ass is with me."

His plan called for the drivers to move away from the trucks once the offloading began and move out of camera range. At that point, they would leave the campus. Once they reached the roadway, the drivers would then detonate the bombs. The result should send a rolling ball of flame down and into the chemical holding tanks located below Blaine's new production facility.

By that time both drivers would be picked up and long gone, but not the employees of Blaine Manufacturing. Both trucks were scheduled to arrive at 1 PM. Lorretta patiently listened as Enzo repeated the timeline to her. All she cared about was causing so much havoc and destruction that Rick Blaine would suffer a tremendous loss and, hopefully, his life and the lives of people he cared about most. She couldn't wait, having planned this attack for the last two weeks. She perked up when she heard Ivan begin to speak. "I will be stationed across from the Blaine campus using a spotting scope to watch for Mister Blaine. The rifle I use has long range capability, so if he is in his office or walking outside, I will see him and make the kill."

When they returned to the Petrula Trucking facility, Lorretta made sure that the two trucks being used in the explosion contained nothing to trace back to her company. For all intents and purposes, the manifests for each truck read: MC Trucking headquartered in New Jersey. The MC was in honor of her beloved Michael Castillino.

§

VENICE BEACH, CA

Rick relaxed alone in one of the most soothing places in the world: his condo in Venice Beach. He looked forward to getting back into his old groove, making regular weekend trips south from Tiburon and San Jose to his beach life. Each trip sent him into a different world, one of carefree living and hanging with friends. The trip down south also gave him time to think, while he challenged the ribboned asphalt of Highway 1 in his Porsche.

On this latest trip he made sure not to road race, choosing to change the tempo and act as tour guide for his passenger. "You see this tunnel coming up?" Abbas nodded. "There's a visitor spot on the other side that I'm familiar with, we'll stop for a few minutes so you can soak up the scenery, it's beautiful." Rick took his time with the young newcomer. The longer he spent with the kid, the more he understood what Jamal saw in him: potential.

He had just returned from taking Abbas to meet Jamal's sister, Shamir, and his brother-in-law, Harood, and their three children, two girls, both older than Abbas, and a son who was half Abbas's age. Shamir taught school in nearby Upton, and Harood was a civil engineer who owned a small construction company.

They met in a park and soon the children were off playing as Rick, Shamir, and Harood sat and ate a picnic lunch. Harood had prepared some questions that pertained mainly to who Rick was, Shamir's questions focused on Abbas. Evidently, Jamal had filled them in on Abbas's background, which they seemed perfectly happy with, but wanted to know how the boy came across to Rick. After less than an hour, they were ready to make a smooth transition. Rick reminded them that he'd known Abbas for a few days, but had quickly become extremely impressed with him. He assured them that, as far as he was concerned, Abbas was ready to make the adjustment into a new life; he had an uncanny ability to absorb new material. Rick gave them a few examples of Abbas's reaction to flying and riding in cars that made them laugh.

As they watched the children play, Rick noticed Abbas look over more than once at the table where the adults sat eating. He even waved as if to send a message to Rick that he was alright. When Rick saw the boy's smile, he felt it was time to take his leave. Time to go, a feeling that Rick was becoming all too familiar with these days.

As Rick rose to leave, he handed Shamir and Harood an envelope that contained documents that outlined the details of a trust account set up in Abbas's name. The contents could be read at another time and he told them so. The trust would provide enough money for Abbas' upbringing and a college education. Shamir looked Rick in the eye and graciously thanked him for all he had done for Abbas. "We will take good care of him, Rick. Inshallah, maybe one day you two will meet again. God is great, my friend."

Rick said good-bye to Harood and Shamir and wished them well. He gave Harood his contact information and told him to call anytime if he needed anything. He then walked over to say good-bye to the boy he had come to know only recently.

"You are leaving now, Rick?"

"Yes, but Harood has my information and knows how to contact me."

Abbas and Rick shook hands and Rick pulled him close as they both laughed. "You will be fine, Abbas. I have no doubt you will enjoy your new life."

Abbas didn't say anything more; he just stood back and nodded as his new American friend turned and walked away.

§

SILICON VALLEY, CA; HANSEN INVESTIGATIONS

Bear sat in his office going over the surveillance reports on Blaine Manufacturing. Something didn't feel right as he read through the eleven-page document. He took another sip of coffee, his drink-of-choice since giving up alcohol three years ago. The more Bear read, the greater his concern grew, especially after what his contacts heard on the street. His intel guys heard that the Castillino clan had a plan to kill Rick and disrupt his business. The Castillinos had made one attempt for Rick in North Africa, a few weeks ago. Shortly after that, Michael Castillino was killed in a failed attempt to kill Rick in northwestern Italy. Bear leaned back in his office chair, hands folded to his chin. He let out a deep sigh. It was clear to him that it was only a matter of time before Rick and his company would be targeted again in the near future.

The reports indicated two current concerns. First, a black SUV had been spotted near the Blaine campus on several occasions over the past two weeks, both day and night. Second, there were now two new guard gate locations that increased access to the area. The gate allowed tanker trucks to enter the campus and offload highly flammable petrochemicals. Both points bothered Bear, but the second one caused his military mind to work overtime. He began to think from a terrorist perspective, and the results were frightening. He picked up his phone. Brenda didn't answer, so he left her a voicemail. "Brenda, we need to meet. You, Rick and your head of security, right away."

After the call, Bear left his office and made his way to an editing bay, in a back area, where one of his technical people was going over the last month's security video of the entire Blaine campus. "How's it going Nigel?" The man had been working most of the day, meticulously looking for any improprieties that would appear to be unusual. "I've noticed two places where Blaine's security could be breached; the production facility guard gate during the night has one less guard, leaving one person to control the entry and exit of each delivery. And the windows on the sixth floor of the main building. They don't have blinds like the other floors do, leaving them open to sniper fire."

Bear made a note and would bring both points up at his requested meeting with Brenda and Rick. "Good work, Nigel. Watch for the black SUV we discussed and report to me if you spot it again." Bear left the building and headed for the Blaine campus. He planned to do some surveilling of his own for a couple of hours, in addition to the team already on duty there.

§

SILICON VALLEY, CA; BLAINE MANUFACTURING

Rick drove up from Venice Beach early the next morning. He arrived an hour before the meeting with Bear. As he walked past Brenda's office, he noticed her standing next to the largest of her birthday bouquets, sniffing the flowers with her eyes closed.

"That wasn't the one I sent you, is it?" ask Rick as he poked his head into her office.

Brenda looked startled—and possibly a little embarrassed—as she stepped away from smelling the extremely fragrant floral arrangement. "Oh…morning, Rick. I…I've never had so many thoughtful gifts, especially this one." Rick held his smile, but he could not back off from pursuing the moment with Brenda. He entered Brenda's office turning his head from side to side until she stopped and looked him square in the face. "What?" Brenda softly uttered as her brow wrinkled over a sweet smile. Rick had to know as he reached over and read the card on the bouquet she'd just walked away from. Rick spoke in a low carefully worded manner.

"Am I to assume there might be some spark of romance included in Ben's gift?" Rick smiled as he walked slowly toward Brenda. She looked at the bouquet as if it were solid gold and then quickly back at Rick. She led him over to two red leather chairs sitting in front of her desk. They both sat down without looking at the chairs.

"Ben and I have developed a special friendship in the last few weeks, since you left," Brenda explained as if she were convincing herself. Rick said nothing as silence filled the room. Then Brenda offered more. "There might be something there, we'll see."

Rick sat back in the chair and looked over his shoulder back at one of the largest groupings of flowers he'd ever seen. "I'm no expert, Brenda, but judging from the size of Ben's present, I'd say he has feelings for you." Rick reached over and took hold of Brenda's hands and moved closer. "Either that or… maybe the florist sent the wrong arrangement." Brenda immediately let go of Rick's hands and punched him a good one his right shoulder. "Ouch, that hurt," Rick stood as they both burst into laughter. "Very funny, Rick." "Hey, I'm happy for you, for both of you. Ben's a great guy."

Brenda stood and hugged Rick, a person who has always believed in her. As Rick started to leave, he turned and offered one more thought. "Oh, and by the way, thanks for having my back as I traveled. I'm not sure what I would have done without you, and your special friend."

Rick left Brenda's office just as Bear and the Blaine security team exited the elevator for their briefing. Bear insisted that he bring Rick up-to-date on the security concerns Bear's crew had unveiled. Bear suggested that Rick consider staying at his condo, close by in Tiburon, and commute from there to work, rather than traveling up and down the coast as he normally did on weekends. In other words, not use his Venice Beach condo until the Castillino threat was resolved. Bear said he would make sure that Rick had a guard 24/7 in Tiburon for the next few weeks.

Brenda could see the wheels turning in Rick's head as he considered having a bodyguard and limiting his lifestyle.

"What do you think, Rick?" asked Bear.

Rick stood and walked over to blind-less picture window in his 6th floor office. "I've never considered someone taking a potshot at me from those hills over there." He was looking out at the foothills of the Santa Cruz Mountains that overlooked the eastern side of the campus.

One of the security people agreed with Bear's assessment that some additional people be added to his force. "I have the names of six current police officers that can be implemented into our crew immediately."

Rick gave his approval for the new force as well as having someone stationed at his condo 24/7. But he still had a lot of questions: "How long is this going to take? When will we know the threat is over?"

His questions hung in the air like a dense fog until Bear finally spoke. "When we find whoever is causing the rumors and bring them to justice, which may include a confrontation. "We have to be ready for that, Rick." The look on Bear's face reminded Rick of the time they first met in Ralph Phillips's law office. The memory of meeting this giant of a man who literally came forward from a corner shadow like a creature out of a horror movie, concerned him then and struck a similar chord now.

"Okay, you're in charge, Bear. Let's do this."

Rick pictured Blaine Manufacturing's campus looking more like a fort than what he'd ever planned years ago.

§

SILICON VALLEY, CA

Enzo and three others carefully laid tarps over the metal containers that had just arrived. The time had come to put the final touches on the two bombs that would be installed in the two tanker rigs. Building bombs happened to be Enzo's favorite pastime. He became infamous for this particular skill, having first learned to work with bombs in the Army. As a first generation Italian-American he received several military honors for his ability to dismantle the most intricate enemy IED devices discovered in Iraq. Enzo learned from some of the best Explosive Ordinance Specialist trainers the Army ever assigned to his unit. There was something different about this tall handsome Italian, who rose through the ranks from Private First Class to become one of the bravest Sergeants in the 52nd Explosive Ordinance Disposal Group. Unfortunately, Enzo had a dark side. People close to him knew that there were multiple Enzos that made getting to truly know him nearly impossible – unless he permitted it. His deepest, darkest secret was when he planned to kill as he was doing now; that is the only thing that made him feel complete

Deep down, Enzo knew it wasn't his bravery that made him learn all he could about bombs, or to carry out missions. He enjoyed the thrill of the kill. One of his personalities could actually visualize people, places and things coming apart at the moment of impact. The exhilaration got him up and out of his bunk every day in Iraq — one of the most God forsaken places he'd ever seen. In fact, he made God a promise that if he survived his deployment, he would put the skills he learned to good use. He figured if God allowed war to happen, he, Enzo, wouldn't have to make an excuse for waging a war of his own.

Two of the four canisters containing the explosive C-4 became the outer casings for the bombs. He had used this method of bomb building before and it never failed. This assignment would also be a training session for two of Enzo's men, who worked alongside as he guided them through the bomb making process. "I need each of you to work slowly. No one, including me, works fast when you work with this material, understood?" Both men nodded slightly as they both avoided his gaze. Enzo's reaction came totally out of nowhere. He walked over to within inches of their faces and restated what he had just said. Only slower and louder: "U-N-D-E-R-STOOD?" The men looked up and nodded again only this time more convincingly. "Good. I thought the both of you might be going deaf or something. Now put your gloves on and pay attention or deafness will be the least of your problems."

§

SILICON VALLEY, CA; THE SWAMP BAR

Bear ordered another round of beers. He and a few friends were relaxing watching college basketball on a big screen television in his favorite drinking place: The Swamp. An out-of-the-way sports bar known to get a little rowdy at times. Despite his hectic schedule, Bear always did his best to unwind and spend some 'Bobby Hansen time' with his buddies. This was a different set of guys who knew the big man as; Big Bobby, going back to their college days.

He would hang with them whenever he wanted to get away from the Private Detective business and just let himself go. But, even after two beers, Bobby couldn't stop thinking about his number one project: Rick Blaine and company. There was just too much happening that required one hundred per cent of his attention. "Guys, guys, I'm going to have to beg off tonight." And just like that, Bobby turned into Bear. None of the eight guys sitting close by said a word. They knew better. A few seconds later, their friend left out the back of The Swamp after picking up the tab.

§

RICK'S CONDO, TIBURON, CA

Rick called Ben to check on the funeral arrangements for Sir Archie. He had a decision to make, whether to return to London or wherever the services were held, or stay and wait things out, hoping the Castillino situation would be resolved soon. Rick sat on his deck looking out over San Francisco Bay, long neck in one hand, cell phone to his ear.

"Rick, good to hear your voice my friend. Are you settling in over there?"

Ben sounded as if a huge weight had finally been lifted off his shoulders since the terrorist threat had been averted. Their conversation changed direction, like an oxbow stream, finally settling on the reason for Rick's call. "What about arrangements for Archie?"

"Yes, well, the Queen in all her majesty has decided to move all ceremony north to Edinburgh."

Rick hesitated before saying anything. The pause lingered until Ben came back with: "That will move any ceremony, parade, whatever, into next month. For now, Kensington Palace will accept floral arrangements at the gates of the Palace and grant interviews with the media. The man was a hero to many, Rick, but not as well-known as Princess Di or Prince Phillip.

Besides, I think, between you and me, she's also avoiding any possibility of violence in London."

Before he hung up, Rick, in an attempt to help nurture the relationship, decided to go fishing for Ben's thoughts about Brenda. When he mentioned her name, it was Ben's turn to take a breath before responding. "Ah, yes, Brenda," which made Rick smile because he pronounced her name more like Brendure. "She and I have had some quality time on the phone the last few weeks."

Rick teased him about the size of the floral bouquet he'd sent for Brenda's birthday. After a good laugh, Ben lowered his voice and added: "She's a special lady, Rick, you of all people know that."

Rick agreed and moved on to another subject before hanging up. He asked to be kept informed as to arrangements for Sir Archie and said that he planned to attend.

Just as Rick hung up he noticed one of Bear's men walk across the back perimeter of the condo's property. Rick understood Bear's reasoning for the guards and became more accustomed to it, he hoped his three neighbors agreed. In the last few months, having been trained in self-defense and use of firearms, he knew how to protect himself. More importantly, he felt confident he could, and would, help others who needed protection. He retreated into the condo to work out on the treadmill for the next hour, then lights out.

Chapter 15

TANGIERS, MOROCCO; GRAND SOCCO MARKETPLACE

Jamal checked his email every morning before going off to the Grand Socco and his spice stand. He prayed to Allah, kissed the head of his sleeping wife, and padded his way across the kitchen floor in his most comfortable slippers to his computer located in a small alcove. He had several messages, but one stood out from the rest, prompting him to skip down and click on Winston's email. It simply read: "Abbas is safe in his new home with Harood and Shamir." The old man sat back as tears flowed, making it hard to see. Jamal reached into his pocket and pulled out a freshly laundered handkerchief. Then dabbed his eyes before replacing his glasses. He felt a surge of pride for the young man, as a father would of a son. The boy who once ran wild in the Grand Socco, trying to survive, now had a much better chance of living a long and happy life.

The old man's smile continued to light up his face all the way to the Grand Socco a half hour later. He had never felt such joy as he hurried to open the stand in time for the travelers who would be arriving soon. The lady and her daughter in the stall next to his greeted Jamal as they arrived. Jamal returned their bows and was so full of joy he wanted to hug them, all the vendors, and share why he was dancing around his spice stand. It would be a good day today. He could feel it.

And there they came, the tourists. Jamal donned his red fez as he had done for the last 35 years, and turned just in time as an older couple came across the centuries-old flagstone, up to his stall. "Good morning and welcome to Grand Socco. Allow me to spice up your day."

§

SILICON VALLEY, CA; HANSEN SECURITY

It was two in the morning at Hansen Security. Bear sat staring at page after page. Something wasn't right, he could feel it. This third attempt to find some sort of clue in two weeks of Blaine surveillance reports had to happen, even if it took all night. What bothered him the most was that the motive for the Castillino's desire to kill Rick became more plausible with the death of Michael Castillino. They had every reason to take Rick out now that he'd returned. Rumors from his sources hinted at some kind of action taking place soon, possibly within days, but that required more verification.

Bear could hear the clock ticking incessantly in his head and the pressure of the moment really pissed him off. He sat back in his oversized ergonomic office chair and rubbed his eyes with his palms. *If anything happened to Rick or his people, on my watch....* Bear let the thought drift without considering the answer. He had lost many friends in battle overseas and even a few here in the states. To him, loss was not an option, it came as the result clues overlooked, mistakes that could have been avoided if one just took the time to pinpoint all the possible scenarios.

Not only did he hear the clock ticking, but Bear also felt his stomach growling and realized he hadn't eaten. Round circles were slowly appearing in his vision. They came in conjunction with a stomach growl that threatened to eat his insides. A symphony of body functions flashing a series of warning signals. He found a protein bar and heated up his lukewarm coffee. That would have to do, he had to keep at it. He put the paper reports aside for the time being and moved to video footage of the campus. The visitors to the Blaine campus matched the schedule logs, so he concentrated on the delivery trucks. It was past midnight when he saw something that nearly made him choke on his last bite of the protein bar. His gaze rose up from the monitor and settled on his reflection in the glass doors straight ahead. The face staring back, older now, suddenly had that same haunted look he hadn't seen on himself for a decade. Bear's memory sprang into action showcasing the military photo of a Russian sniper labeled; top secret. Lieutenant Bobby Hansen had achieved the rank of Marksman, youngest in C Company and found himself part of a three-man squad setting out that morning, in Kandahar, to locate and kill the man in the photo. The words he slowly uttered to his reflection revealed a startling realization: "Son of a bitch, it's him."

Bear recognized one of the most notorious assassins the underworld had in their arsenal: Ivan Yashenko. The man had a reputation that stretched across continents. *So the Castillinos are going outside the family in order to take out Rick Blaine. Damn.* This assignment just became even more concerning, if that were possible. It was too late for Bear to contact everyone at his disposal, but he did call his night crew on duty, along the Blaine campus perimeter. He emailed a directive to his team and the security force at Blaine. He sent attached photos and background information on Yashenko. Bear recognized him accompanying one of the chemical truck drivers on the video footage. It was standard procedure for all occupants to leave their trucks in order to facilitate delivery. Yashenko could be seen assisting the handling of the hose connections, and looking around as if surveying the area while the delivery offloaded. He kept himself fairly hidden from the cameras until a Blaine employee, working with the offload, dropped a glove. Yashenko turned his head just slightly as he picked the glove up and handed it back to the man. It was just a matter of seconds, but Bear caught it.

What bothered Bear the most was why an assassin, a proficient sniper and hand-to-hand murderer, happened to be riding in a chemical rig? Answering that question, he told himself in a whispered voice, *we have two concerns now; a possible explosion or a lone sniper shot.*

§

SILICON VALLEY, CA; PETRULA TRUCKING WEST COAST COMPOUND

Lorretta looked at the man she'd been hearing about. A competitor really. Tall, bald with uneven crooked teeth. He stood next to Enzo, who at six foot two, was two to three inches shorter than the unfriendly looking Russian. She liked attractive men, which this one wasn't, but there was an air about him that her entourage lacked — Ivan was mysterious. He also had an odor that radiated a feeling of not caring what people thought about his appearance. To her, he was a jagged-toothed chameleon with a good eye. No wonder he had a reputation for killing people from afar, he probably didn't show his face much. She held back a chuckle. And if people did see his face, it wasn't memorable enough to warrant a second glance. Perhaps that's why his body count was so impressively high; he blended into the background.

The assassin wore black boots, laces up to his shins, slim

black jeans, a zipper covered leather jacket and a 1980s Guns n' Roses t-shirt, which ironically had the "Appetite for Destruction" album cover on it, featuring grim reaper-like skulls of each band member on a large cross. The whole outfit was so bizarre to Loretta that it reminded her of a character out of a Mad Max movie. "Mister Yashenko, won't you have a seat?"

The two men had joined Lorretta in her new condo facing the ocean. They were standing in her living room, newly decorated with white everything, carpet, furniture, walls, complemented by her outfit of black leather pants and jacket to match. To Ivan Yashenko, she looked like a dark angel standing on a cloud. "I will stand, I am dirty from riding in truck." Ivan then requested a towel, explaining that he always covered his tracks, especially on expensive carpets.

Lorretta sat back into her white leather couch as her assistant brought drinks and a large beach towel that stretched to the door, on which Mr. Yashenko could stand. "You men may stand if you wish, but I need to relax." She accepted a scotch and water and encouraged the men to do the same. Surprisingly, Yashenko declined the offer of an alcoholic drink, settling for hot tea instead. "My, my, Ivan, you are a disciplined one are you not?"

The man smiled back at the lady he considered to be a very nice-looking client. In his mind, he was a contractor for hire, and he was on the clock, so to speak. "I prefer not to drink for pleasure while I'm working." Lorretta smiled and looked at Enzo who had been watching the two of them carefully. "Let's get started, shall we?"

Enzo laid out the Blaine campus blueprint on the coffee table in front of Lorretta as Ivan came closer. Enzo pulled out two dining room chairs for them to sit on.

Ivan pointed out two key areas that he had personally uncovered as potential "kill spots" on the blueprint. "One is here, the windows along the upper floors where this Rick Blaine works. He is an open target for a sniper as well as several of his key people, especially at night should he choose to work late."

Enzo agreed, reminding Lorretta that Ivan, having spent time in the Russian military as a highly feared expert sniper known as the Reaper, had actually spent time on the Blaine campus, having accompanied a recent chemical delivery. "Ivan also confirmed our first thought of using explosives in the petrochemical delivery area," Enzo offered as he went to light a cigarette. Ivan had experience in setting off explosions with a single shot.

"Stop." Lorretta held up her hand and Enzo dropped the cigarette back into a pocket. Ivan looked at Enzo as he reached across the table to point something out on the blueprint. "Having watched them closely for a few weeks, we know the guards at night are not nearly as good as those during the day. The nighttime guards take smoke breaks here, and here, as each delivery is made," he added, stabbing his finger into the blueprints and accompanying map. He then pointed to two areas on the other side of the trucks out of sight of the Blaine video cameras. "The truck drivers can simply disappear by walking that direction while unloading."

Enzo turned his head and smiled, adding: "Ivan will be stationed somewhere in the hillside overlooking the campus. His job is to cover the drivers' escape until the bombs are set off. He'll also be monitoring the executive floor to see if Mister Blaine makes an appearance in his office. If he does, he will be taken down immediately.

The Reaper appeared to be an unbelievable asset to the Castillino family. Someone who showed up at the right time. He also had the reputation of going off-script if given too much latitude, which Loretta found intriguing — adding an element of flexibility to their plan. Enzo gave the appearance of appreciation when it came to Ivan's willingness to provide insight as their plan came together, but something about the Russian spelled trouble. Enzo hoped to tap into that darker instinct and use it to their advantage. That was one attribute he, Enzo, lacked. And he could tell it turned his boss on by the way she smiled at the Reaper. Beauty has a way of admiring a beast.

§

SILICON VALLEY, CA; BLAINE MANUFACTURING

Hansen Services employed six full-time and twelve "freelance" intel officers. The company also had ten military and a dozen police officers, available for extra work, on call. Most of the agents were men, but all of them, men and women, were familiar with the underworld of the mafia and cartels and their profit centers like drug and human trafficking, prostitution, murder for hire and gambling. The six that worked closely with Bear kept close contact with people they knew on the "street." They were like double agent spies, for the right amount of cash, information could be obtained. Street cash became part of the client's fee, and as far as Rick was concerned, money was never an object.

All agents were placed on active assignment at Blaine, the backup agents were called in to support various Blaine security assignments. Bear assigned his A Team full-time on the Blaine project. They were to work in conjunction with the Blaine Security force of eighteen, who patrolled around the clock — three, eight hour shifts daily.

Major Connors met with Bear and two of his team in the basement of the new Blaine production facility. Rick and Brenda also attended the meeting. The room was located near two large holding tanks that held twenty-five thousand gallons of highly-flammable liquid. In addition to the two main tanks were six smaller vats of additive materials, also liquid, that would be blended with other chemicals used in various products for sealing and coloring.

"Rick, just being in this room with all these explosive chemicals makes me nervous. This place is a time bomb waiting to blow," Connors explained as the six walked through the gleaming white facility with concrete floors and LED lighting. He had to shout in order to be heard over the noise of two forklifts carrying pallets of five-gallon containers of coloring additives that had just arrived. As they entered his production office, an associate collected each one of the white hard hats they'd donned earlier three floors up. The warm room temperature comforted the group as they sat at a round, ten top, table. Connors hurried to find a few more chairs. He hadn't expected guests on such short notice.

Rick was the first to speak as the door shut, immediately cutting off all noise. "Bear has some details he feels we need to know, now, Major." Rick had a look of concern that Major hadn't seen for some time. In fact, Major hadn't had the chance to welcome Rick back from his recent trip abroad, like most of the management team. Everyone had been that busy.

"I understand that we are on alert, Rick," said Major Connors, adding, "I'm ready to hear what you and Bear have to say."

Bear stood and began drawing on a long white board that already contained a few diagrams. "These are a few areas of security concern here at Blaine that we feel need to be addressed." In addition, Bear drew a timeline of when he thought the Castillinos could possibly act based on intel he'd received over the last twelve hours. "Rick, I know you can't shut the place down, and I'm not suggesting that, but I think you and a few of your officers should change your work schedules, or even consider leaving town for a few days."

As Bear spoke, Rick remembered making the same suggestion to Sir Archie about the Queen and her family. A smile appeared on his face as the Queen's response came to mind. He looked up at Bear, all eyes were on Rick as it was his turn to speak. "Ah, Bear, I, we, really appreciate your work, and I personally know how effective and thorough you and your colleagues are in your business, but I'm not going anywhere."

Major Connors and Brenda looked at one another as Brenda spoke up and agreed with Rick, speaking on behalf of everyone at Blaine. "One of our largest domestic clients doubled their previous order, which is in the works as we speak. Business is at an all time high right now. It will be business as usual here at Blaine, Bear, I hope that won't interfere with what you have to do."

Major Connors concurred and suggested that qualified employees, those that have gun licenses, arm themselves and serve as backup. The room went silent for a few seconds as Bear considered a response. Connors stood and walked to the front of the room and spoke in a low tone. "I respect everything about you, Bear, you know that. But you have to know that we can't let others dictate how we do business around here. Hope you understand my friend."

§

SILICON VALLEY, CA; PETRULA TRUCKING WEST COAST COMPOUND

Ivan and Enzo had left, and Lorretta was alone. She'd heard all she wanted and it would be up to her to, "Call the Shot." This was an old term among those in the family business. Her father and his partner, Michael's father, used to trade off Calling the

Shot in the old days when someone or some business got in their way, keeping them from expanding their operation. Invoking it merely meant that people, who needed convincing, made the wrong decision. In the case of Rick Blaine, when he decided to kill Michael, that became a problem that needed fixing, so Calling the Shot would be no different in Lorretta's mind than when her father made the same decision. She called Enzo. "You have three days. Do it in the middle of the work day. We want the place to be hopping. Let me know when you're ready, I want to watch."

§

TIBURON, CA; RICK'S CONDO

The sun rose over the San Francisco Bay as Rick finished his workout watching "Good Morning America". He liked to do some yoga poses to warm up, spin on the stationary bike, then finish by pushing some weights. He was wiping the sweat off his face when his cell phone rang. The tune "Eclipse" from Pink Floyd's "Dark Side of the Moon" was his ring tone. He answered, coughing first into his towel. "This is Rick." One of the two guards outside asked if a Mr. Murphy could come to the door. Murphy was his elderly neighbor who lived in the townhouse next door. Rick admired the Irish gentleman who'd been retired from the real estate business for nearly thirty years. His neighbor was extremely active for his age and enjoyed being like a fatherly figure to Rick, providing sage advice, occasionally, with a slight Irish accent.

In the background, Rick could hear his neighbor, who preferred to be called Murphy, ask the guard for identification and what was going on? "Yes, of course, let him pass, I'll meet you at the door." Rick was laughing as he opened the door and saw the little, white-haired man standing next to a tall, ex-Navy Seal, a black man, who reached for the glass screen door as Rick unlocked it. "Thanks, Jim, he's my neighbor. Come in Murphy, I was just about to make coffee." Murphy entered, keeping an eye on the tall stranger until the door closed. Dressed in his familiar orange, green and white jogging suit, Murphy agreed to share coffee with some cream. "Irish Cream if you have it, Rick," he declared with a slight wink.

Murphy stopped by to invite Rick, personally, to his ninety-eighth birthday party. Murphy's daughter would be sending out invitations, but Murphy intercepted Rick's. "I wanted to see you, boy. After all, you've been gone and I missed your smiling face." Murphy spoke with a bright gleam in his eyes and an Irish lilt to his voice, which Rick couldn't get enough of, like now. Murphy was a credit to his ancestry, which, in Rick's estimation, went back to a time when leprechauns roamed the earth, a claim made by Murphy more than once and never disputed by Rick or his neighbors.

The two sat and talked next to a big picture window overlooking the bay with Alcatraz floating off in the distance beneath a foggy halo. The morning light began to make an appearance as the fog crept by, silently heading for the Golden Gate Bridge.

Rick shared his experience in Italy with friends, including the confrontation with the Castillinos. "That's the reason for the guards outside." His neighbor, of short stature, sat tall in a tan colored hotel chair, sipping and nodding taking it all in as he carefully scrolled through a few photos from the trip on Rick's phone. They chatted for a while before Rick noticed Murphy needed a refill and rose from his chair to retrieve the coffee carafe. As he did, Murphy commented. "That's odd, Rick, there's a red dot bouncing around on the back of my coffee mug." Rick, busy with the refill, didn't pay much attention at first, but after pouring two new cups, he turned and proceeded to put them down on the table. That's when he noticed the dot dancing around the room as if searching.

Rick froze in place after setting the carafe down carefully on the coffee table as if it would break on contact. Murphy picked up his mug and returned to drinking, watching Rick react to the dancing dot. Rick motioned for the old man to put the mug down and join him on the floor.

The time between setting the carafe down and noticing the red dot happened so fast Rick had no time to think he simply yelled "Duck" and hit the floor, as the first hole appeared in the 4 by 8 foot plate glass living room window. Several more shots followed shattering the glass — sending fragments all over. One of the shots went through the back of his chair, two others narrowly missed Rick's head creating holes in the wall behind. He looked across the floor at Murphy who had spilled his coffee all over himself as he dove to the ground. His eyes, as big as silver dollars, gave him the appearance of an aging owl that had just crashed landed through the front window. Murphy nodded to Rick that he was okay.

"Stay here, Murphy, and give me my phone." Rick, bent over and breathing hard, grabbed his phone and ran to the front door. He heard shots coming from outside and looked up in time to see his guards returning fire. One of the guards had his phone to his ear as he pointed to a boat speeding away. A few moments later the man who escorted Murphy to the door came rushing inside after Rick unlocked the door. "We spotted a boat speeding off. My partner saw the shooter with a rifle. Harbor patrol and the sheriff's helicopter are looking for a small cruiser last seen heading south. We need to have both of you shelter here for now. Bear is in contact with the authorities and will be in touch." Rick asked that an ambulance call be made in order to check on his elderly friend. Murphy claimed that he was fine, but Rick insisted and the call was made.

§

SAN FRANCISCO BAY, CA. TIBURON PENINSULA

"Stupid, stupid, stupid." Ivan Yashenko's anger could be heard all over the boat as it sped away. He'd convinced Lorretta that Rick could be taken out with one shot from the water, which in turn, would take the focus off Blaine Manufacturing, and make it an easier target. The Reaper had developed the skill of balancing, breathing and shooting from water over years of carefully crafted "Water Kills" as he referred to them. Besides, the Reaper charged more when the assignment specified a WK. Most recently, he leveled his spring-action rifle tripod from a specially designed Zephyr outboard boat in the Suez Cannel and again on a steamer ship in the North Sea. His most successful water kills came when working for a Russian billionaire in the Black Sea who paid the Reaper handsomely for the elimination of two high-ranking Russian officials who were attempting to take over his empire in the newly formed Russian oil industry. That particular assignment required 3 weeks of planning and netted him triple his normal fee of 1 million Euros.

"The target finally sat in his window overlooking San Francisco Bay. I had him dead to rights as the fog lifted and just as I exhaled waves began to hit the cruiser." Ivan's rant fell on deaf ears as the captain and his two man crew had the boat up to full speed attempting to elude the hail of gunfire coming their way and the authorities that were no doubt alerted. Ivan took a moment to steady himself against the galley sink below in the speeding cruiser. He had his trusted Dragunov 7.62x54mm long-range rifle slung on his back and his customized tripod impaled in the bench cushion behind him as he focused his angry facial expression in the galley mirror he'd just broken with his fist. He felt as fractured as he looked in the splintered reflection. He should have held back when the boat began to rise in the previously calm water. The Reaper swore then that, given another opportunity, he would complete his assignment for the Castillinos and their leader the most beautiful witch he'd ever encountered. He rubbed his temples, remembering the meeting recently at Petrula Trucking. The Castillino family had noticed the beefed-up security on the Blaine campus, especially in the last few days. When Ivan heard about more security at Blaine Manufacturing he suggested a diversion: kill Rick where he lives. Lorretta didn't take long to be convinced, she surprised him by being easy to persuade. She appeared to be turned on by the idea, so Ivan decided to go for it. "Listen, my strength as an assassin isn't bombs, it's long-range kills," the mercenary remembered telling the room at a meeting at Petrula Trucking's office two days earlier. The captain's voice brought Ivan out of his thoughts. They were headed toward shore and the four of them would be exiting soon. Ivan needed to make a phone call.

§

LORRETTA PETRULA'S CONDO, SAN JOSE, CA

Enzo paced the floor awaiting a phone call from the Reaper. Lorretta sat looking out at the view, calm, sipping tea. Enzo knew he would have to come to terms with Ivan who seemed to be gaining favor with Lorretta. His opinion didn't count when it came to killing Rick Blaine at his condo, and that bothered Enzo. Lorretta may have been convinced, but not Enzo. Besides, he didn't exactly know how the Russian fit into the family process. The man may have been good at killing, but he was terrible when it came to communicating with others. Enzo believed in working as a team. Ivan was a loner and Enzo couldn't make his piece of the puzzle fit. Enzo had attempted to negotiate with Lorretta by suggesting that the idea of a long-range shot from the bay into Rick's condo had merit. But why now? Why not wait until after the bombing to see if it needed to be done. In the end, Enzo lost out, the shooting attempt was on as was his phone, which began to vibrate as if on cue. Lorretta looked up from across the room at Enzo's face as the bad news slowly transitioned from the phone and into her trusted associate's furrowed eye brows. When the phone was replaced in Enzo's pants pocket, he looked up and briefly explained what had just occurred.

"You have got to be kidding me. Damn that Russian bastard and his can't miss idea." Lorretta's temper was as hot as her figure. She wanted to kill the Russian on the spot, but couldn't. "He's got his sorry ass in one hell of a bind. Where is the idiot?"

Enzo explained that the boat Ivan used had been stolen from the Saint Francis Yacht Club the evening prior to the incident. The plan was to use it and lose it or sink it, if necessary.

"Great. I hope the fool drowns in the Pacific," she yelled.

Lorretta went for another scotch as Enzo answered a second call. When he hung up Enzo explained that Ivan and the crew were okay. They managed to get away and hid the boat in a marshy area near Burlingame. Enzo didn't tell her that Ivan apologized and that the Reaper suggested another idea. Instead, he kept Ivan's suggestion to himself and suggested he disappear for a few hours. Ivan was out-of-breath and sounded like he and the others were running through brush while he attempted to explain his new idea. Although the call would break up as he spoke, Enzo understood that the Reaper wanted to continue to serve the family by securely planting himself and his Dragunov on the hillside east of the Blaine Campus. Enzo had a much better feeling about the Reaper's change in plan and hoped Lorretta would come around and give the sneaky bastard another chance. Lorretta was in no mood to discuss any idea coming from the Reaper. Enzo would wait until they had another drink or two before convincing Lorretta that accepting the Reaper's apology and moving forward would be the more productive course of action. About an hour later, Enzo smiled as he left Lorretta's condo pondering what she would do if she ever saw Ivan again. To be honest, they needed Ivan.

§

TIBURON, CA; RICK'S CONDO

Rick spent part of the morning comforting his old neighbor. "Why would someone want to kill such a fine young man as you, Rick?" Those were the last words Murphy spoke before being loaded into an ambulance. He had sustained some cuts from the window and minor scalding on his face from the hot coffee. Rick let Murphy's comment go, but knew exactly why someone would want to kill him and spoke with Bear about what action needed to be taken.

"You are lucky that those shots were taken from a boat bobbing up and down in the bay, Rick. If that shooter would have been on dry land you'd be in the morgue chillin' out." Bear had driven up in his six-wheeler as the ambulance was leaving. "You don't know how relieved I was when I saw you standing in the driveway just now. Who were you waving to?"

Rick explained what had happened to his neighbor. Bear listened intently and asked, "Wait, the old Irish fella that discovered the girl's dead body last spring?"

"Yep," Rick nodded. "The same."

"Jesus. Your HOA may want to meet with you ole buddy.

I may have to take you out into the desert and hide you in an adobe hut until we get a handle on things."

Bear's big frame shaded Rick from the sun, but his point hit Rick square on. They stood talking in the driveway outside his condo. He knew Bear was teasing—the big man had a way of taking a near tragedy and turning it into a serious comedy routine.

Rick smiled at his trusted associate and assured him that he wasn't going anywhere. "They'll find me wherever I go, Bear. Let's get this over with. You believe they're planning something big, so it couldn't have been this attack." Rick paused for a second and let a deep sigh. "They will be coming for me where I work, Bear. I can feel it and I'm ready."

§

SILICON VALLEY, CA; PETRULA TRUCKING WEST COAST COMPOUND

The two new Petrula tanker trucks were ready to roll. Lorretta stood above on the iron grate outside the trucking office. She wanted a cigarette, but knew better. She opted to obey the red and white sign with the big slash through it off to her right. A quarter of a million dollars was spent on those sleek rigs all because she wanted a successful Silicon Valley entrepreneur dead. The thought of a revengeful success made her smile. *At least there was insurance.* She inhaled, closing her eyes. When she exhaled, drool started to fall from her rosy red lips so she spit and let it go, for good. Good riddance.

Both trucks started up, sending a brief cloud of smoke out the vertical chrome pipes extending past the driver's cab like proud monuments making a statement. Each driver knew their mission and would be carefully monitored as they made their forty-minute drive.

§

BLAINE MANUFACTURING, SILICON VALLEY, CA

Bear and two of his men walked back from Rick's office after escorting him to work in San Jose from Tiburon. Bear had his antenna up, wondering, waiting as they approached the front doors where the head of security for Blaine stood watch. Each step the giant of a man took felt more comfortable as they accompanied Rick to his office, now that a canvas barrier had been erected at the entrance of the main building. Thanks to the quick work of Bear's crew, the line of sight of potential snipers in the nearby hills had been temporarily blocked. "Hey, Billy, your boss is safely tucked away upstairs." The two men fist bumped as Bear and two more of his men continued their way to the production facility on the other side of the campus.

The five men, each armed, wearing dark glasses, walked side by side not saying a word. Walking through the compound reminded Bear of being in Iraq, looking for trouble and expecting the worst. "Let's spread out," he ordered his men. "My gut tells me something is about to go down. Keep your eyes on the hills, and report anything suspicious to me. Let's work as a unit; and don't be a hero."

Each man had been trained in the military to look for breaks in established patterns: a car in the wrong place, a bush that hadn't been there before, a new face who didn't have a lanyard with Blaine identification; anything recognizable as out of the ordinary after having surveyed the security theatre. They would make random checks and ask people what department they worked in and psychoanalyzed their responses. Looking away, blushing, sweating, stammering, were a few of the indicators that the guilty had trouble controlling, especially if they were surprised by the unexpected questioning. Having worked at Blaine for a few weeks, the team had become more familiar with Rick's employees, who were no longer troubled by the increased security presence, so someone new would stand out. Indeed, just two days earlier, Cynthia, one of Bear's top agents, surprised a crew of landscapers with the same line of questions. One of them, an illegal alien, cut and ran. Her team caught him, placed him in handcuffs and was prepared to hand him over to Immigration and Customs Enforcement — commonly called ICE — but Brenda intervened after being alerted to the incident. She then made arrangements to formally hire the worker as a full-time landscaper and sponsor his work permit, which was extended to his family.

Bear caught up with Major Connors and introduced him to two of his men that were going to be stationed in the chemical depot where a series of deliveries were to be arriving soon. The trucks normally made deliveries during the night on Tuesdays and Thursdays, but business had been very good lately and on a newly scheduled Wednesday, trucks would be arriving around 1 PM.

"You said you'd show me your fire suppression system last week; do you have time today?" asked Bear, who was a brave man and proved it many times in combat, but one fear that followed him from childhood was fire. When he was seven years old his family home caught fire, caused by a faulty electrical cord from a space heater left on in the living room. It was a frightening experience for his parents and four siblings. The parents carried out his two sisters, , but Bear and his little brother had to escape out of an upstairs window. He lowered his brother as far as he could and dropped him into bushes below, and then had to jump as the flames broke through their bedroom door. The sight of the flames engulfing their room were etched in his memory.

Years later, when he was training to parachute jump at night over the Mojave desert, he was asked by a soldier if he had any experience jumping at night, he simply nodded. "I was seven, snow on the landing and fire behind me. Very traumatic." The guy just looked at him as the tail of C-121 dropped and the men proceeded to jump into total darkness.

§

SILICON VALLEY, CA PETRULA TRUCKING COMPOUND

Enzo radioed the tanker trucks. Each one was equipped with tracking devices, but he had to know the status of things even though they had rehearsed the run more than once. Timing was vital. That was Enzo. Everyone involved, especially Ivan, appreciated the way he worked. As for Lorretta, she wanted results; for things to happen much faster. She was tired of chasing Blaine, the chase had to end or heads would roll.

"Can't we move the damn date up and get this over with?" she demanded. "I want to get out of here."

Setting off bombs required meticulous timing, charging ahead without careful planning usually resulted in disaster for the team, not the enemy. For Enzo, the matter before them was more than an assignment — knowing how to constructively deconstruct things with bombs happened to be his "calling." And to Enzo's credit, his record was perfect. He'd have to do some convincing in order to ease Lorretta's mind. He also pleased her in other ways in order to take her mind off of planning Blaine's demise. Many times, during their lovemaking, Lorretta would slip and call him Michael. He didn't mind, he, too, wanted the

West Coast job to be over so he could get back to Boston, his hometown. But it had to be done right.

§

BLAINE MANUFACTURING

Major showed Bear how the fire suppression system worked, stopping short of actually activating the process. Bear offered a comment as they walked up the ramp back to the guard gate. "Every home should have one of these systems, Major."

The older man just looked at Bear, then smiled as he caught the joke. "Yes, they should, if they had an extra million dollars in their cookie jar."

Two Hansen agents walked the perimeter of the basement checking exits and areas of concern where an enemy could penetrate.

"Today's first loads of chemicals should be arriving in a few minutes," added Major as he gave Bear a casual salute and then walked off toward the truck entry gates.

Bear walked toward a holding area where the tanker trucks staged, waiting for the call to bring the first truck forward, about a hundred yards to the guard gate. The purpose of the holding area was to keep traffic flowing on the main road leading to the front gates of the Blaine campus, approximately a quarter mile further down the road. There were four tanker trucks waiting to be called forward when Bear looked through a cyclone fence marking the perimeter between the campus and the holding area.

Major told him they expected six trucks today. "Normally, we prefer to process these deliveries at night when there are fewer employees on campus. But because of recent increases in business and supply chain issues, a decision was made to go with a more flexible schedule allowing for earlier delivery times."

Bear made a quick mental note of the schedule change, as he looked over his shoulder and watched dozens of Blaine employees making their way along the campus grounds. He turned back to watch as two trucks entered the holding area. Both rigs stood out from the rest. They looked much cleaner than the others, long black with gleaming silver details and bright chrome wheels. "Nice," whispered Bear to himself, admiring the sleek lines of the big rigs.

A row of red lights, similar to those on an ambulance, flashed over the guard gate as the first truck made its move forward. Bear and the two men who had been with him earlier, watched as a second truck passed through the gate, heading for one of the two pumping stations. The offloading accommodated two trucks at a time, speeding up the process. According to Major, there were three different chemicals being delivered, all of which were highly flammable liquids, so the offloading required both the Blaine employees and the truck drivers to handle things with care. The drivers removed the hoses alongside the trucks and assisted in making sure each hose connection was tight and secure. Once the transfer hose had been set in place, the driver would signal the Blaine employee who would secure their end before the driver opened the tanker valve.

The next two tanker trucks waited patiently in the holding area for the signal to move up to the gate. Bear looked at his Apple Watch as his men began checking in to report. It was early afternoon on a warm blue-bird sky day. The chemical offloading appeared to be going well as each of the four stations reported "all clear." Bear could have left the next two truck offloads for his counterparts to monitor, but he forced himself to stay. Besides, he told Major he'd stick around and maybe they'd go together for a beer later. After the incident with the Castillinos earlier in the year, Major and Bear had become better acquainted. Shared combat experience—with the mob, no less!—drew the two of them together. Over several drinking excursions, they found they had similar military backgrounds, but in different time periods. They clinked glasses, more than once, over the fact that combat is combat, even if the theatre of operation—whether Vietnam or Iraq—happened to be fought in very different parts of the world.

The next two trucks were on their way, with the first making its way through the gate and the second pulling up as the gate arm fell into place. Bear stood behind a retaining wall about fifty feet away talking to one of his men. They watched the two drivers through some neatly-trimmed bushes as Blaine staff fit their hoses into the receiving ports and locked them into place. Bear held up a hand, stopping the conversation. "What?" the man said as looked in the same direction. One of the drivers appeared to be talking into an ear piece as he led the other driver away from the trucks, causing Bear's alert antennae to go up immediately. "What's going on? Where are they going?" Bear whispered to himself. His agent standing beside him immediately raised his weapon as Bear called out a general alarm on the encrypted radio he carried. He told his man to cover him as he rapidly moved toward the retreating drivers.

Brenda was in a meeting, when her assistant interrupted. "There's an alert, we have to leave." Rick looked at Brenda as he jumped up and ran from the room. Brenda, along with the four other people in her meeting, quickly left the room. She headed instinctively to Rick's office and found it empty.

Rick was busy herding employees into the stairwell. Everyone had been briefed earlier on what to do next — walking instead of running out into the parking garage. Rick let them know that this was not a drill having been asked the question a few seconds earlier. From there they would be given instructions on where to stage, waiting for an update.

The alert went to Bear's men and Blaine's security, which included the guard gate behind him, and Brenda's office. As the two drivers came closer to Bear's position, he noticed the one with the earpiece holding a black remote. Bear could hear as they approached, and he could tell the man was nervous about what was to happen next. The two drivers walked quickly behind a row of twelve-foot-tall arborvitae that ran along the border fence to the guard gate.

It was clear to Bear that they were not intending on returning to their respective trucks. Bear didn't hesitate, the men were directly in front of his position. He attacked the two men as another of his men came running up. The driver with the ear piece dropped the black remote. It bounced along the asphalt as all three men hit the ground with Bear in the middle driving them both forward — tackling them from behind. The bigger of the two drivers twisted away, rose up to meet his pursuer and hit Bear in the face with a closed fist, knocking him down to the ground. The driver picked up the remote and began running for the perimeter fence leading to the truck waiting area. Bear rose and literally handed the smaller driver to his man. "Cuff him and clear everyone from the area, immediately," Bear shouted the instruction as he ran after the other driver.

Ivan watched from his hillside position about a quarter mile from the guard gate. He could have easily taken out the big guy working over the Petrula driver, but held back not wanting to give away his position. The Reaper had a bigger fish to eliminate.

Bear shifted his body into third gear and started gaining on the driver who had hit him and run. The man fumbled with another remote. Bear knew the instrument well, having activated and deactivated countless remote bombs in the Middle East and captured more than one bombmaker. The remote had to be turned on and a code engaged before being capable of sending the signal to trigger the bomb. That took time, which the man would have had if he and the other driver hadn't been spotted. The fumbling gave Bear enough time to catch up and take the man down, sending the remote into a grassy area as both men hit the ten-foot high, reinforced, cyclone fence.

Major Connors saw what was developing with Bear and ordered two of his men to uncouple the delivery hoses from the receiving tanks. "Toss the hoses back toward the trucks and run like hell." He knew if the hoses remained connected and one of the trucks were to burst into flames, an explosion could rip through the entire production facility. "Go. Now." His team quickly disconnected the hoses, tossing them back under each rig. Beads of sweat formed across Major's forehead. "We need to move those trucks."

Rick pulled back and ran for the elevator, retracing his steps. He avoided being escorted away from his office and ushered off campus through the parking garage with the rest of his employees. He'd been working with his planning team when the Bear's alert went out and was distracted by the evacuation, but now rushed to see what was happening at the chemical depot. He quickly returned upstairs to his office to gain a better perspective of the campus. Rick raised the new blinds and watched from his sixth-floor window as Bear went into action, atone point placing both hands, overhead, on the window in order to get a better view. He twisted his head to the left after hearing shouts and footsteps running down the hall. As he turned, a shot came crashing through the plate-glass window, just missing his head.

Billy and his security team of four officers came rushing up, checking the Executive Offices, as the shot broke through the window, causing Rick to hit the floor. Billy, with gun drawn, scanned for threats as his men spread out in the hallway behind him. "Have you been hit, sir?" Rick shook his head as he started to rise up, brushing off pieces of glass. "Get down! Crawl to me, sir, and keep low — we have a sniper." Rick did as instructed, but as he raised up to leave the room another shot hit the window. Billy managed to pull Rick around the corner just in time. The high-powered bullet exited out Rick's office door, shattering a planter across the hall next to one of Billy's men. Billy helped Rick up with one arm as he radioed an alert; "We have a sniper, two shots coming from the hillside to the southeast — targeting Mr. Blaine's office!"

Rick cleared his throat, placed a hand on Billy's shoulder. "Give me your jacket, Billy, we've got to help Bear." Without hesitation, the head of security did as he was told. Rick pulled a stocking cap over his head, donned the jacket, gave Billy a pat on the shoulder as he led the group down to the campus grounds.

Rick knew the campus better than anyone. As he exited down the back stairway, two steps at a time, he held his Glock 9mm pistol in his left hand, using his right hand to grab the handrail. He slipped the gun into his back waistline as he ran out of the main building heading for the production facility a football field's distance away.

Ivan changed his position on the hillside, rearranged the tripod and settled in watching for Blaine to reappear. In the meantime, the Reaper would begin to eliminate as many of the enemy as he could. He took another deep breath before proceeding to empty his rifle magazine of high-powered ammunition. He couldn't help but smile as he witnessed the results of his marksmanship.

One of Bear's men led the other truck driver away in handcuffs as Rick, breathing heavily, came up on them from behind. The agent turned to fire as Rick held up his hands, removed the stocking cap, and identified himself. "Sorry, Mister B."

"Where's Bear?"

The man pointed to an area behind the trucks as shots came raining down on their location. All three hit the ground. The driver's head was split open, clearly the driver was dead, removing the possibility of a witness. The agent rolled over and began to return fire toward the hillside as more shots came their way. Rick, along with two other agents, also began firing. Whoever was up there was well-hidden.

Bear's man showed Rick that he had the driver's remote and keys to the second truck as they were both reloading. That gave Rick an idea. "Give me the keys."

Bear's man gave a perplexed look. "You know how to drive one of these rigs?"

Rick didn't take time to tell him how he had driven a Kenworth over two thousand miles earlier in the year, so he just grabbed the keys and ran for the truck.

Ivan's well-trained eye hungered for the target until finally it focused on Rick sprinting to the truck. "Welcome to the fight, Mr. Blaine." Ivan licked his lips, took a deep breath and began to squeeze the trigger as he slowly exhaled. "Stop, yes, right there, shit, shit, move, good. "Ivan took another breath – "Now."

Shots rang out as Rick took off for the second rig. He returned fire toward the hillside and at a black SUV parked lower on the hill just off the road. Rick ran in a serpentine fashion with his gun held in front of him with both hands. Bear's man had identified the tanker truck that Major's men had disconnected hoses from, as the match for the keys. "Where are the shots coming from, over?" Bear radioed his team. They had created coordinates for three sections of hillside facing the production facility and Blaine campus, including the Executive Offices. The sections were divided evenly across the hillside for approximately a half mile in width and 200 feet high. The middle section appeared to be the most active. Three agents responded with visuals for the same section: 2. "Roger, section 2. Billy, you and your team take sections 1 and 3 and that black SUV, I'll lead my team up section 2. Move out."

Rick mounted the step below the driver's door without skipping a beat. He opened the truck door and entered the cab in one motion. There was no time to catch his breath. He had to get the truck off the campus grounds immediately. The rig hadn't begun offloading, so it had a full load, approximately sixty-thousand pounds of gross weight, and fought the need to move quickly at first. Rick looked around for clearance as he headed for the exit gate. He instinctively knew that the closest and most logical location would be the future truck staging area. Bullets ricocheted off the hood and cab as Rick raced east toward the flat open ground.

The land, that would eventually become the staging area for trucks, had been hard to come by when his executive team planned the new production facility two years ago. It was the perfect location, just east of the proposed production facility. But another company, named for one of the largest rivers in the world, had a three-year option on the property. Through clever maneuvering and some stock trading, the land became a big parking lot, large enough to hold up to a dozen rigs end to end and side to side. Bordering the lot was a three-sided concrete runoff canal that laid empty most of the year. Beyond the staging area were ten acres of wetlands with a few ponds and a small grove of birch trees.

Rick shifted through the gears and gained as much speed as possible. The truck responded as it crossed the roadway in a semi-circle fashion like a black and silver snake on the attack. The back two tires on the driver's side actually lifted off the ground as the trailer made the sharp turn toward the staging area. Rick looked back to check the trailer and heard what he thought was the loud ticking of a clock. He glanced behind the seat and saw the backpack. It had been unzipped at the top to allow the numbers on a display panel to be visible. "Holy shit, that's a bomb!"

Bear looked back at the road and saw Rick driving the fuel tanker. He shook his head and continued stealthily up the hillside, heading toward the sniper who, Bear suspected, was moving to a different location. Bear signaled his team to fan out further on the hill and begin to move up. His men responded. As they did, the firing began again, further up the hill, but closer to Bear's location. He tripped over a small boulder trying to keep his eyes trained on where the shots were coming from. "There you are you bastard." He figured it was the Reaper and prepared himself for a confrontation. He could now hear the man moving, shifting, reloading. He even thought he heard him laugh at one point. "That's enough," Bear whispered to himself as he circled in behind Ivan the Reaper. Before he could get off another round, the Bear of a man lunged at the sniper, grabbed the surprised shooter by the neck with his left hand, and delivered a devastating right hook to his ribs. Ivan , dressed in tan camo, matched the ground he rolled into. It was hard for Bear to see the rolling kick that caught him in the stomach, causing him to bend at the waist, gasping for air. As he did, Bear saw a knife flash and raised his arm to deflect the blade. The edge penetrated Bear's jacket creating a deep gash in his arm.

He cried out as he slammed a meaty blow into the right temple of Ivan's head. The Reaper fell harder than one of the mighty pines that surrounded them. Bear decided it made no sense to take this hired gun as prisoner and instead thrust the Reaper's own knife deep into the killer's chest — ending a long history of impersonal murders. "Go to hell, Ivan, they're waiting for you." Bear immediately removed his jacket and wrapped it tightly around his arm, slowing the bleeding. As he stood there, waiting for his men to catch up, he noticed the other remote laying on the ground next to Ivan. He suddenly felt dizzy knowing the destruction this man could have caused if he'd had just a little more time.

Terror gripped Rick as sweat appeared on his brow and began to drip. *Change of plan, the backpack has to go, but where?*

The truck came to a screeching halt. Rick reached for the backpack, but stopped. He hated to think what a bomb would do to the land dedicated to various species of birds and other wildlife if he tossed the backpack into the wetlands. He turned and exited the truck – he had another idea.

Major and his men were pinned down close to the remaining Petrula tanker truck under the canopy next to the offload pump. It was a very uncomfortable place to be with bullets flying all around the depot. Two of Major's men were wounded, but still returning fire. Another was lying, face down, dead, shot from behind as he ran back after disconnecting one of the hoses. The truck had to be moved and Major didn't want to send another person in harm's way. He would be the one to move the truck. He radioed his men to cover him as he adjusted his protective vest. The action had been going on for less than fifteen minutes, but it seemed like hours. As he fastened the last strap on his jacket, Major saw Rick working to unhitch the tractor cab from the tank trailer. "What's he up to?"

Enzo monitored the attack activity through a spotter's scope from the black SUV. They had been taking on more fire in the last few minutes. He had to do it, the last option. What happened to Ivan? Why wasn't he shooting? Enzo ordered his men to move up and increase the attack. They only had a short time before authorities would arrive. Five more minutes and he would have to engage his remote, the last option. He'd held back at first, hoping the other two remotes would have been used by now. He never expected this much resistance, but he was ready to blow this place up.

Bear's men surrounded their adversaries, who were losing ground and suffering more casualties as they began to show themselves. The fight had become more intense.

Rick's heart was racing as he unhitched the trailer and headed back into the cab. Starting the engine, he slowly brought the tractor cab forward off the trailer and headed for the concrete spillway that bordered the holding area. He had no idea what the blast would do or when it would be engaged. All he knew was that the control of the bomb behind him was in someone else's hands. The tractor negotiated the turn and the exhaust stacks sounded as if they were making a final blast as Rick took the truck over the side of the concrete wall and down twenty feet into the concrete slough. The cab tipped to the right as it lost balance, scraping the highly polished black paint. The windshield shattered as the truck tipped on its side with Rick suspended in midair like a puppet ready to dance. The bomb, tied in position, hadn't moved, but Rick could hear new sounds coming from the box. He reached over and tried to free himself from the seatbelt that had tightened against his suspended weight. Rick had rolled the driver's side window down before driving into the spillway, anticipating his need for a way to escape. With his right hand he reached through the window and pulled himself up, releasing tension on the belt. Now all he had to do was reach down and push the red button. Shots began to hit the truck as he tried once, twice, but the button would not engage. His right arm was beginning to cramp, as he reached for the gun at the small of his back. "Ping, ping," the bullets began to hit the underside of the cab like rain. Rick pushed the barrel of the gun into the red button — and it worked. "Snap." And there he hung with one arm up, the gun replaced in his belt and, using both arms, brought himself up and out of the cab. Quickly, he jumped to the ground and ran. He dove behind a log that had washed up from the concrete culvert after a recent storm just as the truck exploded out the roof and left side of the cab. Parts of metal and pieces of glass flew straight up and out toward Rick's position. The fragments were carried by a strong concussive wave that knocked Rick and his log safety barrier back a good three feet. Rick ended up with a few scratches, his ears were ringing, as the gunfire appeared to have slowed. The old birch log had been his only protection, which was ironic because he'd been allergic to birch trees his entire life. Rick's Apple Watch continued to set off an 'unsafe heart rate' alarm. Irritated, he slapped the watch with his right hand shutting the alert off.

From his location, Rick had a good angle on the SUV that was parked about fifty yards further back up the service road he'd just driven past. There appeared to be two shooters at the vehicle and other shots coming from further down the slope. After another round of shots came his way, he returned fire as he ran along the bottom of the spillway heading toward the culvert. He figured the shooters couldn't get a clear shot as long as he stayed below the perimeter fencing. Rick counted to three and began shooting toward the SUV. He had two remaining magazines, eighteen rounds. He reported in and knelt behind a concrete wall listening to his radio. Bear had taken over the sniper's rifle, similar to the one he used in Iraq. He was busy covering his men and picking off the attackers from behind.

Enzo had waited too long enough for the drivers to ignite the bombs. The first truck's bomb didn't work — another opportunity missed. That wouldn't happen with the second truck. Shots hit the SUV, causing the driver to move out and back further into the trees. The motion sent the 3rd remote to the floor and Enzo scrambled for it. The driver finally stopped as did the bouncing. Enzo was on the hunt for the last remote.

Major decided to go for it. He patted his pocket where his assistant shoved the truck keys, radioed his intention to move the truck and asked for fire cover, then took off around the concrete barrier, heading for his black and silver target. He didn't have far to go, it was just a matter of avoiding the shots that appeared to be coming his way. He jumped to the truck's running board and opened the door, inserted the key and started the tanker. Two bullets pierced the cab. Major figured he didn't have time to shift through the drive gears, so he slammed the gear shift down and over into reverse.

The driver yelled to Enzo that someone had entered the tanker and was now moving it – backwards out of the gate. Enzo screamed a profanity as he continued his search and found the remote. He quickly input the code and waited for the red light to turn to green. Looking up, he checked for the rig. "Come on, come on!"

The truck began to jump like a rabbit as if it disagreed with his decision. Enzo could see Rick and three other men firing automatic rounds in an attempt to cover Major's tracks as he maneuvered the truck backward toward the guard gate. The guards stationed at the gate had left their post and were lined up along the roadside returning fire with the other security agents. Everyone watched as the sleek black and silver rig crashed backward through the gate sending the yellow and black guard arm flying along with the concrete pillar it rested in. A corner of the guard station booth was destroyed as the rear tires on the right side became a battering ram. The rig pulled two tankers, one long, which was connected to the truck, and a smaller, pup tank connected to the longer container. Pulling two tanks forward made regular driving a challenge at times, but driving backward made it almost impossible to maneuver in a straight line. The pup bounced twice as a result of Major's challenge to keep the rig in line.

Sitting in the SUV with an increasingly pale Loretta watching on Facetime, Enzo had one eye on the tanker rig driving backward off the property, which was quite a show, and one eye attempting to keep track of the buttons on his remote control. "What's that maniac doing?" Lorretta asked, as Enzo questioned Major's driving skills. Enzo dropped the remote just as he prepared to end Major's wild exit.

Lorretta's confidence was quickly being depleted. Sirens could be heard in the distance; Blaine employees had been evacuated off campus and were safe. This operation was not going as planned. The screen would eventually go dark as Enzo scrambled for the remote, grasped it, and pushed the buttons to engage the bomb. That was his last act on behalf of Lorretta Petrula. The fuel truck came crashing toward the black SUV where Enzo sat alone with a dead driver and the most agonizing look on his face. The explosion blew the SUV back fifty yards in a summersaulting fashion. The tires ignited and the gas tank exploded adding to the flames that started a small grove of trees on fire. Enzo, his driver and one guard were immolated instantly. The chemical solution in the pup trailer did not explode, but the small trailer was sent rolling off into the trees, like an oversized bowling ball, as a result of the explosion.

Chapter 16

BLAINE MANUFACTURING

"He's over here," yelled Billy, who found Major's singed body lying face up in the trees after the explosion and subsequent fire. Major had been blown away from the truck after diving out of the cab, seconds before the bomb went off, causing the entire rig to go up in flames. "Major, Major wake up!" The agent gently shook Major, who was fortunate that the fire didn't burn another twenty yards or he couldn't have opened his eyes as he did, while his associate softly slapped his blackened and swollen face.

"Billy, you slap me one more time and I'll rearrange your face, no charge." Major grumbled, half smiling as he tried to get up, but sat up instead with Billy's help.

"It's good to have you back, boss." Billy had the look of relief as others, including Rick, showed up to help.

As the ambulance crew loaded Major onto the stretcher, Rick came alongside. "Hey, tough guy. That was quite a display on how to drive a big rig." Rick paused as Major gingerly took a big swig of water from a plastic bottle that Billy handed him. Rick continued; "What you did saved a lot of lives, not to mention our production facility."

Before Rick could say another word, Major stopped him with a wave of his hand that appeared to have superficial burns. "How many casualties, Rick?"

One of Billy's men had an updated count that he'd given Rick moments earlier. "Three of your crew were wounded, no one killed from your staff. Two of our security guys were killed, the guards at the gate. Three of our security people were wounded, one woman, two men, but none of our other employees were injured. We haven't a good number on the Castillinos, we're still finding bodies on the hillside and in the trees. Bear said that he had six in custody, confirmed 8 dead, not counting the occupants of the vaporized SUV on the service road." Rick checked for a response, but Major had passed out.

Brenda walked up as Rick sat down on the remains of a concrete pillar near, what used to be, a state-of-the-art guard station. She put her hand on his shoulder as he let out a big breath. "So, you put your long-haul driving skills to good use today."

Rick looked up at her and shook his head. "I know you think it was crazy, but something had to be done."

Brenda looked back at him and nodded. "The question is: did it have to be you, Rick?" Her lips pressed together as she bent down and embraced him as he sat. Rick put one arm up on her shoulder in recognition. "Come on, soldier, let's get you cleaned up."

As they slowly walked together back through the campus, heading for the executive offices, Rick turned to her with a question. "Can you take care of things for another week?" Brenda's look deserved a good reason, even though she enjoyed taking the helm once in a while. "I have a funeral in the UK to attend."

§

SOMEWHERE OVER THE ROCKY MOUNTAINS

Lorretta sat in luxury on her private jet heading back to Boston. By the time she heard the news, the plane was at thirty-five thousand feet over Colorado. She ordered another scotch, neat, not because she was disappointed or sad, Lorretta Petrula was pissed. Next time, and there would be a next time, she would be in charge of taking Rick Blaine and his company down. For now, she wanted nothing better than to get back into what she did best, rule her domain with an iron fist. She'd already poured out more tears over Michael Castillino than she ever expected any emotion would pull from her.

Lorretta's part of the underworld that appealed to her most, trucking, would expand. So far, her reign over the logistics industry was unparalleled. And Lorretta would make damn sure it would remain that way or heads would literally roll. Michael had presented her with an opportunity a few years ago by suggesting she, based on her heritage, take over the family business. Since that time the Castillino/Petrula families were better organized and making more money than she ever projected.

The recent Blaine debacle will never rest until Rick Blaine is dead and his company becomes a forgotten legacy. Her last thought, before reclining into sleep, was reading about herself being proclaimed "Employer of the Year" in a transport industry trade magazine. Killing it, she thought to herself as she drifted off.

§

EDINBURGH, SCOTLAND

Ben picked Rick up at the airport in Edinburgh, Scotland. "Welcome back, Rick. How was your flight?"

"Do you really want to know about my flight, Ben? Or would you rather talk about Brenda?" Ben nearly drove off the road as he wondered how Rick could read his mind, which resulted in laughter.

The drive to the funeral home wasn't far, so Ben heard more about how Brenda handled the after effects of the recent Castillino attack on Blaine Manufacturing. They both agreed that Brenda Johnson possessed amazing leadership skills.

The graveside ceremony took place on the Turlington estate, located on the outskirts of Edinburgh. A larger, more grandiose celebration of Sir Archibald Turlington's life had already taken place through the heart of London, led by the Queen herself, two days prior. Prince Charles gave the eulogy and Archie's symbolic coffin laid in state for the people to see for three days in Westminster Cathedral. The procession through London had people lined up the entire way to the Kings Cross train station.

"Archie loved taking the train back and forth from London to Scotland," Winston said at Archie's funeral. "The ride up north gave him time to think and relax, the ride south was often another matter. God knows he needed those moments."

The man who gave his life, along with other heroes that fateful night in Brixton, had died serving his country. That sentiment circulated throughout the various comments made during his funeral service.

Rick stood that day in Edinburgh with a select group of twenty family and a few close friends. The honor Rick felt changed him. He knew he had to come and be here at that moment in time. Sir Archie challenged Rick, more than once, in the short time they spent together. Of all the people, living and dead, with the exception of his father, Rick realized how one person can create a positive change in another.

The time came for people to toss dirt on the casket in the grave. One by one they lined up. Throwing dirt symbolizes the deceased's return to earth. Family and then friends take their turn. When it was Rick's time, he hesitated over the grave, mumbling something, then making the toss. Later, at the reception, Winston asked about the mumble. "I asked Archie to say hi to my dad. I think they'll get along just fine."

Winston and Ben traveled with Rick back to London where Rick caught his flight back to San Francisco.

"We will be in touch, Rick." Winston thanked one of the most enterprising and courageous people he knew for taking Abbas back with him and helping the kid to connect with his family there.

Ben said that he planned to visit Abbas in the next month. He also added that he and Brenda were just friends, but that he, would like to take the relationship further.

"Well, there you go, Ben. The cat's out of the bag." Rick gave Ben a double-fisted handshake and wished him well. He also said that his lips were sealed, but that he couldn't wait to see how things went with Brenda.

§

ONE YEAR LATER

Rick had been working non-stop since his return from London and Sir Archie's funeral. Blaine Manufacturing Inc. had recovered from the attack on their facility and sales continued to rise, the publicity seemingly causing even more demand for their products. Brenda Johnson became the Chief Executive Officer and selected the West Coast's Businesswoman of the Year, by Forbes Magazine. An achievement that placed her firmly in the realm of women who were not only breaking the glass ceiling, but also changing the corporate culture for businesses in America.

Ben Lamperson now managed the Lamperson International, American division out of a downtown San Francisco office. Lamperson Services was very pleased with the new business they achieved in the United States and Brenda Johnson couldn't have been happier. She and Ben were now engaged to be married to the surprise of every one of their associates, except one. The man who had become their biggest supporter also found himself needing to refresh an old relationship with a dear friend.

Rick Blaine was on vacation, heading to Lake Pend Oreille in northern Idaho, driving his vintage Porsche. He decided to take the long way going north over the same route he and his friend, Jillian, had taken two years earlier. The only difference, this time he wasn't being chased. Rick had taken enough time to figure out who he missed most in his life. And through some recent correspondence, he found that his feelings were more than welcomed. Penny had asked that he take his time, drive carefully, but get there as soon as possible. Evidently, pilots like Penny not only know how to make safe landings, they also know how to cruise through life — even without a co-pilot — so far anyway.

Acknowledgments

Taking Rick Blaine overseas required some deep thinking with people I favor most in my life. First, my wife, Lorrie. Without her support and first edits I'm not sure I'd be writing this sentence. Second, my son-in-law, Bryan. Not only is he supportive, he's also extremely knowledgeable – especially when it comes to matters of international intelligence. And kudos to a true marketing professional who provided insightful final edits, Rick H. Jon and his team at Latah Publishing, including Kevin for the cover design and more. Many thanks to those of you who have taken a moment to post a review on my website: jprobideaux.com. The website has recently been refreshed by our daughter, Ashli, and other reviews of my first novel: "Escape Into Rain" continue to show up on Amazon. Your comments are refreshing and encouraging and keep me going.

Made in United States
Troutdale, OR
06/10/2024

20461228R00206